BOYS of ENGLAND STORIES of SHAKESPEARE

COMPLETE

RICHARD THE IIIrd

No. 1.

STORIES FROM
SHAKESPEARE'S PLAYS.

RICHARD III.; OR, THE BATTLE OF BOSWORTH FIELD.

THE sun had for some time set over the old city of London, as a man passed hastily down one of the narrow lanes which led to the river Thames. Very few persons were about.

The streets and lanes in the vicinity were in fact unusually quiet, although, since the cessation of the wars which had so long desolated the country, the city of London had begun to renew its business habits with redoubled energy.

But yet this man seemed timorous of being seen.

Ere passing from the road into the narrow by-way, he looked around him in every direction to see if he were followed or observed.

The look on his face, and the general nature of his aspect seemed to tell that he had travelled far by road, intent on some fell purpose, and that he had never stopped once except to change horses.

He bore, in fact, the appearance of one whose whole soul was wrapped in eager contemplation of some dark and terrible deed.

However, when he had once made his way from the more busy thoroughfare into the less frequented lane, he seemed to breathe more freely; and with something like a smile on his hard and cruel mouth he hastened on to the spot where he could take a boat on what was known justly then as the silvery Thames.

Arriving at the stone steps leading to the water he had no difficulty in obtaining a boat, for a man was lazily waiting on the landing for one more fare before he turned in for the night; and even if he had been absent there were many others slowly rowing up and down, waiting to be engaged by those gallants and others who desired to journey on some mysterious errand on the grand old river.

In a few minutes he was seated in the skiff.

It was very dark indeed on the river.

However, the waterman knew his way well.

He pulled his boat out into the middle of the stream, and the tide being with him it was not long before he was far on his way.

"Where do you wish me to stop, good sir?" he said to his companion.

"Pull me towards the Tower Stairs," said the one who had employed him; "there I will land."

"His voice sounds strangely like one that I heard once in the City haranguing the City in bands—the voice of Richard of Gloucester. What new and terrible deed can he be seeking in the Tower?"

Those were troublous times.

The war between the rival houses of York and Lancaster had just ended.

Edward IV. had been placed securely on the throne of England, and his unfortunate rival, Henry VI., was now in a dungeon in that very Tower of London whither the man had taken the cloaked stranger whom he supposed to be the Duke of Gloucester.

Peace for a time blessed the distracted nation.

But the man had heard of how Prince Edward had died at Tewkesbury.

News did not travel in those days as in these.

But "murder will out," no matter how long a time it takes in oozing forth.

It was well known at Tewkesbury that Prince Edward, first struck by Edward IV.

in the presence of his mother, Queen Margaret, had been stabbed to death by Richard of Gloucester and the Duke of Clarence, and this was speedily known through London.

The people were used to rough masters in those days.

No man was too high, no man was too lowly for "crook-backed Dick" to strike.

Yet, when the waterman steadied the boat to enable his fare to alight, he was resolved to satisfy his curiosity.

"Have a care, your grace. The tide runs strongly here."

The cloaked personage started at the words, so much that he almost slipped on landing.

"What's that thou sayest, sir?" he cried—"'your grace?' For whom then dost thou take me?"

"For yourself, your grace."

The Duke of Gloucester regarded the man as he doffed his cap.

The other stood back so that the light of the dull oil-lamp on the Tower Stairs fell full on the man's face.

"What is thy name?" he asked.

"Tom Herod, an it please your grace."

"Then be warned in time by one who never forgets a true friend, and never forgives an enemy. Talk not to others of the silly thought that has entered thy mind to-night. I am here on an errand which must remain a secret. Look to it that ye open not thy mouth too wide, else ye may find thy tongue plucked out. And now, thou must remain here awhile; row gently to and fro until I return. Thou'lt know me when I come from out the Tower. Away, before I give the summons!"

The man without a word settled to his oars, and drew off into the centre of the river.

"I knew, I felt 'twas he," he muttered as he did so. "I can see danger to King Henry. Heaven save us all! What battles for a crown! I care not who is king, not I, so that there can be peace and plenty in the land, and not this everlasting bloodletting."

Meanwhile, Richard of Gloucester—for it was indeed he—paused a moment ere he rang the deep-mouthed bell, and looked back at the man who was slowly rowing away.

"What bitter fate is mine!" he muttered. "So marked by nature that, hide my face as I will, my humped back makes me known to e'en the lowliest and basest born. What wonder that I, so lame and unlike others that dogs bark at me, have no delight save in scattering others out of my way that I may ascend to the highest point that man can aim at—England's throne?"

The last thought seemed at once to rouse him, and he pulled vigorously at the big chain which led to the huge and sombre-toned bell within.

In an instant, as if he were momentarily expected, the portal was opened, and a man dressed in dusky garments appeared.

He bowed low to Richard.

"Good night, your grace; you see I did expect you," he said.

"Ay, better than others do!" said the monster, with a grim smile. "Quick, lead me to this king—I'm all impatience."

"This way, my lord," said the man, who had by this time refastened the bolts and locks of the big door, and in a few moments they had reached the entrance of the king's chamber.

On knocking here, the door was opened by the lieutenant of the guard.

He started on seeing the duke.

"My lord," he said, "do you wish to see the king?"

Gloucester smiled grimly.

"King Edward will thank you for your loyalty," he said, drily; "he shall not fail to know it. I wish to see the usurper Henry, the man who took another's kingdom. My business admits of no delay. So let me to his presence; and pray you wait without, for my business is a secret one."

The lieutenant stood aside, scarce knowing how to address his prisoner in the presence of the dreaded Duke of Gloucester, who, in his rude impetuous way, broke into King Henry's presence.

The door was closed at once.

The lieutenant and the gaoler remained outside, walking to the other end of the corridor.

They heard faint sounds of angry voices, and then the door was opened, and Richard came out flushed, sword in hand, and with frowning brow.

"The very model of an avenging demon," thought the lieutenant, as Richard came up in haste.

"How fares it with King Henry?" said he, aloud, though in a somewhat frightened voice.

"So well," said Richard, "that he will

not need aid to-night if thou lackest inclination to give it. But quick, the door, I must to the king."

In solemn silence they opened wide the door, and the boatman quickly rowed his skiff up to the water-gate.

"Farewell, lieutenant. See thou art discreet. Farewell, gaoler; here is thy promised reward. Look to it that ye openest not thy mouth too wide."

And with these words he gave the order to the waterman, and away the boat sped into the sombre darkness of the river.

"Mark you," said the lieutenant, as they took their way back into the gloomy Tower, "King Henry died but now. Let's to his dungeon."

Their fears were fully confirmed.

There, sitting in his chair, his head fallen on the table, a pool of blood around his feet, was Henry VI. of England.

Such was the terrible end of a monarch whose own weak-mindedness wrought half the evils he had suffered, and the terrible misfortunes under which England had groaned so long.

"Who next will die?" sighed the lieutenant, as he laid out decently on the bed all that was mortal of long-suffering Henry.

Who next?

Richard of Gloucester had settled this long since.

Having thus far revelled in blood, the insatiate monster looked fearlessly around to take cognizance of what other impediments stood between him and the throne of England.

That the throne would soon be vacant he did not doubt.

Edward's health was rapidly breaking up, and it was generally accepted on all hands that he could not survive much longer.

Three lives then stood between Richard and the throne. Edward's two infant sons and Clarence.

But Clarence was first to be disposed of.

If Edward died now that the princes were so young, Clarence, as their elder uncle, would of course be named their Protector and Regent of England.

The mere thought of this was sufficient to rouse in Richard's mind the most fierce hatred against his brother Clarence.

The aim of his life had never been lost sight of.

He had wheedled, cajoled, betrayed, murdered, in order that the crown of England might some day adorn his brow; and was a little more blood-spilling to make him pause?

No!

He must hasten to the king and tell him of his deed; and ere the time was too far gone, he must wring from the perhaps unwilling monarch an order for Clarence's arrest.

All these thoughts rushed madly through his brain as the boat was propelled towards Westminster by the silent waterman.

Fit place for such thoughts—this black and rushing river!

But Richard thought not of this.

He had no fear of darkness; ambition stilled the beating of his heart, and sent him dashing more swiftly through blood—through anything—towards the giddy height from which in those days it was so easy to fall.

They paused soon at the stairs at Westminster, and Richard leaped out with eagerness.

"Mark you well, my friend," he said, as he placed a heavy purse in the boatman's hand, "here is a purse for silence. You have told me your name, and royal hands have wondrous long and ready fingers. A babbling tongue means a hangman and a rope, for those same fingers will clutch thee if thou prate, wherever in England you may hide yourself."

"Fear not, my lord," said the man, "I leave all babbling to women; I like it not."

"See that you keep to my words then," cried Richard, and with eager steps he hurried towards the palace.

Lord Dorset was the first nobleman whom he encountered.

"Where is the king, my lord?" cried Richard, in his accustomed rude and abrupt manner.

"He is with the queen, my lord, and other ladies," replied Dorset. "Will you go to him or——"

"Nay, I will not go to him," said Richard; "my news admits of no delay, and it is secret also. Tell my good brother it is of great moment."

"Some direful deed has Dick of Gloucester done," muttered Dorset, as he went, "else would he not be so flushed and eager."

Richard himself paced to and fro with hasty strides.

But he was not kept long.

Edward, in spite of the company he was in, came hastening to him.

"Dear brother," he said, extending both his hands, "what is it brings you in such wondrous haste? Have you good news for me?"

"A king is safer when he has no rival," said Richard with a grim smile.

"What!" cried King Edward, "is Henry dead?"

"Ay, your majesty," said Richard; "his troubles now are over. He awaits but his last journey to the tomb. Short was his shrift, and shorter still his death."

"You are too hasty, brother," said the king, glancing round him almost apprehensively.

"Why, Edward, where's thy courage?" cried Richard. "Pray do not let the weak-mindedness which was Henry's bane o'erthrow the plans that made thee King of England! Has not thy Richard fought for thee in the bloody fields of war? And now would you spoil all?"

"No, no, good Richard," said the king, hastily; "thou hast done well. And now this tide of blood can cease its flowing. King Edward has no rival in the field."

"'Tis well thou thinkest so, brother?" said Richard, gloomily.

"What, sombre again, good Richard?"

"I have good cause, Edward," replied Gloucester. "Our brother Clarence's loyalty is fair in seeming, but I fear it would not bear much sifting."

"Thou'rt over suspicious."

"No, no! And more than that, fair brother, I advise nothing—in spite of the old prophecy."

"What mean you?"

"His name begins with 'G.'"

"Truly. What then?"

"And yet you do not remember, good Edward," said Richard, smiling. "There was a prophecy, most august brother, which said that—'Some one whose name began with "G," of Edward's heirs the

RICHARD III.

murderer should be.' But that may be an old wife's tale. Yet Clarence, were I king, should be close guarded."

"Ah, I have heard that prophecy," said Edward; "and his name is George."

"Yes."

"But you give no other reason."

"No, save report; but then report tells truth. I have heard him myself inveighing against the ill-fortune which made him not eldest brother. What would he not have done? What plans he had for people's benefit! What pillars of the state would flock around him if only he could claim the right of hearing them cry 'Hail good king!'"

The weak and treacherous mind of Edward IV. was roused at this.

"Ah! said he so? Then by St. George——"

"Nay, be not too hasty," cried Richard, plausibly; "we may have both been led by idle rumours, and thus we fashion even our own injuries to our own tastes. You must keep sharp look out upon our brother; have him watched awhile, and if we wrong him, he need never know it. We may heap horror on him, and if he be surprised, say 'Dear Clarence, we knew not half your loyalty.'"

"You counsel well, good Richard," said King Edward. "To-morrow you will see that these words have not fallen upon idle ears. And now, let's to the queen's chamber."

"My gracious brother, I will to rest now," said Richard; "this day has been a busy one with me, and I am tired out in your service."

"If you desire retirement, betake thee to what chamber in the palace it pleases you. I should never like you to leave the royal house, when you are always so ready for counsel and for action."

"Always for you, most royal brother," said Richard; and having raised the king's hand to his lips he retired.

"Ah," he said, when presently he

threw himself into a luxurious chair in his splendidly-appointed chamber, " all things go right at present. How quickly poisoned is royal Edward's ear. Clarence once in the Tower—and go there he will—the world must be rid of him as quickly as may be."

Next morning saw him up betimes.

He knew that King Edward had somewhat of vacillation in his temper, especially since his attack of illness, and consequently he was anxious to see how the poison of his words had instilled themselves into the king's mind.

The very first person whom he met, when he had partaken of a hurried repast, was Clarence himself.

He was not alone, however.

He was surrounded by a guard, and with them was Sir Robert Brackenbury, Lieutenant of the Tower.

" Brother, good day," said Richard. " What means this armed guard which waits upon your grace?"

Clarence smiled grimly.

" His majesty," he said, " anxious for my personal safety, has given me this guard to convey me to the Tower."

" Upon what cause?" cried Gloucester.

" Because my name is George."

" For that he should commit your godfathers," said treacherous Richard; " the fault is none of yours. But tell me, Clarence, what is the matter? May I know?"

" Yes, when I know, Richard, for I protest as yet I know not," replied Clarence. " Still, as far as I can learn, he has been hearkening to prophecies and dreams, and says a wizard told him that by ' G ' his issue should be disinherited; and, as my name is George, I go to the Tower."

" It is that the king is ruled by women," said the treacherous Richard; " 'tis not the king that sends you to the Tower. 'Tis his wife. We are not safe!"

" By Heaven!" exclaimed Clarence, " I think no man is secure but the queen's kindred."

" Ay, truly, brother," said Gloucester; " if we would keep in favour with the king, we must be her men, and wear her livery."

" I beseech both your graces to pardon me," interrupted Sir Robert Brackenbury, " but his majesty had given special orders that no man shall have private conference of any kind with the Duke Clarence."

" Even so, an it please your worship," said Gloucester, " you are free to listen to everything that we say. We speak no treason, man. We say the king is wise and virtuous, and his noble queen well struck in years—fair, and not jealous. We say that Shore's wife had a pretty foot, a bonny eye, and a cherry lip. We say that the queen's kindred are made gentlefolks. How say you, sir? Can you deny all this?"

" I have nothing to do with all this," said Sir Robert Brackenbury. " I beseech your grace to defer your conference with the noble duke."

" We know the king's orders, and will obey," said Clarence. " Lead on to the Tower."

" Yes, we are the queen's abjects and obey," said Richard. " Brother, farewell. I will to the king, and urge my best for your release. Fear not, your imprisonment shall not be long."

" I must perforce, and so farewell, my brother," cried Clarence.

And with the words he passed away.

Gloucester glanced after him with a smile upon his evil countenance.

" Simple—plain Clarence," he murmured; " go tread the path thou'lt ne'er again return. I do love thee so that I shall send thy soul shortly to Heaven."

He was just about to pass out when Lord Hastings came in.

" Good day, my gracious lord," he said.

" What news abroad?" said Richard.

" No such ill news abroad as there is at home," said Hastings. " The king is sickly, weak, and melancholy this morning, and his physicians fear for him mightily."

" By St. Paul! this is indeed bad news," said Gloucester. " Is he in bed?"

" He is, my lord."

" Go, then, and announce my coming. I will follow you."

" Ha!" he added, when Hastings had taken his departure; " I must lose no time. I will take this opportunity while he is hard hit by sickness to pour more lies into his coward heart. If I can but succeed, then Clarence has but another day to live. He dead, Heaven take King Edward to its mercy, and leave the world for me to bustle in."

And with these thoughts he went to Edward's bedside.

As soon as he had by this last interview conclusively effected his brother's

disgrace, Richard began to devise further plots by which he might compass his death.

His own hand was, however, so recently imbrued in blood that his soul shrunk at perpetrating the crime himself, and he therefore resolved to engage two assassins to complete the diabolical project he had formed.

Fearing to be seen in converse with ruffians whose characters were so notorious, he resolved not to hazard the bringing them to his palace, but rather chose to wait on them in their own murky retreat, where he could unobserved give them the necessary instructions.

The worst of London's dens were not unknown to this monster of iniquity.

He noted as he went the names and positions of streets; and having remembered two men who lived somewhere in the vicinity now known as Shoreditch—men whose characters were indisputably ruffianly—he determined to make his way to their haunts, and give into their hands the carrying out of his infamous design.

Having formed this resolution, the Duke of Gloucester set forward on his mission, and after traversing numerous streets and narrow lanes he at length reached the vicinity of Old St. Paul's Cathedral, where he met the funeral procession of his recent victim, Henry VI., who was followed, as chief mourner, by the youthful and beauteous Lady Anne, widow of Edward, Prince of Wales, the heir-apparent of the late monarch, and which gallant prince Richard had basely assisted in slaying after the disastrous Battle of Tewkesbury.

Upon this excellent lady Richard had resolved to urge his love, and the opportunity which now offered was therefore considered by him too favourable to be passed by.

As he advanced towards the coffin bearers, he exclaimed in a peremptory voice—

"Stay, ye who bear the corse, and set it down until ye have answered the questions which I would ask!"

"What black magician conjures up this fiend to interrupt our sacred rites?" cried the Lady Anne, glancing fearlessly towards Gloucester. "Oh! is it thou, monster? who hast destroyed the late good king, over whose immortal soul, however, thou hast no control!"

"Villains! set down the corse," cried Richard furiously, to the soldiers, "or I will make a corse of him who disobeys!"

At this, one of the gentlemen who walked at the side of the body of the murdered Henry, stepped forward respectfully.

"My lord," he said, "stand back and let the body pass."

"Unmannerly dog!" cried Gloucester, "stand thou when I command."

At this the bearers set down the corse and Richard turned to Anne, who seemed upon the point of bursting into a fresh fit of anger.

"Sweet saint! for charity, be not so unkind," he said.

"Foul fiend! in Heaven's name I bid thee hence!" cried the lady, with indignant warmth; "for thou hast made the once happy earth thy hell, and filled it with cursing cries of vengeance, and deep outbursts of hatred! If thou delightest to view thy heinous deeds, look here upon the corse of him who was thy last object of vengeance."

"Oh, gentle lady, spare me," exclaimed the Duke of Gloucester.

"Villainous murderer! thy appeal is vain—thou thyself art destitute of mercy, therefore why shouldst thou ask it of me?" inquired the indignant Lady Anne. "Thou art worse than the beasts of the forests, for even they occasionally know some feelings of pity."

"Yet I am not so evil as thou takest me to be," returned the other; "therefore vouchsafe, divine perfection of a woman, to grant permission that I may exonerate myself."

"Rather reflect, and amend the evil tenor of thy life."

"Nay, gracious lady," exclaimed the duke, "grant me permission to clear myself of the many foul calumnies that have been heaped upon me—thy husband fell not by my hand, but by that of Edward."

"'Tis false," returned Lady Anne. "Queen Margaret saw thy murderous blade in his blood. Besides, didst thou not kill the king?"

"Alas! that I cannot deny."

"Then wilt thou be accursed for that wicked deed," replied the fair mourner, "for he was gentle, mild and virtuous."

"Then was he fitter for the King of Heaven, that now hath him," was the laconic reply.

"But which cruel deed renders thee unfit for any place but hell."

"There thou art wrong," returned the duke, "one place else there is, if thou wilt hear me."

"Some dungeon?"

"Thy bedchamber."

"Ill rest betide the chamber where thou liest!" exclaimed Lady Anne.

"But, gentle madam," returned the duke, "is not she who caused me to commit crime as blameable as myself?"

"Thou wast the cause and most accursed effect also," said Anne. "Let us proceed. There need be no more of this."

be revenged on him who killed my husband."

"Nay, nay, fair Anne," returned Richard; "he who bereft thee of thy husband did it to help thee to a better one."

"A better lives not," cried Lady Anne. "No better man breathes upon this earth."

"He who loves thee now would prove a better," returned the other, "for thine eyes have prompted me to love."

"I would that they were basilisk's to strike thee dead."

"I would they were, that I might die at once," returned the duke, "for now

THE MURDER OF THE TWO PRINCES.

"Your beauty was the instigator," exclaimed Richard. "That it was which ever haunted me in my sleep, and prompted me to sacrifice all considerations, so that I might eventually gain thee."

"If I thought that, I tell you, murderer, I would with these nails rend what I have of beauty from these cheeks. Let me pass!"

"These eyes could not endure such beauty's wreck," said Gloucester in that low gentle persuasive voice—soft as a woman's—which he could use at times. "You should not spoil it if I stood by. As the whole world is cheered by the warm bright beams of the sun, so your beauty cheers my soul. It is my day—my life!"

"Black night o'ershade thy day, and death thy life," said Anne. "I will yet

they kill me with a living death. Those eyes of thine have drawn salt tears from mine—mine that ne'er dreamed of weeping, even when my father, York and Edward wept, to hear the piteous moans that Rutland made when black-faced Clifford shook his sword at him. Not even did they shed a tear when thy warlike father told me the sad story of my father's death, and paused full twenty times to sob and weep. But now teach not your lips such scorn. They were made for kissing, not for such contempt. If thy heart cannot forgive me, take this sword and bury it in my heart. Nay, do not pause, for I it was who killed the king —yet 'twas thy beauty that urged me to the deed. Now then despatch me— 'twas I who stabbed thy husband—but it was thy heavenly face that urged me on."

As he spoke he knelt and bared his breast, and give her the sword.

Twice she made as if to strike, but at length flung it down.

"Arise, dissembler!" cried Lady Anne, "for however I may wish thy death, I cannot be thy executioner—take up your sword."

"Then bid me kill myself, and I will do it," said Gloucester.

ring?" continued the duke, at the same time slipping a rich jewel upon her finger. "And now, dear lady, grant but one more favour and thou wilt confirm my happiness for ever."

"Name it."

"That you will be pleased to abandon your intention of following the cold remains of the king to their last resting-place, and allow me to execute your designs. Repair, therefore, to Crosby Place, where, after I have solemnly interred the

THE HOUSE THAT RICHARD III. SLEPT IN ON THE NIGHT
PREVIOUS TO THE BATTLE.

"I have already."

"That was in thy rage," said Gloucester; "speak it again, and even with the word this hand, that for thy love did kill thy husband, shall take this life thou spurnest."

"I would I knew thy heart," said Anne with a sigh.

Gloucester saw that she was yielding, and he cried eagerly—

"Thou dost—'tis imaged in my tongue."

"Then I fear me both are false—but put up thy sword."

"Say then, that thou forgivest me," exclaimed Gloucester; "shall I live in hope?"

"All men, I hope, live so," returned Lady Anne.

"Wilt thou then vouchsafe to wear this

body of King Henry, I will meet you. I would perform this duty myself, fair lady, that I may wet his grave with my repentant tears. Grant me this boon."

"My lord, I will obey you," returned Lady Anne, "and it gratifies me much to perceive that you are become so penitent—farewell then, till we meet again."

Richard, well satisfied at the success of his artifices, commanded the body of the deceased king to be conveyed to its last home, while he himself pursued his way towards the dwelling of those assassins whom he was about to employ in the murder of his brother, the Duke of Clarence.

Riding off at full speed he dashed towards Shoreditch to meet the murderers.

He had no difficulty, as we observed earlier in our story, in finding them out.

The man who had to pay off so many evil scores had a splendid memory for people and places, and Robert Walton and Richard Hardry were easily discovered in their usual haunt—a tavern standing by itself in Shoreditch.

Richard had no fears.

He drew up his reeking horse at the gate, flung the bridle to the ready ostler and leaping from the saddle strode into the house.

Two sturdy ruffians answered to his summons.

Two men upon whose faces were stamped plainly the brands—

Thief and assassin!

As they came towards him by order of the landlord, they bowed low.

"My lord——"

"Hush, prating fool," cried Richard; "has not experience taught you the value of silence? Lead me to some spot where we can be alone."

"This way, then," said Walton, and in a few moments the three were seated in a wild, deserted-looking back garden.

"And now to business," said Richard; "you know me well?"

"The Duke of Gloucester," said Walton.

"Well, then, I must be brief. My brother Clarence lies within the Tower."

"In the Tower, my lord!" exclaimed both at once.

"Aye, but he must not lie there to-morrow. Dost understand me?"

"Yes, my lord; you have need of our daggers."

"And speedily, this very night in fact. But, mind, in this you must be more discreet than ever."

"Not a word will fall from our lips, my lord. Pray proceed."

"Then, take this purse, and remember, be sudden in the execution of your plan. Do not hear him plead, for Clarence is well-spoken, and perhaps may move your hearts to pity if you list to him."

"Fear not, my lord," said Walton, "we shall not stand to prate; talkers are not good doers. Rest assured we go to use our hands and not our tongues."

"I like you, lads," said the duke; "about your business straight; go, go, despatch! When it is done, come to me at Crosby Place, where I shall give you a heavy reward. But mark you, I wish you

away to Flanders for a time, till matters tide over somewhat."

"It shall be done, my lord; but where is the warrant?"

"Here," returned Gloucester, as he drew from his pocket the document signed by King Edward; "quick, away! lose no time."

And without another word he rose, went to his horse, threw to the ostler a gold piece, and rode away.

In pursuance of the order they had received, and instigated by the rich reward which had been promised in case of their successfully executing the mission, the two ruffians immediately proceeded to the Tower.

By this time the night had considerably advanced, but, affirming that their business was of importance, they were conducted to the apartment of the Duke of Clarence, whom they found reading at the humble table with which the strong room was provided.

A moment before he had been engaged in conversation with Brackenbury, the Lieutenant of the Tower, to whom he had been relating his strange dreams and forebodings.

Brackenbury was at the door as the men came up.

"Who's there?" he cried in surprise; "what wouldst thou, fellows, and how came you hither?"

"I would speak with Clarence, and I came hither on my legs," said Walton.

"What! so insolent, so brief?"

"Better that than tedious. I pray thee read this," and he handed the warrant to the lieutenant.

"I am," said Brackenbury, when he had read it, "commanded to deliver up the noble Duke of Clarence to your hands. I will not reason what is meant by that, because I wish not to know the meaning. I will leave you."

"That is a point of wisdom," said Hardry; "come, Walton."

And pushing open the door they confronted Clarence.

He sprang up as he saw them.

"In Heaven's name what art thou?" he cried, addressing Walton.

"A man, as you are!"

"But not as I am—royal! Tell me, what seek'st thou? Thy voice is thunder, but thy looks are humble."

"Ah," said Walton, "my voice is now the king's, my looks are my own."

"How darkly and how deadly dost thou

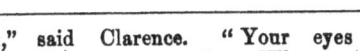

speak," said Clarence. "Your eyes menace me—why look so pale ? Who sent you hither ? Wherefore do you come ?"

"We come from the king, my lord," said Walton ; "you have offended him, and, these being perilous times, you must prepare to die."

"To die !" cried Clarence, "and wherefore ? What is my offence ? I charge you depart and lay no hands on me."

"What we shall do is by the king's command," said Hardry ; "mayhap it be for murder and false-swearing. Thou didst receive the sacrament to fight in quarrel for the House of Lancaster, and like a traitor did break thy vow, and murder thy sovereign's son."

"Alas !" cried Clarence, "for whose sake did I that dreadful deed ? For Edward, my brother, and in that sin he is as deep as I. But if you are hired for gain, go to my brother Gloucester, who will reward you better for my life than Edward will for my death."

"You are deceived, your brother Gloucester hates you. 'Twas he who sent us to destroy you here ! Make peace with Heaven, for you must die !"

"Stay ! Speakest thou of Heaven yet do this awful deed ? Consider, if you do me this wrong, those who set you on will detest you for it."

"What then shall we do ?"

"Relent and save your souls."

"Relent ! 'Tis cowardly and womanish," cried Hardry ; "and more than that, if we were to forego this deed, it would be but a short respite to you, and death to us. Ah, look, look behind you, my lord !"

The incautious and alarmed Clarence was taken off his guard by these words, and glanced behind him.

It was a fatal glance.

In an instant Hardry had sprung forward and struck him to the ground.

There were no words, no lament ; only a deep groan, and Clarence sank upon the floor.

"And now," said Walton, "to disguise the deed. There is a butt of malmsey in the adjoining room; let's drop him in it, so it shall be said he drowned himself in his favourite wine."

This idea was forthwith carried out, and then the two murderers slunk away from the spot, and, as swiftly as they could, made their way towards the place of meeting, Crosby Hall.

Richard of Gloucester was well pleased when he heard of the success of this new act of villainy, and his darkly brooding thoughts were instantly occupied in plotting further deeds of crime, when the somewhat unexpected death of his brother, King Edward IV. placed him in a yet nearer position to the throne of England.

Shortly after the demise of Edward, the youthful Prince of Wales, under the style and title of Edward V. was proclaimed King of England, and his uncle Richard, Duke of Gloucester, as nearest in relationship, was appointed regent.

Having succeeded thus far, the ambitious regent sought to discover means by which to gain over to his cause the nobility.

Among these, the most important to his plans, was Lord Hastings, and fearful of making any advances himself, he sent Catesby to sound the principles of that nobleman.

For a long time Richard awaited the return of his emissary, and when at length he made his appearance, exclaimed hastily—

"So, Catesby, what news have you ?"

"My lord," replied Catesby "according to your commands I have visited the Lord Hastings, to ascertain how far he was affected to your cause."

"Well, well, and how found you the proud lord ?" asked Richard.

"For a while he seemed as though he understood me not," replied Catesby. "At length, as I spoke plainer, he became furious, and declared that, rather than wrong the young head which now wears the crown, he would lose his own."

"Indeed !" exclaimed the Protector ; "then his head shall he lose. Meanwhile, do you, my trusty friend, go hence to Doctor Shaw, and Friar Benker ; bid them both attend me here within an hour. Hence, hence and do my bidding quickly, for my Lord of Buckingham is gone to try how far we may depend upon the citizens of London in our future projects."

Catesby bowed and retired, and the Duke of Gloucester, who already began to feel an antipathy towards his recently married wife, the Lady Anne, betook himself towards her apartment.

As he entered the room he discovered the afflicted lady wrapped in thought, and giving way to her sorrows in copious tears.

"What !" he exclaimed, "still weeping. Let thy tears flow ; they are signs of a substantial grief. You still take care, I see, to let the world believe I love you not. This outward show of lamentation has mischief in it. I would have you tell the world I doat upon you."

"Would that it were in my power," replied the lady; "and even were I to do so it would not be believed. My lord, have I deserved this usage from you?"

"You have—you do not please me as when I first knew you."

"What have I done?" asked Lady Anne; "what horrid crime have I committed that you should thus cast me from your bosom?"

"To me the worst of crimes," replied the duke, "you have outlived my love!"

"If that be criminal," cried Lady Anne, "may Heaven be merciful and take me from thee. Oh, sir, forgive and kill me!"

"Umph!—why no, the meddling world would call that murder," said Gloucester; "and for the present I would have them think me merciful. Now, wert thou not afraid of self-destruction, thou hast a fair excuse for it."

"Oh, name it?"

"Thy husband's hate!" exclaimed the duke; "nor do I hate thee only because appetite is sated, but from the ardent love I bear another—I mean the fair Elizabeth. Some call me hypocrite, what thinkest thou—do I dissemble with thee?"

"Alas! to me thy vows of love were all dissembled."

"Not one," returned Richard. "When I told thee so, I loved. Thou art the only soul I never yet deceived, and 'tis my honesty of heart that prompts me now to declare how much I hate thee."

At this period they were interrupted by the entrance of Catesby, to announce that the Duke of Buckingham was in attendance to crave an audience.

At this intelligence, the countenance of Richard brightened up, and, motioning to Lady Anne to retire, he ordered the visitor to be introduced.

In a short time the Duke of Buckingham was ushered in by Catesby, and as he entered, Richard greeted him with—

"Now, cousin, what say the citizens?"

"By our hopes, my lord, they are senseless stones," replied Buckingham, "for their hesitating fear has struck them dumb."

"Hinted you at the bastardy of Edward's children?"

"I did," returned the other; "indeed I overlooked nothing that might tend to be of service in your cause. As I concluded, I urged those who loved their country's welfare to do you justice and cry, 'Long live King Richard!'"

"And did they so?" asked the duke.

"Not one, by Heaven!" replied the other, "but all stood like statues, pale and speechless."

"Senseless fools!" exclaimed Richard, "will they not speak? Will not the mayor and corporation come to wait on me?"

"The mayor is here at hand," replied Buckingham; "feign you some fear, and be not spoken with, except by the most urgent entreaty. A prayer book in your hand, and yourself standing betwixt a couple of clergymen would add to the delusion."

"My oracle! my prophet! my dear cousin!" cried the Duke of Gloucester; "as a child I will follow thy counsel."

"Hark! the Lord Mayor is at hand. Retire, my lord, and at some fitting moment return to us."

"I obey you, Buckingham."

The Duke of Gloucester retired, and the next moment the mayor, attended by a few aldermen entered the apartment.

These were welcomed by Buckingham, with much apparent warmth, and in compliance with former concert, Catesby made his appearance as though just come on a message from the Protector.

"Now, Catesby," exclaimed Buckingham, "what says your lord to my request?"

"My lord, he would remain in privacy to-day, and entreats your grace to visit him at some other time."

"Return, good Catesby, to the duke," replied Buckingham, "and tell him that myself, the mayor and citizens of London have matters of great importance to communicate to him."

Soon after, with his eyes intently fixed upon a prayer book which he held in his hand, the Duke of Gloucester entered, exclaiming—

"Cousin of Buckingham, I beseech you, pardon me, who, earnest in my meditations, have thus long kept you waiting. And you, my lord mayor, I fear I have acted in some way displeasing to the City's eye."

"Know, mighty prince," returned Buckingham, "that I now come with lowly suit, to move your highness that you would take upon yourself the charge and kingly government of this our land."

Perceiving the boldness with which the duke urged his suit, the mayor and aldermen now knelt at Gloucester's feet to join in the supplication.

"Upon our knees, my lord," exclaimed the mayor, "we beg your grace to assume the real dignity, and thus save your country from anarchy and wild despair."

"Alas! why would you heap this load of care upon me?" asked the artful monster, as though unwilling to accede to their entreaties; "I am unfit for state and majesty. I thank ye for your love, but must decline the honour."

"If you refuse us from unwillingness to depose your nephew," returned Buckingham, "yet know that, whether you accept our suit or not, your brother's son shall never be our king."

"Stay!" cried Richard, yielding with apparent reluctance; "since ye will buckle fortune on my back whether I will or no, I must have patience to endure the load."

"Heaven preserve your grace," exclaimed the lord mayor.

"Then thus do I salute you with your royal title," cried Buckingham. "Long live King Richard, England's worthy king! When will it please your majesty to be crowned?"

"Even when it may please you, since you will have it so," returned Richard.

"Then to-morrow we will attend your grace," said the Duke of Buckingham; "and so, for the present, we take our leave."

On the following day the coronation took place.

At length, however, Richard began to entertain doubts of the loyalty of his subjects while the lawful heir to the throne was in existence.

He therefore resolved that he would at once rid himself, not only of the young king, Edward V. but also of his little brother, the Duke of York.

Full of these diabolical schemes, he one day commanded the presence of Buckingham, Ratcliffe, and Catesby, to whom he could safely confide the secret, and who, he doubted not, would aid him in the crime he was about to perpetrate.

As the duke and his two associates entered the royal presence-chamber, the former, after making an humble obeisance, exclaimed—

"My gracious sovereign, we attend your bidding."

"Buckingham," replied the king, "by thy assistance, we are seated upon the throne of England. But say, shall we wear these glories for a day, or shall they last during the time that Heaven shall give us to live?"

"Long—long may they last," responded the duke.

"Then if thou art indeed my friend," returned Richard, "that which I am about to say will prove a touchstone. Young Edward lives, so does his brother York. Now think what I would speak."

"Say on, my gracious lord," said Buckingham.

"Cousin, thou wert not wont to be so dull," exclaimed Richard. "Shall I be plain? I wish the bastards dead, and I would have it immediately effected. Now cans't thou answer me?"

"None dare dispute your highness' pleasure," replied Buckingham, submissively.

"Indeed, methinks thy kindness freezes, cousin," cried the king, with a darkening brow. "Thou wilt refuse to aid me then?"

"My lord, since it is an act that cannot be recalled," returned Buckingham, "allow me to reflect upon it for awhile."

With these words the Duke of Buckingham, followed by Ratcliffe and Catesby, quitted the chamber.

The emergency in which the king now found himself placed did not allow of very long deliberation; and calling to a page he desired him to summon to his presence a ruffian named Tyrrel.

Obedient to the royal command, Tyrrel shortly afterwards made his appearance, to whom he communicated his desire of having the young princes murdered, promising at the same time a large reward in the event of the deed being executed with despatch and certainty.

Tyrrel at once complied; and it was then agreed that, aided by the royal signet, he should obtain an easy access to the Tower, where, with the assistance of Dighton and Forest, two other assassins, they should enter the apartment of the princes, whom they were to smother in their sleep.

All this was faithfully promised by Tyrrel, who, receiving from the hands of King Richard the royal signet, left the palace, with a promise to return on the following morning and report the success of the infamous task.

Meanwhile as Tyrrel left the presence of the king, Buckingham returned.

"My lord," he said, "I have considered in my mind the matter you but now spoke to me upon."

"Oh, let that rest," said Richard, who was profoundly agitated. "Hast heard the news? Dorset has fled to Richmond."

This was the Earl of Richmond, afterwards Henry VII.

"I hear the tidings, my lord," said Buckingham.

"Stanley—he is your wife's son," said Richard, "well, look to it. See to your wife. If she conveys letters to Richmond, you shall answer for it."

"My lord," said Buckingham calmly, "I claim the gift, my due by promise, the earldom of Hereford, and the moveables which, on your word, I was to possess."

Richard heard him not, or affected not to hear him, and went on—

"I do remember now, Henry the Sixth did prophesy that Richmond should be king when he was but a little peevish boy. Why was not I by to kill him?"

"My lord," said Buckingham, "your promise for the earldom is——"

"Richmond," pursued Richard, pacing to and fro and totally ignoring the presence of the speaker, "when last I was at Exeter the mayor and Courtney showed me the castle, and called it Rougemont, at which name I started, because a bard of Ireland told me once I should not live long after I saw Richmond."

"My lord——"

"Ah, what's o'clock?"

"Upon the stroke of ten," said Buckingham; "but tell me, pray——"

"Thou troublest me, I am not in the vein," cried Richard, "another time. I am not in the giving mood to-day."

"Good," said Buckingham, as he hastened off; "he repays service with contempt. I will be off while yet my head is on."

Faithful to his promise Tyrrel on the next morning presented himself before the king, who was impatiently awaiting his arrival.

"Kind Tyrrel," cried the king, "am I happy in thy news?"

"If to have done the deed which you commanded will give you happiness," returned Tyrrel, "rest content, for the deed is done."

"But didst thou see them dead?" asked Richard anxiously.

"I did, my lord."

"And buried?"

"The chaplain of the Tower buried them," replied Tyrrel, "though where, to tell the truth, I know not."

"'Tis well," replied the king; "but away, away, I hear footsteps approach, and thou must not be seen in converse with me. Meet me an hour hence, and the reward I promised shall be thine."

As the assassin retired Ratcliffe and Catesby entered by another door, the former of whom exclaimed with much alarm—

"Most mighty sovereign, news has just arrived that a powerful army has made its appearance on the western coast; thither, with the intention of revolting, many of your faithless subjects have fled—most notably the Duke of Buckingham. The Earl of Richmond is at the head of the invading host, and purposes to march towards London as your open foe."

"Then not an instant is to be lost," cried Richard, whose countenance betrayed the alarm which the news had occasioned. "Do you, Catesby, instantly hie to the Duke of Norfolk and bid him bring all the men he can, and meet me at Salisbury."

Richard now saw that nothing but the greatest activity could avert the ruin which was impending, and hastily collecting a large army, he, in the course of a few days, was enabled to set forward to meet the foe who had thus suddenly arisen to hurl him from the throne.

His first revenge was the capture of Buckingham at Salisbury, where he was at once beheaded.

A few days more and Richard found himself within a few miles of the enemy at that place which has since become so well-known as Bosworth Field.

Expecting that a battle would shortly ensue, he made all the necessary arrangements to receive any attack which might be made upon him, and at length when night arrived, he was returning towards his tent when he met the Duke of Norfolk, Ratcliffe, and Catesby, to whom he gave their several instructions, and desiring Catesby to visit him in his tent an hour after midnight, he retired thither himself, to snatch a few moments' rest ere the great struggle which was to decide the fate of either himself or Richmond.

As the king advanced towards the couch in thoughtful meditation, he exclaimed—

"'Tis now the dead of night, and half the world is hung in solemn silence. How awful is this gloom, and hark! from camp to camp the hum of either army is distinctly heard, yet in such gentle sounds that the sentinels almost hear the secret watchword of each other. Steed threatens steed in high and boastful neighing, piercing the night's dull ear. Hark, from the tents the armourers are busily engaged in closing rivets up, giving dreadful note of preparation, while some, like sacrifices, by their watch fires sit patiently, and inly ruminate the danger which morning brings. By yon heaven, my stern impatience chides this tardy night, that like a foul and ugly witch limps so tediously away. I'll to my couch and once more try to sleep her into morning."

Richard advanced towards the bed and was just proceeding to lie down when a hollow groan was heard.

At this his soul shrunk within him, and starting back, he exclaimed—

"Ha! what means that dismal voice? Sure 'tis the echo of some yawning grave. 'Tis gone—'twas but my fancy, or perhaps the wind. Away vain fears—my eyes grow weary and I'll lie me down to sleep."

At these words the guilty monarch threw himself upon the couch, and, fatigued as he was with the exertions he had undergone, he was soon wrapped in a deep sleep.

But his slumber was not such as the guiltless man enjoys, for visions of the most terrific nature haunted him throughout the night, each one being succeeded by another even more horrible than that which preceded.

At length he perceived the aerial forms of the late King Henry VI., the young princes Edward and the Duke of York, and the Lady Anne, who had recently died from the effects occasioned by the barbarity of her ruthless husband.

After gazing for a short time upon him, the spirit of King Henry thus addressed the guilty usurper—

"Oh, thou, whose unrelenting thoughts no terror can shake, whose conscience ever sleeps with thy body, sleep on, while I, by Heaven's ordinance, in dreams of horror wake thy soul. Now give thy thoughts to me—let them behold these gaping wounds which thy murderous hands inflicted; let thy devouring conscience gnaw thy heart, and terribly revenge my murder."

As he concluded, the gentle spirit of Lady Anne thus continued to pour agony on his racked soul—

"Think upon the wrongs of thy wretched wife; even in the battle's heat remember me, and edgeless fall thy sword. Despair and die."

Then spoke the shade of the young Prince Edward—

"Richard, dream on, and see—the wandering spirits of thy nephews. Could not our youth, our innocence, prevail upon thy hardened heart to spare us? But for thee, alas! we might have enjoyed many years of happiness and peace. Oh, 'twas a cruel deed, and therefore alone, unpitying, unpitied shalt thou fall."

The spirit of King Henry then resumed—

"The morning's dawn summons us away! then, Richard, wake, in all the hell of guilt, and let that wild despair, which now preys upon thy thoughts, alarm the world—to guilty minds a terrible example."

The spirits now disappeared, and Richard in imagination saw the sanguinary tragedy that closed the mortal career of the mild and excellent Prince Edward.

Next came the deliberate and cold-blooded murder of the young princes in the Tower of London.

Agitated beyond endurance by the scenes he had witnessed, Richard awoke, and rushed with frenzied steps from the tent into the open air, and falling upon his knees, exclaimed—

"Give me another horse, bind up my wounds. Have mercy, Heaven!"

Then recovering himself a little, he continued—

"Ha, 'twas but a dream, but then so terrible, that it shakes my very soul; cold drops of sweat hang on my trembling limbs, my blood grows chilly, and I freeze with horror. Oh, tyrant conscience, how thou afflictest me. Who's there?"

"'Tis I, my lord," replied Catesby, as he entered. "Your friends are up, and buckled in their armour."

"Oh, Catesby, I have had such horrid dreams," exclaimed the king.

"Shadows, my lord."

"Now, by this day's hopes," returned Richard, "shadows to-night have struck more terror to my soul than can ten thousand soldiers, even though led by shallow Richmond."

"Be more yourself, my lord," said Catesby. "Considering, sir, were it known a dream had frightened you, how would your foes presume on it?"

"Perish the thought!" cried the king. "No, never be it said that fate itself could awe the soul of Richard. Hence, babbling dreams; conscience, avaunt. Richard's himself again. And, hark, the trumpet sounds a call. Hence, my soul's in arms and eager for the fray!"

The battle was a most terrible one.

Richard performed prodigies of valour.

He was everywhere encouraging his men, and five times during his tremendous career he imagined he had killed his rival —five gentlemen having been attired in like armour to Richmond, in order to draw him to different parts of the field.

Catesby was staunch to the last, and did his best to keep up the flagging courage of the men, and the doubtful prowess of the leaders.

Again and again had Richard a horse slain under him, and yet on foot he dashed madly into the very jaws of death.

But he saw the day was waning, and that all hope was gone unless he met Richmond and slew him.

The battle was turning in favour of the Duke of Richmond, when at length he met with the object of his hatred, who rushing towards him exclaimed—

"Of one, or both of us the time is come, for I have set my life upon a cast and I will stand the hazard of the die."

"Kind Heaven, I thank thee," cried the other; "if Richard's fit to live, let Richmond fall."

A desperate combat now ensued between the tyrant Richard and Richmond, the latter of whom, possessing every advantage, soon succeeded in inflicting a mortal wound upon his adversary, who, falling to the earth, exclaimed—

"Perdition catch thy arm, the chance is thine. Now let the world no longer be a stage to feed contention with, but let one spirit reign in all bosoms, that each heart being set on bloody actions, the rude scene may end, and darkness be the burier of the dead."

With these words the spirit left the body of the guilty king, and Richmond bending over the body, cried—

"Farewell, Richard, and from thy dreadful end may future kings be warned from tyranny. Hark! the glad trumpets speaks the field our own."

Lords Stanley and Oxford, with numerous others of the nobility now approached bearing the crown of Richard, which, presenting to Richmond, they earnestly begged of him to accept.

The conqueror acceded to their wish, and, a few days afterwards, he was publicly invested with the imperial power.

He subsequently, by authority of parliament, espoused the Lady Elizabeth, the daughter of Edward IV., and the union put an end to the deadly strife between the houses of York and Lancaster.

THE BATTLE OF BOSWORTH FIELD.

IMPORTANT NOTICE TO OUR READERS.—Orders should be given Early for the Next Complete Story from Shakespeare—"HAMLET." The Stories from Shakespeare, when finished, will make one of the Best Works of the Day.

EDWIN J. BRETTS STORIES OF

SHAKESPEARE

COMPLETE

HAMLET

o. 2.

EDWIN J. BRETT'S
STORIES FROM
SHAKESPEARE'S PLAYS.

No. 2. HAMLET.

DARKNESS had fallen over the Royal Castle at Elsinore in Denmark.

Along the battlements paced frequent sentinels, who, in the gloom and silence of the dusky night, looked almost longingly at the lights, dim though they were, of the town below them.

All was very still; and one of the solitary watchers—who walked to and fro at an angle of the castle walls—broke continually the monotony of his weary promenade by glancing furtively round him as if in fear of some ghostly visitation.

Things were not quite as settled as they might have been in the Royal Castle.

But two months before, Hamlet, the King of Denmark, had died—loved in his life and regretted in his death: a monarch who had been the idol of the multitude and of the nobles also.

He had left behind him a son, a widow, and a brother; and, to the astonishment of all, and the disgust of many, the widow had married her husband's brother within a month of the good king's death.

Many and suspicious were the stories which floated about Elsinore when this hasty marriage was concluded, and young Hamlet, whose Uncle Claudius had on his brother's death assumed royal power, had at once hastened home from Wittenberg, where he had been at school, to ascertain the strange mystery which seemed to envelope his father's fate.

Very still, however, was everything in the castle now, for the clocks was close on the stroke of midnight; and the soldier, Francisco, as he paced to and fro, grew more nervous as the witching hour approached.

At length, on the echoing stone pavement was heard the sound of footsteps approaching, and with a sudden start he drew his sword, exclaiming in a voice which was strangely hoarse:

"Who's there? Stand and reveal yourself."

"Long live the King!" said the tall mail-clad officer who approached; "it is I, Bernardo. It has now struck twelve; get thee to bed, Francisco, and if you meet Horatio and Marcellus, the rivals of my watch, bid them make haste."

"I think I hear them," said Francisco. "Stand ho! who is there?"

"Friends and liegemen to the Dane," cried the officer named Horatio, who had been a fellow-student, and was a bosom friend of young Prince Hamlet; "Marcellus is here with us."

"Welcome, Horatio; welcome, good Marcellus," said Bernardo. "Good-night, Francisco; get thee off to bed."

"Well," exclaimed Horatio eagerly, as the soldier hastened off, "has this happened again to-night? Has this ghostly thing which you declare you have seen two nights appeared once more?"

"I have seen nothing," said Bernardo.

"Horatio declares it is only our fancy," said Marcellus; "but, as he is disbelieving, I have persuaded him to watch with us to-night, that he may see it proved by his own eyes, and speak to it."

"Tush!" cried Horatio, with a laugh, "it will not appear."

"You see he will not believe," said Marcellus; "come, let us tell him once again the horrors we have seen these past two nights."

"Yes, we will sit down here," said Horatio. "Come, Bernardo, quickly to your story."

"Last night," began Bernardo, "the

bell was just tolling the hour of one, when——"

"Peace!" cried Marcellus, "see when it comes again."

As they looked in the direction which Bernardo pointed out they saw a shadowy figure approaching—a figure clad in armour, with helmet on, and white plumes nodding on its head.

It came onward—a gray glow rather than a substantial form, and its noiseless tread told plainly that it was an inhabitant of the other world.

It took no notice of them; but marching with martial stride to the battlements, gazed sadly down upon the town.

"See, I was not wrong," said Bernardo; "it is the same figure like the King that's dead."

"Thou art a scholar, Horatio; speak to it," cried Marcellus.

"Looks it not like the King?" said Bernardo; "mark it well."

"Yes, it is most like," said Horatio, "it harrows me with fear and wonder. Yet I will speak," he added, as he walked towards the dread thing: "What art thou that usurpest that fair and warlike form which the late King wore? I charge thee, speak!"

The figure made no answer, but slowly and sadly turned to depart.

"Stay—speak!" cried Horatio, "I implore thee—speak!"

But his appeal was of no avail; the ghost glanced coldly, impassively at him, and stalking away was lost in the gloom of night.

"How now, Horatio?" said Bernardo, "you tremble and turn pale. Is this not more than fancy?"

"I would not, by heavens, have believed it!" returned Horatio, "had I not seen it with mine own eyes. It was as like the King as you are to yourself. Such was the very armour he had on when he fought the Norwegian King. 'Tis wondrous strange."

"Twice, exactly at this hour, has he appeared," said Marcellus; "it must mean something; a warning surely of some coming evil."

"Perhaps," said Horatio, "it has something to do with the expected invasion of Fortinbras. Warlike preparations occupy all the public mind. You remember, mayhap, that our dead King was dared by Fortinbras of Norway to single combat; and that the latter was slain. According to a compact well ratified by law he forfeited his lands to the conqueror. Young Fortinbras, the son of the vanquished hero, has raised a number of resolute fellows to recover the lands his father forfeited. This is the cause of our preparations, and perhaps of this nightly visitation."

"But soft! behold, it comes again! Be still!"

Marcellus and Bernardo withdrew a few paces, and Horatio boldly advanced towards the ghostly figure, which gazed at him with sorrowful eyes.

"Stay, illusion!" cried he; "if thou hast any sound or use of voice, speak to me. If thou knowest anything of the fate which threatens thy country, speak, I pray thee! Ah, it will not stay! Stop it, Marcellus."

"Shall I strike at it with my partizan?"

"Yes, if it will not stand."

But all efforts were useless.

The ghost has departed, vanished suddenly, and only a chillness in the air seemed to mark the spot by which it had passed away.

"'Tis gone," said Marcellus, "and being so majestic, methinks we do it wrong to show it violence. It is invulnerable as the air, and all our efforts to harm it are but vain mocking."

"Well, well! the cock crew as it passed away, and we shall see it no more this night," said Horatio; "see now the russet-mantled dawn climbs over the eastern hill. Let us break up our watch and hasten to young Hamlet. This spirit, which is dumb to us, will no doubt speak to him."

"Yes, yes! Let us hasten to him," said Marcellus. "We will first to breakfast; and then I know where to find him. The King has audience of his ministers early to-day, and Hamlet will be there!"

So saying they left the battlements together; and having partaken of their breakfast, they adjourned to the hall of state, where they found the King and Queen, the Lord Chamberlain Polonius and his son Laertes, with Cornelius, one of the courtiers, some attendants, and young Prince Hamlet, the latter dressed in the deepest mourning, and looking the very picture of sorrow.

When they entered the audience chamber the King was delivering some orders to the ambassadors, whom he was about to send to Norway to inform the King of the levies which young Fortinbras was raising, and to ask him to at once suppress them.

Horatio, when this was over and the

ambassadors dismissed with all necessary credentials, was about to address Hamlet, who, leaning against one of the pillars, surveyed the scene with indifferent sadness.

Laertes, however, the son of Polonius, came forward to ask permission to return to France, whence he had come to be present at the King's coronation; and Claudius having granted it, said (turning to Hamlet):

"And now my cousin Hamlet, and my son, how is it that clouds still hang over you?"

"A little more than kin and less than kind," muttered the Prince; but he added aloud: "No clouds hang over me, my lord, I am too much in the sun."

"Good Hamlet," said his mother, "try, I beseech you, to cast off your sorrow. True, your noble father is dead; but all must die some day."

"Ay, madam," returned Hamlet, gazing at her fixedly, "it is our common fate."

"Why then do you seem so sorrowful, if your philosophy assists thee so far?"

"Seems, madam!" cried the young man. "I know not 'seems.' It is not only my inky cloak, nor my tears, nor my dejection that denotes my grief. These are but the trappings of my sorrow. I have that within me that passeth show!"

And striking his breast forcibly with his hand as he spoke he turned away.

"Why, Hamlet," said the King, "your grief no doubt is most commendable; but death is inevitable. Remember that you are not the only one who has had to mourn a father! You must not forget that you are the immediate heir to the throne, and I love you with a father's love. Your idea of returning to school at Wittenberg is much against our wishes. We beg you to remain."

"Yes, I pray you, Hamlet, stay with us," said Queen Gertrude entreatingly.

"I shall obey you to my best ability, madam," replied Hamlet, bowing.

"A good answer," said the King. "Come, Gertrude, I would speak with you."

Hamlet was now left alone, or at least he thought so, for Horatio, Bernardo, and Marcellus had kept far in the background.

"Oh!" he cried, "that there was no law against self-slaughter! How weary, stale, flat, and unprofitable seem the world and its ways! Oh, does it not appear a dream! My father only two months dead, and my mother married to my uncle! So excellent a King too was he—so loving to my mother, that he would not even let the winds of heaven visit her face too roughly. And this my uncle—no more like my father than Hyperion to a satyr! Oh, how could my mother marry him in such a little time? A beast that has no reason would have mourned longer; and yet with my heart breaking at this treason, I must hold my tongue."

"Hail to your lordship!" cried Horatio, approaching with his two friends.

"Ah, Horatio! or I forget myself," cried Hamlet. "I am glad to see you well. What brings you from Wittenberg?"

"A truant disposition, my lord."

"Ah! you are no truant—tell me what brought you to Elsinore."

"My lord, I came to see your father's funeral."

"Mock me not!" cried Hamlet; "say rather you came to see my mother's wedding."

"Well, indeed, my lord, I must confess," said Horatio, "it followed hard upon."

"Thrift, good Horatio! thrift!" said Hamlet with a strange smile; "the funeral baked meats did coldly furnish forth the marriage-tables! Oh, my friend! Would that I had met my dearest foe in heaven rather than have seen this day! Oh, my father! Methinks I see him now!"

"Where, my lord?"

"In my mind's eye, Horatio."

"I saw him once; he was a goodly King."

"Ay," said Hamlet, "he was a man, take him for all in all. I shall not look upon his like again."

It was now the opportunity which Horatio desired, and yet he seemed to shrink from it.

Hamlet was so pale, so stern, so wrought by pent-up passion!

But it was his duty to speak; and at length summoning up courage he said:

"My lord, I think I saw him yester-night."

"Saw whom?"

"The King, your father, my lord."

"For heaven's sake let me hear! delay not, good Horatio."

"Listen then," returned the Prince's friend. "Two nights running these gentlemen, Bernardo and Marcellus, were encountered during the night by a figure like your father, armed at all points, cap-à-pie, and walking slowly and stately before them. They stood before him dumb with fear; but when they told me this I spoke to it, yet answer made it none. It lifted up its head as if it wished to speak; but at that moment the cock crowed and it vanished."

Hamlet's face was pale and stern as he listened.

The words of his friend seemed, indeed, to have roused up some memory, or awakened some latent suspicion.

"'Tis very strange," he said: "do you keep the watch to-night?"

"Yes; we three."

"Was he armed, you say?"

"Ay, from top to toe, my lord."

"Saw you not his face?"

"Yes, my lord; he wore his beaver up, and gazed upon us more, as it seemed, in sorrow than in anger; his features pale, and his eyes fixed constantly upon us."

"I would I had been there," cried Hamlet; "but I will watch to-night. Perchance 'twill walk again; and, if it assume my noble father's person I will speak to it, though hell itself should gape and bid me hold my peace. But, my kind friends, say naught of this. Let us keep this secret between ourselves, and it may lead to good. Between eleven and twelve to-night I will meet you on the battlements."

"Ah," he added as they left him, "my father's spirit in arms! All is not well! I doubt some foul play! Would that the night were come!"

The wished-for time came at last.

During the day Laertes had departed for France.

His sister Ophelia was his special care ere he went.

A beautiful girl was Ophelia—tall, exquisitely proportioned, with large liquid eyes and masses of waving golden hair, which fell below her waist.

Though she was only the daughter of Polonius, the Lord Chamberlain, it was evident to all that the Prince loved her.

It was a piercingly cold night; and a wind which was keen even for Norway swept round the topmost towers of the castle.

Suddenly, as Hamlet and the others were walking to and fro somewhat quickly to keep out the cold, a loud flourish of trumpets was heard and the report of a cannon.

"What doth that mean, my lord?" asked Horatio.

"The King holds high festival to-night," said the Prince; "and as he drains the draughts of Rhenish wine the kettledrum and trumpet proclaim his pledge. Though I am a native here, and to the manner born, however, it is a custom, I fancy, more honoured in the breach than in the observance. But, stay; what's that?"

"The ghost, my lord; look, it comes!"

As Hamlet had been speaking, the terrible apparition had glided up behind him; and as the Prince turned and saw him, he started and stood in amazement.

But at length he found speech.

"Angels and ministers of grace, defend us!" he cried; "be thou a spirit of health or goblin accursed, thou comest in such a questionable shape that I must speak to thee. Oh Hamlet! King! Father! oh royal Dane! speak to me. Tell me why the sepulchre, wherein we saw you quietly interred, hath opened its marble jaws to cast thee up again. Say, why is this? Why are you here?"

"It beckons you to go away with it, and speak to it alone," said Horatio; "but pray go not."

"Why should I fear?" cried Hamlet.

"What if it were to tempt you to the dreadful summit of the cliff," said Horatio, "and there assume some shape which might deprive you of reason and lead you on to death?"

To this warning Hamlet paid no heed.

His eyes were fixed upon the semblance of his father.

"Ah!" he cried, "it waves me still. Go on; I'll follow thee."

"No, no," exclaimed Marcellus, "you shall not go, my lord."

Both he and Horatio caught Hamlet by the arm.

But Hamlet was determined.

"Unhand me, gentlemen," he cried. "See, see; it beckons me. By heaven! I'll make a ghost of him who hinders me! Go on, go on; I'll follow thee."

"What means this, think you?" asked Horatio, as Hamlet quickly followed his weird visitor.

"Something is rotten in the state of Denmark," said Marcellus; "but, come, let's follow him."

Meanwhile the ghostly visitant had led Hamlet to a remote place upon the battlements, where at last the Prince stopped.

"Whither wilt thou lead me?" he cried. "Speak, for I'll go no farther."

"Mark me!" said the ghost, in clear though hollow accents; "mark me well, for the time has nearly come when I must render myself again to tormenting and sulphurous flames. I am thy father's spirit, doomed for a certain time to walk the night. I am forbidden to tell the secrets of my prison-house, or I could unfold a tale whose very lightest word would harrow up thy soul. But list! If ever thou didst love thy father, revenge his foul and most unnatural murder."

"Murder!" cried Hamlet, starting back in utter astonishment.

"Ay, murder most unnatural. Hear me, Hamlet. 'Tis given out that sleeping in my orchard a serpent stung me. But know, my noble son, the serpent who took your father's life now wears the crown of Denmark; who, to his shameful love, has enticed my Queen. Oh Hamlet, what a falling-off was there!

"But listen. As I slept in mine orchard—my custom always of an afternoon—your uncle poured from a vial into my ear the deadly juice of hebenon, and robbed me at once of life, of queen, of kingdom. And then, thy mother! Oh! that she could have wed mine assassin! But turn not your thoughts against her; leave her to Heaven. To you I leave the rest. And now, farewell. The glow-worm shows the morning to be near, and begins to pale his ineffectual fire. Adieu; remember me!"

And in an instant he was gone.

For a few minutes Hamlet stood still as if petrified by horrid astonishment.

"Oh villain," he cried, after a moment; "oh smiling, damnèd villain! Ah! one may smile, and smile, and be a villain. Ah, my lords," he added, as Horatio and Marcellus came up, "it is all true that you told me. Alas! my poor father."

"What said he, my lord?" asked Horatio eagerly.

"What must not pass my lips," said Hamlet; "and I must beg of you, most excellent friends, to swear that you will not speak of this visitation to anyone. I know what I know, and to carry out my purpose I must be secret. Swear that, until I give you leave to do otherwise, you will be silent."

"Ay; silent as the grave. We swear it!" cried both.

"Then I will leave you. With all my heart I thank you," replied Hamlet. "Keep ever a finger on your lips, I pray. Good night!"

And so he left them.

To them there was nothing but wonder and surmise.

In his heart there was a steadfast purpose.

He would wait, carefully watch for his revenge, and in the meantime he would disarm all suspicion by feigning madness.

"It takes a wise man," they say, "to make a fool;" but Hamlet had wit and courage too, and had no fear of the consequences.

On the next day Polonius was seated in his own house, looking over some papers, when his daughter entered.

He had just sent off to France a messenger, one Reynaldo, with strict orders to inquire into the behaviour of his son Laertes, and sending a letter and money.

Ophelia looked very beautiful on this afternoon, with her long golden hair streaming over her shoulders, and her exquisite form, clad in some light material, which made her appear like some lovely visitant from fairyland.

She was troubled evidently, however, in her mind, for her eyes seemed as if she had been recently shedding tears.

Her father noticed her demeanour at once.

"Ha! Ophelia!" he cried, "why are you so distraught? What is the matter?"

"Oh, my lord, my lord, I have been so affrighted," returned the girl, who at the very remembrance of her trouble began to tremble violently.

"With what, in Heaven's name?"

"My lord, while I was sewing in my chamber, Lord Hamlet came before me. His doublet was all unbraced; no hat was on his head; his stockings fouled, ungartered, and hanging about his ankles; pale as his shirt he was; his knees knocking one against the other, and a look so piteous that it went right to my heart."

"Ah, he is mad for thy love, girl!"

"I do not know," sighed Ophelia, "but I fear it."

"Did he not speak?"

"He took me by the wrist, and held me hard, and gazed long and earnestly into my face. Then he shook my arm, waved his head up and down two or three times, and then, with a sigh so profound that it seemed to rend his heart, he passed away."

Hamlet had soon commenced his acting.

"Ah! I fear me I gave you bad counsel," said Polonius. "I advised you to repulse him."

"And I did, my lord."

"That hath made him mad," said her father. "I feared he did but trifle with you; but as it seems he loves, I must straightway to the King, and let him know."

There were in the castle at this time two persons of the name of Rosencrantz and Guildenstern, who had been at college with Hamlet, and to these the King had spoken in regard to the altered manner of the young Prince.

At the request of Claudius and the Queen, these gentlemen consented to remain at the palace awhile, in order to try and discover the meaning of Hamlet's extraordinary behaviour.

Polonius, who brought him news from Norway that Fortinbras had foregone his expedition, and was craving permission to march his forces through Denmark into Poland, brought him also the welcome news that Hamlet's distraught mind was caused by his love for Ophelia.

This was a relief to Claudius, as he had feared that Hamlet had got scent of his cruel murder of his brother.

"We must see to this," said the King, "for if he loves your daughter, and that love is his only malady, we can soon arrange things properly."

"And see," cried the Queen, "see how my poor son comes sadly reading."

"Away, I do entreat both of you!" cried Polonius; "I'll question him."

"How does my good Lord Hamlet?" he added, as the King and Queen went out; "do you know me, my lord?"

"Excellent well," returned Hamlet, "you are a fishmonger."

"Not I, my lord."

"Then I would you were so honest a man; for to be honest as the world goes is to be one picked out of ten thousand."

"That is true, my lord."

"Have you a daughter?"

"I have, my lord."

"Then look to her well, lest she err."

"Ah, still harping on my daughter! Yet he knew me not at first, but thought I was a fishmonger. He is far gone—far gone," muttered Polonius; "I must contrive a meeting between him and my daughter. My lord, I humbly take my leave."

"You cannot take from me anything I would more willingly part with," said Hamlet.

As he spoke, Rosencrantz and Guildenstern entered, and advanced to meet him.

"Ah, lads!" he cried, addressing his old schoolmates, "how do ye both?"

"Indifferently well, my lord."

"What news then?"

"None, my lord, save that the world's grown honest."

"Then is doomsday near!" said Hamlet, with a bitter laugh. "But your news is not true. What ill turn, my friends, have you deserved of fortune, that she sends you to prison here?"

"Prison, my lord?"

"Ay; Denmark's a prison, though it may be none to you. To me it is a prison. But no more of this. Shall we to the court? for, by my faith, I cannot reason. Yet stay; tell me honestly, were you sent for?"

"We were, my lord," said Guildenstern, after some hesitation, "but we are now here to tell you that the strolling players are coming to offer you service."

"Are they? then they shall be entertained well," said Hamlet.

"They are even now without. I'll fetch them, good my lord," said Rosencrantz.

"Stay," said the Prince, "let me tell you, gentlemen, you are welcome to Elsinore. Give me your hands. You are thrice welcome; and I blame you not for listening to the talk of my uncle-father and my aunt-mother, but they are deceived."

"In what, dear lord?" said Guildenstern.

"Why, I am mad only north-north-west. When the wind is southerly I know a hawk from a hand-saw."

At this moment Polonius again appeared the pompous old Chamberlain.

"Hark, my friends!" said Hamlet, in an undertone, "list to what I say. That great baby there is not yet out of his swaddling-clothes."

"Happily," said Rosencrantz, "has the second time come to them, for they say an old man is twice a child."

"I prophesy he comes to tell me of the players," said Hamlet. "You say right, sir; on Monday morning; 'twas then, indeed."

"My lord," said Polonius, not heeding his words, "I have news to tell you."

"My lord, I have news to tell you," mocked Hamlet. "When Roscius was an actor in Rome——"

"The actors are come hither, my lord."

"Buz, buz!"

"Upon my honour——"

"Then came each actor on his ass."

"The best actors in the world," continued Polonius, getting somewhat red in the face, but still disregarding the interruptions of the Prince, "either for

HAMLET.

OPHELIA.

tragedy, comedy, history, pastoral, pastoral - comical, historical - pastoral, tragical - historical, tragical-comical-historical - pastoral, scene individable, or poem unlimited."

"Oh Jephthah, judge of Israel, what a treasure hadst thou!" cried the Prince.

you play the Murder of Gonzago?"

"Ay, my lord."

"Well, have it then to - morrow night," said Hamlet. "You could, I suppose, study a speech of some dozen or sixteen lines, which I would write out and insert."

"Certainly, my lord."

CLAUDIUS.

"What treasure had he, my lord?"

"Why, one fair daughter and no more, whom he loved passing well."

"Still on my daughter!" murmured the old man.

"Am I not right, old Jephthah?"

"If you call me Jephthah, my lord, I have a daughter whom I love passing well."

"That follows not; but here come the players," said the Prince, as four or five actors were ushered into the room. "Masters, you are all welcome. Polonius, will you see these gentlemen well bestowed?"

"My lord, I will use them according to their deserts," said Polonius.

"Odds bodikins, man! much better, let us hope," exclaimed the Prince; "use every man according to his deserts, and who shall escape whipping?

"Can you," he said, turning to the one player who remained with him, "can

POLONIUS.

"Very well, I'll see to it. Now follow your friends; and you, Rosencrantz and Guildenstern, I'll leave you till to-night. Make yourself at home, for you are very welcome."

When they had bowed themselves out, Hamlet for some time paced hurriedly to and fro in his chamber.

"Ah! I have it," he cried; "Heaven sent these players here to serve my vengeance. I have heard that guilty creatures, sitting at a play, have by the very cunning of the scene been so struck to the soul that they have confessed their crimes. I'll have these players play something like the murder of my father before my uncle. I'll observe his looks; I'll try him to the quick. If he shows signs of guilt, I know my course.

"Yes, the play's the thing whereby I'll catch the conscience of mine uncle. Heaven send me good success!"

The King and Queen in

vain endeavoured to discover from Rosencrantz and Guildenstern the cause of Hamlet's strange distraction.

But the young Prince nursed his secret well; not even to Horatio would he disclose it.

Ophelia, too, had been questioned, and desired to give him all reasonable encou-

for rich gifts wax poor when givers prove unkind."

"Ha! ha!" cried Hamlet; "are you honest?"

"My lord?"

"Are you fair?"

"What means your lordship?"

"This—that if you be honest and fair,

CLAUDIUS AND LAERTES.

ragement; and at last an opportunity came when, in a room in the King's palace, Hamlet might find her alone.

He did not appear to see her at once, but pacing to and fro, went on with his thoughts, then suddenly he said: "Ah! soft, now—the fair Ophelia! Nymph! in thy orisons let all my sins be remembered."

"Ah, my good lord," said Ophelia, "how does your honour for this many a day?"

"I humbly thank you—well."

"I have something here you gave me as a keepsake, that I have long wished to redeliver. I pray you now take them back,

I should admit no discourse to your beauty. I did love you once."

"Indeed, my lord, you made me believe so," said the blushing girl.

"You should not have believed me. I loved you not."

"I was the more deceived."

"Get thee to a nunnery! Why shouldst thou be a mother to sinners? I am myself but indifferently honest, yet I could accuse me of such things that it were better my mother had not borne me. I am proud, revengeful, ambitious. What should fellows such as I am do crawling between heaven and earth? Go thy ways to a nunnery. Where is your father?"

"At home, my lord."

"Then," said Hamlet, "let the doors be shut upon him, that he may play the fool nowhere but in his own house. Fare thee well!"

And with these words he left her.

"Oh! what a noble mind is here o'erthrown," sobbed Ophelia. "Oh! woe is me to have seen what I have seen."

During all this time the King and Polonius had been listening, and they now advanced from their concealment into the room.

"This is not love, Polonius," cried the King. "There is something I fear in all this that means danger to our kingdom. Now listen, Polonius, he must be sent away for a time. He must away to England, to demand our neglected tribute. What think you of it?"

"It will do well," said Polonius, "but yet I believe still that the origin of his grief is neglected love, and I would suggest that after the play his Queen mother shall question him alone. I will be so placed that I shall hear all their conference."

"It shall be so," said Claudius.

Evening came at length, and Hamlet, strolling first into the hall where the play was to be performed, met Horatio.

"What, ho! Horatio," he cried, "I would speak to thee. There is a play to-night before the King, one scene of which comes near the circumstance which I have told thee of—my father's death. I pray you observe my uncle."

Amid braying of trumpets a large company now swept into the room, including the King, Queen, Polonius, Ophelia, and others.

"How fares our cousin Hamlet?" cried Claudius, in a voice of friendship.

"Excellent, i' faith," cried Hamlet; "of the chameleon's dish. I eat the air, promise-crammed. You cannot feed capons so?"

"These words are not mine, Hamlet."

"No—nor mine," said Hamlet. "My lord Polonius, you once played in the university, did you not?"

"That I did, my lord," said the old Chamberlain.

"And what did you enact?"

"I did enact Julius Cæsar: I was killed in the Capitol. Brutus killed me."

"It was a brute part of him, to kill so capital a calf there. Are the players ready?"

"Ay, my lord," said Rosencrantz, "they wait your patience."

"Come here, Hamlet," said the Queen, "and sit by me."

Hamlet smiled, and shook his head.

"No, no, good mother," he said, "here's metal more attractive."

And with these words he threw himself at the feet of Ophelia.

"Lady," he said, "shall I lie in your lap?"

"No, my lord."

"I mean, my head upon your lap."

"Ay, my lord. You are merry to-night."

"Why not?" cried Hamlet. "What should a man do but be merry? Look you how cheerfully my mother looks, and my father died within these two hours."

"Nay, 'tis twice two months, my lord," cried Ophelia.

"So long!" said Hamlet. "Nay, then let the devil wear black, for I'll have a suit of sables. Heavens! Two months dead, and not forgotten yet! But the play begins; I must watch."

As usual with plays in those days, the actors commenced by some dumb show; and in a moment the attention of all present was fixed upon the stage.

The actors' King and Queen entered, very lovingly embracing. She knelt and made protestations to him; and then, after raising her up and embracing her tenderly again, the King lay down upon a bank of flowers, and the Queen, as soon as she saw him asleep, left him.

Presently a man came on the stage, took the crown from the King's head, kissed it, and then, after pouring poison in the King's ear, glided away.

The Queen then returned, and, finding the King dead, made passionate actions, and was found so acting by the poisoner, who entered with some friends, and appeared to lament with her.

The dead body was then carried away, and the poisoner made love to the Queen, who after a time was persuaded by unceasing appeals to accept his love.

"What means this play, my lord?" asked Ophelia.

"Marry," cried Hamlet, "it means mischief; but see, Prologue advances. We shall know by this fellow."

The man who represented the part of Prologue now advanced to the front of the stage, and bowing to all, said:

"For us, and for our tragedy
    Here stooping to your clemency,
    We beg your hearing patiently."

During the prologue the royal pair had seemed greatly disturbed; but this feeling had apparently passed away, or was kept under restraint.

The play now began in earnest, the player King and Queen again appearing on the stage.

"Full thirty years," said the player King, "hath Phœbus' car gone round since love our hearts and Hymen our hands united."

"Yes," replied the player Queen, looking lovingly up into his face; "but, woe is me, you are so ill of late that I sometimes fear for you."

"In very truth, my love," returned her husband, "I must leave thee, I fear, full soon. Yes, thou wilt live on in this fair world, and haply one as kind for husband wilt thou——"

"Such love would be treason to my heart," cried his Queen. "I should be accursed if I took a second husband. No woman weds the second who did not kill the first!"

"That's wormwood," muttered Hamlet to himself, looking at his mother.

"Ah!" continued the player King, "you think you will no second husband wed. Wait until your first one is dead."

"No, no, my husband," cried the player Queen, lovingly embracing him, "let earth not give me food, nor heaven light; let woe and strife pursue me here and hereafter, if, once a widow, ever I be wife."

"'Tis deeply sworn!" said the player King. "Sweet, leave me here awhile; my spirits grow dull, and I would fain court sleep."

With these words he laid himself down upon a bank, and soon slept.

And then with a gentle kiss the player Queen left him.

"Madam!" said Hamlet to his mother, "how like you the play?"

"Methinks the lady does protest too much."

"Oh, she will keep her word!"

"Have you heard the argument, Hamlet?" said the King; "is there no offence in it?"

"No, no; they do but jest—poison in jest. No offence in the world."

"See," added the Prince, as another player appeared on the stage, "this is one Lucianus, nephew to the King."

"You are as good as a chorus, my lord," said Ophelia.

"Ay; but see the murderer's to speak now," cried the Prince.

"Thoughts black," began the actor, "hands apt, drugs fit, and time agreeing! Thou mixture rank, of midnight weeds collected, this wholesome life will instantly destroy."

As he spoke he took from his breast a phial of poison, and poured the contents into the ear of the sleeper.

"He poisons him in the garden for his estate," cried Hamlet, addressing his mother and his uncle. "His name's Gonzago: the story is extant, and written in very choice Italian. You will see anon how the murderer gets the love of Gonzago's wife."

"See, the King rises!" cried Ophelia; "what is the matter?"

Well might she ask.

The King had sprung up, clutching the Queen by the arm.

His eyes glared at the mimic scene of murder; his cheeks were deathly pale; his whole aspect one of trembling confusion.

"How fares my lord?" cried the Queen.

"Give me some light!" gasped Claudius; "and let us go—let us go!"

"Lights! lights! lights!" cried Polonius; "give over the play. The King is not well. This way, most royal sir."

In a short time Hamlet and Horatio were left alone.

"Well, good Horatio, I'll take the ghost's word for a thousand pounds," said the Prince; "didst thou perceive the guilty King's terror?"

"Very well, my lord," replied Horatio; "he looked for all the world like one stricken with death as he staggered from the hall."

"Ay, on the talk of the poisoning; but hush, we are not alone," said Hamlet; "here come Rosencrantz and Guildenstern. How now my friends, what seek you?"

"A word with you, my lord."

"A noble history, one you like, sir," said the Prince.

"The King in his retirement," said Guildenstern, "is marvellously distempered."

"With drink, sir?" said Hamlet.

"No, my lord, with anger; but the Queen, your mother, in great affliction of spirit, has sent for you. Your behaviour has struck her with amazement."

"Oh, wonderful son that can so astonish a mother!" said Hamlet.

"She desires to speak to you in her closet ere you go to bed?" said Rosencrantz.

"We will obey," returned Hamlet; "but here comes Polonius."

"My lord, the Queen would speak with you at once," said the Chamberlain.

"Do you see yonder cloud that's almost in the shape of a camel?" asked the Prince.

"By the mass, and it is like a camel, indeed," said Polonius, looking up with his imbecile smile.

"Methinks it's like a weasel," said Hamlet.

"It is backed like a weasel," said Polonius.

"Or like a whale!"

"Very like a whale."

"Ah me! they fool me to the top of my bent! Pray go on; tell my mother I shall be with her anon. Leave me, my friends."

"'Tis now the very witching hour of night," he murmured, "when churchyards yawn, and hell itself breathes forth contagion on the world! Soft; now to my mother. Oh heart, lose not thy nature! Let not ever the soul of Nero enter this firm bosom! Let me be cruel, not unnatural! I must speak daggers to her, but use none!"

Hamlet was not long in seeking his mother's chamber. Polonius had scarcely given his message and hidden himself behind the arras—as he had promised the King he would listen to Hamlet's words—when the young Prince entered, saying:

"Now, mother; what is the matter?"

"Have you forgot me?"

"No, by the rood," cried the Prince, "not so. You are the Queen, your husband's brother's wife; and—would it were not so!—you are my mother."

"Nay, then I'll send those to you that can speak," said the Queen angrily.

"Come, come," said Hamlet, "sit down; you shall not budge until I have set you up a glass where you may see the inmost part of you."

"What wilt thou do? Thou wilt not murder me? Help, help, oh!"

"Help, oh, help!" cried a voice behind the arras.

"How now, a rat!" cried Hamlet. "Dead for a ducat—dead!"

And in an instant he had made a pass through the hangings with his sword, while a voice behind was heard saying: "Oh, I am slain!"

"Ah me, what hast thou done?" cried his mother, clasping her hands wildly.

"I know not—is it the King?" cried

Hamlet; and, eagerly lifting up the arras, he drew forth the dead body of Polonius.

The Queen was horrified.

"Oh, what a rash and bloody deed!" she murmured.

"A bloody deed, good mother!" said Hamlet, laughing bitterly; "almost as bad as to kill a king and marry with his brother! Nay, answer not. My words are true. Farewell, Polonius, rash intruding fool!"

Then turning to his mother he again addressed her.

"Leave off wringing your hands. Pray sit down and let me wring your heart. Look!" he said, as he pointed at two portraits on the wall—those of Claudius and his murdered father—"look here upon this picture and on this. The counterfeit presentment of two brothers. See, what a grace was seated on this brow. Hyperion's curls, the brow of Jove himself; an eye like Mars, to threaten and command. And this, your husband, like a mildewed ear, blasting his wholesome brother. What devil thus cozened you? Oh shame——"

But here Hamlet paused.

Before him stood once more the spirit of his murdered father.

"Save me and hover over me with your wings, you heavenly guard!" cried the young Prince, starting back. "What would you, gracious figure!"

"Alas! he's mad!" murmured the Queen.

"Do not forget," said the ghost, who though seen and heard by Hamlet, was invisible and silent to her; "this visitation is but to whet thy almost blunted purpose. See, amazement on thy mother sits. Oh, step between her and her fighting soul; speak to her, Hamlet!"

"How is it with you, lady?" asked the Prince.

"Alas," she said, "how is it with you, that you bend your eye on vacancy—whereon do you look?"

"On him—on him. Look you, how pale he glares!"

"To whom," cried the frightened Queen, "do you speak thus?"

"Why look you there?" exclaimed Hamlet, as he pointed across the room. "See how it steals away. My father, in his habit as he lived. Look where he goes, even now out of the portal!"

"Oh, this is madness!" cried the Queen, looking round the room, for still the spirit was invisible to her.

"Mother, for love of grace, lay not that

flattering unction to your soul. It is your trespass, not my madness, speaks. Confess yourself to heaven; repent what's past; avoid what is to come. Good-night. For this lord" (pointing to Polonius) "I do repent. But heaven has pleased it so. Good-night, mother. Come, Polonius, thou art now a counsellor most grave and secret, though in life you were but a foolish prating knave."

And with these words he bore the body from his mother's chamber.

With his departure so also went the fear and the good resolutions of the Queen. She flew at once to the King, and confided in him; and they consulted again with Rosencrantz and Guildenstern as to the means to be adopted.

The preparations for Hamlet's departure were eagerly hurried on; and the two schoolfellows were entrusted with sealed letters to those in England who would compass Hamlet's death.

It is not for one moment to be supposed that Hamlet did not suspect the evil designs of the King against him; but his mind had little fear.

From the moment of her father's death, meanwhile, Ophelia seemed utterly distraught. She was continually to be found wandering to and fro in the palace, singing sad melodies about her lover, and dropping, too, such direful hints, that people's minds began to be set on the rack of wonder.

It was some days after the departure of Hamlet that she claimed an audience of the Queen.

"How now, Ophelia; what ails you?" she said.

The young girl stood still, picking at a flower, and singing a wild sad song.

"Alas!" said the Queen, turning to the King, "look upon her, her reason has fled."

"How do you, pretty lady?" said Claudius.

"Well. God shield you," returned Ophelia, "they say the owl was a baker's daughter. But let's have no more words of this. When they ask what it means, say you this:

"Good-morrow, 'tis St. Valentine's day,
　All in the morning betime;
And I, a maid, at your window
　To be your Valentine.

Hope all will be well; but I cannot choose but weep, to think they should lay my poor father in the cold ground. Come— my coach! Good-night."

"We are in danger, Gertrude," said the King, when the poor mad girl had gone. "Her father slain; your son gone; the people querulous and troubled at this swift burial; Polonius slain; and now Laertes, Ophelia's brother, returned in furious hate!"

It was true; and even as he spoke he could hear the cries of the people shouting "Laertes! Laertes? Down with Claudius!" and presently Laertes, followed by a crowd, came dashing into the room.

It was a hard matter indeed to calm the blood of the furious son of Polonius; but by dint of patience and cunning the King at length succeeded, and they entered into a deadly bond against Hamlet, should he return from England safe.

At this moment news was brought of the death of poor Ophelia, who was found calmly floating among the water-lilies of the palace lake, with her exquisite hair bedecked with flowers.

This maddened Laertes so much that he at once acceded to the King's cowardly counsel, that he should pick a quarrel with Hamlet, and slay him should he return.

Laertes, inflamed with rage, informed the King that he possessed a poison in which he could dip his sword—a poison so violent that if once a man received a scratch from it no human power could save him, and the King eagerly urged him on to this murderous deed.

Close upon this devilish compact came the news that Hamlet had returned.

His ship had been attacked by pirates, and he alone had been taken prisoner, in consequence of leaping too hastily on the vessel's deck.

However, in consideration of his having letters to the King, he had been set on shore unharmed.

He sent at once to Horatio, and returning with his friend, he passed through the churchyard where the funeral of the unfortunate Ophelia was about to take place.

An old gravedigger was already engaged in fashioning her last resting-place—singing as he worked, and throwing up the skulls as he dug them up.

"I will speak to this fellow," said Hamlet. "Whose grave is this, sirrah? What man dost thou dig it for?"

"For no man," said the gravedigger.

"For what woman, then?"

"For none, either."

"Who is to be buried in it?"

"One that was a woman, but, rest her soul, she's dead.

"How long hast thou been a grave-digger?"

"Why here in Denmark I have been sexton, man and boy, forty years. Here's a skull that hath lain in the earth for many a day."

"Whose was it?"

"Ah! he was a mad rogue. He poured a flagon of Rhenish on my head once. This is the skull of Yorick, the King's jester."

"This!" said Hamlet, as he took it in his hand. "I knew him well, Horatio. A fellow of infinite jest. He hath borne me on his back a thousand times. Yet now, how abhorred in my imagination it is. But soft, aside, here come the King and others in procession. We will conceal ourselves and watch."

Horatio, of course, knew nothing of the death of Ophelia, as he had rushed at once from Elsinore to meet his friend the instant he received his letter.

They watched until the body was about to be lowered into the grave, in the presence of the King, the Queen, Ophelia's brother, and a large band of mourners; and it was then seen that Laertes was bandying angry words with the priest.

"Is there no further ceremony, priest?" he cried.

"None," returned the other. "We have gone even now as far as we have warranty. Her death was doubtful, and had not the King's command o'erswayed us, she should have lodged in unsanctified ground till the last trumpet."

"Must there be no more done?"

"No more. We should profane the service of the dead to sing a requiem and such rest to her as to peacefully-departed souls."

Hamlet listened eagerly from his vantage point behind the tombs. He almost already knew the worst from the sad teachings of his own heart.

"Lay her in the earth," cried Laertes; "and from her fair and unpolluted flesh let violets spring. I tell thee, churlish priest, a ministering angel shall my sister be when thou liest howling."

"What!" whispered Hamlet; "my fair Ophelia!"

"Sweets to the sweet. Farewell!" said the Queen, as she scattered flowers over the body of the fair maiden. "I hoped thou wouldst have been my Hamlet's wife. I thought thy bride-bed to have decked, sweet maid, and not thy grave."

"Oh! treble woe," cried Laertes, "fall on that cursed head who of thy life deprived thee. Hold off the earth awhile, till I have caught her once more in my arms."

"Now," he added madly, as he leaped into the grave, "now pile your dust upon the quick and dead, till of this flat a mountain you have made."

"What is he," cried Hamlet, advancing from his concealment, "what is he whose grief bears such an emphasis? Here am I, Hamlet the Dane!"

And with these words he also leaped into the grave.

"The devil take thy soul!" cried Laertes, savagely grappling with him.

"Thou prayest not well," said Hamlet; "I pray thee take thy fingers from my throat; for though I am not rash-blooded, yet I have something dangerous in me, which it would be wise to fear. Hold off thy hand."

"Pluck them asunder," cried the King.

A rush was made, and they were separated, and brought up out of the grave; where they stood gazing furiously at one another.

"Why," cried Hamlet, "I will fight with him upon this theme until my eyelids will no longer wag. I loved Ophelia; forty thousand brothers could not with all their quantity of love make up my own. What wilt thou do for her? Wilt thou weep—or fight—or fast—or tear thyself? I'll do the same. If thou wilt mouth, I'll rant as well as thou."

"This is mere madness," said the Queen, "and thus awhile the fit will work upon him."

"Madness! why should you, Laertes, use me thus?" said Hamlet; "I loved you ever. But it is no matter."

And with these words he left them, followed by Horatio.

"Be patient, Laertes," said the King; "remember our last night's conversation. We'll settle the matter quicker than you think. Forget not the potion that I shall prepare. When you are hot and dry, I'll proffer him the cup, and if he sips, he'll save your sword much trouble. Come, Gertrude, let's away."

"Horatio," said the Prince, "I am sorry I forgot myself to Laertes; but, peace, who comes here?"

It was Osric who approached.

"Your lordship is right welcome back to Denmark," said he. "I bring a message from the King. There is newly returned to court, Laertes—one whom you know well, an absolute gentleman. Now the King has wagered with him six Barbary horses; against which Laertes has gaged six French rapiers and poniards with their assigns, girdles, hangers, and so on. The King hath laid that in a dozen passes between yourself and this Laertes he shall not exceed you three hits. What say you, my lord?"

"I accept the challenge," said Hamlet.

"You will lose the wager, my lord," said Horatio.

"I do not think so," said Hamlet; "but here come the King and Queen and Laertes, with men who carry foils. They're wondrous eager."

"Come, Hamlet," said the King, "come and take Laertes' hand from me."

"Give me pardon, Laertes," said Hamlet, accepting the hand. Farthest from Hamlet's mind was all thought of the vile treachery of Laertes.

"I embrace it freely," he said, "and will this brother's wager frankly play. Come on."

"Give them the foils, young Osric," said the King; "Cousin Hamlet, you know the wager."

"Very well, my lord; but your grace hath laid odds on the weaker side."

"This is too heavy," said Laertes, as he took a foil, "let me see another;" and he adroitly chose the poisoned one.

"This likes me well," said Hamlet, as he examined his; "they are, I suppose, all of a length."

"Ay, my lord," said Osric.

"Set me the stoups of wine upon that table," said the King. "If Hamlet give the first or second hit, or quit the answer of the third exchange, let all the battlements their ordnance fire. The King shall drink to Hamlet's better health. And in the cup he will throw a pearl richer than that which four successive Kings have worn in Denmark's crown. Give me the cup. Come, begin, and you, the judges, bear a wary eye."

"Come on, Laertes!" cried Hamlet.

"Come on, my lord!"

They began to fence admirably, both of them, and presently Hamlet touched his adversary.

"One!" he cried.

"No!" exclaimed Laertes.

"Judgment!" said Hamlet, pausing.

"A hit, a very palpable hit," cried Osric.

"Stay," cried the King, as they were about to recommence. "Give me drink! Hamlet, this pearl is thine. Here's to thy health. Give him the cup."

As he spoke a loud roar of cannon was heard without, and a flourish of trumpets.

But Hamlet would not drink; they crossed foils again.

"I'll play this bout first," he said; "set it down awhile. Come, ah! another hit! What say you?"

"A touch! a touch! I do confess," said Laertes.

"Our son will win," said the King.

"He's fat and scant of breath," said the Queen. "Here, Hamlet, take my kerchief, rub thy brows. The Queen drinks to thy fortune, Hamlet."

"Gertrude, do not drink," said the King in an eager whisper.

"I will, my lord," said the Queen, "I pray thee pardon me."

"It is the poisoned cup!" murmured the King to himself. "It is too late."

"I dare not drink yet, madam," said Hamlet; "I will by-and-by."

"My lord, I'll hit him now," cried Laertes.

"I do not think it."

"And yet it is sore against my conscience," said Laertes to himself.

"Come, for the third, Laertes," cried Hamlet. "I pray you pass with your best violence. I am afraid you only dally with me."

"Say you so? Come on! Have at you!"

This bout was by far the most violent of all; and Hamlet—caught off guard—was wounded.

Then came an unexpected scuffle, in which they changed rapiers, and Hamlet wounded Laertes.

"Part them, they are angry," cried the King. "Ah! the poison works—my Queen! See to her, gentlemen." For as he had spoken, the Queen had fallen.

"How is it with you, Laertes?" cried Osric.

"Why, Osric, I am justly killed with my own treachery."

"How does the Queen?" said Hamlet anxiously.

"She swoons," cried the King, "to see them bleed."

"No, no," exclaimed the Queen bitterly; "the drink! the drink! Oh! my dear Hamlet, I am poisoned."

And with the words she fell dead upon the couch.

"Ho, there!" cried Hamlet; "let the door be locked. There's treachery here, and we must seek it out!"

At this moment Laertes fell to the floor in agony.

"Ah, Hamlet!" he said faintly, "the treachery's here. Hamlet, thou art slain. No medicine in the world can do thee good. In thee there is not half an hour of life. The treacherous weapon is in thy hand. The foul practice hath turned itself on me. So, here I lie, never to rise again. Thy mother's poisoned. I can say no more; the King's to blame!"

"The point envenomed still!" cried Hamlet; "then, venom, do thy work!"

And in an instant he had sprung upon the King, and buried the weapon in his breast.

"Treason! Oh, yet defend me, friend," exclaimed the King; "I am but hurt."

"Ha! here then, murderous, damnèd Dane. Drink off this potion. Is thy pearl in this? Follow my mother!"

As the King fell back in the agonies of death, Laertes spoke again:

"He is justly served. It is a poison tempered by himself. Exchange forgiveness with me, noble Hamlet; mine and my father's death come not on thee! Nor thine on me!"

"Heaven make thee free of it! I follow thee," said Hamlet, as he saw Laertes die at his feet. "I am dead, Horatio. Wretched Queen, adieu! You that look pale and tremble at this scene, had I but time—oh! I could tell you—but let it be. Horatio, thou livest; report me and my cause aright to the unsatisfied."

"Never believe it, Hamlet," cried Horatio, as he seized the cup of poison. "I am more an ancient Roman than a Dane. Here's yet some liquor left."

"As thou'rt a man," cried Hamlet, "give me the cup! Let go—by Heaven, I'll have it!" he added, as he struggled with his friend, and dashed the cup from his hand. "Think, Horatio, what a wounded name would live behind me, if things were not explained! If thou didst ever hold me in your heart, Horatio, tell my story to all. Ah! what noise is that?"

A sound was heard afar off, and a shot.

"It is young Fortinbras," said Osric, "with conquest come from Poland, and to the ambassadors of England gives this warlike volley."

"Oh!" exclaimed Hamlet, "I die, Horatio. The potent poison quite o'er crows my spirit. I cannot live to hear the news from England; but I do prophesy the election of the Danes lights on Fortinbras. He has my dying voice; so tell him. The rest is silence."

And with one last look at his true and tried friend he expired.

"Now cracks a noble heart," said Horatio, in a voice choked by emotion. "Good night, sweet Prince; and flights of angels light thee to thy rest."

Our story is done.

Horatio faithfully fulfilled his promise, and told to the wondering and sorrowing Danes the wrongs and troubles of their favourite Prince.

The election, as Hamlet had prophesied, fell on young Fortinbras, and Horatio was advanced high in office; but one of the things which most delighted the heart of the true friend was the news from England that the two cowardly traitors, who had tried to compass Hamlet's death—his two treacherous schoolfellows, Rosencrantz and Guildenstern—met their death instantly on their arrival on Albion's shores.

THE END.

NOTICE.—"MACBETH," being No. 3 of Stories from Shakespeare, will be ready on Monday, Nov. 21. Orders should be given early, as a large demand is expected.

"COME ON, MACDUFF; THIS STRUGGLE IS OUR LAST."

"Boys of England Edition."

EDWIN J. BRETT'S
STORIES FROM
SHAKESPEARE'S PLAYS.

No. 3. MACBETH.

CHAPTER I.

A WILD heath in Scotland. Bleak, bare, and desolate at all times, it was just now rendered more gloomy and forbidding by the black storm-clouds that had gathered overhead. A fierce tempest was raging; ever and anon the forked lightning flashed forth with fearful vividness, and the deep, rolling, deafening thunder shook the whole earth.

In the centre of the heath stood three figures of weird and unearthly aspect. They appeared to be old women, with hideous and wrinkled countenances, half hidden beneath their hoods as they leant upon their staves in close converse. Sometimes they uttered shrieks or peals of diabolical laughter; sometimes raised aloft their skinny arms and gesticulated wildly, and often broke into snatches of discordant song. Presently they flung aside the long grey cloaks which enveloped them, and joined hands in a wild dance, keeping time to a barbaric chant.

Such an aspect and such actions showed these beings to be witches; aged crones leagued with the powers of evil, and gifted with supernatural knowledge of the future.

Suddenly they stopped in their dance and song, and turned to greet two strangers of warlike and distinguished aspect who were evidently surprised at meeting them. The elder was a man of middle age and haughty mien, with dark hair and somewhat stern countenance. This was Macbeth, Thane or Earl of Glamis, a powerful nobleman of the court of Duncan, King of Scotland. His companion was Banquo, one of the leading generals of Duncan's army. Both were clad in square Saxon tunics and mantles, encircled with cross-garters of ornamented leather; feathered steel skull-caps protected their heads; breastplates and back-pieces of polished steel formed their body armour, and their weapons were a sword and dagger each, fastened by chains to their iron-bound leathern belts.

"What strange weird beings are these?" exclaimed Banquo, gazing in astonishment at the weird figures before him.

"What do they mean by their uncouth grimaces and this barbarous chorus?" added the Thane of Glamis.

In reply, the three witches, with unearthly peals of laughter, joined hands and danced around the two warriors.

"All hail, Macbeth, Thane of Cawdor!" cried the first witch.

"All hail, Macbeth, the future King of Scotland!" added the second.

"All hail, Banquo, the father of future kings!" exclaimed the third.

And then all joined in a chorus of "All hail, Macbeth and Banquo!"

"Stay, ye beldames," imperatively commanded the Thane, "explain your dark prophecies. I know I am Thane of Glamis, but how can I be also of Cawdor, whose thane is still alive and well? Above all, what mean you by calling me the future King of Scotland, to whose throne I have no title? Upon what authority do you tell me this? Speak!"

But the trio of hags only answered by another peal of demoniacal laughter, and then suddenly vanished into the darkness.

"Strange!" exclaimed Banquo, looking round. "They must be but beings of the air; evil spirits of the storm."

"Their words still ding in my ears,"

said Macbeth. "They prophesied that your children should be kings."

"And better still for you, that you should yourself be King," returned Banquo; "but, my lord, why attach any weight to the utterances of beings who may be, after all, but the creations of our own fancy."

"We saw them too plainly for that," answered Macbeth ponderingly, "and their speech was full of meaning, though it may be but lying and deception. King of Scotland! Is it possible that such is the lot in store for me. I cannot think it, and yet——"

"But who comes here?" said Banquo, suddenly interrupting his chief's cogitations.

A flash of lightning revealed Rosse and Angus, two other Scottish nobles, with their attendants.

"Welcome, Lord Macbeth," said Rosse, courteously saluting the Thane. "We were seeking you, but scarcely expected to meet you so suddenly. Our gracious King, the noble Duncan, has received with great pleasure the news of your glorious victories over the Norwegian invaders, whom you have so utterly defeated that Sweyn, the King of Norway, begs for a truce."

"Therefore, our royal master," added the Earl of Angus, "sends you his thanks."

"And what is more," proceeded Rosse, "he bade me greet you as Thane of Cawdor."

Banquo and Macbeth started.

"What!" so ran the thoughts of each, "are the prophecies of the three hags really true, and so soon to be fulfilled?"

"Noble lords," said Macbeth, "I thank the King and yourselves; but how can I have the title of Cawdor, when the thane still lives?"

"He is in disgrace," was the reply, "suspected of conspiring with the enemy, and his rank and fortune are forfeited. But you, most worthy commander, stand highest of all in his favour, and he has, doubtless, still greater honours in store for you."

"Perhaps the highest of all," said Macbeth, in a low tone to his companion. "Banquo, there is destiny in this."

"It truly appears so," said the other. "You may yet wear the crown of Scotland."

"But only by Duncan's death," returned the Thane, "and by the deaths of others who stand near to the throne. Will these all die to make room for me, unless indeed

foul means are used, and then——" But shaking off the dark thoughts that now rose in his mind, the newly-made Thane of Cawdor turned again to the two noblemen, shook them warmly by the hand, and repeated his thanks for their conveying to him the King's favours.

We must explain that it was about the middle of the eleventh century when King Duncan reigned in Scotland, but the country was distracted by the quarrels and intrigues of the turbulent nobles of whom Macbeth was the chief. The King was mild and humane, but scarcely vigorous enough to rule so disordered a monarchy; his son and heir, Malcolm, had many enemies, and his prospects of succeeding might at any time be dashed aside by some bold and unscrupulous usurper.

Macbeth was naturally ambitious; but still more so was his wife, the Lady Gruach, who was of energetic and masculine character, and ever urging her lord to take advantage of his rivals and to rise, by whatever means, in the King's favour. She was capable, as we shall soon see, of inciting him to yet darker deeds, and even of personally assisting in them.

In a richly furnished chamber in Macbeth's massive stone castle at Inverness sat the Lady Gruach.

Her majestic appearance was set off by a magnificent costume of the Anglo-Saxon fashion, and her raven locks were encompassed by a golden circlet, set with gems; but she meditated wearing, ere long, a yet richer robe and a still more costly headgear—the crown and mantle of a Scottish queen.

"Yes," she murmured, laying down the letter in which Macbeth had informed her of his elevation in rank and of the witches' prophecies, "it must be, at whatever cost; the reign of the feeble Duncan shall be speedily ended. Macbeth shall sit upon the throne, and I will share his glory and power. Splendid destiny! but how will it be fulfilled?"

As she was pondering upon this vital point, a knock was heard without, and a messenger, travel-stained and breathless, hurried in.

"Madam," he said with an obeisance, "I have to tell you that the King comes here to-night."

"The King here!" exclaimed the lady; "this is indeed a sudden and unexpected honour. Is your master with him?"

"He is, gracious lady, and desires that

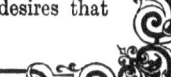

all preparations shall be speedily made to receive his Majesty in a fitting manner."

"It is well," replied the lady, rising. "Summon the seneschal and our other attendants at once, to receive my instructions."

While Lady Macbeth was in the midst of the preparations to receive the royal visitor, Macbeth himself arrived. He also seemed hurried and excited, but not too much so to notice a strange, dark, determined expression upon his wife's face which boded some important resolve.

"Thane of Cawdor," she said, when they were alone, "our master, King Duncan, comes here to-night; but when does he depart?"

"To-morrow—so he intends."

"Macbeth," said the lady, sinking her voice to a whisper, "to-morrow must never come."

"What is your meaning?" asked the Thane, starting back in alarm.

"I mean," she replied, "that Duncan shall never leave this castle alive."

"Great Heaven!" exclaimed Macbeth, "would you have us commit murder?"

"Murder! what is murder? Is it worse to kill one man in a room than a thousand on a battle-field? I say that he must die. Fate has delivered him into our hands, and the witches' prophecy shall be fulfilled."

"But think how horrible a crime it is," said Macbeth, "to kill a King—an old man, and unprotected—who comes here as our honoured guest. Would it not be a deed of double baseness and treachery?"

"Pshaw, my lord! why so scrupulous; is it that you are afraid? These are no times for weakness and gentleness. The welfare of the State demands that the old and feeble Duncan shall be removed; and you, as the most powerful and popular of the Scottish nobles, will be elected to reign in his stead."

"Even if I agreed to the crime," said the Thane, pondering, "how could it be done without strong suspicions against us?"

"Oh, I have laid my plans well," was the reply of his ambitious spouse. "It will seem that he has been murdered by others. Listen, and I will unfold my scheme."

In the midst of the whispered conference that now succeeded, the sound of a bugle was heard without, indicating that the King had arrived at the castle.

Macbeth and his wife now smoothed their wrinkled brows, and, guilty plotters as they were, went forth to meet their monarch in all smiling courtesy and loyalty.

King Duncan of Scotland, a grey-haired man of venerable and benevolent aspect, was attended by several distinguished noblemen and officers, who, with their attendants, formed a considerable cavalcade, but the castle was of extensive size and could accommodate them all.

"Welcome, most gracious King, to our humble home," said Lady Macbeth, with a low reverence to the King. "Let me conduct you to my lord, who is all impatience to pay you his respects."

CHAPTER II.

A GRAND banquet was now prepared; the King's table was placed upon a daïs or raised platform, where he was accompanied by a select few of his favourite nobles, and waited upon by the numerous servants of his host.

Meanwhile Macbeth himself was in a state of mind bordering on distraction. Eager as he was to seize the throne, and egged on as he was by his unscrupulous wife, he yet could not make up his mind to commit the dreadful deed she had planned. He wandered irresolutely in the ante-chamber in deep thought.

"Can I kill him?" he asked himself; "he is my guest, my sovereign, my distant relative; a man of venerable age and of great virtue and meekness? Would it not be a horrid deed to slay him in cold blood? And what would be the consequence to ourselves? Perhaps discovery and death."

"My lord," said Lady Macbeth, "the King has almost supped; he asks why you have left the table so abruptly."

"I scarcely dare to look him in the face," replied the Thane, "with this projected guilt upon my soul. We will proceed no further in this business. Look what honours the King has lately heaped upon me. Can I treat him with such base ingratitude?"

"Would you have me call you a coward?" angrily answered the merciless lady. "One who can plot and resolve, and then, when it comes to action, draw back alarmed? This is mere weakness. There is no danger to ourselves if we act cautiously, so as to throw all suspicion upon his attendants who will sleep in the adjoining chamber."

Macbeth accordingly accompanied his wife back to the hall, and remained until the King was conducted to his sleeping-chamber. The aged monarch was much pleased with his reception, and, besides large gifts to Macbeth's servants, sent Banquo with a costly diamond brooch as a gift to his "kind hostess."

Macbeth, as the time drew nearer for the dreadful deed, was still more irresolute and disturbed in mind. The prophecy of the witches, who hailed him as King of Scotland, rang in his ears, a demon form seemed to hover before him, giving him a dagger, and pointing to the door of the King's apartment.

His wife was again by his side.

"The King sleeps," she said in a hissing whisper. "I have laid the daggers ready. His two chamberlains have had their wine drugged, and are in a heavy stupor; they cannot wake yet awhile. Macbeth, the time has come!"

She held the door of the King's chamber open, and pointed into it with a look of command.

Summoning a desperate courage, Macbeth entered. It was scarcely dawn as yet, and quite dark within the gloomy castle. No one was astir except Macbeth and his wife, and they crept noiselessly along, more like guilty intruders than as the owners of the place. There was a brief interval, during which Lady Macbeth stood eagerly waiting her husband's return.

Then, with face ashen pale, hair dishevelled, eyes wild with horror, and frame trembling all over, the Thane of Cawdor staggered from the dark room into the ante-chamber. In his hands he held two daggers, deeply dyed with a crimson stain.

"I have done the deed," he gasped, leaning against the wall for support, and wiping the drops from his brow. "Oh, the burden of this guilt! Here is a horrible sight!" and, with a shudder, he showed his hands, also stained with blood.

"Calm yourself," said the lady; "the worst is over."

"No; the worst is to come. Oh, Gruach! there is a stain upon my guilty soul which nothing can wash away. Never can I forget the face of my victim, calmly sleeping when he received the fatal blow. I thought I heard a voice say, 'Macbeth hath murdered sleep, and shall himself

sleep no more; but shall for ever and ever be kept awake by the tortures of remorse?'"

"You are over excited," said the lady, "and these are but fancies. Go, get water, and wash the blood from your hands. But why have you brought these daggers from the place? You forget our plan. Go, carry them back, and smear the sleeping chamberlains with blood, that it may appear that they have done the deed."

"I cannot go back again," answered the Thane with a shudder. "I am afraid even to think of what I have done—look on it again I dare not!"

"Infirm of purpose," answered Lady Macbeth in scorn; "give me the daggers. I will go myself. I am not afraid either of sleeping or dead men, for both are powerless. Wait here a moment."

And she fearlessly entered the fatal chamber, while Macbeth, overcome with the horror of the recent deed, stood shuddering, and started at the slightest sound.

"See," whispered Lady Macbeth, re-entering; "my hands are now as blood-stained as yours. Yet my heart is not so pale with terror. Ah! what is that? A knock at the castle gate! Come, my lord, we must to our chamber at once, or we shall indeed be discovered."

And, seizing the arm of the guilt-bewildered Macbeth, his resolute consort hurried with him to their own apartment.

The knocking at the gate which so disturbed Macbeth, awakened also the porter, who had fallen asleep at his post.

It was a wild night. The gale blew fiercely among the forest trees surrounding the castle; but the porter slept through it all, until at length awakened by the repeated summons.

The grey dawn was just breaking, but the clouds were so thick and heavy, it was still almost as dark as midnight, when, the ponderous door of the castle having been rolled back upon its hinges, Lords Macduff and Lennox were admitted.

They had come with tidings of importance, which made it necessary they should at once awaken the King; but first they enquired for Macbeth, who soon appeared.

He had now rid himself of every sign of the dark deed he had committed, and if he seemed somewhat alarmed and dishevelled, it was easily accounted for by his being called up so soon and suddenly.

"Good morrow, noble sir," said Lennox. "We crave pardon for disturbing you; but our business with the King is urgent. Is he awake ?"

"Not yet, my lords," answered Macbeth; "but yonder is his chamber; you may summon him."

Macduff walked to the door and knocked.

"It has been a wild stormy night," said Lennox to Macbeth; "where we lay, chimneys were blown down, trees uprooted, and wild screams and moans heard in the air; the owls hooted all night. All this, I fear, portends some dreadful event."

At this moment, Macduff, who had entered the royal sleeping apartment, rushed out as if panic-stricken.

"Oh, horror! horror!" he exclaimed; "it is too frightful to think of!"

"What is the matter?" asked Macbeth and Lennox in a breath.

"A fearful sacrilegious murder has been committed. The King lies dead upon his bed, bathed in blood."

Macbeth and Banquo, with an expression of horrified amazement, immediately rushed into the fatal room.

"Murder! treason! raise the house!" exclaimed Macduff in great excitement; "ring the alarm-bell! Malcolm, Banquo, Donaldbain, come hither!"

The alarm thus given, all the inmates of the castle were soon hurrying to the spot in great confusion and consternation; among them Lady Macbeth, who had all the appearance of having been, like the others, suddenly roused out of her sleep by the clamour made.

"What has happened? Tell me—speak!" she asked breathlessly.

"Oh, gentle lady," answered Macduff, "the news is too horrible for woman's ear. Oh, Banquo, Banquo," he added, addressing that chief, "our royal master's murdered!"

Lady Macbeth screamed as if horror-stricken by the shock of the dread intelligence.

At this moment, Macbeth, Lennox, Malcolm, and Donaldbain arrived at the spot.

"What is amiss?" asked Donaldbain.

"Your royal father's murdered!" said Macduff.

The Prince recoiled as if struck by a sudden blow.

"Powers of Heaven! is it possible?" he exclaimed. "Who has done it?"

"His treacherous attendants," answered Lennox. "They were found with their daggers and hands stained with blood."

"The sight so filled me with rage and horror," added Macbeth, "that I drew my sword and killed the villains with my own hand. Oh, it was dreadful to see our beloved and venerable King, his white hair and his pillow drenched with blood, like the murderers themselves!"

"Oh! I faint! help me, take me away!" exclaimed Lady Macbeth, who seemed totally overcome by the horrors of the catastrophe.

Her female attendants accordingly bore her from the scene. All the others now crowded into the chamber of death, and thus Malcolm and Donaldbain were left alone in the hall.

"Brother," hurriedly whispered the elder prince, "we must at once escape from here. Our father's death is sudden and mysterious. I have my suspicions; and we know, at least, that Macbeth is our rival, and he will now be our deadly enemy. I will away to England; go you to Ireland. We will seek aid of our friends. Stay not to take leave of anyone, but to horse at once."

Ere the others returned, the two sons of the murdered King had left the castle.

CHAPTER III.

MACBETH'S way to the throne was now easy. Whatever might be suspected, no one could prove that the Thane had any hand in Duncan's death. Prince Malcolm and his brother had fled, and Macbeth, as the chief nobleman in Scotland, and a relative of the murdered monarch, was immediately elected King by the other nobles in council.

He immediately set out for Scone, the coronation place of all the Scottish kings, where he and his wife were crowned with great splendour; and then proceeded to the royal palace at Forres, where a grand banquet was to be given.

Macbeth appeared at this time to treat Banquo with special favour; but that commander had just begun to be jealous of his powerful ally.

"Why should he be King of Scotland, when there are others with more right?" he thought to himself; "and, if the witches spoke truly in this, why not in my case? They foretold that Macbeth should be Thane of Glamis and Cawdor, and, lastly, King of Scotland. It has all come true. But then they said no son should succeed him, but that my descendants should carry on the royal line. Perhaps there is a high destiny in store for me! We shall see."

His distrust of Macbeth was somewhat allayed by the marked attention paid to him by the new King and Queen, who invited him to occupy the highest place of honour at the banquet.

Scarce had Banquo given his promise to be present, and departed, when it was announced to the King that two men were awaiting his commands in a small room adjoining the banqueting-hall.

King Macbeth, having secured the door, seated himself upon a chair, and the two visitors stood waiting at some distance. They were wild, desperate, forbidding-looking fellows, evidently the fitting instruments for any deed of violence.

"Now," said the King, "have you thought over the proposals I made yesterday?"

"We have, so please your Highness," returned the eldest of the two.

"And you agree to do as I said?"

"Yes; we are entirely at your Majesty's disposal."

"'Tis well; the time for action has come. Banquo is my enemy. While he lives he is sure to be my rival. Neither my crown nor my life is safe. It is your work to make away with him, and in order that the witches' prophecy may not come true, his little son Fleance must die with him. Succeed in this, and not only shall a large sum of gold be yours, but I will give you protection against all punishment."

"We will, my lord, perform what you command us," said the younger murderer.

"Throughout our lives we will serve you," added the elder.

"Make good your words, then, by obedience. Within this hour at most I will instruct you where to lay in wait in the palace grounds and attack the chief and his son as they pass. But, mark you, the deed must be done so that there is no breath of suspicion as to my part in it. Go; I will shortly summon you again."

Thus we see Macbeth had made another step along the dark pathway of guilt. One crime had brought on another. He had shed blood to seize the crown. He must now shed more blood to keep it. Remorse was leaving him, his heart being hardened to the perpetration of atrocities he would at one time have shuddered to contemplate.

It was a dark night when Banquo, accompanied by his son Fleance, entered the gateway of the palace park, and proceeded along the avenue of trees leading to the entrance.

The chief had passed the day in hunting, and was to attend the banquet at seven o'clock, according to the monarch's invitation.

Little did Banquo suspect that danger lurked so near; that three murderers—for another comrade had joined them—hid behind the trees near the entrance with their deadly weapons ready.

Banquo's son Fleance walked before him, carrying a torch.

Scarcely had they gone fifty paces up the avenue when a crackling of leaves was heard, and three armed men rushed upon them.

Taken by surprise, the chief had no time even to draw his sword before the foremost ruffian plunged a dagger into his heart.

"Oh, treachery!" gasped Banquo, as he fell heavily to the ground. "I am slain! Oh, my dear son, fly, fly at once from these wretches; and you may live to—to—avenge me!"

With these words he expired. The boy Fleance, terrified almost to death, ran with all his might, dropping, as he started, the pine-torch, which went out, and left the place in total darkness.

"Who put out that light?" asked the first murderer.

"The boy himself," replied the second.

"And got clean away," added the third.

"Curses on it, our work's but half done, after all," growled the leader; "we were specially charged not to let the boy escape, and now there is no chance of catching him. However, away to the King, and tell him how we have succeeded."

The time for the banquet had arrived when the three ruffians again waited upon Macbeth in the small chamber.

"Well, is the work done?" asked the King.

"It is, my lord," returned the first ruffian with some hesitation; "Lord Banquo is safely slain by my hand."

"Bravely done! and one of your companions, no doubt, did the same for Fleance?"

"Most royal sir, I grieve to say it, but the youth escaped."

"Ha!" Macbeth's face fell; "that is bad news. His death is even more important to me than his father's, since 'tis he and his who, by the weird sisters' prophecy, will oust me and mine from

"LIAR AND SLAVE! THUNDERED THE KING.

the throne. But Banquo is removed—that is much. Fellows, attend me after the banquet, and you shall have the reward promised."

Just as the assassins departed, the Queen entered, clad, like her husband, in the regal robes and crown.

"My lord, the feast is ready, and the

THE SACKING OF MACDUFF'S CASTLE.

MACBETH'S DREAM.

guests assembled. Let us go into the banquet-hall."

Entering with a flourish of trumpets, the King and Queen were marshalled up to the regal daïs, where the Queen seated herself on the richly carved chair.

"My friends," said the King, addressing his guests, "there is but one thing as yet wanting on this joyful occasion, and that is the presence of our honoured friend Banquo, who has tarried so late that I fear some mischance for him."

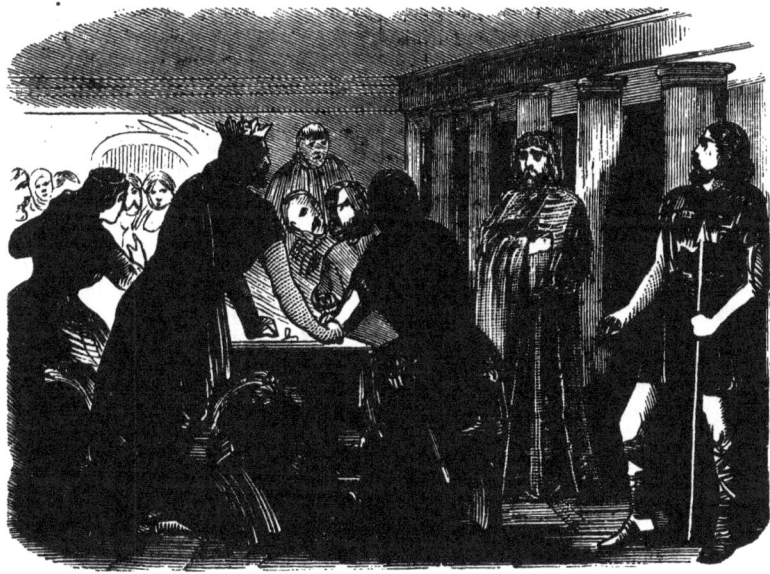

A SHADOWY FORM APPEARED TO RISE.

He was then stepping back to take his seat, when a sudden paroxysm came over him; his face turned ashen pale, and his eyes, wide open with horror and amazement, were fixed upon the empty chair.

A shadowy form, exactly resembling the murdered Banquo, appeared to him to rise and sit in the seat, pointing, at the same time, to its gory wounds.

"Where can I sit?" asked Macbeth in a hollow voice, as he glared around him; "each place is full."

"This one, my lord, is reserved for you," said Lennox, indicating the royal seat.

"I cannot—I dare not come near it," said the King, recoiling; "'tis filled already. He is sitting there—risen from the grave."

All the nobles were much alarmed at the King's agitation, for which they could see no cause, the spectre being invisible to them.

"Pray, my liege, compose yourself," whispered the Queen. "My lords, the King is subject to fits of this kind—visions which soon pass over."

"I am better already," answered Macbeth, as the ghost vanished from his sight. "But, as I live," he whispered to his wife, "I saw him sit there!"

"Hush, my lord; remember our guests observe us."

"True. My friends, pardon this strange manner. I am subject to these paroxysms, but they are soon over. Give me some wine. My lords, charge your glasses; I drink to the general health of the whole table, but more especially to our absent friend Banquo."

"Health to the King, the Queen, our friends, and Banquo!" was the response of the noble guests.

But just as Macbeth raised the golden goblet to his lips, the fit again seized him. He dropped the vessel, and the rich wine was spilt upon the floor. The ghost had again risen, and stood by his side, still invisible to all others, but only too plain to his tortured vision.

"Hence, horrible shadow! unreal mockery!" he exclaimed, addressing the phantom; "glare not at me with those stony eyes! Rather would I face the rugged Russian bear, or raging tiger, than a being in your form! Ha! it has vanished again! My fit is over; pardon me, my lords, again; but these attacks exhaust and weaken me;" and he sank in the chair, covering his face with his hands.

"We had better break up the banquet," said the Queen; "to-morrow his highness may be better. I pray you do not speak to him, it may again bring on his attack. My lords, good-night."

"Good-night; and better health attend his Majesty," said Lennox, as the guests hastily rose and passed out.

"Thus blood calls for blood!" exclaimed the guilty King. "Must I be perpetually haunted by such spectres? There is magic in all this. To-morrow early I will go and seek the three witches; for I am determined to know the worst."

CHAPTER IV.

AGAIN a wild scene, a raging storm; again those hideous and unearthly beings, the three witches, were met together—not on the open heath, but in a dark and gloomy cavern, illuminated only by the lurid glare of a huge cauldron, which was boiling in the centre. Into this the hags in turn flung all sorts of repulsive ingredients, muttering incantations as they did so, and stirring up the mixture with long staves, causing flames of various colours and thick volumes of smoke to ascend. Ever and anon they would join hands and, making a ring, dance round the cauldron, screeching forth this wild chorus:

"Black spirits and white,
   Red spirits and grey;
Mingle, mingle, mingle,
   You that mingle may."

Suddenly they became aware of the presence of a mortal, and stopped their wild dance when they saw Macbeth among them.

"You secret, black, and midnight hags," said the King, "I come to seek from you knowledge of the future, and I charge you answer me truly."

"What dost thou ask?" said the chief witch in harsh accents. "We will answer thee ourselves, or we can call up spirits more potent than ourselves."

"Let them appear," said Macbeth.

The incantation was resumed. The thunder burst forth overhead, and from the cauldron rose the apparition of an armed warrior, who said, in sepulchral accents:

"Macbeth, Macbeth, beware Macduff!"

"Ha!" exclaimed Macbeth, starting, "I suspected he would become mine enemy; I swear he shall not live. Tell me, thou unknown power."

But the apparition had vanished, and was succeeded by another resembling a child crowned, and holding a tree in his hand.

"Macbeth," said the childish voice, "be proud, and bold, and fear no man; for thou canst never be vanquished until Birnam Wood shall move to Dunsinane Hill."

"That will never be!" answered Macbeth exultingly, "for who can uproot the mighty trees, and move the forest? I now breathe freely, yet would I fain know more."

"Seek to know no more," responded the witches.

But Macbeth was resolute.

And now still more surprising sights followed; not only did the child vanish, but the cauldron itself sank into the ground, and there passed before him a long row of figures crowned, of all ages; the ghost of the murdered Banquo brought up the rear.

The King was appalled; he knew from this that the kings were the descendants of Banquo, who were to reign in Scotland in the future instead of the dynasty of Macbeth.

As he recoiled there was unearthly music and a peal of demoniacal laughter; then the whole scene, witches and all, suddenly disappeared.

Macbeth was recalled from his consternation by the voice of Lennox, who said:

"My lord, news has arrived that Macduff has fled to England, and, with the fugitive Malcolm, is plotting thy destruction."

"Traitor! He shall suffer for it," exclaimed Macbeth. "I will seize his Castle of Fife, and put his wife and children to the sword. Come what will, I will still be King of Scotland."

Meanwhile Malcolm Canmore, Prince of Cumberland, and heir to the murdered Duncan, had fled to England, resolved to seek the assistance of his grandfather, Siward, the great Earl of Northumberland, and of the pious King Edward the Confessor.

It was at the palace of that monarch that Macduff found the fugitive Prince, and they conferred together, both in deep concern at the woes of their native land.

"Can nothing be done," asked Macduff, "to purge poor Scotland of this tyrant and usurper?"

"I am promised," replied Prince Malcolm, "the assistance of an army to march northward and conquer him."

"Heaven grant you may succeed," said Macduff, "in regaining your just rights."

"Yet I fear I am not worthy of them," said Malcolm. "Macduff, as a friend, I trust you, and will not spare myself in the confession I make to you. Our country groans under the weight of Macbeth's tyranny, but how if, when he is conquered, I were to prove even a worse tyrant than he?"

"Impossible!" answered the chief. "Macbeth is a fiend in human form; how can you compare yourself to him?"

"Alas!" said the prince, "I fear I am, if possible, even more diabolical. By nature I am capable of any crime. There are no bounds to the evil I would perpetrate had I the chance; there is not a deadly sin I would not commit were it in my power, and there is not a single virtue that I have the least spark of. Such is my character, though I have hypocritically concealed it until now. Is such a one as I fit to govern?"

"Fit to govern? No—not even fit to live!" answered Macduff, whose noble nature recoiled from the depravity of his companion. "Oh, Scotland, Scotland! how wretched is thy lot; the prey of a cruel tyrant, while even the real heir to thy throne owns himself a monster of villainy!"

"Macduff," said the prince in a changed manner, "your indignation shows your virtue and patriotism. I did but say this to try you. I am, thank Heaven, guiltless of the crimes I have just now acknowledged. If I can deliver my country from Macbeth's tyranny, I hope to deserve the crown by my own merits."

At this moment the Earl of Rosse was announced, and then ushered in. The Prince and Macduff cordially welcomed their friend, and eagerly questioned him as to the state of Scotland. Gloomy, indeed, was Rosse's account of the country, oppressed as it now was by the savage despotism of Macbeth and his inhuman Queen.

"What is the last calamity you have to tell us?" asked Macduff.

"We are so full of calamities that one can scarcely count them," was the reply.

Rosse's manner as he spoke thus seemed troubled, evasive, and his companions began to suspect that he was keeping back something he dreaded to tell.

"How is my wife?" asked Macduff.

"Oh, very well," replied Rosse slowly, and turning his face from his questioner.

"And my children?"

"Well, too."

"The tyrant has not interfered with their peace?"

"No; they were quite at peace when I saw them last."

"Kinsman," said Macduff, "I scarcely like the tone of your replies; do not be so sparing of your speech, but relate all you know."

"The country is in such a state of disturbance," answered Rosse, without directly replying to this appeal, "that we can never be sure one minute of peace or safety. If we could only collect a brave and powerful army."

"We will," said Malcolm enthusiastically. "Earl Siward has promised himself to join our cause, and lead ten thousand men to the field. Is not that good tidings?"

"It is. I wish I had as good to relate in return," responded Rosse; "but, instead, I am the messenger of woe and terror."

"Ah!" said Macduff, "your manner convinces me there is some dark trouble yet unrelated. Does it concern our cause in general, or any special person?"

"It is a calamity we must all feel," was the reply, "but the main fact of it pertains to you alone."

"To me? Quick! let me have it," answered Macduff eagerly, yet fearful to hear the worst.

"Macduff," said Rosse solemnly, "prepare yourself for the most horrible tidings your ears ever listened to."

"Ah! I partly guess what is coming. Speak on."

"Your castle was surprised, your wife and children savagely slaughtered. Even the servants did not escape; the murderers sent by Macbeth left none of their horrible work undone."

The effect of this intelligence upon Macduff was so powerful as to terrify his companions. So ghostly and powerless was his aspect that it seemed as if he would sink beneath the blow; for some moments he was utterly speechless.

"My children murdered!" he gasped at length.

"Wife, children, servants, all that could be found," answered Rosse.

"And to think that I should be away! My wife, too, slain?"

"Alas, it is too true!"

"All; did you say all?" repeated the agonised man, even yet scarcely able to grasp the extent of his misfortune. "All my dear children and their mother, at one fell blow?" and covering his face with his hands, he gave way to an agony of grief.

"Revenge it like a man," said Malcolm.

"I will do so, but I must also feel it as a man," returned the chief; and then, rousing himself, he sprang to his feet in a fury of wrath. "Hear me, oh, mighty Power!" he exclaimed, kneeling and gazing upwards; "upon my knees I make a deadly oath of revenge upon Macbeth for this cruel wrong. One boon alone I crave: bring me face to face with this fiend of Scotland at my sword's point, and if he escapes, then may Heaven forgive him too!"

"Amen!" added his companions solemnly, and they swore to aid him in his just revenge.

CHAPTER V.

MACBETH and his wife had now reached the summit of greatness and power. They were absolute King and Queen of Scotland, obeyed and feared by all; the rebellious nobles were quelled, the wild Scots utterly brought to subjection.

But discontent still existed in secret, and only needed a chance to show itself. Macbeth, urged to tyranny by the fear of losing his throne, made fresh enemies each day, and at length received intelligence that a large army commanded by Malcolm, Macduff, Earl Siward, and his son Osbert, had entered Scotland from the south.

This was a great blow to the usurper, who was scarcely prepared for the invasion. Ever haunted by the memory of his crimes, the fear of deadly retribution now fell upon him. He summoned a large army, and further strengthened his strong fortress of Dunsinane to resist a siege.

The Queen, to whose instigation the crimes of Macbeth were principally owing, felt all the force of the dangers now menacing them.

She saw that their ill-gotten royalty was

tottering, and might soon fall; remorse perpetually tormented her; her sleepless nights were haunted with dreadful anxieties, and when she slept it was to dream horrible dreams. During the time when her husband was absent in the field her health gave way, and it was feared her reason was deserting her.

The Queen's physician was in constant attendance, and he heard with anxiety that she had lately taken to walking in her sleep, rising in the dead of night, taking paper, writing, reading, and sealing the letters without waking.

"And does she speak when so engaged?" asked the doctor of the lady-in-waiting, who replied:

"Frequently!"

"What have you heard her say?"

"That which I dare not report," replied the attendant, sinking her voice to a low tone, and glancing uneasily at the door of the Queen's chamber. "All I can tell you is, that on several occasions, about this time, I have known her rise, walk in her sleep, and mutter words to herself. Hush! she is coming now; stand back and watch her."

The door opened slowly and the Queen appeared, clad in a long white dressing-gown and hood, which, with her pale haggard face and fixed eyes, gave her a ghostly appearance. She held a small lamp in her hand.

"Fast asleep," whispered the lady-in-waiting.

"Her eyes are open," observed the physician.

"Yes, but their sense is shut."

"What is it that she does now?" asked the doctor. "Look how she rubs her hands."

"Yes, that she frequently does," replied his companion. "I have known her continue at it a quarter of an hour at a time."

The Queen, in effect, had set down the lamp, and was rubbing her hands together as if washing them, sometimes pausing to examine them intently.

"Yes, here's a spot," she murmured in a hollow voice, "a spot of blood! Will nothing wash it away? Out, accursed spot; out, I say! Hark! the clock strikes; 'tis time to do the deed. Fie, my lord, fie," she added, as if addressing the King, "you, a soldier, and afraid? What need we fear when no one knows of our guilt? Yet, who would have thought

that the old man had so much blood in him?"

"Do you mark that?" whispered the doctor to the attendant.

"The Thane of Fife had a wife," proceeded the somnambulist; "where is she now? More murders, more blood! What, will these hands never be clean?"

"I greatly fear," said the doctor, "that this disorder arises from remorse at some guilty deed."

"Heaven knows," replied the other, "but there is some dark mystery in it."

"Here's the smell of blood still," cried the Queen. "All the perfumes of Arabia will not sweeten this little hand;" and she heaved a deep sigh of anguish which almost froze the blood of the listeners.

"This disease is beyond my practice," said the doctor.

"Wash your hands," continued the sleep-walker, as if to her husband. "Look not so pale. Banquo's buried, he cannot come out of his grave. To bed! to bed! there's knocking at the gate. Come, come, come! give me your hand, we must not be found here. What's done, cannot be undone. To bed, to bed!"

And still gazing with a stony stare at vacancy, she turned, took up the lamp, and slowly re-entered the sleeping-chamber.

"Alas!" said the doctor, "here are signs of a mind disordered, I fear, by the memory of some dreadful crime. There are some who suspect that King Duncan died by foul play at the hands of our present King and Queen. I know not what to think. God forgive us all! Look after her, and take care that she has no dangerous weapon by her, for fear she might commit some desperate act. I fear the worst!"

The English forces pursued their way triumphantly into the very heart of Macbeth's territory.

He led his army against them, and some miles from his castle a desperate conflict took place. Macbeth's men fought bravely, but numbers and superior discipline were against them.

The battle raged long and furiously, and great numbers were slain on either side.

At length Macbeth retreated to his strong Castle of Dunsinane, which he had put into a thorough state of defence. Even here, however, reports of fresh disasters to his forces were continually reaching him.

"I do not despair," he said to his favourite, Lord Seyton, "the witches' prophecies will yet hold good. They said I could never be defeated until Birnam Wood shall come to Dunsinane, and that can never be. Ah! what cream-faced coward is this?" he exclaimed in anger, as a young soldier, with terror-stricken countenance, hurried into his presence.

"My lord!" he said, "there are ten thousand English soldiers in sight!"

"Away, bird of evil omen!" thundered the King, in a rage. "Just as I was thinking of future victory, dare you come to dash my hopes? Seyton," he added as the soldier fled his presence, "is this messenger's news true?"

"Too true, my lord," replied the noble. "The English force is everywhere successful!"

"Get my armour," said the King, "I will fight all hacked to pieces ere I yield. How does your patient, doctor?"

"Not so ill in body, my lord; but her mind, I sadly fear for it, and day-haunting visions disturb her rest."

"Cure her of that," said the King. "Cannot your skill deal with the mind as well as the body? Can it not make us forget our troubles, and, perchance, our crimes?"

"Alas, my lord, 'tis beyond the power of physic to do that."

"Then throw physic to the dogs!" said Macbeth impatiently. "Is my armour ready, varlets? Help me on with it, and get me my weapons. Doctor, if you could but cure the complaints of this distracted land of Scotland, you would be a physician indeed. Now," added Macbeth, when fully attired in warlike array, "we will forth again to meet the foe; I will fear nothing until Birnam Forest come to Dunsinane."

Fully aware of the witches' prophecies, Malcolm and his friends determined that they should be fulfilled, but in a manner disastrous to Macbeth. The army had now penetrated within sight of the Castle of Dunsinane, and halted at Birnam Wood.

"My men," said the Prince, "we will break the wizard charm that guards this tyrant. Let every soldier cut down a bough, or uproot a small tree, and carry it with him on the march. Thus Birnam Wood shall come to Dunsinane."

The soldiers immediately set to work—being provided with woodmen's tools—with such good will that ere long the fine forest was thickly strewn with branches and saplings. Then each man took up one of these, and the force proceeded on its way to Macbeth's Castle, hidden and protected by this huge leafy screen.

The usurper saw that he would have to stand a siege, but confident in the strength of his castle and the witches' prophecies, he awaited the attack without apprehension. He was anxious, however, for the Queen, whose malady had that day taken a turn for the worse, and a deep wail, as of many female voices, coming from the door of her apartment, gave him a shock in the midst of his fancied security.

"Go, Seyton, and see what has happened!" he said. "I am now so used to horrors and evil tidings that I am almost hardened against everything."

Seyton returned in a few minutes with a very grave face.

"What meant that cry?" asked the King.

"The Queen, my lord, is dead."

This intelligence, though not unexpected, gave Macbeth a deep shock, and for a few moments he seemed overcome.

"Death ever hovers over us," he said. "What is life but a candle that soon burns out—a walking shadow—an actor who plays his part, and then dies, and is forgotten? Ha! what fresh intelligence?" he asked as another soldier entered.

"My gracious lord, I scarcely dare to speak it," answered the messenger.

"Speak, speak!" said the King.

"As I stood at watch upon the hill I looked towards Birnam Wood, and presently the wood began to move."

"Liar and slave!" thundered the king.

"I swear what I say is true," protested the man. "Look, my lord, yonder, and you can yourself see the wood moving!"

Macbeth gazed from the battlements, and, indeed, to his amazement, beheld what appeared to him to be a forest of small trees coming straight towards the castle.

"Fate fights against me!" cried Macbeth. "Curses upon the hags whose words seem true, yet but lie and deceive—Birnam Wood is coming to Dunsinane! I am driven desperate. What ho! Ring the alarm-bell, muster our forces for

a last effort; at least I'll die with sword in hand and armour on my back!"

Arrived at the foot of Dunsinane Hill, directly in front of the castle, the opposing party again halted.

At the command of the Prince the trees and branches they carried were thrown down, and what had appeared a moving wood revealed itself to the dismay of the castle garrison as a vast army at close quarters.

Resolved to make one more stand against them, King Macbeth, at the head of a strong body of men, issued forth.

The opposing armies were drawn up upon a plain, and were soon in full order of battle.

A flourish of trumpets gave signal for the engagement, and then it commenced, a desperate hand-to-hand fight, too fierce and unequal to last long.

Macbeth was overmatched in numbers, several of his best generals were killed, he had lost his faith in the witches and their prophecies, being so deceived. Yet never did he fight more valiantly, for he had the courage of desperation. He seemed, indeed, to bear a charmed life, for, even in the thick of the fray, he emerged unwounded. But he soon saw that the day was against him, his forces were routed, the enemy, easily overcoming the garrison, burst into the castle, headed by Malcolm and Earl Siward.

Macbeth, powerless to prevent this, was obliged to retreat to another part of the battle-field, and soon found himself, cut off from all his followers, standing watching his flying army.

"I am at bay, at last," cried the desperate usurper; "like the baited bear, tied to the stake, I cannot fly, but must turn and grapple with my foes. But many shall fall ere I yield or die. Who comes here?"

"Osbert of Northumberland," replied the youthful chieftain, who now advanced. "And what is your name?"

"You'll be afraid to hear it."

"Not I; no name can make me tremble."

"My name's Macbeth!"

"The devil himself could not pronounce a title more hateful to mine ear," exclaimed Osbert. "Abhorred tyrant, now I will revenge my kinsman's wrongs."

And he furiously attacked the King, but Macbeth stood on the defensive, and his comparative coolness gave him an advantage over the fiery young warrior; a few desperate strokes, and then Macbeth's sword was plunged into the heart of Siward's son, who fell without a groan.

"You, at least, bear no charmed life," murmured Macbeth, gazing at the body in grim triumph.

Yet it was but small satisfaction to slay one enemy when so many others were ready to avenge him.

Desperate thoughts of suicide crossed the mind of the tyrant, but he shook them off, and resolved, come what might, to fight to the last.

And now, looking up, he perceived another enemy approaching him, a man of middle age, of stalwart form, his eyes flashing with rage, his expression that of one thirsting for revenge.

The King knew that face but too well.

It was Macduff.

Despite his desperate courage, the tyrant turned pale and recoiled, for here he knew was his mortal foe, who would never leave him till one or both were slain.

"Turn, hell-hound, turn!" fiercely exclaimed Macduff, seeing Macbeth retreat.

"Macduff," replied the other, stopping short, and confronting him, "beware of me, I am desperate! I have avoided you most of all men. Back, on your life; my soul is too much stained with blood of yours already."

"I cannot stay to parley," replied Macduff, "my sword alone must speak for me. Execrable villain! murderer of all I held dear! I have prayed and longed for the hour of revenge, and now it has come!"

"Beware, again I say; I am under supernatural protection, and bear a charmed life."

"Despair your charm!" said Macduff; "for Birnam Wood has come to Dunsinane, and the spell is broken."

"Accursed be the tongue that tells me so," hissed the King, "and doubly accursed be the lying fiends who have deceived, me. I'll not fight with you!"

"Then yield, coward, and be a prisoner chained in a cage, and mocked and hooted at by the vilest crowds."

"Never!" exclaimed Macbeth. "A king I have lived and I will die a king; though fortune desert me, my death shall be that of a hero. Come on, Macduff, this struggle is our last!"

The two chiefs, armed only with broad-sword and target, commenced a deadly combat—a fight for life. Blow succeeded blow in rapid succession, fire flashed from the quick-clashing claymores, the iron-bound shields were cut and dented; it was less like a combat of men than that of two fiends.

At length a false pass threw Macbeth off his guard, and he fell to the earth, literally transfixed through the throat by his enemy's sword.

Macduff drew a long breath of relief as he drew out his dripping blade, and gazed upon his fallen foe.

At this moment the Prince and his victorious followers reached the spot.

"See!" exclaimed Macduff. "My vengeance is slaked at last, the murderous tyrant is slain, our country is delivered! Long live Malcolm, King of Scotland!"

"THUS BIRNAM WOOD SHALL COME TO DUNSINANE."

THE END.

NOTICE.—"KING HENRY THE FOURTH," being No. 4 of Stories from Shakespeare, will be ready on Monday, Nov. 28. Orders should be given early to your Booksellers.

No. 4.]   [Price One Penny·

EDWIN J. BRETTS STORIES OF SHAKESPEARE

COMPLETE

HENRY THE FOURTH

FALSTAFF DESCRIBING HIS FIGHT WITH THE ROBBERS AT GADSHILL.

"Boys of England Edition."

EDWIN J. BRETT'S
STORIES FROM
SHAKESPEARE'S PLAYS.

No. 4.—KING HENRY THE FOURTH.

IT was after years of strife and blood-shed, that Henry the Fourth, King of England, was enabled to lay aside the red sword of war, and enjoy those blessings which peace ever brings in her train.

Yet still there was one care that pressed heavily upon his soul, which was the wildness and dissipation in which his eldest son, Prince Henry, afterwards the justly celebrated King Henry the Fifth, was too wont to indulge.

Possessing the true nobility of soul in a most exalted degree, he had yet, in some manner, debased himself by associating with some men of loose character and intemperate habits, whose riotous excesses had frequently led him into scenes which would have disgraced a man of far inferior grade.

The King, having secured an honourable peace for his country, now resolved upon proceeding with a powerful army into Syria, the sovereign of which country had latterly proceeded to great extremities against the unfortunate Christians, who had been left there for the protection of former conquests.

Incensed at this conduct, Henry vowed to take an ample vengeance upon the Saracen Prince, and having called a council at his palace in London, for the purpose of deliberating upon the subject, he thus addressed himself to the assembled persons :

"My faithful friends, shaken as we are with the terrible effects of the wars but just terminated, we must yet find means for the punishment of those who have taken advantage of our occupations in other conquests. Therefore, friends, we must now proceed to the sepulchre of the Saviour of Mankind, whose soldiers we must henceforth be. Gentle cousin of Westmoreland, what did our council decree in yesterday's conference on this important business ?"

"My liege," answered the Earl of Westmoreland, "while we were most earnest in consultation, a messenger arrived from Wales, bearing heavy news, that the noble Mortimer, at the head of the Hereford-shire men, has been overthrown and taken prisoner."

"What now ?" exclaimed the King.

"This," replied Westmoreland. "From the north we learned that, on Holyrood Day, the gallant Hotspur and brave Archibald met at Holmedon, where they engaged in a bloody fight, but how it terminated we have not yet learned."

"The news I have already heard from Sir Walter Blount," exclaimed the King, "and he assures me that young Harry Percy overthrew the Scot, killing a great number, and taking many prisoners. This is welcome news, cousin, is it not ?"

"It is a conquest for a Prince to boast of," replied the other.

"Ha !" cried the King. "There thou makest me envious of my Lord Northumberland, that he should be the father of such a son—a son who is the theme of honour's tongue, whilst I behold nought but riot and disgrace in my young Henry. But what think you of this Hotspur's arrogance who sends me word that he shall keep all the prisoners, with the exception of the Earl of Fife, who alone is to be my share of the victory ?"

"This is his uncle, the Earl of Worcester's advice," returned the other, " who has ever opposed himself to you in matters of importance."

"But I have sent to young Percy," observed the King, "desiring that he immediately commits his prisoners to my charge. If he refuses this, I will so proceed against him that he shall bitterly repent ever having set himself in array against me. Therefore, retire, my lords, for the present, and in the meanwhile continue your considerations upon the affairs of which I have spoken."

The council now broke up, and as soon as the King found himself alone, he retired to the privacy of his closet, where he could meditate undisturbed upon the various matters that had so suddenly arisen to overthrow the projects he had formed.

In the meanwhile, Henry, Prince of Wales, was engaged in another apartment of the palace, with his old friend and companion, Sir John Falstaff, the latter of whom, growing weary of his lengthened visit, was about to depart for the Boar's Head, in Eastcheap, when Poins, another companion, made his appearance, who was greeted by the Prince with his accustomed familiarity, exclaiming :

"Good morrow, Ned."

"Good morrow to thee," answered the other. "What says Monsieur Remorse ? What says Sir John Sack-and-Sugar ? Jack, how agrees the devil and thee about thy soul that thou soldest him on Good Friday last for a cup of Madeira, and a cold capon's leg ?"

"Sir John stands to his word, and the devil shall have his bargain," exclaimed the merry Prince ; " for he was never yet a breaker of proverbs, and will give the devil his due."

"Good," returned Poins ; " but to the business that brought me hither. By tomorrow morning at four o'clock, we must be at Gadshill. There are pilgrims going to Canterbury with rich offerings, and traders riding to London with fat purses. I have visors for you all, you have horses for yourselves. I have bespoke supper tomorrow night in Eastcheap, so you may do it as secure as sleep."

"Hal, wilt thou make one ?" exclaimed Falstaff.

"Who ! I rob ! " cried the Prince indignantly ; "I a thief ! Not I, by my faith."

"There's neither honesty, manhood, nor good fellowship in thee," returned Sir John ; "nor thou camest not of the blood royal, if thou darest not stand for ten shillings."

"Well, come what will, I'll tarry at home," answered the Prince.

"By the lord, I'll be a traitor then, when thou art king," cried Falstaff.

"Sir John," interrupted Poins ; "I prithee leave the Prince and me alone. I will lay him down such reasons for this adventure, that he shall go."

"Well," answered Falstaff ; "may'st thou have the spirit of persuasion. Farewell, you will find me in Eastcheap."

"Now, my good lord, ride with us tomorrow," said Poins, addressing himself to the Prince as soon as Sir John Falstaff was gone ; " I have a jest to execute, that I cannot manage alone. Falstaff, Bardolph, Peto, and Gadshill shall rob those men of whom I spoke. Yourself and I will be there, and when they have the booty, if you and I do not rob and frighten them, cut this head from my shoulders."

"But how shall we part with them in setting forth ?" asked the Prince.

"Why, we will set off before or after them," replied Poins.

"Well," exclaimed the Prince, overcome by his love for fun, " I will go with thee ; provide us all things necessary, and meet me in Eastcheap. Farewell."

Upon receiving this order, Poins left the chamber, when young Henry looking after him as he retired, continued :

"I know ye all, and will for awhile enter into your wild adventures—imitating the sun, however, who permits the gathering clouds to hide his beauty from the world, that being wanted he may be the more admired, by breaking through the foul vapours that seemed to smother him."

Thus communing with himself he retired to another apartment, where he might remain unobserved until the hour arrived when he was to be joined by Poins.

At length the moment came, and with it the lawless companion of his night's adventure, when both of them mounting their horses, they took the road leading towards Gadshill.

On reaching that place our two travellers secured their horses in the adjoining wood, when sallying forth in quest of their companions, they soon discovered them lurking near the roadside.

Secreting themselves they now watched the motions of Sir John Falstaff and his followers, and in a few moments the sounds of footsteps being heard, the robbers pounced upon their prey, and driving the affrighted travellers off, succeeded in despoiling them of a large booty.

The next business was to share the booty, and for this purpose Sir John and his companions seated themselves by the

roadside to divide the spoils, but scarcely had he commenced operations, when the Prince and Poins, rushing out from their place of concealment, demanded the prize.

So effectually had they contrived to disguise themselves, that even their companions knew them not, and Falstaff, after a blow or two with the Prince, ran away, as his friends had already done, leaving their booty behind them.

Having thus succeeded in their designs, the Prince and Poins remounted their horses, and taking the road that led towards London, they, after a swift journey, reached the Boar's Head, in Eastcheap, where Dame Quickly had prepared a substantial meal against the return of her company.

In about half an hour afterwards, Sir John Falstaff and his party arrived, when, having greeted the Prince, they all sat down to the evening's meal, which being at length finished, Sir John began to exclaim vehemently against all cowards.

"Why, what's the matter now?" asked the Prince.

"What's the matter!" returned the other with a feigned anger. "There are four of us here have taken a thousand pounds this morning."

"Where is it, Jack? Where is it?" asked Prince Henry.

"Where is it?" responded the jolly Knight; "why, taken from us it is—a hundred upon four of us!"

"What! a hundred, man?" exclaimed the Prince of Wales.

"Aye!" shouted Falstaff; "and I'm a rogue if I were not at half sword with a dozen of them, two hours ago. I have escaped by a miracle. I was eight times thrust through the doublet; four through the hose; my buckler cut through and through; my sword hacked like a handsaw, *ecce signum*. I never dealt better since I was a man; all would not do. A plague of all cowards! Let them speak who were my companions, and if they speak more or less than truth, they are villains and the sons of darkness!"

"Speak, sirs; how was it?" cried the Prince, addressing himself to those around.

"We four!" replied one named Bardolph, "set upon some dozen——"

"Sixteen, at least, my lord," interrupted the Knight; "and captured and bound every one of them—else I'm a Jew!"

"As we were sharing the booty," continued Bardolph, "some six or seven fresh men set upon us——"

"What! and fought ye with them all?" exclaimed Henry.

"All!" returned Sir John. "I know not what ye call all; but if I fought not with fifty of them, I am a bunch of radishes! If there were not two or three and fifty upon poor old Jack, then am I no two-legged creature."

"Pray Heaven you have not murdered some of them," said Poins, with much assumed gravity.

"Nay, that's past praying for," returned the swaggering knight; "I have peppered two of them—two, I am sure I have paid; two rogues in buckram suits. I tell thee what, Hal, if I tell thee a lie, spit in my face, call me horse. Thou knowest my old way—here I lay, and thus I bore my point. Four rogues in buckram let drive at me——"

"What, four!" interrupted Prince Henry; "thou said'st but two, even now."

"Four, Hal! I told thee four; who came all a front, and mainly thrust at me. I made me no more ado, but took all their seven points in my target, thus!"

"Seven!" exclaimed the Prince; "why there were but four, even now."

"Seven, by these hilts!" returned the other, "or I am a villain. Well, these nine in buckram, that I told thee of——"

"So two more already," thought Prince Henry.

"Well, their points being broken," continued Falstaff, "they began to give me ground. But I followed close—came in foot and hand, and with a thought, seven of the eleven I paid."

"Oh, monstrous! eleven buckram men grown out of two!" again ejaculated the Prince.

"But, as the devil would have it," continued the unblushing bragster, "three misbegotten knaves, in Kendal green, came at my back, and let drive at me—for it was so dark, Hal, that thou could'st not see thy hand."

"These lies are like the father that begets them," replied the Prince of Wales, "they are gross as a mountain, open and palpable. Why, thou clay-brained knotty-pated fool! Thou——"

"What, art thou mad, to rail at me thus?" cried Sir John. "Is not the truth the truth?"

"Why, how could'st thou know these men in Kendal green, when it was so dark thou could'st not see thy hand?" continued the Prince; "what sayest thou to this?"

"Aye, explain, explain!" interposed Poins.

"What, upon compulsion?" returned the Knight, anxious to creep out of the error he had committed. "No, were I at the strapado, or all the racks in the world, I would not tell you on compulsion. Give you a reason on compulsion! If reasons were as plenty as blackberries, I would give no man a reason on compulsion."

"Why, thou coward, thou bed-presser, thou huge hill of flesh!" exclaimed the Prince.

"Away, you starveling," interrupted Falstaff, "you elf-skin, you dried neat's-tongue, you stock-fish! Oh, for breath to utter what is like thee! You tailor's yard, you sheath, you bow-case, you——"

"Well, breathe awhile," exclaimed Henry, "and then to it again; and when thou hast tired thyself in base comparisons, hear me speak but this. We two, Poins and myself, saw you four set on four, you bound them, and became masters of their wealth. Mark, now, how plain a tale shall put you down. Then did we two set on you four, and, with a word, outfaced you from your prize, and have it, yea, and can show it you here in this house, Falstaff. Why, what a slave art thou to hack thy sword as thou hast done, and then say it was in fight!"

Falstaff stood for a few minutes astounded at this exposure, but recovering his self-possession, he replied:

"By the Lord, I knew ye as well as he that made ye. Why, hear me, my masters. Was it for me to kill the heir-apparent? Should I turn upon the true Prince? Why, thou knowest I am as valiant as Hercules. But, by the Lord, lads, I am glad ye have the money. Hostess, clap to the doors; watch to-night, pray to-morrow. Gallant lads, boys, hearts of gold, all the titles of good fellowship come to you. Shall we be merry? Shall we have a play extempore?"

"Aye," answered the Prince, "and the argument shall be thy running away."

"Ah! no more of that, Hal, an thou lovest me!" cried Falstaff.

After pursuing this conversation for some time longer, they were interrupted by the entrance of a domestic, who, with much alarm, informed them that the officers of justice were at the door, demanding admittance.

On learning this, the whole party made their escape by a secret entrance, when the Prince, returning to the palace, threw himself upon the couch to obtain a short repose after the excesses he had so thoughtlessly committed.

On the following morning the Prince of Wales arose, and having learned that his father was about to set forth immediately with a powerful army, to check the insolence of young Hotspur, who was already in battle array against him, he proceeded to the royal closet, where he found the King busily engaged in concerting his measures.

Upon the entrance of his son, a frown overshadowed his brow, and motioning him to advance, he exclaimed:

"I know not whether Heaven thus afflicts me for some crime that I have committed, but the evil courses that thou hast pursued have given much grief to my aged heart."

"So please your majesty," answered the Prince, "though I must plead guilty to many offences, yet there are others that have been charged against me that are most untrue. If, however, I have given uneasiness to your grace, I now hope to find pardon on my sincere repentance."

"Heaven pardon thee!" returned the King. "Yet I cannot but wonder that thou should'st have followed a course so unworthy of thy noble ancestry."

"Henceforth, my gracious liege," answered the Prince, "I will be more myself, and prove a worthy scion of thy noble blood."

"Why, this is well," exclaimed the King, clasping him to his bosom, "for young Hotspur is already in the field against us, and I have much need of thy assistance. The Earl of Westmoreland, with thy brother, Prince John, have set forward with an army to oppose him, and to-morrow thou shalt lead a gallant party on the same glorious enterprise. Therefore, away, and make all necessary preparations, whilst I conclude the business I have in hand."

Bowing in submission to his royal parent's command, the Prince retired, and having despatched a note to Sir John Falstaff, informing him that he must be prepared to lead a company against Hotspur, set himself busily to work in order to retrieve the character he had so thoughtlessly lost.

Gratified at this mark of friendship from the Prince, Falstaff at once commenced his task, which was immediately to proceed through Warwickshire, in which county he was to enlist as many recruits as possible to strengthen the army which was to meet so formidable a foe as Harry Percy.

On the following morning, in strict adherence to the orders he had received, Falstaff set forward on his march, and having by the way picked up some forty or fifty recruits, he at length pushed on for Coventry, where it had been appointed he was to meet the Prince.

On the day that had been named, leaving his men to the care of one of his officers, he set forward, accompanied by Bardolph, and having advanced within a short distance of the town, he desired his companion to hasten on, in order that he might conduct his men into the town.

Bardolph obeyed his orders, and Sir John, being thus left alone, was soon interrupted by the near approach of the Prince of Wales and the Earl of Westmoreland, the former of whom, hastening to meet his old friend and companion, exclaimed, "Why, how now, Jack—how now?"

"What, Hal!" cried Sir John, highly delighted at again meeting the Prince. "Why, what the devil dost thou in Warwickshire? My good lord of Westmoreland, I cry you mercy; I thought your honour had already been at Shrewsbury."

"Faith, Sir John," replied the Earl, "'tis more than time that I were there, and you too; but my soldiers are there already. The King looks for us all, and we must march all night."

"Tut, never fear me," replied the other, "I am as vigilant as a cat to steal cream."

"But who are those fellows we overtook, marching?" asked the Prince.

"Mine, Hal, mine," returned Sir John, with much evident satisfaction.

"Then never did I see such pitiful rascals," answered the Prince.

"Tut, tut, good enough to toss," returned the jolly knight, "food for powder—food for powder—they'll fill a pit as well as better. Tush, man! mortal men—mortal men!"

"Aye, but Sir John," interposed the Earl of Westmoreland, "methinks they are exceedingly poor and bare — too beggarly!"

"Faith, for their poverty," answered the other, "I know not where they had that, and for their bareness, I am sure they never learned that of me."

"No, I'll be sworn," exclaimed the Prince, laughing heartily at his friend's humour, "unless you call three fingers' depth on the ribs bare. But we must proceed onward, for Percy is already in the field."

"What! and is the King encamped?" asked the Knight.

"He is," replied the Earl of Westmoreland, "and I fear, unless we hasten onward, we shall be too late."

At these words, the Prince and his noble friend, bidding Sir John farewell, again set forward on their journey towards Shrewsbury, leaving the Knight to make what speed he could with the miserable squad of ragged soldiers whom he had enlisted to engage against the hot and impetuous Percy.

In the camp of Hotspur, the promptitude displayed by the King had occasioned the greatest confusion and dismay, and no sooner was it known that Henry's army was within sight than a general feeling was entertained that their cause was hopeless.

Some were for an immediate retreat, others for submission to their royal master, and others for the postponement of the battle for a few days.

But the fiery Hotspur, heedless of all dangers, would not listen to their suggestions, and bidding those that feared to depart, expressed his own determination to try the issue of an engagement on the following morning.

No sooner was this resolution expressed than an officer entered the tent to inform them that some Royalists waited without, who had come on a message from the King.

Hotspur, who yet hoped that some terms of accommodation might be offered which he could, without dishonour, accept, commanded them to be admitted, and in a few seconds Sir Walter Blount, with two attendants bearing a flag of truce, made their appearance, and delivered the King's message, promising forgiveness to them all on condition that they would lay down their arms and submit themselves to his mercy.

Percy listened patiently till Sir Walter had concluded, when, suspecting some treachery to be masked under these fair promises, he returned an answer that he would take time to consider of them, and send a message on the following morning to convey his final determination.

With this reply, Sir Walter Blount retired, intimating, however, that if the

reply came not at an early hour, the royal forces would be set in motion to enforce that submission which the King had hoped to have effected by pacific means.

By sunrise on the next day King Henry had left his couch, and after giving some necessary directions, returned to his tent, accompanied by his two sons and Sir Walter Blount.

Seating himself at a table to await the answer of Hotspur, Henry exclaimed thoughtfully:

"How bloodily the sun begins to peer o'er yonder hills, making the day look pale and sickly."

"The southern winds, too, moan as though foretelling a tempestuous day," rejoined the Prince Henry.

At this moment a trumpet was heard without, sounding a parley, and in the next the Earl of Worcester, attended by Sir Richard Vernon, entered on their mission.

As soon as the King saw who was the messenger, a frown of indignation overspread his countenance, and fixing a look of great displeasure upon him, he exclaimed:

"My lord of Worcester, it is not well that you and I should meet thus. You have deceived the trust I had reposed in you, and made me doff the easy robes of peace, to ensconse my aged limbs in warlike mail. This is not well! What say ye to it?"

"Hear me, my liege," answered Worcester: "this quarrel was not provoked by myself, and but for the treatment I have received, would never have placed myself against you."

"Name, then, in what I have offended you," returned the King.

"It hath pleased your Majesty," answered the Earl, "to turn your looks of favour from myself, and those of my family. And yet I must remind you that we were the first and dearest of your friends. For you, in King Richard's time, I was the first to break my staff of office, and swore allegiance to you, when scarce a friend beside embraced your cause. In a short time, fortune showered upon your head, and you became the King of England. Your favour towards me then began to decrease, till coldness began to usurp the place of royal favour. Then it was that I resented your ingratitude, and embraced the cause of him who now disputes your right."

"It is an impotent excuse," exclaimed the King; "and such as traitors ever urge to palliate their rebellion."

"But it shall be punished as the crime deserves," cried the Prince of Wales. "Tell your nephew, Hotspur, that though I esteem him for his gallantry, yet for this treason I will risk my life against his. For my own part, and I speak it to my shame, I have been a truant to chivalry, and so, I hear, he, too, considers me; yet this, in the presence of my royal father, I now declare, that I am willing to take the odds against his warlike reputation, and to save the unnecessary effusion of blood on either side, and will meet him in single combat."

"No, Worcester, no!" exclaimed the King; "we love our people well, aye, even those who have been misled into this rebellion, and if they will take the offer of our clemency, we promise them our pardon. But if they will not yield, our vengeance light upon them. Therefore, retire to your leader, and warn him of his peril."

Upon this command, the Earl of Worcester quitted the royal tent, and almost immediately afterwards, the King, accompanied by the Princes and their retinue, proceeded towards the field of battle, leaving Sir John Falstaff alone to reflect upon the dangers he was about to undergo.

Personal safety was ever the first consideration with our worthy Knight, and he would have gladly betaken himself to some place of security.

Now this was a consideration that weighed rather heavily with him.

"Well," he said, "honour pricks me on, yea, but how if honour pricks me off when I come on? How then? Can honour set a leg? No. Or an arm? No. Or take away the pain of a wound? No. Honour hath no skill in surgery, then? No. What is honour? A word. What is that word honour? Air; a trim reckoning. What hath it? He that died on Wednesday, doth he feel it? No. Doth he hear it? No. Is it insensible? Yea, to the dead. But will it not live with the living? No. Why? Detraction will not suffer it; therefore I'll none of it. Honour is a mere scutcheon, and so ends my catechism."

Having thus logically convinced himself of the emptiness of honour, the Knight left the tent to take what care he could of his own person.

Soon after this the battle commenced with the greatest fury, and continued for some time with the most uncertain success.

CORONATION OF HENRY IV. (FROM A SCARCE OLD PRINT IN THE BRITISH MUSEUM).

Finding himself unexpectedly in the midst of dangers which he could scarcely hope to escape, Sir John at length laid himself upon the ground among the slain, and covering himself with his shield, resolved to await the result in security. After he had remained there for some time, the Prince of Wales and Hotspur met within a few yards of where he lay, and engaged in a most desperate single combat, which was concluded by the Prince Henry mortally wounding Hotspur, who, falling on the earth, instantly expired.

The Prince was now about to proceed in search of other foes, when perceiving as he supposed the dead body of his old Falstaff, he paused for an instant to express his sorrow, and having given utterance to his feelings, turned away to reap fresh honours in the bloody strife.

As soon as he was gone, Sir John slowly arose, and seeing the corpse of the impetuous and noble Hotspur lying near, he resolved to take the merit to himself of having slain him.

With this design he drew his sword when Prince Henry returned with his brother and a party of soldiers.

ARTISANS (TIME OF HENRY IV.).

COURTIERS (TIME OF HENRY IV.).

PRINCE HENRY RETURNING THE CROWN TO HIS FATHER.

HENRY IV.

"Thou alive!" he exclaimed. "Sir John alive?"

"Aye," replied the Knight; "and there is Percy, whom I have slain. If your father will reward me for the service, it is well. If not, let him kill the next Percy himself."

"Why, Percy I slew myself," cried the Prince; "and saw thee among the dead."

"Didst thou?" returned the Knight. "Lord, Lord! I grant you I was down, and out of breath, and so was he; but we rose both at an instant, and fought a long hour by Shrewsbury clock."

"Well, the honour shall be contested elsewhere," answered the Prince; "but in the meantime, Jack, I have the gratification of informing you that the day is our own. The trumpet of the enemy has sounded a retreat, and we now hasten to my father's tent to learn what steps he means to pursue."

"Then I'll follow for my reward," answered Sir John; "and he that rewards me, Heaven reward him. If I do grow great, I'll leave sack, and live cleanly as a nobleman should do."

They now proceeded together towards the appointed place, where they found the King in council, having before him the Earl of Worcester, Vernon, and several other persons of distinction, who had been taken prisoners. Upon entering the tent the King thus addressed the assembly:

"Thus is rebellion ever checked. Worcester, we offered thee mercy and pardon, but thou didst reject our terms with scorn."

"What I have done," answered the Earl, "I was compelled to for safety, and now, since ill-fortune has befallen me, I am willing to take the consequences, be they whatsoever they may."

"Then bear him to the death," exclaimed the King, "and let Vernon suffer with him; as for the other offenders, I will pause ere I give sentence. Rebellion is now checked, but much yet remains to quell it, and it is meet, therefore, that we now use every means to restore that peace which has been so rudely broken. With to-morrow's dawn, prepare to march for London."

After the battle of Shrewsbury, tranquillity reigned for some time throughout the kingdom.

At length, however, War again reared his gory head, threatening the entire subversion of those institutions which peace had given birth to, for the King of France, taking offence at some trivial affair, attacked our possessions in that country, which required a powerful army to be sent thither.

In the north of England, the Archbishop of York, aided by Lords Mowbray and Hastings, stirred up a rebellion against the monarch; while in Wales, Owen Glendower obtained several advantages over the royal troops.

Full of years, and afflicted in the evening of life by so many cares, Henry the Fourth gradually sank under his misfortunes.

In this extremity, a favourable peace was made with France.

Prince John of Lancaster and the Earl of Westmoreland were to be sent with an army against the rebels in the north, and it was proposed to send Henry Prince of Wales to subdue the discontented Welshmen.

Placing the most implicit confidence in the valour and discretion of his sons, whom he had thus appointed to these important commands, the mind of the dying sovereign became more calm, and he contemplated with pleasure the success that would crown their victorious arms.

In one of Sir John's rambles through the London streets, accompanied by his page, he unexpectedly met the Lord Chief Justice Gascoigne, the intrepid administrator of the laws under Henry the Fourth.

"Sir John Falstaff, I would speak a word with you," said the Judge.

"My good lord," exclaimed Sir John, "I am glad to see your lordship abroad. I heard say your lordship was sick, and I most humbly beseech your lordship to have a reverend care of your health."

"Sir John, I would speak with you concerning——"

"I hear his majesty is afflicted with a grievous sickness," interrupted the wily Knight.

"Well, Heaven mend him," exclaimed the Judge impatiently; "but I pray you let me speak with you."

"It hath its origin from much grief," continued Falstaff; "from much study and perturbation of the brain. I have read the cause of the effects in Galen. It is a kind of deafness."

"I think you are fallen into the disease," observed Gascoigne, "for you hear not what I say to you."

"Very well, my lord—very well."

"I sent for you when there were matters against your life," continued the Lord Chief Justice.

"And following the advice I received," returned Falstaff, "I did not come."

"Well," exclaimed Gascoigne, "the truth is, Sir John, you live in great infamy. You follow the young Prince up and down like his ill angel."

"My lord," cried the Knight, "you that are old consider not the capacities of us that are young."

"Do you set down your name in the scroll of youth, that are written down old with all the characters of age?" exclaimed the Judge. "Have you not a moist eye—a dry hand—a yellow cheek—a white beard—a decreasing leg—an increasing belly? Is not your voice broken—your wind short—your chin double—your wit single—and every part about you blasted by antiquity, and will you yet call yourself young?"

"My lord," answered Falstaff, "I was born about three o'clock in the afternoon, with a white head and something of a round belly. For my voice, I have lost it with holloaing anthems."

"Well, Heaven send the Prince a better companion!" cried Gascoigne.

"Heaven send the companion a better Prince!" retorted the Knight. "I cannot rid my hands of him."

"However, you are now to be severed," exclaimed the Judge, "for the King has ordered that you proceed with Prince John of Lancaster against the Archbishop of York and the Earl of Northumberland."

"Ah! thus it ever is," cried Sir John, alarmed at this intelligence. "There is not a dangerous action can peep out its head, but I am thrust upon it. I would to Heaven my name were not so terrible to the enemy as it is. It were better to be eaten to death with a rust than to be scoured to nothing with perpetual motion."

"Well, Heaven speed you," exclaimed Gascoigne as he turned away, "and when you see my cousin of Westmoreland, commend me to him."

"If I do, fillip me with a three-man beetle," returned Sir John, as the Lord Chief Justice left him; then, turning to his page, he said: "Boy, what money is in my purse?"

"Seven groats and twopence," answered the other.

"Well," cried Falstaff, "go, boy, and deliver this letter to my Lord of Lancaster, this to the Prince of Wales, this to the Earl of Westmoreland, and this to old Mistress Ursula, whom I have weekly sworn to marry since I perceived the first white hair in my chin. About it—you know where to find me."

The page immediately obeyed the injunction of his master, and the Knight was about to return to his home, when Dame Quickly, hostess of the inn called the Boar's Head, accompanied by Fang and Snare, two sheriff's officers, advanced towards him.

As they approached, Fang stepped forward, and laying hold of the Knight, declared that he was arrested at the suit of Mrs. Quickly.

At this moment Bardolph arrived on the spot, who, seeing the trouble into which his friend had fallen, commenced an assault upon the officers, when a general scuffle ensued.

Alarmed at the outcry, the Chief Justice Gascoigne speedily returned, and seeing the affray that had thus taken place, he commanded them to desist, and having succeeded in restoring quiet, enquired the occasion of the disorder.

"Oh, most worshipful lord, an't please your grace," cried Dame Quickly, "I am a poor widow of Eastcheap, and he is arrested at my suit."

"For what sum?" asked the Judge.

"It is more than for some, my lord," answered the hostess. "It is for all I have. He hath eaten me out of house and home, and hath put all my substance into that fat belly of his."

"What is the gross sum I owe thee?" asked the Knight.

"Marry, if thou wert an honest man, thyself and thy money too," answered Dame Quickly. "Thou didst swear to me upon a parcel-gilt goblet, sitting in my dolphin chamber, at the round table, by a sea-coal fire, on Wednesday in Whitsun-week, when the Prince broke thy head for comparing his father to a singing-man of Windsor—thou didst swear to me then, as I was washing thy wounds, to marry me, and make me my lady—thy lady. Canst thou deny it? And didst thou not kiss me, and bid me fetch thee thirty shillings? I put thee now to thy book oath—deny it if thou canst."

"My lord," cried Falstaff, addressing himself to the Judge, "this good woman has been in better circumstances, and the truth is, poverty hath distracted her. But, for these foolish officers, I beseech you I may have redress against them."

"Sir John, Sir John," exclaimed Gascoigne, "you have, as it appears to me, practised upon the easy yielding spirit of this woman, and made her serve your uses both in purse and person."

"Yea, in truth, my lord," interrupted the hostess.

"Pay her the debt you owe her," continued the Judge, "and unpay the villainy you have done with her."

Seeing at length that all hopes of an accommodation were at an end, Sir John now called the dame on one side, and endeavoured to prevail upon her not only to drop her suit for the present, but to lend him a further sum of money till he returned from the wars, promising upon the word of a gentleman to pay her then.

"By my troth, to do that," replied the hostess, "I must be fain to pawn both my plate and the tapestry of my dining-chamber."

"Glasses will be better to drink out of," returned the Knight; "and for the walls, a pretty slight drollery, or the story of the Prodigal, in water-work, is worth a thousand of these fly-bitten tapestries. Come, if it were not for thy humours, there is not a better wench in England."

"Pray, Sir John, let it be but twenty nobles," said the hostess, overcome by the flattery of the Knight, "for I am loth to pawn my plate."

"Let it alone, then," replied Sir John; "I'll make other shifts, since thou art still a fool."

"Well, well, you shall have it," exclaimed Dame Quickly, "even though I pawn my gown."

As she came to this resolution, she turned towards her home for the purpose of fulfilling her words, accompanied by Bardolph, who was to bring back the required sum.

Gascoigne then ordered the officers to release their prisoner.

At the tavern in Eastcheap Sir John met the worthy hostess, Dame Quickly.

A few days afterwards, the Knight set forward towards Yorkshire, where the rebels were mustering their forces.

The first person whom he officially visited was Justice Shallow, a Gloucestershire magistrate whom he had known in earlier times, when they were both starting in life together.

As the Knight approached, Shallow received him with the greatest cordiality, and grasping his hand with fervour, exclaimed:

"Welcome to Gloucestershire, Sir John Falstaff. By my troth, you look well, and bear your years excellently."

"I rejoice to see you well," returned the Knight. "Now, then, to business. Have you provided me half-a-dozen efficient men?"

"Marry, have we, sir. Will it please you to see them?" returned Shallow, and receiving a nod of assent from the Knight, he continued, addressing one of his attendants: "Call Ralph Mouldy."

The person named now made his appearance—a raw awkward country youth—when the Justice, turning towards Sir John, asked:

"What think you of him? A good limbed fellow, young, strong, and of good friends."

"Is thy name Mouldy?" asked Falstaff, disregarding the encomiums of his friend.

"Yea, an't please you," returned the fellow.

"Then 'tis the more time thou wert used," observed the facetious Knight.

"Ha, ha, ha!" vociferated Shallow, tickled at the conceit; "most excellent, i'faith! things that are mouldy lack use! Very singular good! Well said, Sir John, very well said."

"Let him be pricked for one," exclaimed Sir John.

"My dame will be undone now," cried Mouldy, "for who's to do her husbandry and her drudgery; there are other men fitter to go than I."

"Peace, fellow, peace!" roared the Justice. "Stand aside; know you where you are? Now call Simon Shadow."

"Here, sir!" cried that person, answering as soon as his name was uttered.

"Shadow, whose son art thou?" asked Sir John Falstaff.

"My mother's son, sir," answered the countryman.

"Thy mother's son! like enough," returned Sir John, "and thy father's shadow; so the son of the female is the shadow of the male, but not much of the father's substance, however. Shadow will serve for the summer, so prick him."

Thomas Wart, another rustic, was next called, who was addressed in a similar manner by the Knight.

"Is thy name Wart?"

"Yea, sir."

"Then art thou a very ragged wart," returned Sir John, "and to prick thee would be superfluous, therefore stand back awhile."

Then turning towards Francis Feeble, who was next brought forward, he continued:

"What trade art thou?"

"A tailor, sir."

"Well said, tailor! well said, most forcible Feeble!" cried the jolly Knight. "Thou wilt be as valiant as the wrathful dove, or most magnanimous mouse. Prick him, Master Shallow."

Peter Bullcalf, of the Green, was the next in succession, who, having made his clumsy obeisance, the Knight eyed him from top to toe, observing:

"A likely fellow that; come prick me Bullcalf, till he roar again."

"Oh, Lord! Good my lord captain!" cried the alarmed countryman.

"What! dost thou roar because thou art pricked?" exclaimed Sir John.

"Oh, Lord, sir! I am a disabled man," returned Bullcalf. "I have a cold, sir; a cough, sir, which I caught when ringing on the King's coronation day, sir."

"Come, come, sirrah!" vociferated the Knight, "thou must away with me to the war, and I will see that thy friends shall ring for thee."

"Well, Sir John," cried Justice Shallow, "our business is now done, and we will therefore think of dinner. Come, come!"

As he spoke, he conducted his guests into the hall, where the mid-day meal was already spread.

The afternoon and succeeding evening were spent by the worthy trio in the most riotous excesses, and each was finally carried to his couch, most gloriously drunk.

On the next morning Sir John Falstaff arose at an early hour, and once more partaking the hospitality of his friend Shallow, he started towards the north, accompanied by his raw recruits.

We must now quit the Knight, and travel to the camp of the rebel Archbishop, who had encamped his army on the borders of a large forest near the confines of Yorkshire.

By this time the army of Prince John of Lancaster had taken up a position a short distance off, and as the Royalists were desirous of concluding the civil commotion without having recourse to bloodshed, negotiations were immediately commenced between the contending parties.

At length everything appeared to be nearly accomplished in a most favourable manner, when the Earl of Westmoreland was despatched by the Prince to settle the preliminaries for a meeting between himself and the warlike Churchman.

On arriving at the outposts, a messenger was sent to the Archbishop announcing the embassy that was awaiting his pleasure, and in a short time afterwards an answer was returned, desiring him to follow the bearer of the message, and meet the parties as he desired.

Westmoreland hesitated not for an instant.

"My Lord Archbishop," he cried, "I bring health and fair greeting from our general, Prince John of Lancaster."

"Say on, my Lord of Westmoreland," replied the dignitary. "What news bring you now?"

"I come on business from my general," answered Westmoreland, "and to your grace I address myself. You, Lord Archbishop, whose see is maintained by civil peace, whose learning peace hath tutored, why do you transform yourself to rebellion?"

"I have carefully weighed what mischief our arms may do," returned the Primate, "against what wrongs we suffer, and thus have found that our griefs are heavier than our offences. We have the summary of our grievances to show, which we endeavoured to present to the King, but were on all occasions refused an audience. When we are wronged, and would point out our sufferings, we are denied access to his presence, even by those very men who have most deeply injured us."

"When was your appeal ever refused?" asked the Earl of Westmoreland. "In what have you ever been oppressed by the King? I am now come from our royal general to learn your complaints; to tell you that his grace will give you audience, and that he will grant all your just demands."

"He has been compelled by our perseverance to make this offer," exclaimed Lord Mowbray; "and it is from policy, not love, that it proceeds."

"Mowbray, you do my royal master wrong," returned Westmoreland; "this offer proceeds from mercy, and not from fear; for lo! within a short distance from hence, lies our army, which, upon mine honour, is too full of confidence to admit a thought of fear. Our ranks are more full of names than yours; our men are more perfect in the use of arms; our armour as strong, and our cause the best. Say not, therefore, that our offer is compelled."

"If I had my will, we would admit no parley," cried Mowbray.

"That argues but the shame of your offence," returned the Earl.

"Hath not Prince John," asked Lord Hastings, "full commission to hear and determine upon what conditions peace shall be restored?"

"Such is indeed the case," answered the Earl.

"Then, my lord of Westmoreland," exclaimed the Archbishop, "take this packet, which contains our grievances, each one of which is there specified. If he will indeed fulfil the promises you have made in his name, we will each return to our separate homes and henceforward dwell in peace."

"This I will show the Prince," answered the Earl of Westmoreland; "and, if it please ye, lords, we will meet one hour hence in sight of both our armies."

"It is enough," cried the Prelate; "we will await the Prince without fail."

Having thus far succeeded in his mission, the Earl now bent reverently before the rebellious Primate, and retired, accompanied by his attendants, towards the camp of the Royalists.

As soon as he was gone, Mowbray, who had all along looked on with distrust, exclaimed:

"My lord Archbishop, there is a something within my bosom tells me no conditions of peace can stand between yonder Royalist general and ourselves."

"Fear not for that," answered Hastings, "for if we obtain the terms we ask, our peace shall stand secure."

"Aye," returned Mowbray; "but we shall no more be honoured by the King, and we shall be winnowed with so rough a wind that our corn even shall seem as light as chaff, and the good will experience no difference from the bad."

"No, no, my lord," interrupted the Archbishop. "Mark this—the King is weary of our complaints; his foes are so mixed up with his friends that, in endeavouring to root out an enemy, he shakes his surest friend."

"Besides," continued the Lord Hastings, "the King hath wasted all his rods on recent offenders, so that now he is destitute of the very instruments of chastisement, so that his power, like a fangless lion, may try, but cannot hold."

"True!" cried the Archbishop; "and therefore, my good lord, be assured that if we make our atonement well, our peace, like a broken limb that has been united, will be the stronger for the breaking."

The lords now separated for the present, to make arrangements for the meeting that was to take place between the leaders of the two armies, and by the time the hour was elapsed, they were all arrived on the spot appointed for the adjustment of their several grievances.

The Prince, with his adherents, was first on the ground, and as he beheld the rebel nobles approaching for the purpose of parley, his brows contracted with ill-concealed anger against those who had raised the standard of revolt in opposition to his father.

However, concealing his anger as well as he could, he bowed to them with cold civility, and thus accosted each of them by turns:

"You are well encountered here, my cousin Mowbray; good day to you, my lord Archbishop; and so to you, Lord Hastings; and to all. My lord of York, it was a fairer sight when your flock, assembled by the bell, encircled you to hear with reverence your exposition of the holy text, than now to see you here, armed in proof, and cheering an army of rebels with your drum, and converting the word into a sword, and life to death."

"My Lord of Lancaster," answered the Archbishop mildly; "I sent your grace the particulars of our many grievances, which had been scornfully rejected from your father's court. On these causes the hydra son of war is born, whose watchful eyes can only be lured to sleep by the granting of our just and righteous demands."

"Which, if not fulfilled," exclaimed the fiery Mowbray, "we will fight for them to the last man!"

"Will it please your grace," said the Earl of Westmoreland, addressing Prince John, "to answer them directly how far you approve their propositions?"

"I like them all," answered the Prince, "and will allow them; and here I swear, by the honour of my blood, that my father's purposes have been mistaken, and that those about him have been too harsh in the administration of the laws. My lords, these grievances shall be immediately redressed."

"If it may please you, my lord," exclaimed the Earl of Westmoreland, addressing the Archbishop, "I think it would be well if you discharge your army upon the instant, as we will ours, and here, in sight of them both, let us embrace, that all men may behold the tokens of restored peace and amity."

"I take your princely word for these redresses," said the Primate.

"I give it you," answered the Prince, "and will maintain my word."

"Go then," cried Lord Hastings, addressing two of his attendants, "and deliver to the army this news of peace. Let them have their pay, and instantly depart for their several homes."

"I have bestowed great pains to bring about this peace, my lord Archbishop," said Westmoreland, "and my regard to you shall show itself more openly to you hereafter."

"I doubt you not," replied the prelate; "peace is of the nature of a conquest, for then both parties are nobly subdued, and neither party loser."

"Behold our army is dispersed already," exclaimed Hastings, "like youthful steeds unyoked, they take their way east, west, north, south, each hastening towards his home."

"These are good tidings, my lord of Hastings," cried the Earl of Westmoreland in a tone of exultation, "for which I arrest thee as a traitor; and you, my lord Archbishop, and you, my lord Mowbray, I attach you both of the crime of high treason!"

Several guards now approached, who having surrounded and disarmed the prisoners, Mowbray asked:

"Is this proceeding honourable or just?"

"Why do you thus break your faith with us?" asked the captive Archbishop.

"I pledged thee none," returned the Prince. "I promised to redress those grievances of which you complained, and, which, by the honour of a Christian knight, I will perform. But for you, rebels, look to receive the just punishment of your crimes. Guards, lead these traitors instantly to the block, and see that ere the sun goes down they die the death of traitors."

A flourish of trumpets and drums was now sounded, and the rebellious lords were conducted from the presence of the Prince to the place where their crimes were to be expiated.

It is unnecessary that we here describe the manner of their exeution, and, therefore, passing over the melancholy scene, shall merely observe that they died with the same degree of fortitude that had ever marked them while living.

The dangerous rebellion being thus brought to an end, news reached the camp of the alarming illness of the King, who was now said to be lying on the bed of death, without even the smallest hopes of recovery.

On receiving this alarming intelligence, Prince John gave the command of his army, for the present, to one of his best esteemed officers, and hastily taking his departure from the North, he returned with all possible speed to London.

Leaving him to pursue his journey, we will at once proceed to the chamber of the sick monarch, who now lay in almost the last extremity of death, attended only by two pages.

The King, after a restless night, had, as the morning dawned, sunk into a quiet repose, from which, however, he shortly awoke, when calling to the pages, he exclaimed :

"Who waits there ? "

"We, your faithful pages."

"Is my son, Prince Humphrey, gone to rest ? "

"Not yet, my liege," replied one of the attendants ; "a short time since he retired to his closet to offer up prayers to Heaven for your recovery."

"Seek him and bring him to our presence," cried the afflicted monarch.

The pages at once retired to execute the commands of the King, and in a short time returned accompanied by Humphrey, Duke of Gloucester, Thomas, Duke of Clarence, the Lord Chief Justice Gascoigne, and others of the Court.

Prince Humphrey knelt beside the couch of his illustrious parent, and enquired what he was sent for.

"Where is your brother, the Prince of Wales ? " asked the King.

"He dined yesterday in the City, and is not yet returned."

"And by whom was he accompanied ? " again enquired the monarch.

"By Poins and his usual riotous companions."

"The foulest soil is most subject to weeds," returned the King ; "and he, the noble image of my youth, is overspread with them. On this account my grief extends even beyond my death, and my heavy heart weeps blood when I reflect upon the days that he shall look upon when I am sleeping with my ancestors."

"My gracious sir," exclaimed the Lord Chief Justice, "you mistake the Prince, who only studies his companions as men do a strange tongue. In time he will cast off those followers, and the recollection of them will serve as a guide or pattern by which to shape his future course."

"I rejoice to hear the favourable opinion from your lordship," cried the King in a low tone, "but now my sight fails me, and my brain is giddy. Oh me ! come near me, I am dying."

As he spoke he sunk back exhausted on his couch, and fell into a gentle slumber, when the crown being placed upon his pillow, all retired in order that he might not be disturbed.

The Prince of Wales now entered the chamber, and believing that his royal father was dead, he wept over him with tears of real sorrow and anguish.

Seeing the crown, he took it from the pillow, and believing it to be now his, he placed it upon his own brow, and hastily quitted the apartment to mourn in private the death of one whom he had ever loved so fondly.

In a short time afterwards the King awoke, and missing the crown from his pillow, he called to one of his attendants to know by whom it had been taken away, and, being informed that the Prince of Wales had only just before left the chamber, he desired that he might instantly be sent for.

This summons the Prince most willingly obeyed, and throwing himself upon his knees before his royal father, he exclaimed :

"Alas ! my liege, I never thought to hear you speak again."

"Thy wish, Harry, was father to that thought," exclaimed the King. "I stay too long for thee. Dost thou so hunger for mine empty throne, that thou must needs invest thyself with my honour ere thy hour be ripe? Get thee home and dig my grave thyself, and bid the merry bells ring, that thou art crowned."

"Oh, pardon me, my liege," cried the Prince, much affected by this rebuke from his dying father. "There is your crown."

On the day following the death of the King, Falstaff, accompanied by his friend Justice Shallow, arrived in town, and the first news he heard was that his former companion, Prince Henry, was now the King of England.

Delighted at the prospect that thus seemed to open for his future fortune, he resolved to throw himself in the way of his Majesty, who was expected to visit Westminster Abbey in the course of the day.

"Heaven save thy grace! King Hal! my royal Hal!" exclaimed Sir John as the King approached.

"Are you in your senses?" cried Gascoigne, stepping between the King and his former companions; "know to whom you speak!"

"Aye," replied Sir John, "to my King! my Jove! I speak to thee, my heart!"

"I know thee not, old man," exclaimed Henry with dignity. "Fall to prayers. How ill white hairs become a fool and jester! I have long dreamed of such a man, old and profane as thou art; but, being again awake, I despise thee. Presume not I am the thing I was, for Heaven knows I have turned away from the follies I was wont to commit."

Falstaff and his companions now retired, when Gascoigne, whispering to Prince John, said:

"I like this fair beginning; yet still I fear it will bring no grace to me."

SIR JOHN FALSTAFF.

"You have indeed great cause to doubt," answered the Prince.

The King now approached Gascoigne, exclaiming:

"My lord, you are assured I love you not."

"I am, my liege," answered the other; "yet your Majesty hath no just cause to hate me."

"No?" cried Henry. "Think you, then, I have forgotten the indignities you have offered me, when you rebuked and sent to prison the heir of England?"

"I then supported the person of your father," answered the Judge; "and in the administration of his law, your Highness was pleased to forget my place, and struck me on my seat of judgment; whereupon, as an offender against your father, I committed you to prison. Suppose the case your own, and then condemn me as I deserve."

"You are right," exclaimed the King; "and therefore you shall still bear the sword of justice. And I wish your honours to increase till you see a son of mine offend and obey you as I have done. You committed me; for which I commit into your hand the unstained sword that you have so long and honourably borne. There is my hand, in token of forgiveness."

The royal party now arrived at the Abbey, where having attended mass, they afterwards returned to the palace. Then the young King, retiring to the privacy of his closet, mused thoughtfully on the heavy responsibility that had fallen upon him, and resolved henceforward to earn the love of his subjects by the excellence of his government.

THE END.

NOTICE.—"ROMEO AND JULIET," being No. 5 of Stories from Shakespeare, will be ready on Monday, Dec. 5. Orders should be given early to your Booksellers.

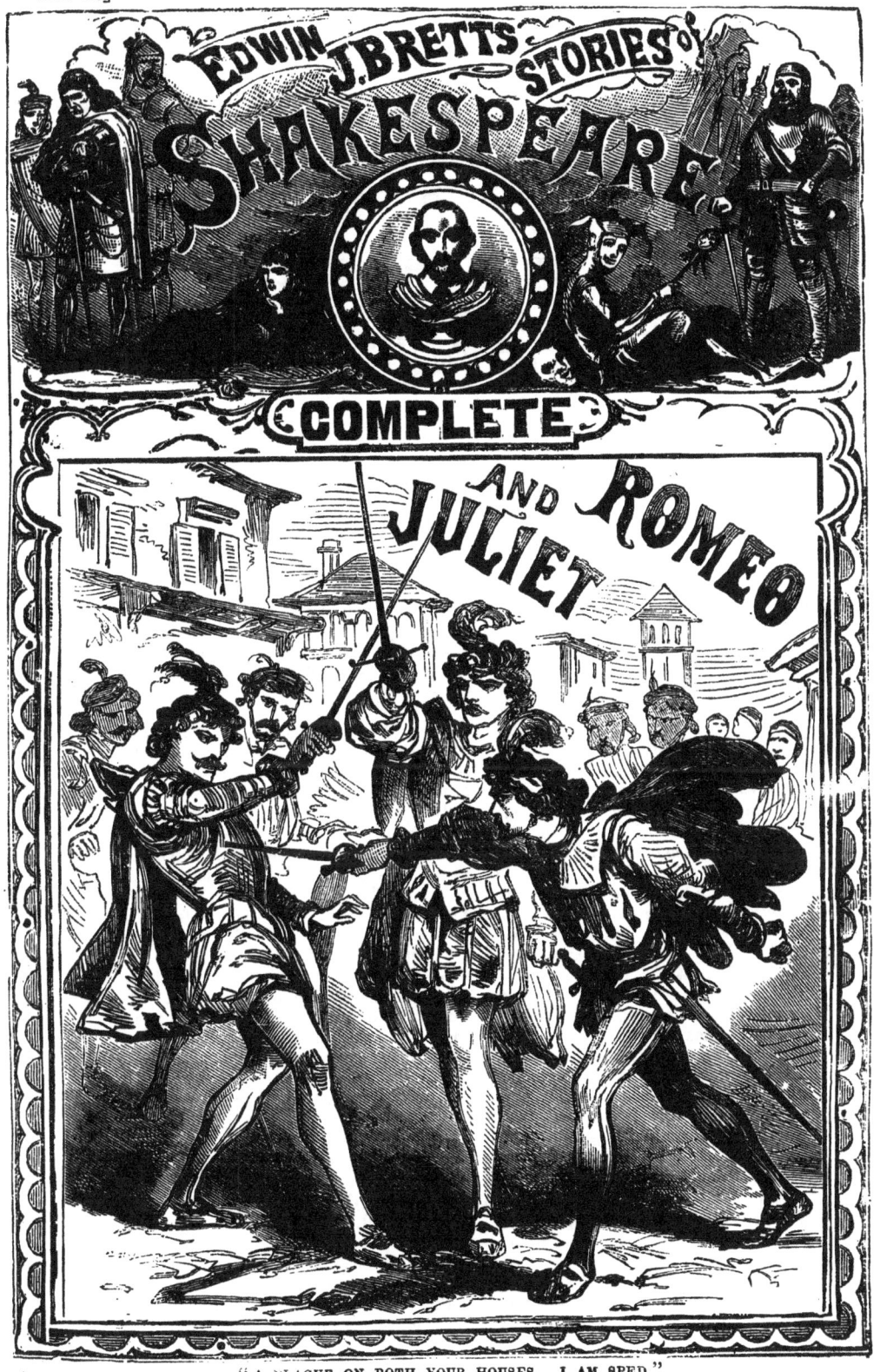

"A PLAGUE ON BOTH YOUR HOUSES. I AM SPED."

EDWIN J. BRETT'S
STORIES FROM
SHAKESPEARE'S PLAYS.

No. 5.—ROMEO AND JULIET.

"THOU art unkind to-night, Rosaline. Yet woman is ever thus; wilful and wayward as the wind."

The speaker was a young man of not more than twenty summers; tall, well-built, handsome, of distinguished mien; a face and form on which nature had set its seal of nobility.

The young girl was fair also, both in form and feature; but there was a weakness and irresolution in her expression, and a coyness in her manner which was not that of a timid maiden, but of a confirmed coquette.

The spot where they were standing was the terrace of a house near Verona, built on the slope of a hill, with exquisite views of varied landscapes, vineyards and cornfields, and pleasant streams, and white cottages and olive groves, with here and there the spire of a church or the towers of some stately mansion.

Sunset was casting its golden shafts over the scene, bathing all equally with its glowing light, the humble cottage of the lowly peasant, and the marble palace of the noble, and falling softly on the figures of the youth and maiden who stood on the terrace, he bending forward in anxious doubt and entreaty, she with downcast mien, and an evident desire to quit his presence before he pressed her further.

" You are so jealous, Romeo," she said, in low timorous accents. " Only the other night you fumed and fretted because I spoke to Count Paris. And then young Gonzalvo; because I danced with him your hand was on your sword-hilt, and it is only Heaven's mercy you gave him not his passport straight to heaven."

" Ay; Gonzalvo! I like him not," said Romeo; " he is a kinsman of the Capulets. How should I wish to see him hold your hand and breathe his hated love in your ear?"

" He spoke not of love," said the young girl, though her cheek grew more rosy, and her bosom trembled with some re-awakened emotion. " I fear me, Romeo, we are sadly unsuitable to one another. You are so fierce a wooer that you frighten me."

" Fierce! when I love you, Rosaline!" cried Romeo, clasping her hand in both his own, and gazing into her eyes with ardent passion. " Am I not right to guard my promised treasure? Oh, Rosaline, do not pretend this coldness. It is but feigned I know, for you cannot, if you possess a heart at all, fail to see how much I love you. My love is like yonder sunset which gilds all nature with its golden beauty; were I to lose it, it would grow dim and dull and colourless as yonder valley, where the rays of the day-god have ceased to fall."

He passed his arm around her as he spoke, and bending, pressed a kiss upon her lips.

She shrunk from him as he did so, but he observed not the action, or if he did he attributed it to that shrinking timidity which made her often seem cold and impassive.

At the moment that he imprinted a kiss upon her lips, a voice was heard calling her.

The sound came to her evidently as a great relief, and so plainly was this demonstrated by her manner that he dropped her hand, and a painful flush overspread his cheek.

"Your mother calls, and I will away," he said, in a voice rendered deep with anger. "I will come again when you are in better mood, Rosaline. As to Gonzalvo, let him beware. No Capulet shall wear a flower which a Montague has nearly plucked. Good night, and pleasant dreams. I will come again to-morrow."

With these disjointed sentences, and with a heart bursting more with anger, perhaps, than jealousy and disappointment, he strode from the terrace, and passed into the high road.

As he did so the young girl leaned over the balustrade of the terrace, instead of answering the call within, and gazed after her lover with some sadness.

"Alas," said she, "alas! He fears Gonzalvo will win my love. That no man will. Never shall husband call me wife; not long will it be now ere I am the bride of Heaven, and bolts and bars will keep my eager lover out. Poor Romeo! To-morrow, when he comes, my mother must tell him all."

She watched him until he was swallowed up in the gloom of the twilight, and then with a sigh she entered the house.

Meanwhile the lover, to whom her timid heart had feared to tell the truth, went angrily on towards the city gates.

His mind was in a tumult of contending passions and emotions.

There had for many years—for more than one generation—been a deadly feud between the houses of Montague and Capulet, to the former of which Romeo belonged, and of the latter of which Gonzalvo was a distant relative.

This family quarrel, commenced through some political jealousy, had culminated now in incessant wranglings and sword-drawing in the public streets; for now that the heads of the several houses were too old to carry on more than wordy warfare, the younger ones were more fierce and desperate than ever in their attacks upon each other.

Knowing nothing then of the real cause of the young girl's behaviour, he was in a state of furious passion, vowing vengeance on the supposed lover if he met him, when, as he passed through the city gates, he came full butt against a tall and handsomely-dressed gentleman, who was hurrying round the corner of a street.

"How now!" cried Romeo angrily. "Whither goest thou? Ha! Mercutio."

"'Tis even I," cried the other, who was a relative of Escalus, Prince of Verona, and a friend of Romeo's.

He was a young, gay-hearted, true, and generous fellow, brave as a lion, taking life merrily withal, but apt, like others of those days, to take offence at the least affront.

"But what gets thee in this state, my Romeo?" he added; "you look as angry as an old man whose wife has run away with a young one. I grieve to see you always so sad. Tell me, my friend, is Rosaline still the cause?"

"The cause is Gonzalvo, for she favours him."

"Nay, then, as much as the hawk does the dove. 'Tis said that Rosaline will never marry. If she let you believe so, 'tis because she fears to tell the truth. But why think more of one who loves you not? There are brighter eyes, and prettier forms, and more neatly-turned ankles in Verona than hers. Tut, man! are you to waste your life and the famed name of Montague in sighing for a wench who knows not her own mind?"

"I know you speak in all kindness, Mercutio," said Romeo, "else I might feel angry with you. But I feel oppressed and ill—I know not how."

"Love-sick — love-sick, my friend," said Mercutio, patting him on the back; "it is a disease that is easily cured by finding a more complaisant damsel. I warrant me that in Verona, could you only make up your mind to discover her, there is a lady (or shall I say hundreds of them?) who would make your heart beat with a warm passion that would soon eclipse all thought of pale Rosaline. But let us on. I came here to meet you; we will have a cup of wine together, and drink to the health of the fair unknown who will banish care from your heart, and make you again the Romeo of old."

And so, linking his arm in that of his friend, the light-hearted young nobleman drew him away.

The manner of Romeo had, in fact, caused great anxiety to his friends of late.

Instead of being gay and happy-hearted, he moped about alone, taking long, solitary walks early and late, avoiding the company of those who on other occasions were his chosen friends, sometimes remaining in his room all day with closed windows, and refusing to speak to any one.

But a great change was at hand—a change of which no one would have dreamed, and of which Mercutio had touched the key-note when he spoke of other loves.

Sooner would the generous fellow have cut off his right hand than said the words had he but known to what they would innocently lead—the terrible catastrophe which was to startle all Verona, and plunge whole families in mourning.

Two days passed, on the first of which Romeo again sought Rosaline, though in vain.

On this occasion he learned from her mother the truth—that she had devoted herself to a life of chastity, and that she had permitted his allusions to Gonzalvo because she had feared to tell him her real meaning.

On the morning of the second day the early morning sun was pouring down in unclouded beauty on the Place or Square of St. Mark.

It glistened brightly on the splendid palaces, and on the marble fountains, converting the crystal water into myriads of diamonds, as it was sent up to an immense height towards the blue heavens, and descended in broken masses to the ground.

The few shops that were included in the buildings of the great square were already open.

At the windows of the various mansions fair faces began to peep, while here and there a graceful form leaned over the balustrade of a balcony to catch the balmy air of morning.

Presently from a side street there came two men, dressed in the attire of servants to some noble family, and armed with swords and bucklers.

They had much of the appearance of bullies about them, with their swaggering gait, bloated faces and restless eyes, which seemed to wander round as if in search of a quarrel, but those of the townspeople who saw them knew them at once to be Sampson and Gregory, two servants to the noble house of Capulet.

They paused when they came near the benches of a wine shop, and were presently engaged in testing the quality of some ruby liquid, which seemed to make them more aggressive in their aspect still.

"I wonder," said Sampson, as he wiped the wine from his long moustache with the sleeve of his doublet, "I wonder if we shall meet any of the Montagues this day, for the quarrel of the masters is between the men too."

"Ay; and, marry, if we do meet them we'll attack them," said Gregory, "for I strike quickly when I am moved."

"And I also, for they are an insolent lot," said Sampson; "and see, by St. Peter, here come two against whom we have a special grudge — Balthazar, Romeo's servant, and Abram, who is old Montague's."

Gregory leaped from his seat.

"Then draw thy sword, Sampson," he cried, "and let's be ready for them."

"My naked weapon's out," cried Sampson, as he followed his companion's example; "fear me not. Let us keep on the right side of the law, though; let them begin."

"Ay, so let it be," said Gregory. "I will frown as they pass by, and let them take it as they like."

"Nay, as they dare," said Sampson. "I will bite my thumb at them, which is a disgrace to them if they bear it."

And he suited the action to the word.

In an instant it had its effect, for Abram advanced with an angry mien, and with his hand upon his sword-hilt.

"Do you bite your thumb at us, sir?" he said, staring at Sampson aggressively.

"I do bite my thumb, sir."

"Do you bite your thumb at us, sir?" repeated Abram.

"No, but I bite my thumb," said Sampson significantly, "but yet if you want to quarrel, I am ready. I serve as good a man as you do."

"No better."

"Say better," whispered Gregory, for at this moment Benvolio, the cousin of Romeo, appeared turning into the square; "here comes one of his master's kinsmen."

" Ay, a better man than you serve," said Sampson loudly.

" You lie !" cried Abram.

" Then draw, if you be men," exclaimed Sampson. " Gregory, remember thy swashing blow."

They went at it now with good will, and, as may be expected, a crowd was quickly collected around them.

The citizens of Verona, in fact, were becoming disgusted with the frequent brawls which this deadly feud between Montague and Capulet brought about, and looked with little favour on either ; but a murmur of approbation ran through their ranks as Benvolio appeared, and beat down the swords of the disputants, crying—

" Part, fools ! Put up your swords. You know not what you do !"

But a new element of mischief soon appeared upon the scene.

The houses of both Montagues and Capulets were close to the great square, and, at the very moment that Benvolio had to a certain extent succeeded in restoring peace, Tybalt, nephew to Lady Capulet, rushed, sword in hand, upon the scene.

He was a young and handsome nobleman, full of fire and courage, and, like Romeo, maddened by the foolish feud which had long so unrighteously existed between the two families.

He waited not to reason, but seeing Benvolio with his sword drawn between the serving-men, he drew his rapier fiercely.

" What !" cried he, " are you drawn among these heartless hinds, Benvolio ? Turn, and look upon your death !"

Benvolio, brave as he was, had no desire to recommence a quarrel which would inevitably draw into it his already excited and exasperated cousin Romeo.

" I do but keep the peace," he said. " Put up your sword, unless you aid me in parting these men."

Tybalt laughed scornfully.

" What ! drawn, and talk of peace ?" cried Tybalt. " I hate the word as I hate hell, the Montagues, and you ! Coward, come on !"

Benvolio could stand no jeers such as these, and in an instant their swords had crossed in deadly combat.

And now a tumultuous scene resulted.

The news had spread rapidly that the old feud had broken out once more, and

that a fierce battle was being waged in the market-place, and so from every street which led into the square came pouring an angry crowd.

" Ho, there ! Clubs and partisans !"

" Strike ! Beat them down !"

" Down with the Montagues !"

" Down with the Capulets !"

These and other cries resounded loudly through the Place of St. Mark, and the battle waged with unprecedented fury.

The unexpected struggle was just at its height, when Capulet and Montague, and their wives appeared on the scene—the old men forgetting their grey hairs and their dignity, and striving to reach each other for a deadly conflict.

But at this moment, Escalus, followed by a number of soldiers, came hurriedly in the square.

In an instant the scene had changed as if by magic.

Escalus was a just prince, but he was a severe one, and he ordered his men at once to clear the streets.

The order was obeyed without any compunction, the soldiers driving the crowds before them without distinction into the streets and byeways until the square was cleared.

To neither Capulets nor Montagues would the prince listen.

" This is not the place for explanations," he said. " I have had too much of these family brawls, and will endure them no longer. I warn you, if you disturb our streets again, your lives shall pay the forfeit of the peace. If there is aught on either side to complain of, you know where my palace is, and there I will listen to you both. And now, on pain of death, depart."

The prince was known to be one who would not be trifled with, and it was surprising with what rapidity the place was cleared.

" Uncle," said Benvolio, as he passed away with his uncle Montague, " Heaven is kind to us to-day. See, yonder comes Romeo. Had he been a moment sooner he would have seen the fray, and had he seen any of the Capulets, Heaven only knows what might have happened. By your leave I will meet him. He seems in sore trouble again."

" Yes ; pray go to him," said Romeo's father. " My grateful thanks to you, if you can but find his trouble, and help to cure it."

Benvolio smiled.

"I think I know it well," he said, "and have in view already the way to make him well. How now, Romeo," he added, as he advanced to meet his cousin; "you are sad again to-day, but I have good news for you."

"I fear me not," said Romeo, "for I am out of favour with the one I love. Love is all tyrannous, and I am but its slave."

"Does she deny thee, then—refuse thy love?"

"Ay, you are right," said Romeo; "and she is so exquisitely fair. Rich, indeed, in beauty, yet poor in the fact that when she dies she leaves no likeness behind her."

"She has sworn, then, to live chaste?"

"Yes; I did imagine her in love with Gonzalvo," said Romeo, "but I was wrong; she feared to tell me the truth."

"Come, man, be ruled by me," cried Benvolio; "forget to think of her."

"Ah! teach me how I can forget to think."

"By giving liberty to your eyes," said his cousin; "examine other beauties."

"If I do that, it will only make me think her more beautiful," said Romeo. "Show me a damsel who is passing fair, and she will only make me think how Rosaline does surpass her. Farewell! thou canst not teach me to forget."

"Nay, not farewell, good cousin," said Benvolio. "I must speak to thee awhile. I have ever been thy friend—not only cousin. My word and my sword have ever been at thy service. And now I have a favour to ask. To-night a grand feast is given by old Capulet, and I have gleaned from the serving-man, who took through the town the notes of invitation, the names of the principal guests. Among them is the fair Rosaline, whom thou lovest so much. Be just, then, Romeo; go with me to-night, and see her there among all the beauties of Verona. Compare her face with some whom I will show you, and I will forfeit my life if you do not confess yourself wrong,"

"Good Benvolio," said Romeo, smiling, as he pressed his friend's hand, "I will do you this favour since you so urge me. But, mark me, not for the reason you give; no, I go simply to see again my Rosaline—alas! my Rosaline no longer— to bask once more in the sunshine of

those features, whose beauty exceeds those of every woman in the world. And now, farewell! At six o'clock I will be ready."

"And look you, Romeo, forget not your domino. We must go masked to Capulet's."

And so with a friendly grip of the hand they parted.

Benvolio's honest heart was much rejoiced, for he knew not how surely, how awfully, the shadow of Fate was darkening over the devoted head of Romeo.

The household of the Capulets meanwhile was in a most unusual state of excitement.

The feast truly was one which was held every year, and to which invitations were scattered broadcast through the town, at any rate to all the notabilities; but on this occasion there was another interest attached to it; for Count Paris was to be there—a young nobleman, a kinsman of Prince Escalus, and a relation therefore to Mercutio; and to him it was understood that Juliet, the only daughter of the house, was to be soon married.

Juliet, though only fourteen, was well worthy of the doting love and admiration of her parents.

She was of medium height, with a form ripened into roundness and exquisite symmetry by the sunny breezes of Italy; her hair of rich chestnut brown waving luxuriantly over shoulders white as snow, and carved into such perfect contour that no sculptor's chisel could hope to imitate them; eyes of melting tenderness, blue as the cloudless skies above her native land; and a mouth whose pouting red lips seemed to smilingly invite the pressure of a lover's kiss.

Robed as she was now in a low-necked velvet and gold dress, with a deep blush rose nestling at her breast, the flush of pleasure and innocent excitement causing her cheeks to outvie in colour those of the noted beauties of Verona, she was indeed something to be proud of; and many were the glances of admiration which were cast upon her by those among the guests to whom she was a new revelation of loveliness.

The scene around her was well calculated to excite the wonder and delight of any one not much used to the brilliant sights of society.

The feast was over, the splendid banquet disposed of, and, merry with good things and wine, the company were joining in the gay dance or promenading around the splendid hall, whose marble pillars were decorated with garlands of real flowers—the richest and rarest that money could procure.

Bright were the lights that cast a magic glow over all; and gorgeous indeed were the dresses of the throng, among whom were noticeable many maskers in fantastic dresses.

Among the latter were Mercutio, Benvolio and Romeo.

Persuaded much against his will, the latter's eyes had glanced in vain around the room for Rosaline, until presently they lighted upon Juliet.

Oh, how his pulses beat! how his heart quickened as he beheld her!

Here was beauty indeed unalloyed! Loveliness, purity, innocence combined; and his heart went out to her in an instant, worshipping at her shrine as at that of a superior being.

Rosaline was forgotten; his dream of passion dissipated, as if by the stroke of an enchanter's wand.

"Fellow," he said, in an undertone, as he turned eagerly to a serving-man, "what lady's that who leans upon the arm of yonder knight—the one in velvet, whose pure angelic presence casts lustre over this scene of gaiety?"

The man to whom he addressed these words was not one of the regular servants of the house, and had never seen Juliet before.

"I know not, sir," he said respectfully.

"Oh, how beautiful she is!" murmured Romeo, as he crept behind one of the marble pillars, where he could observe her better. "Her loveliness sanctifies the place; and beside her all others seem as dross to purest gold. When this dance is over I will speak to her. Ah, I have never loved till now! I never saw true beauty till this night."

Unobserved by Romeo, who had neither eyes nor ears for anything or any one but Juliet, Tybalt had meanwhile crept near him, and recognised his voice, though he could scarcely distinguish his lowly murmured words.

"By Heavens!" he cried, to Capulet, who stood near, "that voice—it is a Montague's! Uncle, this is our foe—'tis he, that villain Romeo."

"Content thee, gentle cousin," said the host. "Let him alone. He bears him like an honourable gentleman, and in very truth Verona boasts of him as a well-grown and a virtuous youth. I would not for the world's wealth that any evil should befall him in this house. Be patient; take no notice of him. It is my will."

"I cannot endure him."

"He shall be endured," cried his uncle angrily. "Am I the master here or you? What, will you not be quiet? By Heaven, I'll make you!"

"I will withdraw then, since you wish it," said Tybalt, as he saw his uncle's ire rising. "Never shall it be said that Tybalt would breathe the same air as Romeo in your house. Farewell, sweet uncle, and a fair good night."

While this scene had been going on, and Tybalt had withdrawn from the festivities with a heavy and wrathful heart, Romeo had sought Juliet, and stood with her near one of the marble pillars, conversing.

The daring which had prompted him to address her had not been resented; it was enough for this pure-hearted girl that he was her father's guest, and his voice was so gentle, yet so eloquent, that it at once found an echo in the heart of one who had been so little tutored in the world's ways.

They looked a strange pair—the one so young, so exquisite, the other attired in the sombre garb of a pilgrim.

In the bustle of the scene they remained long unnoticed, retired to the recess of a window looking out upon the square.

Such a brief time of happiness neither had ever tasted before, and it was rudely indeed dispelled when the voice of Mercutio said—

"'Tis close on midnight. At that hour all must unmask, and we, my friend, must go, lest we be known."

"A sweet five minutes more, Mercutio," said Romeo, as he took Juliet by the hand. "I must away, fair goddess, but even a pilgrim has lips to show his reverence, and thus do I salute thee."

He raised her hand to his lips and kissed it softly.

"Good pilgrim," said Juliet, "you do err. Palm to palm is holy palmer's kiss."

"Have not saints lips and holy palmers, too?"

"Ay, lips that they must use in prayer."

"Nay, dear saint," said Romeo, "let lips do what hands do. Move not, sweet one, while I my prayer do make."

"'COME, MAN, BE RULED BY ME,' CRIED BENVOLIO; 'FORGET TO THINK OF HER.'"

And the daring youth bent over her and kissed her on her lips.

Mercutio was now in a terrible state of impatience; he knew well what would be the result of an open discovery in the banqueting hall of Romeo's identity, however much Capulet might wink at the fact of his being there in disguise.

Seeing this daring act of Romeo's, he hurried towards the pair again—loving already, though she had caught but little glimpse of his face, and had only read his heart through the strange glamour of his eyes.

"Come, come," he said; "you know not what you do. We must be gone. Another time this lady and you can meet again. Away, my friend. Sweet lady, fare thee well!"

At this moment Juliet's father was seen approaching, and, with a tender pressure of the young girl's hand, Romeo reluctantly departed.

"Mad youth," cried Mercutio, as they went away in the direction of the exit, "it was not for this that I and Benvolio brought you hither. Know you not who it is, whose bright eyes have lured thee from Rosaline towards thy death?"

"I know not, unless she be an angel?"

"She is the Lady Juliet, the daughter of old Capulet. Seest thou thy danger now?"

"I see no peril save in losing her," replied Romeo. "But here comes Benvolio, let us haste away."

All was bright and splendid as they hastened down the marble staircase and across the grand hall, but once out in the street, along which ran the high wall of Capulet's orchard, it was black as pitch, and here Romeo suddenly disappeared.

"CAN IT BE POSSIBLE! IS IT YOU, ROMEO?"

In vain his friends called him; in vain Benvolio shouted—" Romeo! Cousin Romeo!" in vain Mercutio conjured him in one of his merriest speeches to show himself."

He was nowhere to be seen or heard of.

" He ran this way and leaped the orchard wall; call him again, Mercutio," said Benvolio.

" Nay, he is wise, and has stolen him off to bed," said Mercutio, " to forget Rosaline, and dream of Juliet. Come, let us to bed too."

The fair object of all this love and mystery had not been long in discovering who it was who at a first meeting had so taken her heart by storm.

It was from her old nurse she learned the news, but, as with Romeo, it had no effect in quenching the flames of a love so swiftly awakened.

When all had retired after the feast, the young girl, whose heart was beating with an emotion which, until now, had been a stranger to her, passed out upon her balcony in the balmy air of night to think of the events of the evening—of her proposed marriage with Count Paris, and the coming of Romeo, which had changed all the current of her feelings for ever.

She knew all the difficulties of her position—the deadly enmity of the Montagues and the Capulets, and the impossibility of even hoping for their consent to such a union.

But she must be forgiven if these considerations had any or little weight with her.

She was only fourteen, a child to our English notions, but in Italy a woman just cognizant of the nature of love, with blood warmed by the sultry clime, all her nature aglow with passion for this lover who had suddenly appeared to her and taken her heart by storm. .

As she leaned upon the balcony thinking of her lover, she had little idea that he had, as Benvolio had said, scaled the orchard wall in the face of desperate danger, and was even now beneath her resting place, eagerly drinking in the beauty of her face and form, and listening to the words which ever and anon she gently murmured to the echoes of the night.

Presently, however, as he clambered to a spot where, by hanging on to the thick vine branches he could contrive to be near enough to speak to her, he ventured to say softly—

" Juliet !"

The word, though spoken so lowly, startled her in the extreme stillness, but she recognised the voice.

" Can it be possible? Is it you, Romeo !"

" You know my name then," he said; " alas ! it is hateful now to me, because it is an enemy of thine."

" Then be some other name," said Juliet; " that which they call a rose would smell as sweet by any other name ! But, how camest thou hither ? and wherefore ? The orchard walls are high, and hard to climb, and the place—death, considering who thou art, if any of my kinsmen find thee here."

" With love's light wings I overleaped the wall," said Romeo ; " and as for kinsmen ! There lies more peril in thine eye than twenty of their swords."

Shaded by the night from observation the lovers held sweet converse for long hours.

Their youth must be their excuse, if when the morning dawned they had plighted their troth, and even arranged for an early and secret marriage.

They had another and more cogent reason for haste, moreover, for there was no doubt that her parents, though they had consulted her so little, were making preparations for an immediate marriage with Paris.

It was touching, indeed, to hear the pleading way in which Juliet spoke to her lover—to respect her youth, her innocence, her trust.

" Romeo," she said, " you may think me too easily won. In truth, fair Montague, I am too fond; but trust me I will prove more true than others who have more cunning and affect to be perverse and coy. Therefore, my Romeo, you must pardon me, and not impute this yielding to light love."

" I think thee all that is pure and good in woman," said the enraptured lover; " would that we could exchange this night one kiss of love !"

" A few more words, my Romeo, and then I must away. If your love is honourable, and thy purpose marriage, send me word to-morrow by one whom I will send to meet you at nine in the morning in St. Mark's Square. Let me know when and where the rite is to be performed, and that done, I will leave all and follow you, my lord, throughout the world."

Again and again they bade each other adieu, and as often returned to exchange a few words more.

" Oh, Romeo, you must go !" cried Juliet, at length; " peril surrounds thee here ! I have forgot why I did call you back."

" Let me stay here then till you remember it."

" No, no! You must away," said Juliet ; " yet parting is such sweet sorrow that I could say good-bye until to-morrow ! Farewell, and Heaven's blessings attend you !"

Romeo lost no time.

During their converse at the feast of Capulet, he had learned about the preparations which were being made for the early wedding of Juliet with Count Paris.

In the days of which we write any denial on her part would have been of no avail.

No questions would be asked by any priest; the only thing necessary was that the young girl's parents should desire the union, and the ceremony would be performed whether the lady wished it or no.

Elopement and a secret marriage, therefore, was the only course open to Romeo and Juliet, if they desired the marriage in spite of the mighty obstacles which confronted them.

So without waiting to obtain any rest, Romeo got rid of his palmer's costume and proceeded to the monastery of St. Antonio, where resided a holy friar, who had been Romeo's friend from youth, a man of devout habits, but generous mind.

The old man was in his cell, tidying it up and talking to himself when Romeo made his appearance, and in his impetuous way told him his errand and his purpose.

Surprised indeed was Friar Lawrence

when he heard how quickly Romeo had forgotten Rosaline, whom he had so often spoken of in tender accents; but still more was he astounded when he heard that Romeo was intent on a union with the only daughter of his father's deadly foe.

But he was by no means averse to this match.

It seemed to him to promise a happy ending to the feud which had so long been the pest of the city.

And so it was arranged that Juliet should obtain leave to come to confession that afternoon, and there and then be married to her ardent lover.

All seemed to go well now.

Juliet's nurse, an old servant whom she could trust, was punctual to her appointment at nine, when Romeo's message was taken to the anxious girl, and at the appointed hour the young couple met at the friar's cell, and were united.

There they parted until night, Juliet to return to her father's house, and Romeo to wander to and fro in Verona to think of the strange lot which had made him in one day the lover and the husband of the handsomest girl in the city, and to pass away the time until darkness took her to his arms.

Both were very happy, but the clouds of coming evil were gathering thick and fast, and but half-an-hour after the strange marriage they began to fall.

After an early dinner, and having in vain sought for Romeo at his father's house, and through the streets of the fair city, Mercutio and Benvolio with their pages and servants came out upon the Place of the Four Angels, a large square not far from that of St. Mark, but on the other side of the houses of Montague and Capulet.

"Let us adjourn to our homes, Mercutio," said Benvolio, halting; "the day is hot, the Capulets are abroad, and if we meet they will certainly be a brawl. The mad blood stirs in these hot days."

Mercutio, light-hearted Mercutio, upon whom the world's troubles seem to fall so gently, laughed at his friend's words.

"Why, Benvolio," he cried, "you are like one of those fellows, who, when he enters the precincts of a tavern, claps his sword upon the table, and says—'God send me no need of thee!' and after the second cup, draws it on the first person who is near him without provocation."

"Am I like such a fellow?" said Benvolio, somewhat fiercely.

"Come, come," cried Mercutio, with his radiant smile, "you are as hot a man as any in Italy. If there were two such, we should have none soon, for one would kill the other. Why, Benvolio, you would quarrel with a man who had a hair more or a hair less in his beard than you had. You will quarrel with a man for cracking nuts, for no other reason than you have hazel eyes. Your head is full of quarrels as an egg is full of meat. But see, here come the very ones we wanted to avoid."

"Ay, by my head, here come the Capulets!"

"And, by my heel, I care not," said Mercutio.

"Gentlemen, good-day," cried Tybalt; "a word with one of you."

"And but one word with one of us?" said Mercutio, with insolent gaiety. "Pray couple it with something—make it a word and a blow."

"Who loves quarrels now?" said Benvolio, under his breath.

"You will find me ready enough at that, sir," said Tybalt, "if you will give me occasion. Mercutio, you consort with Romeo?"

"Consort!" cried Mercutio hotly. "What, do you make minstrels of us? If you do, look to hear nothing but discord. Here's my fiddlestick!" he added, tapping his sword-hilt. "Here's that will make you dance. Zounds! Consort indeed!"

"Stay," said Benvolio; "we are in a public haunt; let us withdraw to some more private place—here all eyes are upon us."

"Men's eyes were made to look," cried Mercutio, whose blood was up; "let them gaze, say I. I will budge for no man's pleasure."

At this moment Romeo appeared, hastening along from the wedding, gay and cheerful of aspect, no longer moody and ill at ease.

"Ah! peace be with you, sir," said Tybalt to Mercutio; "here comes my man. Romeo, the hate I bear thee can be expressed by no other words than these— Thou art a villain!"

"Tybalt," said Romeo, with a smile, "the reason that I have to love thee I cannot now explain. I am no villain. Thou knowest me not. Farewell."

But these words—with which Romeo

sought to avoid a hostile meeting with one to whom he was now so closely allied—were of no avail.

Prevented by his uncle Capulet from venting his spleen at the feast, Tybalt was now boiling over with fierce anger.

"Boy," he cried, "this shall not excuse the injuries that thou hast done me. Therefore, turn and draw."

"I do protest," said Romeo, "I never injured thee. I love thee better than you can imagine. And so, until I can explain my meaning, rest satisfied."

Mercutio's face was flushed now, and expressive of contempt and fiery anger.

"Oh, calm, dishonourable, tame submission!" he cried, as his bright blade flashed in the sunlight. "Tybalt, you rat-catcher, turn on me!"

"What wouldst thou with me?" cried Tybalt; "my quarrel is with Romeo."

"What want I with you? Nothing, king of cats," said the brave and gallant Mercutio, "but one of your nine lives. Make haste and draw your sword, or mine will be about your ears."

"So be it, your life or mine!" and in an instant Tybalt's weapon was out, and the conflict began.

In vain Benvolio and Romeo endeavoured to separate them; in vain they urged the anger of the prince.

The two—once at it—were too hot to part; and as Romeo at length intercepted his body between them, Tybalt, by a cowardly thrust under the arm of Romeo, ran the gallant Mercutio through the chest, and was then dragged instantly away by his friends.

"I am wounded by a cowardly thrust," cried Mercutio, as he staggered back. "A plague on both your houses. I am sped. Is he gone, and hath nothing from my true sword?"

"What! are you hurt?" cried Romeo.

"Ay, ay; a scratch, a scratch! But 'tis enough," said Mercutio. "'Tis not as deep as a well or as wide as a church-door, but 'twill serve. I am peppered, I warrant, for this world. A plague on both your houses. Why the deuce came you between us, Romeo? I was hurt under your arm as you struck our blades up."

"I thought all for the best to stay the fight," said Romeo sadly.

"Ah! help me to some house, Benvolio, or I shall faint," said the gallant young nobleman. "A plague on both your houses! They've made worm's meat of me. I have it, and soundly too here," and he placed his hand over his heart.

Only a few moments elapsed when Benvolio came back to Romeo, who was watching, with the news of Mercutio's death.

This intelligence aroused a new feeling in his heart.

His brain burned with rage, and with his drawn rapier he was about to hasten in search of Tybalt, when the latter, who had escaped from the hands of his friends, came running back again into the square.

Romeo thought no more of relationships.

Juliet was no bar to his deadly feeling of revenge against the one who had slain his best and bravest friend.

He sprang, with glistening weapon, towards his foe.

"Now, Tybalt," he cried, "take the 'villain' back again that thou so lately gavest me! Mercutio's soul is but a little way above our heads, staying for thine to keep it company. Either thou or I, or both, must go with him."

"Thou, wretched boy, shalt go with him hence," cried Tybalt, and again the echoes of the square were awakened by the clash of steel.

The conflict was short but terrible.

Tybalt in his fancied wrong was as eager as was Romeo, who had his friend's death to avenge, but the latter quickly proved the better swordsman, and in a few moments Tybalt lay dead upon the pavement, pierced to the heart.

It was but just in time.

Already the clamour of voices was heard, and the rush of feet.

"Romeo, away—begone," cried Benvolio. "The citizens are up. Stand not amazed! Thy certain doom is death if thou art taken. Begone—away!"

He almost dragged him to the entrance of a side street, and had hardly done so when the prince appeared with some soldiers and a throng of citizens.

The prince was in terrible anger, both at the manner in which his commands had been set at nought, and at the bloodshed which had ensued upon the disobedience.

But he was a just man.

At first he would hear of nothing but Romeo's arrest and death, but when he had listened to the eloquent pleadings of Ben-

volio, when he had heard how Romeo had striven to preserve peace, and had even foreborne to draw his sword until after Mercutio's death, his mood changed and he calmed down.

"I will never look upon his face again," he cried. "Your eloquent and friendly pleading has saved his life, but my judgment, and that an unalterable one, is that he be banished for ever from Verona. Let him go hence in haste, for if he's found that hour will be his last!"

The death of Tybalt made no difference in the preparations which were being made at the house of the Capulets for the early marriage of Paris and Juliet.

In the very hour of the young man's death the subject was broached to the young girl, who gave evasive answers, and contrived to send to Romeo a message by her nurse, begging him to come to her as soon as night fell, that she might have at least an hour or two of his company before he quitted the city, and that they might concert measures also for her speedy flight to join him.

That night, when the household of the Capulets was in darkness, and all save Juliet and her nurse had retired to rest, Romeo once more scaled the wall, and by the aid of a rope-ladder reached his young bride's chamber, where he remained till daybreak.

Fain would she have kept him longer, fain would he have stayed, but the peril was too great.

It was agreed between them, at the very hour of parting, that he was to go to Mantua, and there remain until, through the agency of his friends, Romeo had obtained permission to return, or if this was impossible, she was to arrange to quit the city by stealth and fly to him.

Kiss upon kiss, embrace upon embrace followed; the newly-wedded pair seemed unable to tear themselves from each other; but presently a loud knocking at the door of the bed-chamber, and the cough of Lady Capulet, warned them of the danger of further delay, and Romeo went.

Little did they dream, when lips were last pressed to lips, how they would meet again.

For some reason which they did not explain to Juliet, the marriage between her and Paris was hurried on more rapidly than ever.

Even the early visit of Lady Capulet,

which had disturbed the wedded lovers, was for the purpose of informing her daughter that her union was to take place in three days—that was on Thursday.

Tears, entreaties, refusals, were alike of no avail; both her mother and her father stormed and raved and threatened, until at last, for the sake of peace, she pretended to consent.

That very afternoon she hastened to her only real friend, Friar Lawrence.

The old man truly pitied her and Romeo, but it was a long time before he could see even a glimmering of hope.

The time was short, and against the power of the Capulets and that of Prince Escalus, whose kinsman Paris was, he was but weak to fight.

There was, however, a strange notion in his brain, which he revolved in silence, walking in agitation up and down his cell, while poor Juliet, seated on a stool, watched him with eager and tear-dimmed eyes.

At length approaching her he took her hand, and gazing down into her face with tender compassion, said—

"My child, there is a way which comes into my mind, but it is one which demands of you great courage."

"Courage!" cried Juliet; "it cannot be so bad as to be forced to the arms of Paris, when I am the newly-made bride of Romeo? Nothing will alarm me, for if you fail me, I shall take my life, and yield it willingly a sacrifice to my husband's love. Oh! pray, pray speak, good father; until you do the world is full of woe."

"Good then, fair Juliet, since you fear not——"

"Fear!" cried Juliet; "bid me—rather than marry Paris—leap from the battlements of the highest tower of Verona—bid me go into a new-made grave, and hide me with a dead man in his shroud, and I will do it without fear or doubt."

"It is good then," said the priest; "listen carefully to me."

Juliet listened with eager ears and wonder-stricken eyes to the words of the holy man.

His was indeed a strange revelation, yet never once did her young heart revolt against the danger.

His plan was this.

In a phial which he gave her was a curious potion which, once imbibed,

enabled the person who drank it to simulate death to such perfection that none could suspect the presence of a fraud.

When the liquid was taken, the pulses ceased to beat, all warmth left the body, not a breath came from the pale and deathly lips, and for two-and-forty hours the patient lay apparently lifeless with cold and rigid limbs.

The marriage being arranged for Thursday, Juliet was to drink the potion on the Wednesday night, so that on the morning of the wedding-day, she would be found dead, and be borne on a bier, covered only in her best apparel, to the ancient vault of the Capulets.

In the meanwhile the priest undertook to send to Romeo to apprise him of all that had been done in order that he might hasten back to Verona in disguise.

"He and I," added the friar, " will watch your waking, and we will contrive then to effect your escape together to Mantua."

Juliet raised the friar's hand to her lips ere she went.

"May Heaven bless you," she cried; "you have filled my heart with joy. Farewell, till I meet you and Romeo once more."

"Yet stay, my daughter," said the priest, as she was passing from his cell; "in order to obtain freedom in your actions, pretend to change your wayward mind, and consent to this marriage. Let not your nurse lie with you in your chamber, but say that on the eve of your marriage you wish to be alone. Farewell, be brave and cautious."

Juliet acted her part to perfection.

Her gloom was cast aside, her tears dried, and though she still said that it was strangely soon after the death of Tybalt she yielded that her mother and father knew best.

By these means she had her way, and was permitted on the night before her marriage morn to lie in her chamber alone.

Alone!

To her it had now a fearful sound.

When the door closed on her mother and nurse, a sudden sense of desolation overcame her, so much so that she was on the point of calling out to them to come back.

But her love for Romeo, and the knowledge that if she drew back now she would inevitably be married to Count Paris on the next morning, overcame her fears, and throwing herself on the bed, dressed as she was, she prepared to drink the wondrous potion.

Naturally there were a few moments of hesitation.

Doubts of the priest, fears of the charnel-house, where Tybalt had been but newly laid; visions of spirits which might rise around her when she awoke, perhaps before the friar and Romeo arrived, all tormented her brain; but at length she raised the phial to her lips.

"Romeo, I come!" she murmured; "this do I drink to thee."

And drinking the potion at a draught, she laid her head upon the pillow and was soon wrapped in oblivion.

All was preparation during nearly the whole of the night at the house of the Capulets, and all the greater therefore was the consternation when the awful event was discovered.

Very early the Lady Capulet came to her daughter's room.

Both the mother and father had had little rest, thinking of the unexpected consent of Juliet, and full of the anticipated connection by marriage with the Prince of Verona, which would place them in the foremost position among the citizens of that city.

But in an instant all congratulations were changed to grief, so sudden and so terrible that it is almost impossible to describe it.

At first, of course, when Juliet would not answer, they imagined, naturally, she had lain awake thinking of her coming marriage, and had now overslept herself with weariness, but when they approached nearer to the bed they saw what seemed the truth at once.

The pale and marble face, the blue lips, the heavy veined eyelids drooped over the splendid orbs which had been once the most beautiful in all Verona, the cold and listless hands, all told the sad tale of death.

The mother, struck dumb with amazement, could not utter a word until old Capulet himself hurried into the room.

"Oh, husband, Juliet is dead!" she cried then; "for some evil that we have done Heaven is punishing us. Oh, fairest flower! Oh, only daughter!"

And the Lady Capulet—who but a brief moment before had been doing her best to force her daughter into a hateful marriage —fell sobbing, half-fainting at the side of Juliet's bed.

To describe accurately the sorrow and consternation which prevailed in that house that morning would be almost an impossible task.

This marriage-day had been looked forward to and prepared for in such a manner as to outshine any festival which had been given in Verona.

What mattered it that the body of Tybalt, newly slain through his own unbridled passion, lay yet but newly buried in the gloomy vault of St. Peter's.

A marriage with the kinsman of Verona's prince must not be delayed.

So musicians were ready, friends invited, and everything done to render it a day to be remembered in the town.

And now all was changed.

The place was hushed and still.

Those who had been going about with gay and happy faces were grave and sad, knowing that, as was the custom in those days, the corpse would be buried at once, and a solemn funeral take the place of a gorgeous wedding.

Within a few hours the body of Juliet, arrayed in her best garments, was borne to the Church of St. Peter's, where, in a tomb just without the walls, a magnificent marble monument with a strong wooden door, the fair Juliet was placed upon a stone slab, where they imagined she was to rest for ever.

How could they think in their wildest dreams that she was going to meet a husband?

A solemn terrible rite it was; one at which even servants wept, and Paris was distracted; for the count was a noble, generous-hearted man, and loved Juliet with a true and holy love.

But even such sorrowful scenes as this must end—sorrow like joy cannot be long extended—and presently the monument was quitted, the door locked, and Juliet left, living among the dead!

Poor Juliet!

Confident in her lover, confident in the friar, she had done as she was directed— drinking in perfect faith what might have been a death potion—and yet all the gentle plans of love, the earnest hopes of two fond lives, the exquisite happiness of a married life which promised unprecedented success and rapture, was to be crushed, blighted, set at nought, by the blunder of a servant and the folly of the multitude.

Romeo, while these sad and unexpected things were progressing, was at Mantua, reviling every one for delay, imagining every kind of trouble, but none so awful as that which had happened.

The priest, Lawrence, had given in charge to a brother priest some letters for Romeo, which were to be sent on at once.

But, unfortunately, Balthazar, the servant of Romeo, reached Mantua long before, and met his master full of the evil news.

He met him in one of the public places of Mantua, and Romeo advanced to him with a joyous mien.

"Ah, Balthazar," he said, "you are soon after me. We gave them nicely the slip. Do you bring news from the friar for me? How doth my lady?"

So joyous looked his master that the servant had hardly heart to tell him; but with many a stammer and blunder he at last told the truth.

Romeo's grief approached the borders of madness.

He ordered horses to be got ready at once to return.

"What matters to me," he said, "the prince's anger? To-night in death I'll lie with Juliet."

Armed with a bottle of deadly poison, which he obtained by an immense bribe from an old apothecary who, according to the law of the place, risked his life in selling it, he dashed off to Verona as swiftly as post-horses would carry him.

But disastrous things had already happened.

The priest to whom Friar Lawrence had entrusted the letters to be forwarded to Romeo, brought them back, saying that in consequence of fear of contagion from Juliet, who had died so suddenly, no one could be persuaded to take the letters to Mantua.

In consequence of this, Romeo, mad with his love's new terror, arrived at the tomb without receiving the friar's explanation, and commenced, by the aid of Balthazar, to break open the tomb of his young wife before the appointed time.

It was night, and all was dark. Weird shadows hung over the tombs; in doleful cadence rustled the misty trees.

"Leave me," said Romeo at length. "I will finish this task myself. No other eyes but mine shall desecrate this meeting."

At the moment that the servant retired, Paris, unseen and unnoticed in the dim light of the torch by which Romeo was working, approached to strew flowers on her grave, and fearing that Romeo was—in his hatred of the Capulets—about to desecrate the tomb, he seized him by the arm.

"Stop thy unhallowed work, vile Montague!" he cried. "Condemned villain, obey, and come with me!"

"Fly hence!" cried Romeo hoarsely; "fly hence whoe'er thou art—be warned in time. I beseech thee, youth, heap not another sin upon my head. Begone!"

"Turn, villain, I do defy thee!"

"Then have at thee!" said Romeo, as he dashed furiously at him. "Thank thy own folly if thou diest this night, and by my hand."

The fight was short and fierce, and Paris, no match for the maddened Romeo, soon fell mortally wounded at the side of the grave.

Romeo lost now no time.

He feared the noise might have attracted attention, and he might, at the last moment be dragged away.

Not that he feared death, but he wished to die with Juliet in his arms.

In a few moments the lover-husband, delirious with grief, had clasped the body of his girl-bride in his arms, showering upon her voiceless lips showers of kisses and calling on her to awake and hear him.

Then saying, "Thus do I come to meet you, dear Juliet," he, with the courage of a Spartan, raised the poison to his lips and drained it.

FRIAR LAWRENCE.

There was just time to press one more kiss on Juliet's statue-like face, and he fell on her breast—dead!

Juliet soon after awakened to learn her awful fate just as Friar Lawrence appeared.

As she saw the horror-stricken face of the good old priest her words seemed frozen on her lips, and yet in the dim light she could not see that her young husband Romeo lay beside.

"Ah, good priest," she said, "you have not deceived me. Where is my Romeo?"

"Alas, my child! Ill-fate and thou are mates. Thy husband in thy bosom there lies dead; and Paris, too—see where he silent sleeps. Oh, haste away from this death vault!"

"Go, get thee hence," cried Juliet; "from this I will not move. My place is here, by my lost husband's side. I might have known my love was too strong—too quickly happy to last. Ah! there is Romeo's dagger. Happy dagger, this is thy sheath. Romeo, I come to thee!"

And with the words, before the priest could spring forward to prevent her, the weapon was buried in her bosom, and Juliet, the bride of a day, had fled to join the one whom she had loved even unto death.

We must draw this story to a close.

The Capulets and Montagues were reconciled by these sad events, which had descended upon them like thunderbolts of Heaven's vengeance; but of what avail was that?

Who could restore those fair and gentle lives, Romeo and Juliet? Who could give back to earth such perfect beauty?

Childless and in grief the Capulets and Montagues went to their last home; but the loves of Romeo and Juliet live for ever in song and story.

THE END.

NOTICE.—"OTHELLO," being No. 6 of Stories from Shakespeare, will be ready on Monday, December 12. Orders should be given early to your Booksellers.

"I THANK THE HEAVENS YOU ARE SAFE, FAIR DESDEMONA."

EDWIN J. BRETT'S
STORIES FROM
SHAKESPEARE'S PLAYS.

No. 6.—OTHELLO, THE MOOR OF VENICE.

CHAPTER I.

THE soft silvery moon had just risen over the blue waves of the Adriatic one glorious summer's night in the year 1568, when a gondola, after passing beneath the Bridge of Sighs, turned aside out of the Grand Canal of Venice into a smaller water-way and disembarked its passenger at a landing-place from which ran a narrow street.

"Wait for me, Bembo," said the passenger.

"Certainly, Signior Iago," responded the gondolier.

The Signior Iago was about twenty-six years of age, his dress showed signs of long wear, as though his tailor knew the measure of his purse as well as his body, but it was of military pattern.

A soldier certainly, well-made and well set-up, and had it not been for a subtle look in his dark eyes, one would have pronounced him a handsome man.

"Give me the guitar," said Signior Iago, returning when he had taken a step or two.

And Bembo handed the guitar to Iago with a very polite bow.

Having received the musical instrument, Signior Iago tucked it beneath his mantle, walked up the narrow street a little way and then turned into an open square.

"Yonder the fair Emilia lives," he muttered, pausing. "As arrant a flirt as ever lived. Were it not that she has money I should little care to waste my time on her. Yet she is a handsome wench, and I suppose I must pay her the Venetian compliment of a song."

He placed his fingers on the strings of the instrument, and was about to begin playing when something happened that drove all thoughts of music from his mind.

For a man came slowly and silently from the house wherein dwelt Emilia, the fair object of Iago's love.

"Again that Moor," he muttered. "Twice this week he has been there, and yet she vows she has no liking for him."

Past Iago's hiding-place came a man whose dark skin betokened him of Moorish birth.

A tall, stately, and handsome man, clad in a full gown of crimson velvet with loose sleeves, over which he wore a mantle of cloth of gold, buttoned upon the right shoulder with massive gold buttons.

"Othello the Moor! as I am a Christian," muttered Iago.

Unconscious of the fact that one was at hand ill-disposed towards him, the stately African general of the Venetian soldiery stalked out of the square.

Iago looked after him for a minute, then leaving his guitar in the doorway where he had been hiding, he advanced to the house the Moor had just quitted.

There was a light in one of the upper windows, and the shadow of a female form appeared on the blind.

"Ho, Emilia!" cried Iago.

"Who calls?" responded a soft female voice.

"'Tis Iago, thine own lover."

"Wait but a moment, I will open the side door, dear Iago."

"Humph! Othello had the front door opened to him," Iago muttered, as he walked round to the side entrance, where a few seconds later Emilia appeared.

Iago caught her in his arms; but instead of kissing her and calling her by a variety of endearing names, he asked rather savagely—

"Who was it left this house but ten minutes ago?"

"Who but Othello the Moor, old jealous pate!"

"What wanted he?"

"He would win me if he could; but, good faith, I would as soon be wooed by Satan. He has great power in the city and the senate, though, so one must not be uncivil to him."

"True; but you love him."

"I hate him, Iago! as I have a soul to be saved!"

Emilia said it with such an appearance of sincerity that Iago believed her, and altering his tone began to tell his own love.

And when, an hour later, he returned to Bembo the gondolier, it was as the affianced husband of Emilia.

A month later they were married, and then Iago found to his great disgust that his wife was as poor as himself.

True, Emilia had a few hundred ducats, which Iago quickly dissipated in taverns and gaming houses.

When those were gone he once more joined the army of Venice.

He had been relieved from guard one evening, and was returning home, when again the Moorish general was seen emerging from the house in which Emilia lived.

"The jade is false, faithless to me!" he muttered. "Shall I kill her? No, 'twere best to kill him, then I may stand some chance of promotion."

He drew back in the shadow of an archway which Othello must pass, and unsheathed his dagger.

But the black general, when he came to the place where the intending assassin was concealed, stepped aside and kept his own hand upon his scimitar, as though aware that some danger lurked in that darksome spot.

Iago knew too well the Moor's uncommon strength and skill with his weapon to venture on an attack when he was unprepared.

"A thousand curses on him! He visits my wife when I am away!" exclaimed Iago. "But he shall pay for it right dearly. Ah, who comes here? The most illustrious and silly Signior Roderigo."

Up came a youth of one and twenty or thereabouts, clad in the height of the fashion of that period.

"How now, Signior Roderigo! What brings you abroad?"

"Utter weariness, Iago."

"You weary? The handsome Roderigo, the pride of Venetian cavaliers, and the delight of all fair signorias, complains of being utterly weary! Do the pretty moths, the ladies, fall too readily a prey to your persuasive manners?"

"No, no; but there is one I have seen I would give the world almost to have speech with."

"Then speak to her."

"I know not where to find her."

"Ho, ho! but you have seen her?"

"Ay, in front of the ducal palace. By my soul, hither she comes!"

Attended by a page, who lighted her steps with a torch, came the brightest flower of Venice.

Barely eighteen years of age, much fairer-complexioned than most daughters of the City of the Sea, perfectly shaped and exquisitely attired, Desdemona—the daughter of old Senator Brabantio—was the acknowledged belle of Venice.

Iago pulled off his cap and saluted her.

"Who is she?" whispered Roderigo.

Iago told his weak-minded friend.

"And you have the felicity of knowing her?"

"I have indeed."

"Good Iago, procure me an introduction to her, and all I have shall be yours,"

"Hush! who comes here? 'Tis the Moorish general again."

Both Iago and Roderigo saluted the general, who, giving them a courteous bow in return, asked—

"Who was that lady who passed—she with the torch-bearer?"

Iago had no intention of answering; he did not love Othello well enough to do him any service.

But Roderigo blurted out—

"That, noble Othello, is Desdemona, the daughter of Brabantio, the Senator."

"She is indeed peerless," said Othello. "I ne'er saw her before, but I know her father well, and—— good evening, gentlemen."

Thus saying Othello walked away again.

"And now that Moor hath fallen in love with the divinity I worship. Truly, Iago, I am most unlucky," said Roderigo.

"Truly you are nothing of the kind. Why, man, I can procure you an introduction to her father's house, and it will then be strange if you cannot keep the Moor out of her favour."

"You will introduce me?"

"Yes. You unlucky!—nothing of the kind. But I am, if you like, an unlucky dog."

"How so?"

"Why, I have looked all day, and looked in vain for fifty ducats, which I must have before noon to-morrow."

"I'll lend thee a hundred, honest Iago. Here, boy, my purse."

"Fifty ducats, say you? Here, take a hundred," Roderigo repeated, forcing the money on Iago. "But mind, I am to be introduced in her father's house."

"Meet me here to-morrow at noon," said Iago.

The meeting took place, and Roderigo found himself within the doors of old Brabantio's house.

But the Moor was there also, and the handsome but weak-minded Venetian could not help seeing that the dark-skinned African was preferred.

CHAPTER II.

ABOUT the latter end of 1568 the Doge of Venice, by the advice of the senate, appointed Othello to the chief command of the Venetian army, giving him power to appoint his own subordinates.

"Now is my time," said Iago. "I must even be second in command, for I am well recommended by three of the senate; and Othello's very supicious friendship for my wife should have some weight in influencing his decision. But here again comes my noble gull, Roderigo."

That youth languidly sauntered up, and Iago asked where he had spent the morning.

"I was at the house of Brabantio—but I shall never go there again."

"Why not, man?"

"The senator has given his servants strict orders to bar the door against me."

"Humph; it must be your fault, Signior Roderigo. Good morrow, Signior Angelo."

The person Iago thus addressed was an elderly man, whose robe betokened him one of the senate or ducal council.

"Good morrow, friend Iago. I fear my intercession with the Moor on your behalf is useless."

"How so?" Iago demanded.

"Why, he has already appointed his lieutenant. One Michael Cassio, of Florence, has just arrived with recommendations from Colonel Hercules of Pisa, Sebastian of Modena, and other great captains, and has obtained the post."

"Cassio! I know him. A mere theorist—a man who has never seen a battle. He lieutenant!"

"Ay, but the general is well disposed towards you."

"My wife rather," Iago muttered.

"And has appointed you ensign. 'Tis but a small appointment, but it may lead to better things."

"I humbly thank him, and shall accept the office," responded Iago.

Whereupon Senator Angelo went on his way to the ducal palace.

"Cassio! why, that is the man who once or twice has been at old Brabantio's house with letters or presents from the Moor to fair Desdemona!" said Roderigo.

"The Moor himself oft visits her. 'Tis only when duty keeps him from her that his new lieutenant goes a wooing for him."

"Do you know that?"

"Ay, as well as I know my own sword."

"Then, Iago, I think it very unkind that you, professing to be my friend, and using my purse as though it were your own, should not have told me of this."

"Hush! here comes Cassio himself; and I will wager my ears he comes from Brabantio's house. Stand aside while I speak to him."

The gull Roderigo suffered himself to be pushed away, while Iago saluted the lieutenant and asked what news.

"By my soul! the news will stir all Venice in the morning, for it cannot be concealed. The fair Lady Desdemona has

eloped from her father's house, and but an hour ago was safely married to Othello."

"That's news, indeed. But, lieutenant, you have often been at the senator's house?"

"Ay, but only as ambassador on behalf of my general, for you know I have as fair a wife as any man. However, I cannot stay now, ensign, but next time we meet we'll drink to the health of the happy couple."

Cassio hurried away, and Iago returned with his additional news to Roderigo, who was intensely angry at hearing that his hopes were thus nipped in the bud.

"But can we do nothing?" he asked. "You, Iago, have no cause to love the Moor; cannot you suggest something?"

"We'll get Othello in disgrace with the senate. Let us call up her father, and accuse the Moor of having used witchcraft to beguile her away."

"Good!" exclaimed Roderigo.

And away they went together to the street in which Signior Brabantio's house was situated, and there made such an outcry that one would have imagined the city was on fire.

"What means this outcry?" Brabantio demanded, showing himself at an upper window.

"It means that thieves have been about, and have stolen your daughter," said Roderigo.

"Drunkards, begone! I know you, Roderigo, and in proper time will have you punished for this disturbance."

"Poor thanks we get for trying to do you a service," observed Iago. "Pray, reverend signior, search your house; if you find your daughter within doors, hand us over to the watch as brawlers."

"Humph! I can soon do that. Give me a light there within."

"The rest I leave to you, Roderigo, for it will not do for me to be seen acting against my general."

Iago slipped away, and ten seconds later Brabantio with some of his servants appeared at the front door.

"Now, sir, my daughter is not within. Tell me instantly what you know about her absence."

"Simply that but a short time since she was seen entering the Sagittary, the official residence of our Moorish commander."

"The Moor! Othello! Heaven pre-serve us! Think you, Signior Roderigo, they are married?"

"It is so reported. But the Moor must have used witchcraft or spells of some kind to persuade her to leave all her kindred for him."

"True. But the Doge shall do me justice. Will you come with me to the ducal palace?"

"Would it not be best first to visit his house and take back the poor girl? Let us go search for the poor deluded Desdemona."

When Iago departed he soon reached the arsenal, and calling for his commander told him some tale that induced him to quit his bride, and go out into the town.

Nor had they gone far before they encountered Cassio, who was searching for the black general.

"Now, lieutenant, what brings you abroad?" said Othello.

"The Doge and senate require your instant presence at the council-chamber."

"It must be something of great importance," said Othello, "to make them sit in council at this hour."

"Great news from Cyprus as I understand. But who comes here with torches?"

"'Tis old Brabantio," whispered Iago. "Signior Othello, I take it he is no friend of yours."

"He is, but knows it not."

Up came the other party, with whom was Roderigo.

"Villain!" cried Brabantio. "Where is my daughter whom you, by subtle charms and magic spells, have stolen? Seize him there, you who are my friends."

"Lay not a hand upon me!" exclaimed Othello. "You accuse me of having used magic to take your daughter from you. I am going to the palace of the Doge on most important business—there, and before him, I will answer your accusation."

Brabantio assented to this proposition; so away they all went to the council-chamber, where the Doge and most of his senators were already assembled.

For most important news had that night reached Venice.

The Turks were reported to have resolved to subdue the Isle of Cyprus.

The Venetian ambassador at Constantinople and the governor of the Isle of Cyprus had sent home letters to the Doge and senators, warning them that the attempt would soon be made. Those letters had just arrived.

"How say you, noble Othello?" said the Doge, as the black soldier entered the council chamber. "Will you defend Cyprus against the Turk?"

"Ay, reverend signiors, but reinforcements are much needed there."

Just as Othello spoke, the Doge noticed the presence of Brabantio, and spoke to him.

"Welcome, Signior Brabantio; we need the aid and counsel of all wise citizens, and I am glad you heard the senators had met."

"Sir, I heard nothing of your affairs of state; it was my own private woe that brought me here at your feet."

"What great grief is it that so disturbs Signior Brabantio?"

"My daughter!" the old man sobbed.

"Signior Brabantio, surely the charming Desdemona has not fallen a prey to death?"

"I would she had died first! No; but she has been lured from me by magic spells of witchcraft, and by this very man —this Moor, whom you have trusted with the chief command of your army."

The Doge and senators looked grave, for witchcraft was a very serious crime, and the Moors were reputed to be very proficient in all kinds of diabolical art.

"Othello, what answer can you make to this charge brought against you by the Signior Brabantio?" asked the Doge.

"I have used no witchcraft, great Doge. I often visited Brabantio's house, and spoke of all my former life, my travels, battles, and strange adventures. Fair Desdemona heard me, pitied me, and said she would Heaven had made her such a man to undergo such dangers; and that he might most expect success in wooing, who such a tale as mine could tell. I told my tale again, grave signiors, and found the gentle Desdemona loved me for the many dangers I had encountered. I loved her, and 'tis true that I have married her, but no other witchcraft have I practised. See where Desdemona comes; let her say how I won her love."

Escorted by Iago and some servants, Desdemona entered the council chamber.

Blushing like the dawn of morning, she corroborated all that the Moor had said, and left her father's side to stand by him.

"My duty is divided," she said; "but my lord Othello claims and has the best part of my heart. He used no spell save his own eloquence to win me; but it must be more than witchcraft that parts me from him."

CHAPTER III.

THE affairs of state that had delayed the Doge were, as we have already seen, the threatened attack upon Cyprus.

Pietro Loredano, the Doge who ruled between 1567 and 1570, had in his pay a variety of ambassadors and spies to inform him of what was going on in the Turkish empire.

But the Turks also had their spies in Venice, and one of them had but a short time before sent word of the almost total destruction by fire of the Venetian arsenal.

Hence, the maritime power of the Venetian republic being very much crippled, the Turks judged that a good time to attack the island of Cyprus.

And, as we have seen, their fleets were already at sea.

"Noble Othello," said the Doge, "you have heard of these mighty preparations of the foe, and the state demands your services. True, we have already in Cyprus a brave commander, Signior Montano, but the general opinion of the senate points to you as the fittest man to act against the foe. We therefore ask, will you command the expedition we intend to send thither?"

Othello was silent for some few seconds, then he replied—

"Most grave and reverend senators, 'tis not the kind of honeymoon I hoped to spend, but I am so used to war and its constant changes, and will therefore undertake your war against the Ottomans, only requiring of you fit accommodation for my wife during my absence."

The Doge at once suggested that her father's house would be Desdemona's best residence while Othello was away, but old Brabantio objected, as did Desdemona herself, and the Moor also would not hear of it.

But Desdemona had her plan, and she at once proposed it.

"Noble senators," she said, " in marrying Othello I have consecrated my life to him; for better or for worse I have vowed to share his fortunes; therefore, if he goes to Cyprus let me go with him."

After a very brief consultation with the senators, the Doge replied—

"Be it as you two shall decide, whether Desdemona goes or stays. But you, Othello, must away at once—this very night."

The Moorish soldier of fortune was used to prompt action, and agreed to start that very night.

Iago was to remain till the next day to take the written instructions of the council, and also to escort Desdemona, who required a little more preparation for travel than her warlike lord.

And Emilia, Iago's wife, was, by Othello's particular request, to accompany Desdemona as her principal attendant.

These arrangements being made, Othello at once proceeded to the arsenal to embark himself and the troops destined for Cyprus.

The long quays were in a blaze of light with torches and lanterns.

And drawn up on the wharf were two thousand of the finest foot soldiers in Europe.

As Othello appeared they gave him a general salute, accompanied by the roll of drums and the loud braying of trumpets.

"Soldiers," cried Othello, "we go to meet a furious foe. Be brave, for your courage will be severely tested; and, above all, be obedient to command, and keep good discipline."

One and all shouted a promise of obedience, and then, at the word of command, the various detachments marched on board the vessels, which before the sun had fairly risen had left Venice many a mile behind.

Othello oft looked back, thinking doubtless of the fair Desdemona, but the storm arose, and increased to a furious tempest.

Unable to keep company, the Venetian fleet was soon dispersed.

Meanwhile at Cyprus all was expectancy.

Signior Montano, the governor, had sent messenger after messenger to Venice for assistance; and the morning after the great storm that dispersed Othello's fleet, he was standing with two gentlemen of the island on the beach near Famagusta, the chief port of Cyprus, looking out to sea.

"Can you see anything, gentlemen?" the governor asked.

"Nothing at all," replied one of the gentlemen; "not a sail is in sight."

"We shall hear sad news, I fear; pray Heaven our fleet be safe."

Bang!

A gun from the fort in which the governor's house was situated, then six others.

And then another gentleman of the town was seen hurrying towards them.

"What is the news?" Montano demanded.

"Good news, signior; the guns have just saluted a Venetian ship which brings as its chief passenger one Michael Cassio, second in command to Othello, who is sent to our aid."

And following close upon the heels of this gentleman came Cassio himself, who then related how the tempest had separated him from the general.

"But," added Cassio, "this same tempest hath saved us much bloodshed, for as we came along we saw several of the Turkish vessels disabled and being towed by others back to Rhodes. Let us hope, though, that our general Othello is safe."

They all hoped so, but knew not.

It was early morn when Cassio landed; other vessels, filled with the rank and file of the expedition, came in one by one; but at noon the guns of the fort again thundered out a salute, showing that some person of importance had arrived.

"Iago, the general's standard-bearer," was the report of the messenger Montano sent to the quay.

"Our general's general has arrived," Cassio exclaimed—"Othello's wife. She left not Venice till some twelve hours after ourselves, but the sea and the wind have been civil to one so fair and virtuous, and brought her here in safety. Let us go out to meet her."

Desdemona was soon landed and established in her new residence, where all the afternoon Cassio, Roderigo, Montano and others endeavoured to keep her thoughts from becoming melancholy.

It wanted an hour of sunset, when for the third time the guns of the fort thundered out their warlike greeting to some new arrival.

The ramparts of the castle where Desdemona was lodged overlooked the water, so they could see who it was that had arrived.

"Othello's here!" exclaimed Iago and Cassio, starting to their feet. "That is his trumpet."

"WHAT GREAT GRIEF IS IT THAT SO DISTURBS YOU,
SIGNIOR BRABANTIO?"

"Let us go down to the quay to receive him," said Desdemona.

Cassio was very ready, and Iago appeared ready.

But the latter, as he walked down by the side of Montano, whispered to the former governor—

"'Tis by the vilest fraud and falsehood the Moor has persuaded the senate to send him hither. You good sir, have no cause to love him."

Montano made no reply, but the poison of Iago's words sank into his mind.

On the quay were assembled a number of soldiers and some of the townspeople to greet the new governor, who very soon appeared, clad partly in armour, but with his official mantle about his shoulders.

He was bareheaded, but close at his heels followed a page bearing his plumed helmet.

Desdemona, as soon as she saw her dark lover, stepped forward to meet him, and the next moment she was clasped in the arms of the Moorish warrior.

"Thank the heavens you are safe, my fair Desdemona! though it fills me with wonder, as well as pleasure, to see you here before me," said Othello, kissing her.

"My dear Othello, I have known no comfort since I parted from you at Venice till now," she responded.

"And it is little comfort you shall either of you know henceforth," muttered Iago. "It will be no hard task to turn this love to loathing, to fill the Moor's heart with jealousy of Cassio, and so hurry all three to perdition!"

"EMILIA BEGS DESDEMONA TO PLEAD WITH OTHELLO ON BEHALF OF CASSIO."

CHAPTER IV.

AT half-past nine that night Cassio and Iago met in the guard-room.

The subtle Iago was full of his scheme for the downfall of Cassio; and the general festivity had put another notion into his brain, namely, to get Cassio into disgrace for some military fault.

There was plenty of wine in the guard-room, for the general's wedding was to be celebrated, as well as the deliverance from the Turks.

Iago pressed Cassio to drink.

"No, I thank you, good ensign. Besides, we must hasten to make our rounds, and see that all is safe in the town."

"Plenty of time yet, for the general has given orders that the gates and all the offices shall remain open on this oc-casion an hour later than usual. Here is Roderigo, and just outside are a couple of gentlemen of Cyprus, who will gladly join us in drinking happiness to the bride and bridegroom."

Cassio suffered himself to be persuaded, and they were drinking together when Montano entered.

Cassio was not a seasoned toper like his companion, and so it happened as the artful Iago had expected—the lieutenant became intoxicated.

At length he staggered out to visit the sentinels, and Roderigo, prompted by Iago, followed to try and egg him on to some mischief.

Iago himself remained with Montano, both of them expressing surprise at Othello employing such a drunken officer.

In a very short time there was a great

outcry, and next moment Roderigo hastily returned, pursued by Cassio, who was evidently very angry, and inclined to punish the youth.

"Insolent varlet!" exclaimed Cassio, striking Roderigo with his staff; "I'll teach you!"

"Hold, lieutenant," said Montano, "Pray do not strike him! What is the matter?"

"A rascal! He pretends to teach me my duty!"

And again the staff was raised.

But Montano caught the arm of the lieutenant, who thereupon turned fiercely upon him.

"Let me go, sir, or I will break your head!"

"Come, come, lieutenant; it is very easy to see that you are the worse for liquor."

"Liar!" exclaimed Cassio, dropping his stick and drawing his sword.

"Away, and raise an alarm," Iago whispered to Roderigo.

Then turning to the combatants, he made some pretence of trying to separate them.

But the alarm bell sounded, and a minute later Othello entered the place, just as Montano received a severe wound from Cassio's sword.

"Hold! What means this disturbance?" he asked. "Hold! I say again. He that strikes the next blow sets but little value on his life, for by this sword of mine he dies!"

Iago had by this time thrust himself between the combatants, just as Montano sank fainting into the arms of a bystander.

"Tell me, Iago, who began this brawl?"

"I hardly know. They were on most friendly terms till a short space ago, then suddenly their swords were out, and they in desperate conflict."

Iago, though pretending to speak favourably of Cassio, managed to let the general perceive very plainly that the lieutenant was intoxicated, and Othello turned sternly on his subordinate.

"'Tis monstrous that in a town threatened with war such uproar should arise. Go, Cassio, never more be officer of mine."

The angry general stalked off.

Montano was carried away to have his wound dressed, and Cassio, considerably sobered by the affair, remained alone with Iago.

"All's lost!" he moaned; "all reputation is gone through the accursed drink."

"Nonsense, man," replied Iago. "The general is angry now, no doubt, but that will pass away. Seek Desdemona in the morning, ask her intercession with the general. He will deny her nothing, and, my life on it, you will within a week regain his favour."

Cassio argued against this plan for some time, but Iago persuaded him, and at length the lieutenant promised to act upon the advice of his false friend.

And as the disgraced lieutenant walked away, the villain grimly laughed—

"I have given him the best advice man could give, and yet it suits my project; for whilst she pleads for Cassio, I'll persuade the Moor that it is because she loves the lieutenant; and then the demon of jealousy, which oft has racked my breast, shall raise a storm in Othello's bosom."

In the morning Cassio lost no time in sending a message by Iago's wife to Desdemona, begging her to intercede on his behalf, and soon afterwards, meeting the fair lady in the grounds of the castle, the lieutenant repeated in person his request.

While thus engaged, Othello and Iago appeared in the distance, and Cassio, not wishing just then to have an interview with the general, slipped away.

"That looks not well," said Iago.

"What is it?"

"Cassio but this moment parted from your wife. I did not think he could steal away so like a guilty man on seeing you."

Othello, who was full of military matters, thought very little of this circumstance, even when Desdemona came up and began to plead for the disgraced lieutenant.

"I can deny thee nothing," said Othello, when she reminded him how Michael Cassio had assisted in their courtship, and Desdemona, happy to have served a friend, departed with Emilia.

But when Othello was about to resume his inspection of the fortifications, he found Iago had grown strangely thoughtful, and questioned him about it.

"Pardon, general, but did this Cassio know the Lady Desdemona before you wedded her?"

"Ay, from the first, and often went from

me to her to bear my messages or appoint a place of meeting."

"Humph! Many a man would not hesitate to take advantage of such friendship to his friend's injury, but Cassio, I do not think him one of that base sort. I believe him honest."

But as Iago seemed to be pondering very deeply over this matter, Othello demanded—

"What means this strange mood and these strange words? By Heaven, I'll know!"

"My lord, I pray you give not way to jealousy—a fiend that preys upon his victim's mind. Heaven defend me and all I love from that."

"Jealous? Not I. I'll have proof before I doubt, and then—But why should I be jealous?"

"'Tis said that one deceit breeds another," said Iago, in a low tone, as if he did not wish the Moor to hear his words, though the exact opposite was his intention. "The lady who deceives her father may prove false to her husband."

"What mean you?"

"Nothing, my lord. Cassio, I will swear, is true to you. But I see my words have disquieted you. Farewell, my lord."

And so the villain went away, leaving, as he had intended, the first pangs of jealous doubts in the mind of Othello, who at the same time entertained the highest opinion of his ensign's honesty and other merits.

*   *   *   *   *

And that same day Othello, walking in the castle garden, encountered his wife and Emilia.

Desdemona noticed that her husband looked ill, and as he complained of a pain in his head, she wished to bind her handkerchief about his head.

"'Tis too small," he answered, pushing it away. "Come, I will rest indoors awhile."

The handkerchief dropped to the ground, and Emilia, who lingered behind, picked it up.

It was one Othello had given Desdemona in the first days of their courtship, and was embroidered in strange patterns.

Iago had for some time past, notably during the voyage from Venice to Cyprus, expressed a desire to obtain possession of this handkerchief—he had even urged Emilia to steal it.

At that moment he appeared, and his wife, anxious to please him, mentioned that the handkerchief was in her possession.

"Then you have stolen it? Give it me."

"I steal? no, she dropped it; but tell me, Iago, why are you so eager to obtain it?"

"Question me not," said he, rudely snatching it from her hand.

"Give it me back, she will be almost mad when she misses it."

"Begone! say nothing, but leave all to me."

Then, as his wife departed, he said—

"This handkerchief, I will contrive, shall be seen in Cassio's possession. It is but a slight matter; but the Moor is already so filled with jealous doubts that this will confirm his suspicions. But here he comes."

And the general returned with a most haggard expression upon his countenance.

"How now, general? I fear you think too much of some chance words I dropped."

"As well I may, when racked with doubts," responded Othello, with a dismal sigh.

The jealous man paced up and down the garden twice or thrice; then in a furious passion he seized Iago by the throat, exclaiming—

"Villain, you have put me to the rack; but be sure you have good cause for making me suspect my wife, or you had better never have been born."

"Is it come to this? Then henceforward will Iago hold his peace, since speaking out in friendship is a sin."

"The proof?"

Iago paused a moment, then said—

"It is a task I like not—yet I must. Listen, last night this Cassio shared my room. I could not sleep, and as I lay awake I heard him talking in his slumber of stolen kisses with fair Desdemona. 'Be cautious, love,' he muttered, 'we must deceive the Moor.'"

"Ten thousand curses light upon him!"

"And pardon me—have you not seen Desdemona with a handkerchief of peculiar fabric and pattern?"

"I gave it her—it was my first gift, and sent by that villain's hand."

"And Cassio had it but an hour ago. I saw him use it."

Othello vented a fearful curse.

"The love I had for her is gone, and naught but hate remains. But I will be revenged both on the faithless woman and the false villain!"

"But, good lord general, you had best make certain. Your mind may change."

"Never! and here, kneeling in the sight of Heaven, I vow a deep and terrible vengeance."

"And I vow heart and hand to aid you in all that you may command, no matter what."

"Say you so? Then let me know within three days that Cassio is dead."

"It shall be so."

"But long ere that you'll hear of Desdemona's death; when your task is done, you shall be my lieutenant."

"I'll do it—for I have for ever devoted myself to your service," said the villain, who then left his enraged superior to his own bitter thoughts, while he went away to find Cassio, and leave the handkerchief in his possession.

Iago accomplished this part of his business by dropping it upon the floor in Cassio's lodgings; he had the satisfaction of seeing him take it up, and after a few fruitless inquiries as to its ownership, gave it to Bianca, a lovely Venetian girl, whose father had fallen in the wars, and who was in fact a kind of adopted daughter of the regiment to which both Cassio and Iago were attached.

The villain also repeated his advice that Cassio should continue to ask Desdemona's intercession.

It was not till next day, however, that Desdemona had a chance, for, under pretence of seeing to some of the more distant fortifications, Othello was away from his official residence.

However, they met on the parade before the castle, he pretending to greet her with as much love as usual, and she, noticing that his manner seemed strange, attributed it to overwork and thought concerning the defence of the island.

At length she said—

"And now I must rebuke you that you have not kept your promise."

"What promise?"

"Concerning Cassio. You promised he should be restored to his office, therefore I have told him to be here this morning to speak to you."

But instead of replying to this, Othello complained that something in his eye annoyed him, and demanded her handkerchief.

"Not that," he said, rejecting what she offered. "Let me have the one I gave you."

Desdemona explained that she had not got it with her; whereupon Othello's brow contracted as he told her that it possessed certain magical properties, and the loss of it would be attended with the most direful consequences.

"Then I wish that you had kept it yourself," responded Desdemona.

"You have lost it?" Othello demanded.

Desdemona protested she had not lost the handkerchief, and the Moor bade her fetch it, or send for it.

But Desdemona, thinking this was some trick to keep her from speaking in Cassio's behalf, kept pleading for the absent lieutenant, thereby increasing Othello's rage and jealousy, till at length, in a furious passion, he left her.

CHAPTER V.

OTHELLO, after the stormy interview with his wife, of which we have just spoken, sought out his subtle ensign.

"What news, my lord?" demanded Iago.

"I believe 'tis true she gave him that handkerchief—a thousand furies! She has it not!"

And he sank down upon a couch in something like a fainting fit.

But that soon passed over, though Cassio entered while the Moor was in that condition.

At a motion from Iago he went away, promising to return soon.

And then Iago told Othello that Cassio had admitted having received the handkerchief from Desdemona, and promised that if he (the Moor) would conceal himself behind some curtains, he should, on the lieutenant's return, hear him speak of Desdemona in a most familiar way.

"But," he said, "be still, be patient; for if you disclose your presence you will mar our plot."

"I will be most cunningly patient," said the duped Moor, as he hid himself behind the hangings.

Now Iago's plan was this—to keep Cassio at the other end of the room and get him to laugh and talk about Bianca; the Moor not hearing all that was said, would imagine that his wife was the subject of discourse.

Full well the villain played his part; easily Cassio fell into the snare, and, as though to aid the plot, who should come in but Bianca, carrying the handkerchief in her hand and making a pretence of jealousy, because it was evidently one that Cassio must have received from a lady.

The wilful girl, however, was soon appeased, and Cassio went away with her.

And Othello, more mad with rage than ever, came from his place of concealment.

"A thousand fiends!" he exclaimed. "Cassio must die! And she—my wife—little does she guess with what contempt he treats her, to give the handkerchief she gave him to that girl."

"You saw it then?"

"I did! Oh, Heaven! but I'll kill them both."

Iago was about to say something more, when a boat was observed to land some persons at the water-gate, and the next moment a trumpet was heard.

"'Tis a state messenger from Venice! 'tis Lodovico!" exclaimed the ensign, when he had gazed from the window. A few minutes later the gentleman in question entered, and with him Desdemona and a number of attendants.

After the stately greetings, common at that period, had passed, Lodovico, who was Desdemona's kinsman, produced a letter from the doge. While Othello was reading it, questions were asked on all sides; and Lodovico inquired how it was that Cassio was not in attendance upon the general.

"There is some misunderstanding between them," responded Desdemona; "but perhaps your coming will set all right. I am sorry for Cassio, and would give much to see him restored to his place and office."

"Devil!" exclaimed Othello, striking her.

"Why, what is the matter?" Iago demanded.

"Begone, woman! When I need you I will send for you. Signior Lodovico, this letter commands my return to Venice, leaving Cassio as governor. I obey the mandate. You will sup with me to-night."

"With pleasure, sir," responded Lodovico, though he had little liking for the Moor after witnessing the way in which he had treated Desdemona.

And Othello walked away, whispering to Iago—

"To-night! It must be done to-night."

"I will undertake to do for Cassio," the villain replied. "By midnight you shall hear more of it."

"'Tis well—'tis ill—'tis all too horrible to think of!"

Then Iago sought out his weak-minded gull, Roderigo, who was still in Cyprus, in the desperate hope of being able, with Iago's aid, to win the affections of Desdemona.

At the same time Roderigo could not help thinking that his friend was not doing all he could.

"Here have I wasted my fortune in the purchase of pearls, diamonds, and other precious jewels for the fair Desdemona. You say she has received them, and sent word that she would see me?" said he.

"Ay, but Othello has been so jealous of late it is not safe for her to look at any other man."

"What is he so angry about?"

"The senators have sent to relieve him of his charge, and Cassio becomes the governor."

"Then he and Desdemona will return to Venice?"

"No; they go to his native home in Morocco, unless they are hindered."

"What can hinder them?"

"Should anything happen to Cassio, why then Othello must remain till the senate can hear of it and send out a fresh governor. Come, you have no cause to love him — he is your rival for Desdemona's love—so, I say, kill him!"

"Can it be done safely?"

"Ay, he sups to-night with Bianca; he will return about midnight, perhaps the worse for wine. I shall be near and will aid you."

The weak-minded youth suffered himself to be persuaded, and time and place for a future meeting were arranged.

*   *   *   *   *

The ill-matched pair then parted for the time; but a few minutes before midnight they met again, and Iago pointed out to Roderigo the path Cassio must take in returning to his quarters.

"Stand here, behind this buttress, and you cannot miss seeing him; keep your sword in readiness and make a home thrust," Iago said.

"Keep close at hand lest I should fail."

"Fear not, I shall be close by, and 'twixt the two he is certain of his death."

And the villain retired a little distance, hoping that each would kill the other; for if Roderigo lived there would be awkward disclosures concerning the gold and jewels which had *not* reached Desdemona. And on the other hand, should Cassio escape, there was hourly danger lest his vile plot should be exposed.

Roderigo had not been in ambush a minute when some one was heard approaching.

"That's Cassio," he muttered. "I know his footstep. Die, rascal!" he added, in louder tones, leaping forward and making a thrust at the lieutenant.

Next instant Cassio's sword flashed out and was buried in the body of his would-be assassin.

Iago watched his opportunity, and springing out of his concealment, aimed a blow at Cassio which he intended should be mortal.

But in the darkness and excitement he missed his mark, and the blow intended for Cassio's heart did but inflict a deep wound upon his leg.

Cassio fell calling out—

"Help! thieves! murderers!"

A man came very near the scene, wrapped in a long cloak.

It was Othello, and in low tones he said—

"That was Cassio's voice. My good friend Iago has kept his word. Noble Iago, you have set me an example that I must profit by. Now let me do my part in this dark work."

He hastened home to the castle, leaving both Roderigo and Cassio upon the ground, calling for help.

The first wayfarers that passed along were none other than Gratiano, Desdemona's uncle, and her other kinsman, Lodovico.

Gratiano suggested that Lodovico should go and see who it was that groaned so piteously.

"Nay, there are two or three about; I fear it is a trap to draw us on to our destruction. But here comes one with torches," responded Lodovico.

The person who approached was Iago, who, with a light in one hand, and his drawn sword in the other, pretended to have been just disturbed from his sleep.

"Who makes this noise? What is the matter?"

"We do not know, but there was a great outcry and shouts of murder," said Lodovico.

"This way," cried Cassio. "Aid me for the love of Heaven!"

"Whose voice is that? Where are you?"

"Iago, it is your old friend Cassio, set upon and sadly wounded by ruffians."

"Lieutenant Cassio! Which way went the villains?"

"One of them cannot be far off, I think. I gave him a good home thrust."

At this instant a groan from Roderigo called attention to him.

"This must be one of them! Come Signior Lodovico, come in with me and see to this man."

"Here, help, here!" Roderigo moaned.

"There is the assassin!" exclaimed Gratiano.

"So he is! Die, villain!" cried Iago, as he thrust his sword through the body of Roderigo, who, with an exclamation against the ensign's inhumanity, died.

"How fares it with you, Signior Cassio?" Iago then asked.

"Maimed—crippled for life, I fear."

"No, pray Heaven it be not so bad as that. Lend me your handkerchief for a bandage, Signior Lodovico."

The lieutenant's wound having been dressed in a rough manner, he was removed while Iago and the others examined the corpse of the supposed bravo.

"Good Heaven! it is my friend and countryman, Roderigo!" Iago exclaimed. "This must have been some accident or sudden quarrel; there was no malice between them."

By this time a number of people, roused by the noise, had gathered round.

Amongst them was Iago's own wife.

Seeing her, he exclaimed—

"Emilia, hasten you to the castle and tell the Lord Othello what has happened while I see that means are taken to apprehend the murderers."

CHAPTER VI.

OTHELLO, as we know, had returned home to the castle in the full belief that Iago had slain Cassio.

The Moor's heart was filled with black and vengeful thoughts against the fair wife whom Iago had so foully slandered.

He now approached her chamber, muttering to himself—

"Fair but faithless one, your time draws nigh. Your lover Cassio is dead, and soon you must pay the penalty."

Opening the door he softly entered and approached the bed where Desdemona, utterly broken down by grief, had fallen into an uneasy slumber.

But some of Othello's muttered expressions disturbed her.

She awoke—

"Is that you, my lord Othello?" she cried,

"Ay, Desdemona, 'tis I who have come to be your executioner; so repent, I pray you, of all your sins, for I would not destroy your soul, though I kill your body."

"Sins! executioner! What do you mean, my lord? What madness is this?"

"Madness! yes, 'tis madness; but your faithlessness has made me mad."

Then, in a torrent of impetuous language, he told her how the missing handkerchief had been seen in Cassio's hand, how his suspicions had first been awakened, how Iago had induced Cassio to confess.

Poor Desdemona denied the charge, and pleaded hard for a little respite.

" 'Tis too late," the stern Moor replied, and snatching up a pillow he pressed it down with all his force upon Desdemona's face to smother her; for he had made a fantastic vow that he would not shed one drop of her blood, or wound her alabaster skin.

But before life was extinct, there came a loud knocking at the chamber door, and Emilia's voice was heard calling him.

Othello paused in his cruel work, looked first at the door, then at his victim,

The knocking was repeated.

"It must be so," said the Moor. "Thus—thus—I end thy life, and with it my revenge!"

Unsheathing his dagger, Othello plunged it twice into Desdemona's bosom.

Again Emilia was heard knocking.

"My lord Othello, open the door, I pray, for I must speak with you at once."

He drew the curtains closely round the bed, and then opened the door.

"Oh, my lord, here's a sad tragedy has taken place; Cassio has slain young Roderigo."

"But Cassio himself is slain?"

"No."

"Falsely — falsely murdered!" said a low sweet voice, that of Desdemona.

Emilia at once rushed to the bed, drew back the curtains, and saw what a fearful deed was done.

"Gracious Heavens! My dear, dear lady, who has done this?"

"No one; 'twas I myself."

And thus, attempting to screen her cruel husband, the fair Desdemona's spirit took its flight.

And now that the deed was done, Othello seemed to have little care for himself.

"The false, treacherous devil, she died with a lie upon her lips. It was I that killed her."

"Saints above! Help here! murder!"

At the outcry, Lodovico and Gratiano came running in, followed by Iago, and to them did the Moor recount his reasons for the foul murder.

"Oh, monster!" exclaimed Emilia, when the incident of the handkerchief was related. " 'Twas I that found the handkerchief, and gave it to my husband."

Then Othello's wrath turned backwards, and with drawn sword he rushed at Iago, who, however, managed to evade the stroke and escape from the room, after he had plunged his dagger into Emilia's back, killing her almost instantly.

But Gratiano, Montano, Lodovico, and others immediately wrested Othello's sword from him, and then quitted the chamber, setting a guard outside to prevent the Moor's escape.

"I have another sword within this chamber, though," said Othello to himself. "Here it is, and sure a better weapon never graced a soldier's hand."

He then glanced at the couch, and knelt beside it, bewailing bitterly the rash deed he had done.

Then there was a noise without, and some of those who had gone returned, bringing with them Iago and also Cassio.

Then, by the aid of some papers found on the body of Roderigo, the whole of the infamous plot was revealed.

"Oh, fiend incarnate! why have you ruined me both body and soul?" Othello asked.

"Remember my wife, and think of my vengeance," was the sneering reply.

"Devil! You have not cloven feet, but a devil you must be!" said Othello, making a pass with his sword at Iago, wounding, but not killing him.

Lodovico then spoke.

"Signior Cassio, you are now the duly appointed ruler of Cyprus, and in your hands rests the punishment of that villain Iago."

"Doubt not that he shall receive a punishment greater than was ere inflicted upon mortal man.

"As for the Signior Othello, his rank demands that his offence should be dealt with by the senate; therefore you had best keep him in close custody till we return to Venice, and report the whole affair to the Doge and his council."

"Stay," said Othello. "When you make your report to that grave body, I pray you let it be a fair and impartial one, setting forth how I was tempted and led on by that fiend. Remind the grave senators that I have done the state some service; and tell them that, even as I once smote the Turk, so now I smite myself."

The desperate Moor plunged his dagger —which he had been allowed to retain— into his heart, and fell dead by the side of the bed on which lay Desdemona.

And so, through unfounded jealousy, perished the warlike and otherwise noble Moor Othello.

THE END.

DESDEMONA AND EMILIA WATCHING ON THE RAMPARTS FOR OTHELLO'S ARRIVAL AT CYPRUS.

NOTICE.—"KING JOHN," being No. 7 of Stories from Shakespeare, will be ready on Monday, December 19th. Orders should be given early to your Booksellers.

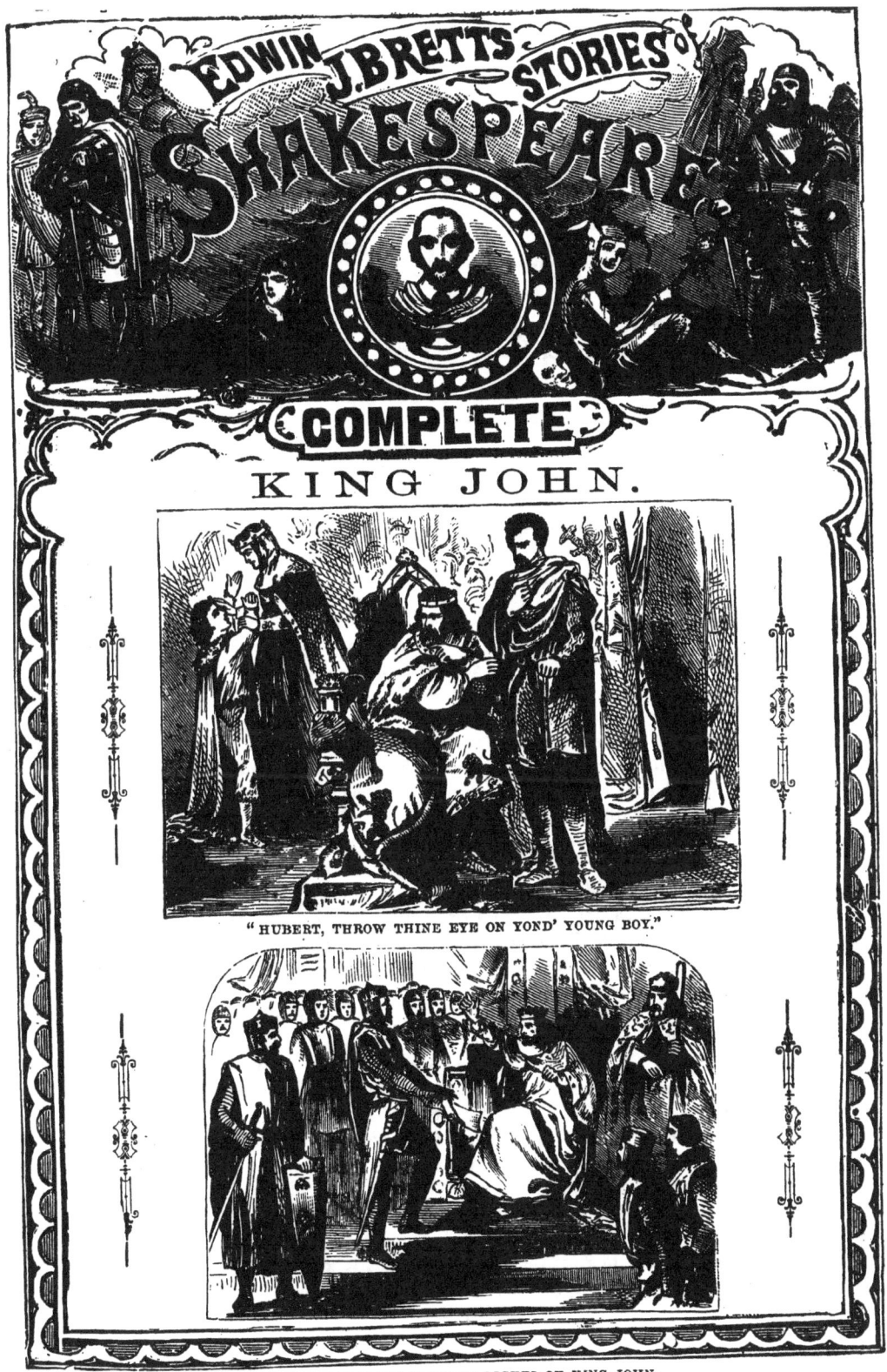

KING JOHN.

"HUBERT, THROW THINE EYE ON YOND' YOUNG BOY."

THE BARONS DEMAND THEIR RIGHTS OF KING JOHN.

"Boys of England Edition."

EDWIN J. BRETT'S

STORIES FROM

SHAKESPEARE'S PLAYS.

No. 7.—KING JOHN.

CHAPTER I.

IN a splendidly-furnished room of state in Northampton Castle sat John, King of England.

He wore his crown and royal robes; in his hand was the sceptre, his seat was the throne of England; noble knights of high degree were grouped around to receive, in due state and magnificence, the Count de Chatillon, special ambassador from Philip Augustus, King of France.

By the English monarch's side, upon a seat little inferior in splendour to the throne itself, sat his mother, the Dowager Queen Eleanor, noted for her beauty (which, though she was now old, was still remarkably striking), for her brilliant abilities, and her resolute and imperious character.

Preceded by heralds sounding a flourish of trumpets, and accompanied by several followers and attendants, the French ambassador entered the royal presence.

Making a formal but not very profound obeisance to the king, he said—

"My august master, Philip, King of France, has commanded me to greet you, John, the so-called King of England——"

"The so-called king!" echoed the Queen Dowager indignantly.

"Peace, good mother, and listen to the ambassador," said John.

"—— and calls upon you," continued Chatillon, "to abdicate your throne, and relinquish your territories on behalf of your nephew, Prince Arthur of Brittany, true heir to the crown of England."

"And what if I decline to fulfil this most unreasonable demand?" said King John angrily.

"Then," said the ambassador, "my royal master will declare war to enforce Prince Arthur's claim to the kingdom of England, Ireland, and all the English territories in Normandy."

"I will not relinquish one square inch of them," said the king, rising in a rage from his royal seat. "What right has Philip to dispute my possession of the throne? If he is bent on war, let him declare it; we will give him war for war, and blood for blood."

"Then, John of England," said the ambassador, in nowise cowed by the king's anger, "I am commanded, in King Philip's name, to give you defiance."

"Tell your king that I defy him too," replied John. "Go, return to your

country, but, almost as soon as you arrive, I will be there too, with a large army to chastise the insolence of France. My Lord of Pembroke, see that the Count·of Chatillon is honoured and protected on his journey as befits an ambassador. Farewell, sir !"

The envoy again bowed, but more profoundly than before ; and then turned, and, with a flourish of trumpets, quitted the presence with his attendants.

" I know whose doing this is," said the Queen Dowager, turning to her son. "Constance, the refractory widow of your brother Geoffrey, who has set France against us, and would rouse the whole world, if she could, in favour of her boy Arthur. The consequence will be a fierce war."

"I do not fear it," replied the king. "Our army is large and brave, and I'm strong enough to defy the fiercest threats of France. As for Constance and Arthur they shall bitterly repent their rebellion."

There was now a commotion at the entrance of the Hall of Audience, and the Earl of Essex entered, accompanied by the Sheriff of Northampton, who announced that two gentlemen were without, humbly praying that a certain controversy between them should be settled by his majesty in person

" Let them approach," said King John. Accordingly the suitors were ushered in.

The elder was a man of soldierly presence and stalwart proportions ; the younger of lower stature and meaner appearance, but both had the aspect of persons of rank and station.

" What men are you ?" asked the king, as they bowed before him.

" So please you," said the elder, " I am your majesty's faithful subject, a gentleman, born in Northamptonshire, and, as I suppose, eldest son to Sir Robert Faulconbridge, a soldier knighted on the field by King Richard Cœur-de-Lion."

" And I," added the younger, " am second son, and heir to the same Sir Robert."

" How comes it the younger is heir ?" asked John.

" Because," said the elder, " my brother here declares that I am not truly the son of the late Sir Robert ; therefore I am illegitimate and disinherited, and men call me the Bastard Faulconbridge."

" This too to thy dishonour, and thy parents' also ?" said the Queen Dowager.

" Ay, madame, and to my disprofit likewise ; for if my brother Robert here speaks truth, his claim deprives me of an estate of full five hundred pounds a year." (A sum equal to at least five thousand pounds in the present day.)

" This is a matter of moment," said the king ; " but if thou art not really a Faulconbridge, who then was thy respected father ?"

" No less a personage, my liege, than the great Cœur-de-Lion himself," answered Philip Faulconbridge.

" Indeed !" exclaimed the king, " wouldst thou then claim royal descent ? This touches us nearly."

" And I make bold to add," said Philip, drawing himself proudly up beside the insignificant form of his half-brother, " that if we are to judge by likeness I more resemble the royal Richard than I ever did the late Sir Robert, or his successor, the present claimant here."

The contrast between the two reputed brothers was indeed striking, and all to the disadvantage of Robert. King John and his mother were both favourably impressed with the blunt soldier, Philip, and they looked upon him with still more interest now that he claimed a sort of relationship to themselves.

Philip, who was shrewd as well as bold, knew that he was pretty sure of some advantage from his appeal. If he were proved legitimate he would get the estate instead of his brother. If otherwise he might still count upon getting some preferment from the king.

"He certainly resembles Richard," said the Queen Dowager aside to her son.

"He resembles him so much," acquiesced King John, "that I am certain his story is true. I like him well, his looks give promise of an able warrior, and such a man deserves encouragement."

Having examined the documents, Robert Faulconbridge produced a proof of his claim.

The king gave judgment that he was the only legitimate heir to the estate.

"As for you," said the king to the disinherited Philip, "you are by this sentence deprived of your estate, and it leaves also a stain upon your birth. This deserves some compensation. How say you, will you enter my service as a soldier of fortune, and follow me to France?"

"It is my proudest wish!" said Philip, bowing low.

"That is well: and as I am convinced that you are really Cœur-de-Lion's son, and thus my own kinsman, I think you should bear a better name. Kneel down."

Philip knelt before the king, who raised his sword.

"Be no longer called Philip the Bastard," said John, giving him the knightly stroke; "but prove yourself worthy of your illustrious parent. Rise, Sir Richard Plantagenet!"

Thus honoured, the brave soldier rose to his feet quite a new man.

CHAPTER II.

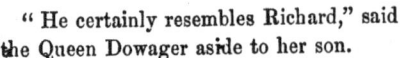

KING JOHN collected a large army, and at once set out for his territories in Normandy.

King Philip was no less ready for action.

He had also a considerable force, and was joined by his powerful ally, the Arch-duke of Austria, noted in history for having captured and imprisoned the great Richard Cœur-de-Lion.

The French forces assembled before the walls of Angiers, and were met by those of Austria, both led by their respective sovereigns.

In the king's pavilion were also Constance, Dowager Duchess of Brittany, who, had her husband lived, would have been Queen of England.

She was a lady of great beauty and dignity of aspect, though careworn by many troubles and anxieties.

Her son Arthur was a fair-haired noble-looking youth of about fifteen.

When introduced to the Archduke of Austria by King Philip, young Arthur stepped forward and said—

"I greet you well, most honoured archduke; and although through you it was that my uncle, the great Richard, met captivity and death, you will atone for that by thus helping me to regain my rights. Welcome to Angiers!"

"A noble boy!" exclaimed King Philip, while the archduke embraced the youthful prince, and declared that he would not rest from the toils of war until John was vanquished, and Arthur had become King of England.

Arthur thanked him, and in this was joined by his mother, the Duchess Constance.

"So now to work," said the French king. "All is ready for besieging this town. I am only waiting till my embassy returns with an answer from England."

No sooner had the king uttered these words than the Count de Chatillon was announced.

Of course every one was eager to hear what news he had brought.

"My liege," he said, "John of England regrets your demands. He has put himself in arms, and followed me so closely that he reached France almost as soon as myself. He in person leads his troops. He is accompanied by his mother,

Queen Eleanor. His forces are strong, his soldiers confident, and he is already on the march hither."

"Thank Heaven we are prepared for them," said King Philip.

Anon the beat of drums was heard in the distance, and a vast force, in all the glittering panoply of war, came marching over the plain.

They bore the colours of England, and in the foremost cavalcade was King John himself, in full armour, with his mother and his niece, the Princess Blanche.

Although deadly rivals, the two kings greeted each other cordially in outward appearance, but their words showed that neither was inclined to give way.

"Peace be to France," said King John, "if France in peace permits me to enter my just and lawful territories in Normandy."

"Peace be to England," replied King Philip, in the same tone, "if England will in peace accept the rule of Arthur, her lawful king. As for you, John Lackland, I can never recognise your claims. Your elder brother, Geoffrey, was rightful heir, but he being dead, his son succeeds. How comes it, then, in the name of Heaven, that you dare wear the crown, and call yourself a king?"

"Who made you a judge over me?" asked John haughtily.

"There is a Judge greater than either of us," answered the French monarch solemnly, as he pointed towards Heaven. "That Judge has made me guardian of the boy; therefore I dispute your sovereignty, and will uphold my opinion by force of arms."

"You are usurping an undue authority," said John.

"Excuse me, I am, on the contrary, opposed to an usurper."

"What usurper?" asked the Queen Dowager eagerly.

The Duchess Constance, who had received her mother-in-law with a cold dignity, equal to her own, now arose,

drew herself to her full height, and answered—

"The usurper, madame, is your son."

"Insolent minion!" retorted the queen. "You would then occupy my place by securing the crown for your son, who, for aught we know, may be but a base-born impostor, and not of true royal blood!"

"This insult, madame, is more than I will endure!" said Constance fiercely.

"Peace, I command you both!" said the King of France. "This is no time for war of words between women, but for war of swords between men. John of England, in this boy's name, I demand that you shall at once lay down your arms, and yield up to him the kingdoms of England and Ireland, and the duchies of Anjou, Touraine and Maine."

"I would sooner yield my life," was John's answer.

But, although fierce and bold, he did not forget caution.

He was crafty as he was cruel, and thought he would do well to try coaxing the youthful prince.

"Arthur of Brittany, my dear nephew," he said, assuming a kind tone, "give me your hand in friendship; and out of love for you I will give you more than all you can ever get by fighting against me. Come, submit, boy, and trust me as your father."

"Yes, dear child," chimed in Eleanor hypocritically, bent on assisting her son's efforts, "come to your kind grandmother."

"Yes; come to your kind grandmother," echoed Constance, in sarcastic mockery. "Give up to your kind grandmother your kingdom, and she will give you a plum, a cherry, and a fig. Very good of her, in sooth!"

"Peace, dear mother!" said the boy; "I would sooner be dead than be the cause of so many disputes."

His voice here faltered, and he turned away his head.

"Poor child! His mother shames him so, he weeps!" said Eleanor maliciously.

"No; it is more likely he weeps with grief for having so evil a grandmother as you," retorted the duchess; "but, by Heaven's assistance, his wrongs shall be righted, and you punished!"

This angry contention between the two royal ladies was only ended by a flourish of trumpets to summon to the walls of Angiers the citizens of that town, who were to decide whose claim they recognised—Arthur's or John's.

The principal men of the town appeared on the battlements.

King John was the first to speak. He represented that the French had everything ready to besiege the city, and lay it in ruins, unless the people acknowledged Arthur; whereas he (John) came as their friend, protector, and lawful sovereign."

King Philip, of course, flatly contradicted this.

Holding Arthur before him, he called upon the men of Angiers to own the boy as their rightful monarch, in which case he promised at once to withdraw the French and Austrian forces, and leave the town in peace; but, if they refused this offer, they would soon have the walls about their ears.

The citizens conferred among themselves in this dilemma, and came to the conclusion that their fortifications being strong enough to resist either of the monarchs, they would defy both.

The chief spokesman therefore answered—

"We acknowledge ourselves subjects to the King of England."

"You hear them?" said John, looking round triumphantly; "they choose me. 'Tis well; open the gates to let in your lawful monarch."

"Pardon me, great prince," replied the chief citizen. "I said we acknowledged the King of England, but we did not say which king. Whichever gains the victory let him be our king; but until that is

settled we will close our gates, and let you fight it out."

Both monarchs were taken aback by this bold decision.

Each immediately despatched a herald commanding the gates to be opened, but these received the same reply as before.

At this crisis, Sir Richard Plantagenet, who was high in his sovereign's favour, made a suggestion of which John approved.

"He says right, for, by Heaven, brother of France," exclaimed John, "there is but one way to bring these refractory citizens to reason, and that is for us to join our forces, and attack their city till we've laid it level with the ground. After that we can fight who shall be king of it."

"Agreed!" said Philip Augustus. "The English, French, and Austrian troops shall each attack it at different points. Come, we will place our forces in position at once."

"One moment," interrupted Hubert de Burgh, Chamberlain to King John. "Condescend, O mighty king, to listen to a proposal I have to make. I will show you a way to win this city, and to heal your differences without bloodshed."

"Speak; we listen," said King John.

"I suggest," proceeded Hubert, "that a marriage be arranged between the noble and gallant Prince Louis, heir of France, and yonder young and lovely princess, King John's niece, the Lady Blanche of Castille."

This proposal was favourably received, and the august party proceeded to discuss it.

The young prince, when appealed to, professed an admiration for the lady, although she, in return, merely said that she was bound in duty to fulfil her uncle's commands as to the marriage.

King John offered to give up five Norman provinces, and the sum of thirty thousand marks as a dowry.

The French king approved, so did the

Austrian archduke, and it was arranged that the wedding should be shortly solemnised in St. Mary's Chapel.

"As for Lady Constance," said King John, "we'll create her son Arthur, Duke of Brittany, Earl of Richmond, and Lord of Angiers. She shall be acknowledged Dowager Duchess, with a large revenue. If this will not quite content her, it will at least stop her complaints. Let us send a messenger to invite her to the wedding of the Dauphin and Lady Blanche."

The party now broke up to prepare for the ceremony.

Thus by the timely suggestion of Hubert, war was averted, and the city saved, but at the same time young Arthur was unjustly deprived of his right.

CHAPTER III.

GREAT was the indignation of Lady Constance when she heard of the treaty that had been made between the Kings of England and France.

"Can I believe my ears?" she exclaimed. "The Dauphin to marry the Princess Blanche, in whose right he will claim to be heir of England? What then becomes of my son's chance of inheriting the crown? Oh, my poor boy!" she added, drawing Arthur closer towards her; "there are those who would take not only thy crown, but thy liberty—even thy life. What are you—what am I—against the combined power of tyrants?"

She refused to attend the wedding, even though the two kings, the Queen Dowager, and the other royal and noble personages came in a body to the pavilion, and sought to prevail upon her.

"King of France," she said, "you have deceived me. You came here with your army to fight my enemies, and now you have turned and leagued with them against us. I am a widow, and unprotected, and I can only invoke the help of Heaven against you."

"Peace, peace, Lady Constance!" said the Archduke of Austria.

"Say rather war—war to the death! You, too, perjured prince, have turned against me."

His Eminence Cardinal Pandulph, legate of the pope, was now announced, and entering with his train of ecclesiastics in great pomp and ceremony, he greeted the two monarchs.

He then solemnly called upon King John to submit himself to the power of the pope on pain of excommunication.

"Away, meddling priest, I disclaim the pope's authority!" exclaimed John.

"Then, King of England," said the cardinal, "in the name of the Holy Church, I pronounce you accursed and excommunicated, and blessed be he who takes away your life!"

"Amen to that!" exclaimed Lady Constance.

"King Philip," pursued the prelate, "King John being thus proved an arch-heretic, you must break off your alliance with him, on pain of the same penalty."

The French monarch was much dismayed at this sudden demand.

He protested that it would interfere with all the arrangements just made.

But the cardinal was obdurate; and the power of the Church being so formidable in those days, the French king gave a reluctant consent.

His son Louis, and his young bride Blanche, in vain tried to interpose in favour of peace, though Lady Constance clamoured still more vehemently for war.

The result was that the cardinal prevailed.

King Philip formally renounced King John's alliance.

"Then, King of France, you shall bitterly repent this day," exclaimed the enraged English monarch.

"I defy your threats," exclaimed Philip.

"And I yours," retorted John. "Sir Richard, summon our forces at once. To arms, to arms!"

SACKING A FRENCH TOWN.

So the war commenced.

Sir Richard Plantagenet, formerly the bastard Philip Faulconbridge, was rapidly rising in favour with the king, who treated him more as a relative and equal than as a subject.

Much bravery had Sir Richard displayed during the campaign, and proved himself worthy indeed of his asserted descent from the great warrior, Cœur-de-Lion.

In the king's most private councils he had always something to say, and his bluff honesty often paid but scant respect to the proud nobles in King John's camp.

In this way the newly-made knight had greatly offended the imperious Archduke of Austria.

ENGLISH KNIGHTS ENTERING A FRENCH TOWN.

During an engagement between the two armies a few days after the events just related, Sir Richard and the Archduke found themselves face to face.

Plantagenet attacked the Austrian prince with all his might, and being a much younger and stronger warrior, he had all the advantage in a hand-to-hand contest.

Both fought desperately, till a mighty blow from Plantagenet's sword stretched the archduke upon the earth.

"Yield or die!" exclaimed the victor, as he placed his foot upon the other's breast.

"I will never yield to a base-born adventurer," gasped the archduke.

"Then die by the hand of a king's son,"

DEATH OF KING JOHN.

thundered Plantagenet. "Thus I avenge the death of my royal father, Cœur-de-Lion."

So saying, he plunged his sword into the heart of the fallen warrior, who died instantaneously.

Then the slayer cut off his head, and bore it as a trophy to King John.

Sir Richard also rescued the queen-mother, who had fallen into the hands of the French; and his bravery was much commended by the king, who further commissioned him to return to England to raise

ENGLISH ARCHER.

funds from the churches and abbeys to carry on the war.

John had now succeeded in an important point, that of getting the boy Arthur into his hands; and he had still darker designs on him than mere imprisonment.

"Hubert, a word with you," said the monarch to his chamberlain, while young Arthur was conversing with his grandmother, Queen Eleanor.

Hubert retired with the king to a corner of the royal pavilion where they conversed in a low tone.

"My worthy Hubert," said John, "I know I can trust you as a good friend and faithful subject."

"I am heart and soul devoted to your highness," was the response.

KNIGHT OF THE TIME OF KING JOHN.

"I am sure of it ; and I had something to propose—but no matter."

"What is your majesty's wish ?" asked the chamberlain uneasily.

"Good Hubert," answered John, looking askance in the direction of the young prince, "cast your eye on that young boy. I tell you, my friend, he is a very serpent in my path." The king's voice sank to a hissing whisper, and he stamped his foot as if crushing some deadly thing. "Do you understand, good Hubert ?"

"You have appointed me his guardian, and I will take care he shall not offend your majesty."

"Death !" hissed the king, as if speaking to himself.

"My liege !" exclaimed the chamberlain, startled at the king's fierce manner.

"A grave !" exclaimed John, in sepulchral accents.

"Ah, I understand," said Hubert ; "he shall not live long to trouble you."

"Enough," said the king. "Hubert, you shall be rewarded. Be secret—remember !"

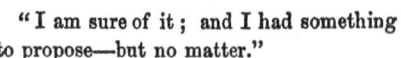

In the tent of the French King sat the Lady Constance, distracted with a frenzy of grief.

Her boy—her only child—her beloved and beautiful Arthur, had now been taken from her, and was in the power of the usurper, who, she knew, would show him no mercy.

She sat upon the ground, her hair was streaming dishevelled over her shoulders, she clasped her knees, and bent down her gaze, and had at times the demeanour of a maniac.

King Philip, who took a fatherly interest in the young widow who had seen so much misfortune, in vain tried to console her for this new bereavement.

"No, I defy all counsel, all redress," she exclaimed. "Death — death alone can bring me comfort and oblivion."

"This is mere madness," said the king.

"Not so ; I wish to Heaven I were mad," replied the afflicted mother, "for then I might forget my woes. Oh, Arthur —Arthur ! my only comfort and joy !— I shall never see you more !"

And rising up, she rushed frantically from the tent.

"I will follow her," said the French King, "for I fear, in her present state, she will do some mischief to herself."

"I too sympathise with her grief," said the Dauphin ; "for I am as grieved that Prince Arthur is a prisoner as King John is rejoiced at capturing him."

"It will go hard indeed with the boy, your highness," said Cardinal Pandulph. "While he lives, the usurper John cannot have a moment's rest, for he who snatches a sceptre by treachery can only maintain it by vigilance and violence. Arthur must die if John must reign ; yet out of evil good may come, for then in right of your wife, Lady Blanche, you can then claim the crown of England in his stead."

CHAPTER IV.

MEANWHILE the boy Arthur had been conveyed to the castle at Northampton, where he was kept strictly imprisoned, in the charge of Chamberlain Hubert de Burgh.

Arthur was not only distressed at his separation from his mother, but full of apprehension for his own fate, for he was now thoroughly in his uncle's power, and he feared the worst that cruelty or violence could do.

Hubert had hitherto treated him with kindness, and was much impressed by the affectionate disposition of the young prince.

In spite of this, stern duty compelled Hubert, against his better nature, to fulfil King John's heartless commands.

Still Arthur was kept in ignorance of the fate in store for him.

"My men," said Hubert, one evening, to the two rough peasants who acted as under gaolers at the castle, "I have work for you to do. Take these irons," he said, producing two long pieces of thick iron wire, similar to skewers, "heat them red hot, then stand yonder behind the tapestry, and when I stamp my foot, rush in and bind the boy fast to the chair."

"I like not the work, master," gruffly responded the first attendant. "Have you a warrant for it?"

"Of course I have, knave; the responsibility of the deed rests with myself. Fear nothing, but do as I command you."

The men obeyed, and when they had left the room, Hubert called to the young prince.

The tapestry was drawn aside, and Arthur entered.

In spite of his anxieties, the fair face of the child was wreathed in smiles, as he bade good morrow to his kind keeper.

"Good morning, little prince," said Hubert, in a strange constrained tone.

"Hubert, you are sad," said Arthur, approaching him.

"Yes, I have been merrier in my time," said the chamberlain.

"Indeed, good Hubert! I think nobody should be sad but I. Ah! if I were only out of prison, and could see my dear mother again; if I were no prince, but only an humble shepherd, I would be as happy as the day is long. But I fear my uncle means some terrible harm to me. He is afraid of me and I of him; but is it my fault that I am the son of his brother, and rightful heir to the throne? Oh, Hubert! I wish I were your son, so you would love me and protect me."

Hubert turned away as the young prince spoke thus, and held fast clenched the hand which Arthur attempted to take.

"If I talk to him," he murmured to himself, "his innocent prattle will awake

my pity. I shall not have heart to do the deed. I must be sudden, and despatch it quickly."

"Are you ill, Hubert?" asked Arthur, looking up at him in concern; "in truth, I wish you were a little ill, for then I would watch beside you and attend to you, and prove that I love you more than you do me."

"His words pierce my soul," said Hubert, to himself, "but I must be firm. See here, young Arthur; read this," and he showed him a paper with writing upon it, and with the royal seal and signature attached.

Arthur turned pale with horror as he read the letter.

It was from the king, and commanded Hubert to burn out Arthur's eyes with hot irons.

Hubert watched the terror-stricken face of the boy as he read this fatal missive, and compassion was more and more stirred in the chamberlain's heart.

He even felt the tear of pity rise to his eye, but he dashed it aside.

"Oh, Hubert, do you intend to burn out my eyes with hot irons?"

"Yes, boy, I must."

"Have you the heart? When your head did but ache I bound it with my handkerchief—given me by a princess— and watched by your side, and attended you all night. Many a poor man's son would not have done this, but you had a prince to attend on you. And now will you burn out my eyes—the eyes that never even frowned on you?"

"I have sworn to do it," answered Hubert, assuming a sternness of tone to disguise the pity he really felt. "Boy, entreat me no further. It is useless;" and stamping his foot he exclaimed, "My men, come forth!"

The two myrmidons appeared, one carrying a long stout cord, the other holding the irons, whose points now glowed with a red heat.

At the sight of these rough men, armed

as they were with these terrible materials of torture, the young prince uttered a cry of terror, and clung to De Burgh for protection.

"O, save me, Hubert! save me for mercy's sake!"

"Give me the irons," said the chamberlain, in a hoarse voice; "do you bind the boy."

The men then seized Arthur, who was powerless in their strong grasp.

"Why do you seize me so roughly?" he asked. "I will not struggle; I will stand stone still. For Heaven's sake, Hubert, do not let me be bound. I promise I will not stir, nor wince, nor speak a word till you permit me, only send these dreadful men away."

"Go, stand in the inner room, and leave me alone with him," said Hubert to the two men, who at once withdrew.

Hubert de Burgh took up the hot iron spikes from the table and advanced threateningly towards Arthur.

"Now, boy," he said gruffly, "no more trifling. Prepare yourself."

"Is there no remedy?" asked Arthur.

"None, but to lose your eyes," and he seized the arm of the youth with one hand, while with the other he pointed one of the irons towards his face.

"Oh, merciful Heaven!" cried Arthur, shrinking back, "is there no hope? Hubert, Hubert! once again I implore you——"

"Silence!" thundered the chamberlain. "Is this how to keep your promise? Be still and hold your tongue."

"Hubert, if I had two tongues, they would not be enough to plead for my eyes. Oh, Hubert, if you will, cut out my tongue, so that you will let me keep mine eyes. Oh, spare mine eyes, if only to look on you and know you for my friend. See, the iron is already cold, and will not harm me."

"I can have it again heated," answered Hubert, looking at the iron, from which the red glow had indeed departed.

"But you will not, Hubert—say you will not," pleaded Arthur, who, finding his keeper's hold relax, had thrown himself at his feet, and continued his entreaties. "Can you be so cruel, so fierce, as to torture one so young and unprotected as I am?"

"Well, see to live; I will not touch your eyes—no, not for all the treasure your uncle owns," returned Hubert de Burgh, who, overcome by the child's implorings, raised him from his kneeling position, and embraced him tenderly.

"Oh, now you are my own good Hubert once more!" exclaimed Arthur in delight.

"Peace, boy," was the reply. "I must leave you now. Rest contented; you shall never be harmed by me. But your uncle must not know but what you are dead. I must hatch up some tale to tell him."

King John sat in state in Northampton Palace.

He had become very unpopular since Arthur's disappearance, which was generally attributed to foul play.

Several powerful nobles surrounded him; notably the Earls of Pembroke and Salisbury, who, professing loyalty, were still suspicious of the king, and disapproved his recent measures.

They were especially displeased at the captivity of Prince Arthur, and took upon themselves to remonstrate with the king upon it.

"My liege," said the Earl of Pembroke, "in the name of my noble friends and your subjects generally, it is my duty to tell you that your seizure of the young prince is causing great discontent, which may prove dangerous to your royal safety. We heartily request that he shall be liberated at once."

Enraged as was the despot at this demand, he yet feared his powerful barons too much to refuse it, so disguising his resentment, he said—

"Let it be so, my lords. I will confide the youth to your care. Here comes his

guardian. We will speak to him of this."

The chamberlain, Hubert, as he entered the royal presence, had an anxious and downcast expression, which did not escape the notice of the noblemen.

After making his obeisance he approached the king, and conferred with him in a low tone.

"This is the king's minion," said Pembroke, aside to Salisbury. "Has he not a cut-throat look? I fear he has already slain the poor boy."

"I think so too," answered Salisbury; "look how the king changes colour at Hubert's tidings."

"My lords," said the king, "I would be willing to do all you ask with regard to my nephew, but it is too late. His keeper here tells me he died an hour ago."

"Ah!" exclaimed Salisbury. "I had heard he was ill, and I feared his disease would be fatal."

"We all feared he was very near death," added Pembroke, both in a sarcastic and suspicious tone, which greatly angered the king.

Then making a stiff obeisance to him, they turned and left the audience-chamber.

"There is evidently foul play here," said Salisbury to his noble colleague.

"We will inquire deeply into it," was the reply. "Such deeds must not be borne. Ere long the king will find retribution will seek him out."

"Now they will go and plot against me," said the king to himself. "What a life is mine! Evil was the day I first mounted this throne. Ah! more troubles. Here comes a messenger from France."

The officer who was now announced brought indeed evil intelligence.

The French with a large army were even now on their way to invade England.

Following close to this news was that the Lady Constance, in grief at losing her son, had died in a mad frenzy, also that the Queen Dowager had died a week later.

The king was naturally much shocked at this, for evil as had been his mother's character and example, he had never been wanting in affection as a son.

Besides, he knew that Queen Eleanor's death would greatly imperil his territories in France, of which she had been guardian.

"Who leads the advancing force?" asked the king.

"The Dauphin," replied the officer, "who comes as claimant to the English crown."

Sir Richard Plantagenet was next announced.

Zealous in the king's service, he had collected a large sum from the abbeys and monasteries for the royal use.

But John was much concerned to hear that the nobles had revolted and joined the invader.

He entreated Sir Richard to go at once and use his utmost endeavours to arrange matters, then sinking into a seat, weary with these numerous anxieties, the king sank into a reverie, till looking up after a while he saw Hubert de Burgh before him.

"My lord," said the chamberlain, "the air is full of signs and wonders; old men and women in the streets gather in groups and foretell disastrous events. Every one is murmuring, and above all they talk of Arthur's death."

"Why am I thus to be continually plagued about Arthur's death?" asked the monarch angrily. "It was you, not I, who murdered him; I, indeed, had cause to wish him dead, but you had no cause to kill him."

"Is it possible your majesty can speak thus to me?" asked Hubert, displeased at the king's endeavour to shift the guilt to himself. "See this paper? Here is your hand and seal for what I did."

The king turned pale at the sight of the document.

"Put it away," he exclaimed; "'tis damning evidence against us. I protest

that if I did command you to slay him, I should not have done so had it not been your cut-throat aspect and evident eagerness to do a deed of blood egged me on to a reluctant consent. Out of my sight, and never let me see you more; see what has been the result—not only foreign invasions, but my own nobles are in revolt against me."

"Then arm yourself against your enemies, my liege," said Hubert; "but as for Arthur, he need not trouble either your conscience or mine any more—he is alive!"

"Alive?" exclaimed the king, in astonishment.

"Yes, I had not the heart to kill him."

"This is good news indeed," said the monarch, "for it may yet reconcile me to the powerful barons, and make them aid me against the French invader. Go, my good Hubert, ride post haste to the Earls of Pembroke and Salisbury and the other nobles, tell them that Arthur is alive, and summon them to a privy council at once, for the time is urgent. Speed, Hubert, speed! my throne and kingdom may be safe yet."

In the absence of Hubert de Burgh, young Arthur had proceeded to put into execution a plan of escape.

Of late his captivity had been relaxed, and he had been permitted to roam at large through the upper apartments.

He obtained more freedom and exercise day by day, walking on to the balcony outside, protected by huge stone battlements, and commanding a view of a large space of the surrounding country.

It was by means of this that he intended to escape, climbing down the ivy that grew thickly upon that side of the wall.

But he knew that in his princely attire he would be at once recognised, so he contrived to get hold of some clothes which had belonged to a son of one of the warders of the castle, and disguising himself in them, chose the hour of twilight for his perilous descent.

As he looked down the dizzy height he shuddered, yet the love of liberty was so strong within him that he resolved to risk it.

Once safely on the ground he knew he could easily complete his escape.

Committing his soul to Heaven, he at length commenced his terrible task; for some distance the ivy was strong enough to bear his weight, but he came to one part where it was weaker; in the uncertain light he missed his footing.

There was a wild shriek, a crash, and the young prince lay crushed and bleeding upon the stone edge of the castle moat, death being instantaneous.

Sir Richard Plantagenet had scarcely overtaken the two incensed nobles, when the party was shocked by discovering the body of the unfortunate boy.

"Oh, Heaven!" exclaimed the Earl of Pembroke, "how soon and sudden is this death!"

"Not death alone, but murder!" answered the Earl of Salisbury.

"A villainous and accursed deed!" added Richard, kneeling down by Arthur's corpse.

At this moment Hubert de Burgh, little dreaming of what had happened, came up.

The sight almost paralysed him with horror.

"Villain!" cried Salisbury, rushing at Hubert and seizing him by the throat, "behold your work!"

"I swear to you, noble lords, that I am guiltless of this deed," replied the chamberlain. "I would give my life to restore that of this poor young prince. I know not who killed him; but an hour since I left him alive and well."

In spite of his assurances, the others were with difficulty dissuaded from dealing signal vengeance to Arthur's guardian.

Thus the way in which the young prince died was for ever after enveloped in

mystery, but all in their hearts laid his death at the door of King John.

CHAPTER V.

THE king's affairs were now in a most disastrous state.

Detested as a tyrant by his subjects, opposed by his powerful nobles, unsuccessful in his expedition to France, he was compelled also to acknowledge himself the vassal of the pope, and even to give up his crown into the hands of the imperious Cardinal Pandulph.

"Take it again," was the reply of the papal legate, as he handed the king back his crown. "In the name of the pope I confirm you in your royalty, on the condition that you remain faithful and obedient."

King John bowed humbly, though rage and mortification swelled within him, and he replaced the crown upon his head.

Sunk in depression and anxiety, he was not reassured when Sir Richard Plantagenet, still his faithful follower, returned.

"I grieve to say, your majesty, that the French are carrying all before them. London has yielded, all Kent is theirs, except Dover Castle, which still holds out, and all your nobles have gone over to the enemy."

"Would they not return to their allegiance when they heard Arthur was alive?"

"Alas, my liege! they found him lying dead outside his prison."

"That villain Hubert told me he was alive," said the king, much dismayed at the intelligence.

"Be not cast down, great king," said Sir Richard; "all may yet be well if we are up and doing at once."

"I have made friends with the cardinal," said John, "and he has promised to make the King of France withdraw his troops."

"And shall we, as Englishmen, in our own land, thus humbly beg for peace?" scornfully replied the bold warrior. "Shall a beardless boy, like the Dauphin of France, invade England unchecked? Not so, King John, we must fight them to the death!"

"Then go, kinsman, and marshal my army for resistance," said the king.

Negotiations, however, were first tried. Upon a plain near St. Edmundsbury, the Dauphin, Louis, and his forces assembled, and they were joined by Pembroke, Salisbury, and the other disaffected nobles.

Cardinal Pandulph was shortly announced, and in great pomp, attended by various other ecclesiastics, he entered the open space between the circle of tents, where the leaders of the army were assembled in council.

"I greet you, Prince of France," he said, "and now inform you that King John of England has reconciled himself to the pope, who, therefore, commands you to be reconciled to him likewise, and to withdraw your invading forces from England."

"In the name of my father, the king, I refuse," returned the prince indignantly. "We are not slaves to Rome, whatever King John may be; and young Arthur being dead, I, in right of my wife, claim to be heir to the throne of England."

"You decline, then, to retire?" said the cardinal.

"Most emphatically," replied the Dauphin; "but who comes here?"

It was Sir Richard Plantagenet, who, in great state, and attended by many knights, entered the council.

"I bear a message from King John," he said, looking disdainfully around. "He commands me to say that he utterly despises this army of boy leaders, and undisciplined rebels, and that he has raised a mighty force which shall chastise you all, just as unruly brats are whipped at school."

" You beat us at one thing, Sir Knight," answered the prince, " that is, at bragging. We have no time to listen to you now."

" Let me speak," said the cardinal.

" No, I will speak," protested Plantagenet.

" We will listen to neither of you," said the Dauphin. " It is no time to parley, or draw back. Strike up, wave flags, and beat the drums."

" And get beaten yourself, vaunting Frenchman !" retorted Sir Richard.

In spite of this boast, however, the battle that followed went hard with the English.

Plantagenet's bravery alone prevented it from being a disastrous defeat.

King John's fortunes were at their lowest ebb, and he would have been involved in utter ruin, but that the rebel nobles, hearing that the French king intended to take away all those liberties which they had gained from John, by the famous Magna Charta, began to think they had made a mistake in thus deserting to the enemy.

Many of them, therefore, returned to their allegiance.

The French retired at last and matters seemed becoming more favourable.

PILGRIM FROM THE HOLY LAND.

But King John was in no position to enjoy prosperity.

Worn out by anxieties, he had been stricken by a fever, and Sir Richard, who wished to find him out, was shocked, on meeting Hubert, to hear that the sovereign he had so faithfully served, was at that moment lying sick unto death in Swinstead Abbey.

Sir Richard immediately took horse, and making his best speed to that place, found the king almost at the last gasp.

He was attended by only a few friends, and his son and heir, the youthful Prince Henry.

" Oh, kinsman, you have only just come in time," said the king in a faint tone, as Sir Richard approached the arm-chair in which he reclined. " I am dying — poisoned, I fear, by a false monk, who was leagued with my enemies; and I have just heard that all my carriages and baggage have been lost in the floods in Lincolnshire. This is the last straw. What am I now? —a king without a crown, or friends, or wealth, or strength to cope with dangers and with sorrows. I am devoid of hope, all is dark—dark—farewell !"

Such was the end of King John.

NOTICE.—" KING LEAR," being No. 8 of Stories from Shakespeare, will be ready on Friday, December 23rd, on account of Christmas Day. Orders should be given early to your Booksellers.

EDWIN J. BRETT'S STORIES OF SHAKESPEARE

COMPLETE

KING LEAR.

DESPERATE WAS THE COMBAT THAT ENSUED BETWEEN EDMUND AND HIS UNKNOWN CHALLENGER.

"Days of England Edition."

EDWIN J. BRETT'S

STORIES FROM

SHAKESPEARE'S PLAYS.

No. 8.—KING LEAR.

CHAPTER I.

IT was on a warm June day, towards the close of the seventh century, that troops of gaily-dressed horsemen might have been seen advancing by different routes towards Kingstonne, then a town second only in importance to London itself.

Wild Norsemen from Northumbria marched under their chieftains, swinging their battle-axes loosely, eyeing askance the stout, stern hillmen from the fens of Lincolnshire, as though a word were but needed to fan a quarrel.

And scrambling over the hills, chatting and laughing, but in movement incessant, like so many kittens at play, the lithe active restless Cambrians, over whom stern Gloster held sway, ruling the marches with an iron hand that could even strike terror to the heart of the tributary King Llewellyn, even in his mountain fastnesses.

"So, my lord of Kent," exclaimed a tall stately-looking man, reining in his horse and motioning his attendants to come to a standstill; "so, my lord of Kent, it seems that we are to have high jinks and junketings. Are you the originator of these mad freaks of our royal king?"

"Marry! that I am not, my lord of Gloster. Heaven wot I did try my very hardest to prevent it, holding that if a man do give away the substance and hold but the shadow of power, he but lays up for himself years of misery."

"What excuse doth he give for this resolution?"

"Marry! that he is old, and would fain have done with the cares of state."

"Well, well, we will see what comes of it; but I promise you I like it not."

"Nor do I, foreseeing nothing but mischief in it for the future. Is this your son?"

"It is, my lord; the second son, and, sooth to say, so much the more my favourite than my first-born that I wish he had come first into the world."

"That he might inherit your broad lands, earl, is it not?"

"It is, my lord of Kent, seeing that he hath stout limbs and a stout brain to keep them, whereas his brother is womanish, more fitted for the cowl than the sword."

"And it will go hard with me but I make my dainty brother Edgar give place, too," muttered the young man to himself. "There be more ways than one of removing an obstacle"

"Edmund," cried the earl, who did not notice this soliloquy, "this is my friend, the noble Earl of Kent, the king's adviser and trusty servant. I have not seen him these five years, but now that we have come to court I trust you will find him to be a friend to you, and perhaps push your interests and fortunes."

"That I will gladly, young sir," replied

the old earl, "and I hope we shall soon put you in the way of promotion."

"My services to your lordship," exclaimed the young man whose name was Edmund. "I shall study to deserve your approval."

And causing his horse to make a demi-vault, he bowed until his head almost disappeared in the flowing mane.

"A comely youth; perhaps a trifle too glib of tongue for my liking," continued the old earl.

His reverie was broken by a flourish of trumpets announcing that the king was come into the state apartments.

Hastily dismounting, the two earls entered the throne-room.

On a throne made of solid gold, and covered with a purple cloth, sat Lear, King of Britain.

His long white hair fell in profusion over his shoulders, and gave him a noble and venerable appearance.

But at times there would come across his face a quick impatient movement as-if he were not used to being crossed in the slightest degree.

At the foot of his throne stood his three daughters—Goneril, Regan and Cordelia, the latter being the youngest as well as the loveliest of the three.

Both Goneril and Regan were dark imperious looking beauties, what one would call splendidly handsome women.

But Cordelia was as fair as a lily, with bright golden hair, and a winning smile that seemed to creep into every heart at once.

It was evident that if she was a favourite with her father the reverse was the case with her sisters.

From time to time they threw glances at her of almost positive hate.

By the side of these two stood two handsome men—the Dukes of Cornwall and Albany.

They looked mistrustingly at one another as though each was afraid that he might be less in favour with the king than his rival.

As the Dukes of Kent and Gloster entered, the king stamped his foot impatiently.

"Gloster," he said, without even greeting him, "I have almost been obliged to wait. Away at once and attend the lords of France and Burgundy."

The nobleman bit his proud lip at thus being spoken to so sharply, but he left the throne-room without saying a word, followed by Edmund.

Not, however, before Edmund darted a bold look of admiration on the two princesses—a look which they returned with interest, for Edmund was the comeliest youth about the court.

"I mean to marry one of those haughty beauties," said the youth to himself as he followed his father; "which one it will be I know not. As for the fair-haired thing, she is too lackadaisical for me, so she may go hang."

"And now, my lords and ladies," said King Lear, "listen to me while I tell you the purpose for which I have summoned you here. Give me the map, there."

He ran his hand over the map of England and continued—

"Know that we have divided our kingdom into three divisions, and it is our fast intention to shake all cares of business from our old age, conferring them on younger strength, while we quietly prepare for our latter end. We have no son, and therefore, that all strife in future may be avoided, it is our intention to partition the kingdom out between the husbands of our three daughters, Regan, Goneril, and Cordelia; that is to say, our son of Cornwall and of Albany. The Princes of France and Burgundy are rivals for our youngest daughter's hand, but I know not which will find favour in her sight.

"And now," continued the king, "tell me, my daughters, which of you doth love me the most? For be assured, that the one who loves me the most shall have the largest and fairest share of my kingdom. Goneril, you are the eldest born, you speak first."

A smile of contempt for her father's childishness flashed for a moment over Goneril's proud lips.

But she quickly suppressed it, and turned to her father with a most dutiful expression of countenance.

"Sire," said she, while her sisters had much ado not to laugh outright, "I love you more than words can wield the matter; dearer are you to me than eyesight or liberty; beyond what can be valued rich or rarer; even life itself, together with grace, health, beauty, honour; as much as child ever loved, or father found; a love that makes breath poor and speech unable; beyond all manner of so much I love you."

"What shall I say?" muttered poor Cordelia to herself. "I cannot insult my father with such extravagances to his face, though I love him far more dearly than she. I must be silent."

The silly old king looked immensely gratified by what his daughter had said, and running his finger down the map, said—

"Of all these lands from this line to this, with forests, and mead, and town, we make thee lady, to thine and thy husband the Duke of Albany's children, and this shall be perpetual."

The duke and his wife bowed low at receiving this gift, as the king, turning from them, said to his second daughter—

"And now, Regan, how much do you love me?"

"I am made of the same metal as my sister," said she, "therefore prize me at her worth. In my true heart I find she names my very deed of love. Only she comes too short—that I profess myself an enemy to all other joys except that of your highness's dear love."

"Alas!" said Cordelia to herself, "how can I tell such miserable lies as that?"

But the king swallowed this gross flattery with evident relish.

Turning to his daughter Regan, he said—

"To thee and thine, hereditary for ever, take this third of our fair kingdom, no less in space and profit than that conferred upon Goneril. Now, our joy, although last, not least, Cordelia, for whose hand the vines of France and milk of Burgundy strive, what can you say to draw a third more opulent than any of your sisters?"

The two elder ones, hearing this, cast a malignant glance at Cordelia, being jealous that she was probably going to have more than either of them.

"Nothing, my lord," replied Cordelia.

"Nothing?" cried the king, astonished.

"Nothing," repeated Cordelia, in a downcast voice.

"Nothing can come of nothing," cried the king, in a rage. "Speak again."

"Unhappy that I am," replied Cordelia, "I cannot heave my heart into my mouth. All I can say is that I love your majesty according to my bond."

"How, Cordelia!" cried the king, in a perfect rage, while a look of gratified malice was plainly visible on the faces of her elder sisters. "How, Cordelia! mend your speech, lest it mar your fortunes."

"I cannot help that," replied Cordelia. "You have begot me, bred me, loved me. I return those duties, obey you, love you, and most honour you. Why have my sisters husbands, if they say they love you most of all? Haply, when I marry, my husband will have half my love, half my care, and half my duty. Sure I shall never marry like my sisters, to love my father all."

"Are you speaking from your heart, Cordelia?" asked the king, in amazement, and looking as if he hardly believed his ears.

"Yes," replied Cordelia, "I must tell you the truth."

"So young and yet so heartless," cried the king, whilst his brow grew black as midnight.

"So young and yet so true," cried Cordelia firmly. "I cannot lie to you as my sisters have done."

"Then let it be so," cried the king, in a paroxysm of passion. "Let truth be thy dower, since you are so fond of it. For by the sacred sun, I swear I here disclaim all paternal care, and as a stranger to my heart and me, hold thee from this time forth — for ever. Begone from my presence!"

"My liege, my liege, you are unjust!" cried the old Earl of Kent.

"Peace, Kent!" cried the king, white with passion. "Cornwall and Albany, take Cordelia's third and divide it between you. Let her pride, which she calls plainness and truth, marry her. I do invest you jointly with my power, and divide the kingdom equally between you. I, on alternate months, will live with each of you, accompanied by one hundred knights, and still retain in name only the rank and additions of a king. This crown part between you."

"Royal Lear," cried the Earl of Kent, "what fearful injustice would you do? I will not hold my tongue; I have been your faithful counsellor for years, and my duty bids me to speak fearlessly. When power to flattery bows, to plainness honour is bound. Check this rashness. Thy youngest daughter does not love thee the least because she does not flatter your vanity. Revoke thy gift, or while I have tongue to clamour, I will tell thee thou dost evil!"

"Oh, vassal, slave, recreant!" cried the king, laying his hand on his sword; "since thou hast sought to make us break our kingly vow, and with strained pride to come between our sentence and our power, take thy reward. Turn thy hated back upon our kingdom. If ten days from now you are found in our kingdom that moment is thy death."

"Fare thee well, my royal master," cried Kent, "you will live to repent this act."

And so saying, the stout old nobleman bid them all adieu.

Just at that moment the King of France and the Duke of Burgundy entered the room.

"Burgundy," cried the king, "will you take our daughter from us now that she has no power or riches?"

"That will I not, your majesty."

"Then, your majesty," cried the King of France, "give her to me."

Then, turning to Cordelia, and before the astonished court, he said—

"Fairest Cordelia, thou art most rich being poor, most choice since thou art forsaken, and most loved because most despised. These and thy virtues I here take. I take up what was cast away. Thy dowerless daughter, king, is queen of us, of ours, and of all fair France. Bid them farewell, Cordelia, for what thou losest here, I will make up to thee a thousandfold."

"Farewell, sisters," said Cordelia. "Use well our father, to your professed bosoms I commit him. But alas! if I was not out of favour with him I could wish him a better place."

"Do not dare to prescribe our duties to us!" screamed both sisters.

"Time will unfold your cunning, sisters," said Cordelia. "Fare ye well, both, may you prosper."

And without a word of blessing, away she went with her lover.

Hardly had her back been turned ere the two elder sisters began to wrangle about who should support the king for the first month.

Each being desirous of throwing his support on the other's shoulders.

However, they were mutually agreed that he must be deprived of further power lest he might revoke the gift he had made them.

So they went away to their castles to plot against him.

CHAPTER II.

WE must now transport our scene to the castle of the Earl of Gloster about three months after the events took place which we described in the last chapter.

Edmund had devised several means for getting rid of his elder brother Edgar.

But so far these schemes had proved abortive.

As he was walking in the corridor of the castle, a new idea occurred to him.

If he could only make his father hate his brother, all would be well with him.

Accordingly he wrote a letter, imitating his brother's handwriting as nearly as he could.

Then he concealed it about his person and waited until he heard his father coming.

Then he appeared to be reading it; but as soon as his father perceived him, he put it away with every appearance of haste and confusion.

"How now, Edmund," cried the earl; "why so earnestly do you seek to put up that letter, as if you were afraid I might read it?"

"'Tis nothing, my father," replied Edmund.

"Let me see it?"

"I had rather not."

"I insist."

"I shall offend either to detain or give it," said Edmund, with well feigned reluctance as he handed the letter, "but I hope, for my brother Edgar's justification, that this is but an essay or taste of my virtue."

The old earl took the letter and read as follows—

"This policy and reverence of age makes the world bitter to the best of our times, keeps our fortunes from us till old age comes upon us and we cannot thoroughly enjoy it. If our father would sleep till I waked him, you should enjoy half his revenue for ever, and live the beloved of your brother Edgar. Come and see me that we may talk more on the matter.

"EDGAR."

"Could my son Edgar have the heart to write this?" asked the old earl, in tokens of anguish. "How did you come by it?"

"It was thrown in at my window."

"You know the handwriting to be your brother's?"

"If the matter were not so vile, I could swear to it."

"Has he ever mentioned anything of this to you before?"

"Never, my lord. But I have heard him maintain that when the son arrives at manhood, the father should give him up his estate."

"Oh, villain!" exclaimed the old earl; "his very opinion to the letter. Abhorred villain, unnatural detested brutish villain! I'll apprehend him—where is he?"

"I do not know, my lord, but I will seek him, and see if I cannot find you proofs of his innocence."

But it was for a very different purpose that Edmund sought his brother.

He found him in the church attached to the castle, praying, and at once addressed himself to his task.

"When did you see my father last, Edgar?" he asked.

"The night gone by."

"Did you part from him on good terms? Found you no displeasure in him?"

"None at all."

"Bethink wherein you may have offended him, and at my entreaty forbear his presence until some little time hath elapsed."

"Some villain has wronged me."

"That is what I told him, but he will not hear me. Now I pray you go with me now to my lodgings until his rage abates; stir not abroad, and if you do go, go armed."

"Armed?"

"Ay, your life is in danger. I have told you what I have seen and heard but faintly; pray you go."

And so he induced his credulous brother to leave the castle unobserved.

Edgar had scarcely gone ere a messenger arrived from the Duke and Duchess of Cornwall to say that they would arrive at the castle that night, having left their own in order to avoid having to entertain the king, who had left the Duke of Albany's castle in a rage.

Almost as soon as the messenger was gone, Edgar reappeared.

"Edmund," he said "I have resolved to see my father and face this matter out. I am guiltless of aught of evil towards him."

"For the love of Heaven, fly!" cried Edmund, assuming an appearance of terror. "I never saw my father so inflamed with passion. He swears he will slay you off hand. But just now a band of men came here searching for you."

Even as he spoke, there was a great noise as of the tramp of armed men.

"See, they come! Fly, my brother, fly!" cried Edmund. "Ah," he added, "it may be too late. Pardon me; in cunning, I must draw upon you."

Then raising his voice he shouted—

"Yield—come before my father. Light ho! torches, torches!"

Then in a lower voice—

"Fly, now, I will see you righted."

Foolish Edgar, panic-stricken with sudden fear, rushed away, and Edmund wounded himself in the arm.

"Father, father!" he shouted, "help—help!"

In a few moments his father rushed in, sword in hand.

He found Edmund apparently in a fainting condition.

"Where is the villain, Edmund?" he cried.

"Look, sir, I bleed; he fled that way when he could not persuade me to——"

"What?"

"The murder of your lordship."

"Let him fly far," replied the duke in a terrible rage, "not in this land shall he remain uncaught, and found—by the authority of the noble Duke of Cornwall, who comes to-night, I will proclaim that he who brings this murderous coward to the stake shall deserve our thanks; he that conceals him, death."

He had scarcely ceased speaking when the Duke of Cornwall and his wife Regan entered, and to him he communicated the news of his son's attempt upon his life.

"Ha!" said Regan, "he was companion to the riotous knights that waited upon thy father."

"Yes, madam," cried Edmund, with ready cunning, "he was."

"No marvel, then, that he were ill affected towards you," she said, turning to the earl. "'Tis they who have put him on to your death. For you, Edmund!" she continued, "you shall be ours. And now we must tell you, noble, why it is we have come to you."

Upon this Regan told the earl that King Lear and his hundred knights were on their way to pay them a visit, and that her sister had sent a messenger to say that she had turned them out of the house.

But the cause of their leaving we must leave for another chapter to explain.

CHAPTER III.

FOR nearly a month everything went well with King Lear at the castle of Goneril the Duchess of Albany.

By that time she had got the power firmly in her hands, and resolved that her father should not have the chance of taking it from her again.

She was a perfect vixen of a wife, and in her heart despised her husband, the easy-going Duke of Albany.

Ungrateful that she was, she was heartily sick of her father's retinue of knights and followers, and resolved that she would take the first opportunity of transferring the burden of their keep upon her sister Regan.

However, the great thing was to find a pretext for quarrelling, and accordingly she instructed her servants to be saucy and insolent to King Lear's followers, and even to be saucy to him.

The result of this very soon became apparent.

Wrangles became more frequent every day, and the passionate old king was not long in perceiving that he was not treated with the respect due to his dignity, and that he had, in fact, worn his welcome out.

Affairs culminated one day when he returned from hunting with his followers.

Meanwhile, the Earl of Kent, who had been banished from the kingdom for speaking up for Cordelia, came back from his banishment, and disguised as a yeoman, took service with the king, who liked his good honest bluff manner of speaking.

"I tell you," cried the king, in a rage, "on this particular day that I will wait dinner for no one. Let it be served at once. Where's my fool?"

At that moment the steward entered.

"You, sirrah, where's my daughter?"

"She is not well," mumbled the steward, "and not likely to get much better with all this riot and noise."

Two knights caught the steward as he was hastening away and brought him before the king.

"You cur, you dog! Who am I?" bawled the old king in a passion.

"My lady's father, my lord; and look you, I am none of these things."

"Would you bandy words with me?" asked the king, and struck him on the mouth.

"I'll not be struck, my lord," replied the steward.

"Nor tripped either," cried Kent, tripping up his heels.

Away went the steward in high dudgeon, to acquaint his lady with what had happened to him.

Meanwhile the king's fool had very much enraged him by wittily pointing out to him that he was nothing better than a pauper depending on the charity of his daughters.

When Goneril arrived, he was in a high state of indignation and rage, and she was in no mood to calm him down.

In fact, the carefully planned opportunity had come at last.

"How now, my daughter?" cried Lear, perceiving her approach. "Methinks you are somewhat too much on the frown lately."

"You strike my people," promptly retorted Goneril, "and your disorderly rabble make servants of their betters. I would have you know that this I will not permit for the sake of humouring an old man in his dotage."

The effect of such a speech on the old king may be imagined.

He stormed and raved, and finally ordered his horses to be saddled that he might go to his other daughter, saying to Goneril as he left the room—

he despatched the Earl of Kent to announce his advent.

But Goneril determined that she would let her sister know why he had left her house, that she might take her measures accordingly.

She despatched her steward to her with a letter, saying that she had reduced his followers to the number of fifty for fear that in one of his sudden fits of anger he might have the power of doing her harm.

"UPON THESE EYES OF THINE I'LL SET MY FOOT.'

"Ingratitude, thou marble hearted fiend, more hideous when thou showest thee in a child than the sea-monster. Detested kite, my train are men of choicest parts that all particulars of duty know. May you have a child to treat you as you have treated me, and learn from her how sharper than a serpent's tooth it is to have a thankless child."

When Lear prepared to go, he found that Goneril had taken away half his followers, so that he had now only fifty.

Certain that his other daughter, Regan, would only be too glad to do him honour,

Goneril's messenger arrived first, and Regan determined to go and visit the Duke of Gloster, so that she might have an excuse for telling her father that he could not live with them.

The Earl of Kent met Goneril's messenger as he was coming out of the presence of the Duke of Cornwall and his wife, and a quarrel ensued between them, which brought the duke and Regan on the scene.

Taking the part of her sister's messenger, Regan ordered the Earl of Kent to be put in the stocks pending the arrival of King Lear.

"'FAIREST CORDELIA,' SAID THE KING OF FRANCE, 'THOU ART MOST RICH BEING POOR.'"

This was done in spite of the protests of the Earl of Gloster, who was still full of reverence for his king, although the power had passed from him.

Meanwhile far and wide went the proclamation of the Earl of Gloster, offering a reward to any one who would kill his son Edgar, who was a fugitive.

Edmund was in high favour with his father and with Regan, who had fallen in love with him.

CHAPTER IV.

WHEN King Lear and his diminished train arrived in front of Gloster Castle, where he discovered the Earl of Kent in the stocks, he could not at first believe his eyes, but then demanded in a fury to see his daughter.

"THE MURDER OF CORDELIA.'

The Earl of Gloster came back with an answer to say that she was too weary with her journey to see him, and the duke was too busy.

He bade Gloster go back and tell them that he insisted upon seeing them, but in the midst of his furious passion his daughter Regan and the duke made their appearance, and greeted the king with cold welcome.

However, they released Kent from his uncomfortable position.

"Oh, Regan!" exclaimed the king, "thy sister is naught; I scarce can speak to thee of her. Thou scarce can think how depraved a quality——"

Regan interrupted the king rudely, and informed him that he was very much mistaken if he thought she would listen to complaints about her sister; on the contrary, she was of the opinion that her sister had acted quite justly, and that he had much better return to her.

"Never, Regan," replied the proud old man; "she hath abated me of half my train. May all curses in nature fall on her!"

"So will you curse me presently," cried Regan, "when the mood is upon you."

"Never, Regan; thou shalt never have my curse; thy tender nature shall not give thee over to harshness——"

"Good sir," cried Regan, interrupting him, "to the purpose. Hark! I hear my sister's trumpet."

"Who put my man in the stocks?"

"I did, and will do so again if he should so deserve. Here is my sister. I pray you, father, being weak, seem so. If till the expiration of your month you will return and sojourn with my sister, dismissing half your present train, then come to me. I am now from home and out of that provision which shall be needful for your entertainment."

"Return to her, and fifty men dismissed!" cried King Lear, in a fury. "No, rather would I abjure all roofs ——"

"At your choice, sir," said Goneril coldly; "besides, if you come to me now I see no need of so many followers."

"Nor I," added Regan sharply. "I spy a danger. What need you with any followers at all?"

"You see me here, you gods," cried the poor king, utterly broken down, "a poor old man, as full of grief as age—wretched in both. No, you unnatural hags, I will have such revenge on you both that all the world shall wonder. You think I'll weep. No, I will not weep. Oh, I shall go mad!"

And uttering a torrent of imprecations, the old king turned away.

"Let's go in; there will be a storm," said one of the sisters. "This house is little; the old man and his people cannot be well bestowed."

"'Tis his own folly," said Goneril; "he hath put himself from rest and must needs taste his folly."

"As far as he is concerned, I will receive him gladly," said Regan, "but not one of his followers."

At this moment the Earl of Gloster returned with the news that the king was going away.

"Oh, sir," cried Regan, "let him go by all means, and see you that the castle doors are safely shut. Who knows what his desperate train might do?"

Accordingly they both retired within the castle, leaving their aged father out in the storm.

——

CHAPTER V.

IN the meanwhile the faithful Kent, who had in reality come back as a spy of Cordelia's to see how her father was getting on, no sooner found out the way he was abused by his two elder daughters than he despatched a gentleman to a seaport, where he was to hasten over to France and beg the French king, Cordelia's husband, to come over to King Lear's assistance, adding that, though professing friendship for each other, the Dukes of Cornwall and Albany were really ready to pit with each other for possession of the whole kingdom.

He then went after the poor old king, who he found half crazy, wandering about the wild heath, in the pitiless rain, and attended only by his fool.

As he drew near he heard him say—

"Rumble thy bellyful! Spit, fire! spout rain! Nor rain, wind, thunder, fire, are my daughters. I do not tax you with unkindness. Why then let fall your horrible pleasures? Here I stand, your slave, a poor, weak, and despised old man; but yet I call you servile ministers that have with two pernicious daughters joined your battles against a head so old and white as mine."

It was with extreme difficulty that good old Kent managed to get the king into a house that stood hard by.

In the meanwhile the Earl of Gloster sought out his son Edmund, and informed him of his pity for the king.

"But when I desired their leave that I might pity him," he continued, "they took from me the use of mine own castle, and charged me, on pain of their perpetual displeasure, neither to speak for him nor mention his name again."

"Most savage and unnatural!" exclaimed Edmund the arch hypocrite.

"Say nothing," said the Earl of Gloster cautiously. "There is division between the dukes, and a worse matter than that, I have received a letter this night. 'Tis dangerous to speak about it even; I have locked it up in my closet. These injuries the king has received will be revenged home. We must take care of the king. I will go and seek him out while you keep the duke in talk. If they ask for me, say I am gone to bed."

So Gloster went out to seek the king in the storm.

But the door had scarcely closed on him ere Edmund clapped his hands with joy.

"The earldom is mine," he cried. "I will get that letter and show it to the Duke of Cornwall. He is sure to behead my father and put me in his place. Besides, I see that the Duchess of Cornwall is sick of her husband and almost in love with me."

Thus scheming against his father's life as he had against his brother's, young Edmund went up to his guests with the letter that he had abstracted from the desk, in his hand.

It announced that the French king had landed at Dover, and would be glad of the assistance of the disaffected nobles.

That was Gloster's death warrant, and his son knew it.

CHAPTER VI.

AFTER a good deal of trouble the Earl of Kent persuaded the now nearly crazy king to enter the cowshed.

From a whim the king bade his jester enter before him, but the jester, or fool, as they were called in those days, ran out again, with all the wit taken out of him, and in a terrible state of fright, to say that there was a spirit there.

But King Lear was not in a condition of mind to fear spirits or anything else.

Fortune and his two ungrateful daughters had about done their worst.

The alleged spirit, indeed, was none other than Edgar, the Duke of Gloster's eldest son.

Seeing that it was impossible to escape his father's vengeance, having heard the proclamation read against him, he had stripped himself naked and rubbed cow-dung upon his face and body.

Then with a blanket only about his loins, he enacted the *role* of a mad beggar, hoping that this disguise would effectually screen him from his father's anger.

Of course he was fearful of his retreat being discovered, and renewed his endeavours to make the wanderers seek elsewhere for shelter.

"Away!" he cried; "the foul fiend follows me!"

"Hast thou given all to thy two daughters that thou art come to this?" asked King Lear.

"Who gives anything to poor Tom?" cried the pretended lunatic.

Talking to this fool King Lear, to Kent's horror, gradually went crazy and tried to tear off his clothes, but in the midst of the wrangle they saw a torch through the blackness of the night, and the Earl of Gloster appeared, and expressed his deep sorrow for the state of the unhappy king.

Although he talked several times with his son Edgar, he still mistook him for Mad Tom, and Edgar was too bewildered to take advantage of the opportunity thus offered, and clear himself of the imputation cast upon him by Edmund.

The king took a great liking to Edgar; and when Gloster announced that he was going to a farmhouse where they would be well cared for, the king insisted on taking Mad Tom, as he called him, with them.

Arrived at the farmhouse, Gloster made them as comfortable as possible ere he took his way back to the castle, never dreaming of his son Edmund's treachery.

But notwithstanding the warmth and comfort of the farmhouse the king continued to be quite mad, and would talk to no other than Mad Tom.

They were preparing for bed when the Earl of Gloster once more made his appearance.

"Where is the king?" he asked eagerly.

"Here," responded Kent; "but trouble him not. His wits are quite gone."

"Good friend," said Gloster, "I pray

thee take him in thy arms. I have over-heard a plot of death upon him. There is a litter ready. Lay him in it, and drive towards Dover, where thou shalt meet both welcome and protection. Take up thy master; if thou shouldst dally half-an-hour his life and thine, and all who would protect him, will be forfeited."

Having said this, he hastened back to the castle, and Kent, assisted by the fool and Mad Tom, lost no time in carrying out his wishes.

CHAPTER VII.

LET us return to the castle, and see how it fared with the nefarious schemes put into execution by Edmund.

"How malicious is my fortune," cried the wily Edmund, "when my loyalty compels me to betray my father. Here is the letter he spoke of, noble duke, and it proves him to have intelligence of the French king's landing. Oh, Heaven! that this treason against your grace were not, or I the detector."

"Go with me to the duchess," cried the duke. "If this matter be so, you have weighty business on hand, and whether it be true or false it hath made thee Earl of Gloster. Seek out thy father that he may be ready for apprehension. Go; although you lose your father you will find a dearer father in my love."

"Fool!" exclaimed Edmund, as he left the room; "I see myself not only Earl of Gloster, but Duke of Cornwall; perchance, if fortune holds, King of England."

So saying, he followed the duke to where the two sisters were.

Servants were instantly despatched to the Duke of Albany, acquainting him with the plot.

"And now," said Cornwall, "what shall we do with that traitor Gloster?"

"Hang him," shrieked Goneril.

"Pluck out his eyes," hissed Regan.

"Leave him to me. Edmund, keep you our sister company. It is not fit that you should see the justice I am about to execute upon your father."

Edmund was only too glad of an opportunity of getting away, more especially as he was to accompany Goneril, who had shown great partiality to him.

Edmund had scarcely left the castle ere his father was brought in, pinioned.

"What means your grace?" exclaimed Gloster.

"Filthy traitor!" exclaimed the vixen Regan, and tore out his beard.

"What letter is it you have from France?" asked the duke, striking him across the face.

"I have one that comes from one of neutral heart."

"Where is the king?"

"I have sent him to Dover."

"Wherefore to Dover?"

"Because I would not see thy cruel nails pluck out his poor old eyes. But I shall see winged vengeance overtake such unnatural children."

"That thou never shalt," cried the Duke of Cornwall, with a fearful oath. "Fellows, hold the chair. Upon these eyes of thine I'll set my foot."

Scarcely were the words out of his mouth ere he tore out his right eye.

"The other too," cried the Hecate Regan. "One side will mock the other."

And inserting her long nails, she drew out the quivering orb, and stamped upon it.

"You villain!" exclaimed one of the servants.

The duke with a fierce oath rushed at him.

But the servant caught his point on his rapier, and thrust his sword into the duke's body.

His triumph was, however, a short one, for Regan, the she fiend, caught up a sword, and plunged it into his bowels.

Fainting from loss of blood, Regan led her husband out; but he expired ere he reached the hall.

This only gratified her the more, for she now saw her way clear to marry Edmund.

As for the poor Earl of Gloster, the servants had pity on him, and leading him to the gate of the castle, bade him find his way to Dover if he could get any one to lead him.

He had not gone very far ere his son Edgar came up with him, and volunteered to lead him to Dover.

The poor duke, still thinking it was Mad Tom, offered him all the money he was possessed of if he would lead him to a high cliff, whence he might leap and kill himself.

This Edgar pretended to do, but in reality kept him from his purpose day after day until they arrived near Dover.

Then he led him to a little hill not above a foot high, and bade him jump.

The earl only fell a few feet, and Edgar hastened to run and pick him up, asking, in his natural voice, how he came to tumble from such a height.

The earl replied that he was a mad fellow—that he was so full of despair, he resolved to commit suicide.

Then Edgar told him his life had been miraculously preserved, and that it was the fiend who had tempted him to commit suicide.

Upon this the stout old earl endeavoured to forget his misery, and bear himself like a man.

While they were thus conversing, the old King Lear entered, quite mad, and dressed up fantastically with flowers.

The earl recognised him by the sound of his voice.

While they were talking, both bewailing their misfortunes, one of Cordelia's gentlemen-at-arms came searching for the king; but Lear, being quite mad, thought that he meant to take him prisoner, and ran away.

In the meanwhile, several people crossed the country, and informed the fugitives that a great battle was pending, as the Duke of Albany and Edmund, Earl of Gloster, who was acting in the place of the dead Duke of Cornwall, were advancing, in battle array, against Cordelia, who had come over with her husband from France to help her father be revenged on his two unnatural daughters, Regan and Goneril.

Edgar and the old earl made up their minds to go to Cordelia's camp, when the steward of Goneril entered.

He had been in pursuit of the old Earl of Gloster, having received orders from Edmund to despatch him.

"That eyeless head," he cried, "was first framed to raise my fortunes! Thou old unhappy traitor! Briefly the sword is out that must destroy thee!"

"Now let thy friendly hand put strength into the blow!" cried the earl.

"By no means!" cried Edgar. "Take yourself, wretch! or it will be the worse for thee!"

"Out, you slave!" cried the steward, whipping out his sword.

But ere he could use it effectually, Edgar hit him on the head with his cudgel, wounding him to the death.

"Slave!" cried the steward, "thou hast slain me! Give the letters, which thou wilt find upon me, to Edmund, Earl of Gloster, who is with the British forces."

So saying, he expired, and Edgar took the following letter out of his pocket, which was from Goneril to Edmund—

"DEAR EDMUND,—Let our reciprocal vows be remembered. You have many opportunities of secretly killing my husband, the Duke of Albany. There is nothing done if he return a conqueror of the French—then I can never be yours. Your wife, I would say, and

"Yours affectionately,

"GONERIL."

"A plot upon her husband's life!" exclaimed Edgar, "and the exchange, my brother!—my dastard brother? Come, father—a battle approaches! I will bestow you with a friend, and then to show the world what wronged Edgar can do!"

CHAPTER VIII.

EDMUND found his position an extremely embarrassing one. Both sisters were in love with him.

When he arrived at Goneril's castle, she sent him back to Regan, so that her husband should not suspect anything.

But in the meanwhile, the Duke of Albany had heard about the treachery practised upon the old Earl of Gloster and King Lear.

The Duke of Albany collected his forces to act in unison with Regan and Edmund against the invasion of the

King of France; and meanwhile, Goneril sent that letter to Edmund with which the reader is acquainted.

But it was never destined to reach him, for the crafty steward disclosed its purpose to Regan, and she sent Edmund another letter, in which she informed him that she was a widow.

On the fourth day after that both forces joined to offer battle to the forces of Cordelia.

And now the eventful day draws on apace.

CHAPTER IX.

THE gentleman sent in search of Mad King Lear had not much difficulty in overtaking him, and in spite of protestation, they took him before Cordelia, who was overwhelmed with grief at the sad spectacle her father presented.

She had him conveyed to a chamber, where they gave him a sleeping potion, and then she left orders that when he woke the whole court should assemble to do him homage.

For four hours the exhausted king slept, and when he gave signs of waking, the whole court assembled round his bed, with Queen Cordelia and the noble Earl of Kent at the head of the bed ready to support him.

"How does my royal lord?" asked Cordelia, twining her arms about his neck as he woke up.

"Where have I been? Where am I?" cried the king, and then attempted to kneel before his daughter Cordelia.

But she prevented him and invoked his blessing.

It was a long time before the king could be brought to believe that Cordelia was not mocking him, as he maintained that she had grounds for ill-treating him, whereas the others had not, but he is finally convinced, and is overwhelmed with joy and gratitude.

Meanwhile, though on the eve of battle, the British forces did nothing but quarrel amongst themselves, the two sisters each intriguing as to who should have Edmund for a husband.

They were going to a council of war, in the Duke of Albany's tent when Edgar, disguised as a beggar, entered the camp.

"Your grace," he said. "Before you fight this battle open this letter. If you have victory, let the trumpet sound for him that brought it. Wretched though I seem, I can produce a champion who will avouch for the truth of everything that is there written."

So saying, he bowed and withdrew, leaving the letter revealing the plot against the Duke of Albany.

The following day the two forces met in a general action, and thanks to the superior generalship of the Duke of Albany, the French forces were routed, and King Lear and Cordelia taken prisoners.

As they went away to Derward Castle, closely guarded, Edmund called a captain to him and gave him a note which contained secret instructions that the king and Cordelia should be put to death.

Hardly had he done so when the Duke of Albany entered, and inquired for the captives.

Edmund answered him saucily that he was as good as he, and that he did not choose to give up the king.

The Duke of Albany disputed the fact, but his wife and sister-in-law both clamoured who should give Edmund the most power.

Suddenly in a terrible voice the Duke of Albany cried out—

"Edmund, I arrest thee on capital treason; and in thine attaint this gilded serpent—pointing to Goneril his wife—for your claim, fair sister, I bar it in the interest of my wife. 'Tis she is subcontracted to this lord, and I, her husband, contradicted your bans. Thou art armed, Gloster. Let the trumpet sound; if none appear to prove it upon thy person, there is my gauge. I'll prove it on thy heart that thou art traitor!"

"There is my gauge," cried Edmund. "He that names me traitor, lies."

"A herald! A herald!" cried the Duke of Albany.

And immediately one came forward, and after sounding the trumpet, read as follows—

"If any man of quality or degree within the lists of the army, will maintain upon

Edmund, supposed Earl of Gloster, that he is a manifold traitor, let him appear at the third sound of the trumpet."

CHAPTER X.

HARDLY had the sound of the trumpets died away when, spurring down the lines of brilliant corselets, came a young knight in black armour.

A shout of pity, not unmixed with admiration arose for him as he came along making his splendid charger curvet, and prance and demi-vault.

"Alas!" cried several, "'tis a noble-looking youth, but he is too slender and frail to fight against such a champion as Edmund."

By this time the heralds and pursuivants were busy, and had hastily cleared the improvised lists.

Riding slowly up, the unknown knight came opposite the Duke of Albany, and cried, in a loud voice—

"What's he that speaks for Edmund, Earl of Gloster?"

"Himself," cried Edmund.

"Draw thy sword," cried Edgar; "that, if my speech offend a noble heart, thy arm may do thee justice. Thou art a traitor, false to thy gods, thy brother and thy father; conspirant against this high and illustrious prince. And from the extremest upward of thy head to the dust beneath thy feet, thou art a most toad-spotted traitor. Sayest thou no, this arm and sword are bent to prove it on thy heart, thou liest."

"I should in wisdom ask thy name," said Edmund, "but since thine outside looks so fair and warlike, and thy tongue speaks of breeding, I scorn to delay answering thee. Back on thy head I fling thy challenge."

Desperate was the combat that ensued between Edmund and his unknown challenger.

Though broad and sinewy-limbed, the disproportion did not seem so great after a little bit as it at first appeared, for the unknown knight made up by skill and adroitness with his weapon what he lacked in mere brute strength.

At length, after a fierce combat, Edmund's foot slipped, and in an instant the nimble blade of his unknown antagonist pierced through the joints of his armour and stretched him on the ground.

"Save him! save him!" cried the Duke of Albany.

"You are not bound to fight any more, Gloster," cried Goneril. "Haste away from the field while you have yet life."

"Hold your tongue, dame," cried the duke, "or with this letter I'll stop it. Do you recognise your own handwriting?"

Goneril made a snatch at it which was ineffectual, and in her rage she fled from their presence.

"What you have charged me with that have I done, and more, much more. The time will bring it out. 'Tis past, and so am I. But who art thou that hast this fortune on me? If thou art noble I do forgive thee."

"Let us exchange charity," returned Edgar the champion. "I am no less in in blood than thou art, Edmund. My name is Edgar, and thy father's son. The gods are just, and of our pleasant vices make instruments to scourge us."

"Thou hast spoken right. The wheel has come full circle. I am here."

"Methought thy very gait did prophesy a royal nobleness, Edgar," said the Duke of Albany. "Let me embrace thee."

At this moment a gentleman came in hastily, crying—

"Help! help!"

"Why, what further misery is the matter? asked the Duke of Albany.

"Your lady, your grace, the noble Goneril, has slain herself, having previously poisoned her sister."

"Oh, most horrible!" cried the duke.

"I was contracted to them both," cried Edmund, "and now all is over. Stay! Some good I may do yet ere I am sped. Quickly send to the castle, for my writ is on the life of King Lear and Cordelia."

But even as he spoke the dead march was sounded, and King Lear entered, bearing the dead body of Cordelia in his arms.

"Howl, howl, howl!" cried the king, in accents of frantic grief. "Had I your tongues and eyes I'd use them so that the heaven's vault should crack. Oh, she is gone for ever! I know when one is dead,

and she is dead as earth. Lend me a looking-glass. If that her breath will mist or stain the glass, why then she will live."

"Oh, my good master," cried the good old Kent, overwhelmed with grief, "she is dead!"

"Go away," cried the king; "away, and leave me alone with her."

"'Tis noble Kent, your friend," cried Edgar.

"A plague upon you, murderers, traitors, all!" cried the king, in a paroxysm of grief. "I might have saved her; now she has gone. Cordelia, Cordelia, stay a little. Her voice was ever gentle and low. Cordelia, I killed the slave that was hanging thee. Who are you?" he demanded, turning to Kent. "Are you not Kent?"

"Your servant, Kent, and also, dear master, your servant, Caius."

"Ah!" said the king, "Kent was a traitor, but Caius was a good servant. He'd strike, and quickly, too; but now he is dead and rotten."

"No, my good lord," cried Kent. "I am the very man that, disguised, have followed your fortunes."

The old king's eyes gradually grew dark and glazed.

It was evident that he did not know what was passing round him.

A gentleman came in upon their grief to inform Edgar that his brother Edmund was dead.

"Know all of you present," said the Duke of Albany, "that during the life of his Majesty King Lear, we resign back to him the power we gained through his daughter Goneril. Would that we had

never attained it. You, my noble Edgar, and you, my noble Kent, have more than merited additions to your high honours. Should he die, you and old Kent here will rule this realm between you."

"Alas, your grace," said Kent, "I want not the honours you would force upon me. I have a long journey to go upon."

"A long journey?"

"Yes. See, my master dies, and I must follow him ere long. Let Edgar take the power."

It was true.

Amidst the silence which prevailed—a silence only broken by the low sobs of the noble Kent—the poor old King Lear was gasping out his life over the dead body of his daughter Cordelia.

He died of a broken heart, holding her corpse in his hand to the last.

The King of France, who had been detained in France prior to the battle in which the French forces were defeated, arrived with an overwhelming force to avenge the death of his wife.

But he found all who were implicated in her death either slain or banished the kingdom.

By his consent Edgar was raised to the supreme rule as King of Britain, and a treaty was made between France and England.

The Earl of Kent scarcely survived the loss of his beloved master a month ere he followed him to the grave, and the Duke of Albany ended his days in a monastery.

Thus ended the melancholy story of King Lear, the moral of which is that we should not always believe in those who make the loudest protestations of affection.

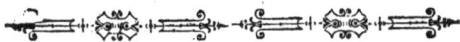

NOTICE.—"AS YOU LIKE IT," being No. 9 of Stories from Shakespeare, will be ready on Monday, January 2. Orders should be given early to your Booksellers.

EDWIN J. BRETTS STORIES OF SHAKESPEARE

COMPLETE

AS YOU LIKE IT.

THE BANISHED DUKE HOLDING COURT IN THE FOREST.

"Boys of England Edition."

EDWIN J. BRETT'S

STORIES FROM

SHAKESPEARE'S PLAYS.

No. 9.—AS YOU LIKE IT.

PART I.

BANISHED FROM COURT.

TOWARDS the end of the fifteenth century, there lived a certain duke, one of those powerful nobles who, while owning allegiance to the King of France, were like absolute sovereigns within their own domains, and kept court with scarcely less splendour than the king himself.

This duke was mild and humane, but not resolute enough for a ruler in those troublous times. He got into political difficulties, and his younger brother, Frederick, who was unscrupulous and ambitious, secretly plotted his downfall.

By much intriguing Frederick at length got his brother deposed, and usurped his title and authority.

The elder duke was banished, and forbidden to come within twenty miles of the capital under pain of death ; so he took up his residence in the forest of Arden, a large, wooded, and mountainous region to the north of France.

But it is not of the duke we have to speak at present, but of a young gentleman in his former dominions, who had also been badly treated by his brother.

A certain Sir Roland de Bois had recently died, leaving three sons. The eldest, Oliver, took all the estates; the next, Jaques, was sent to college, the third, Orlando, a youth of much promise, was kept at home in inglorious idleness by his elder brother and guardian.

It was of this treatment that young Orlando complained to Adam, an old and confidential servant of the family, who had known all the brothers from their infancy.

Adam and Orlando were in the garden of Oliver de Bois' mansion, when the young man thus confided his troubles to the aged retainer.

"Yes, Adam," he said, " I am discontented with my lot, and truly I have reason to be. Why am I, the son of the rich Sir Roland de Bois, thus kept in poverty and obscurity, while my brother Oliver has all this large estate? It is true he is the eldest, but by my father's will he was bound to make me a fair allowance, and bring me up as a gentleman, instead of which he allows me nothing, neglects my education, and treats me no better than a peasant or servant. I tell you, Adam, I will not endure it."

"Hush, Master Orlando," exclaimed the old man, " for here he comes !"

Oliver de Bois was some ten years older than Orlando, and there was some family likeness between them, but Oliver was taller and more set in figure, his dress was richer and his demeanour more haughty than was the case with Orlando.

"Stand aside, good Adam," said the latter to the old man, " and notice how my brother will treat me."

On seeing the youth, Oliver stopped

short, eyed him from head to foot, and said sternly—

"Well, sir, what do you do here?"

"Nothing," answered Orlando sullenly, "and that is all I am permitted to do."

"What do you mean, sir?" said Oliver.

"Shall I be like the prodigal son, and keep your hogs for you, and live on their husks?" asked the younger brother in bitter mockery; "that is all you seem to think I am fit for."

"Do you know where you are, sir, and to whom you are speaking?" asked Oliver angrily.

"Oh, perfectly well; I am in your garden, and I am speaking to one who is my brother, though he doesn't treat me like one. Ah!" he added, "my wrongs rise within me, and I burn for revenge!" and with both hands he seized the throat of his brother.

"Will you lay hands on me, villain?" exclaimed Oliver, dismayed at this sudden attack.

"Dare you call me a villain?" retorted the other. "If you were not my brother I would not take my hands from your throat until I had torn out your tongue for saying so."

Adam now rushed between the contending brothers, exclaiming—

"Oh, my good masters, I entreat you be patient. For the sake of your dead father's memory, do not quarrel like this!"

"Let me go, I say," cried Oliver, struggling.

"Not till you have heard me," replied the young man. "My father charged you in his will to give me a good education; you have trained me like a peasant, with no gentlemanlike accomplishments, and mewed me up in this life of obscurity. I am weary of it and will bear it no longer. Give me the thousand crowns my father left me, and I will go and seek my fortunes."

"And where will you find them, rash boy?" asked the senior brother scornfully. "What will you do when your money is spent? Beg, I suppose. Well, sir, get you in, I will not long be troubled with you. You shall have part of your money at least. I shall be only too well quit of my bargain. And as for you," he added, turning to Adam, "as you evidently take part with this young scapegrace, and have probably set him on against me, you may just go with him, and shift as you can."

"And is this how I am treated in my old age," cried Adam, uplifting his hands, "dismissed without warning after a life spent in the services of the family? Ah, my old master, Sir Roland, would never have behaved to me like this."

"Presumptuous varlets, they shall suffer for this!" said Oliver, as Orlando and the old man Adam went into the house. "But here comes Charles the Wrestler."

A man of tall stature and herculean build, in aspect and garb like a bluff peasant, now approached.

This was Charles, the famous Norman wrestler in the duke's service, and said to be the strongest man in the whole country.

"How now, Monsieur Charles? What news from court?" asked Oliver.

"So please you, Master Oliver, no news at all. The old duke has gone into banishment, the new duke reigns in his stead."

"And what has become of the old one?" asked Oliver.

"Gone to live in the forest of Arden, sir, he and a few of his faithful nobles; they mean to live there like Robin Hood and his merry men did in England."

"And is his daughter Rosalind banished with him?"

"Oh, no; for her cousin, Lady Celia, loves her too much to part with her, so she still remains at court."

"I hear, Monsieur Charles, that you wrestle before the duke to-morrow."

"Just so, your honour; and that is why I came to speak with you. I understand that your younger brother, Master Orlando, prides himself on his wrestling, and has a mind to try conclusions with me. Why, sir," added the athlete, stretching out his brawny arm, "I could double up such a stripling like a lath."

"I'm quite sure you could," acquiesced Oliver; "and to tell you the truth I'd just as soon you broke his neck as his little finger. I tell you, Charles, this youth is the stubbornest fellow in all France, and a perpetual plague to me. I would give something to be quit of him; and remember too, if you only injure him without settling him altogether, he will be sure to plan some deadly vengeance, and never rest till he has had your life."

"Thanks for your hints, sir," replied the Hercules, "I'm glad I came to you. Now I know what to expect, our young hero shall find his match to-morrow, and if he

is able to get about after the lesson I shall give him, I'll never call myself a wrestler any more, that is all. Good-bye, your worship."

And with a bow the burly Norman departed.

The wrestling match was to take place upon the broad lawn in front of the duke's palace.

About an hour before the time appointed for it, and when none of the company had as yet assembled, two young ladies emerged from the palace and walked round the lawn in close conversation.

Both were richly clad, and their aspect denoted high rank.

The elder was tall and fair, with long wavy golden hair falling from her shoulders.

This was Rosalind, daughter of the banished duke.

Her companion was a brunette, smaller in stature, and with brilliant dark eyes.

This was Celia, the daughter of the reigning Duke Frederick.

"Why do you look so sad, my dear Rosalind ?" asked Celia.

"Have I not cause," replied Rosalind, "when my poor father is deposed and in exile ?"

"True, sweet cousin ; but your grief shows you do not love me as I do you. Had my case been yours, I would try to forget my woes, and be merry for your sake. It is true my father has usurped the dominion of yours, but I am his only child, and when he dies, I will make amends by giving up my rights to you. Therefore, my dearest Rose, be merry."

"I will try, coz, for your sake," returned Rosalind. "Let us think of some amusing sport. What say you to falling in love ?"

"'Tis too dangerous a pastime," answered Celia ; "but look, here is friend Touchstone ; he is the one to devise sport and mirth."

Touchstone was the duke's favourite fool or jester, a man of grave features, but with a merry twinkle in his eyes.

He was clad in motley or parti-coloured garments of fantastic cut, with a hood decorated with imitation donkey's ears, and in his hand a bauble, or short staff, with a comical head carved on the top.

There were little bells all over his attire which jingled as he walked.

Touchstone, in his quaint language and with many puns and jests, informed the ladies that they would soon have sport enough, for the great wrestling match was to come off immediately at this very place.

"Shall we stay and see this wrestling, cousin ?" asked Rosalind.

"Oh, yes, I should like it above all things," was the reply.

The garden soon echoed with a flourish of trumpets, and the duke, with several of his nobles and attendants, essayed from the palace.

In the centre of the group, giving himself all the airs of the victor of the day, was the strong man, Charles the Norman.

He might well be confident, for he had of late won many glorious victories.

Behind, and bearing himself much more modestly, came the young Orlando de Bois.

Both were in close fitting attire, convenient for the struggle.

"What, is this the man ?" exclaimed Rosalind.

"He looks far too young and slight to cope with Charles !" observed Celia.

"How now, girls ?" said Duke Frederick, approaching ; "must you also see the wrestling ? Well, be it so ; but there will not be much sport in it, the combatants are too unequally matched. The victory is certain from the start. I told this young man he would stand no chance with Charles, but he is obstinate ; see if you can dissuade him."

Orlando was introduced to the ladies, and in spite of his rustic education and homely garb, the first impression he produced was favourable.

"And so, young man," said Rosalind, "you have challenged Charles the Wrestler ?"

"Pardon me, madam, I did not challenge him ; but as he professes to stand against all comers, I have come to try my strength.

"Young gentleman," said Celia, "your courage is evidently beyond your years ; you have seen what this man can do. You have no chance with him ; therefore, I pray you, give up the attempt."

Rosalind added her entreaties, but nothing could prevail with Orlando.

"I grieve to deny you anything, ladies," he said, "but I have sworn to engage in this struggle. If I succeed, so much the better ; if I fall, I have few or no friends to lament my loss."

"If it must be so, farewell," sighed Rosalind.

"We wish you success," added Celia.

"Now," said Charles, placing himself in the centre of the lawn, "where is this young gallant who is so anxious to be levelled with mother earth?"

"Only one struggle, mind," said the duke.

"No, your grace, he shall find one quite enough for him," said Charles, with an insolent laugh.

In a moment the two combatants were engaged in a deadly struggle.

Though apparently so unequally matched, Charles soon found the youth a tougher antagonist than he had expected. If he had not so much strength and weight, he was yet more muscular than he looked. He had more agility and evident skill in all the science of wrestling.

Charles tried in vain to throw him.

All the spectators watched the contest with breathless interest.

Rosalind and Celia inwardly prayed for the success of Orlando, though without much hope of it; and indeed the bravery of the young man had now impressed a majority in his favour.

The gigantic Charles, who had counted on an easy victory, was so taken aback by this unexpected resistance that his usual skill deserted him, and all his vast strength seemed brought to naught by the skill and agility of Orlando.

At last, a feint on the part of the latter caused Charles to make a false move, whereof his foe at once took advantage.

The burly Norman fell heavily to the earth.

The spectators applauded loudly, but the duke absolutely commanded that the struggle should not be resumed.

"Fear not on my account, your grace," said Orlando, as he now stood over his fallen foe; "I have yet breath left for another bout."

"How fares it with you, Charles?" asked Duke Frederick, bending over the fallen Hercules.

But Charles answered not.

The heavy fall had stunned him, and he lay quite insensible.

"Carry him away, and see him attended by our physician," said the duke. "Young man," he said to Orlando, while this last command was being obeyed, "you have won a surprising victory. What is your name?"

"I am Orlando, my liege, youngest son of Sir Roland de Bois."

"I wish you had been the son of somebody else," said the duke. "The world esteemed Sir Roland, but he was one of my enemies, and so I bear no friendship to your family. But farewell; you are a gallant youth, and deserve a better father."

With this the duke and his attendants returned to the house.

"Better father, eh?" muttered Orlando bitterly. "Why, I am more proud to be Sir Roland's youngest son than I should be heir to a usurping duke."

"He is offended," whispered Rosalind to her cousin. "My father would not thus have treated the son of Sir Roland, who was his friend."

"I grieve that my father treated him thus abruptly," replied Celia. "Sir," she added, to Orlando, "you have acquitted yourself in a manner deserving of all praise."

"And of reward also," added Rosalind. "Young gentleman, I am not rich now, but if you will accept this slight token of our appreciation of your bravery——"

With this, she unclasped a slender gold chain from her neck, and gave it to Orlando.

He stood confused at this unexpected acknowledgment from one whose beauty and sympathetic manner had from the first made a deep impression upon him.

He could not find words to express his thanks, and could only bow respectfully as the ladies passed on.

"Why do I feel thus?" said Orlando, to himself. "Why am I so tongue-tied in her presence? Let me beware, or I shall soon be overcome by that rosy god, who, though so little, is far stronger than Charles the Wrestler."

At this moment one of the duke's nobles approached.

"Good sir," he said, "allow me to give you some friendly advice. The duke is of an uncertain temper, and though you deserve applause and reward, he has a prejudice against you. He is also displeased with his niece, who appears to take some interest in you. Altogether, it will be better for you to quit this place as soon as possible."

"I thank you for your advice," replied the young man, "and will not fail to act upon it. What with a tyrant duke and a tyrant brother," said Orlando to himself, as the other bowed himself out, "this place will grow intolerable to me. But, oh, this heavenly Rosalind!"

And he fell into a romantic reverie.

The Lady Rosalind was no less smitten with Orlando, a fact observed by her lively cousin, Celia, who rallied her upon it.

"Is it possible, cousin," she said, when they were alone together, "that you should so suddenly fall in love with old Sir Roland's youngest son?"

"The duke, my father, loved his father dearly," said Rosalind.

"But that is no reason why you should love his son dearly," answered Celia; "for by that rule, I should hate him, because my father hated his father. Yet I do not hate him."

"No, cousin; please do not hate him, for my sake. Let me love him for having done well, and you must love him because I do. Look, here comes the duke."

"He is angry," said Celia, in alarm.

Duke Frederick, with a stern expression, entered with several noblemen, and approached the young ladies.

"Now, madam," he said abruptly to Rosalind, "I command you instantly to leave our court."

"Me, uncle?" exclaimed Rosalind.

"Yes, you. If within ten days you are found within twenty miles of my court, you die the death!"

"But I beseech your grace," pleaded Rosalind, "what have I done to offend you?"

"No matter; I have sufficient reasons. You are your father's daughter; that's enough. Go and join him if you will, but do not stay here to plot against me. My command is given; obey it."

It was in vain that Rosalind entreated; and her friend Celia interposed in her favour, and declared that if Rosalind must be banished she must go also, for she could not live away from her.

The duke resolutely repeated his commands and departed.

Thereupon the two cousins came to the conclusion that they would run away together.

"But where shall we go?" asked Rosalind.

"To join my uncle in the forest of Arden," answered Celia.

"Think of the dangers of the journey," said Rosalind. "Two females alone and unprotected."

"We will assume poor attire as peasant girls," suggested Celia.

"You may, cousin," assented Rosalind,

"but I know of a better plan with regard to myself. As I am tall and resolute, I will dress myself as a man, and you can go under my protection."

"Excellent, excellent!" exclaimed Celia. "But what shall I call you when you are there?"

"Ganymede would be a good name," was the reply.

"And I will be Aliena," said her companion. "We will be a shepherd and shepherdess. It will be rare sport."

"Agreed!" said Rosalind. "Let us get all our wealth together, and see about our disguises. Then hey! for the forest of Arden!"

Early the next morning they both left the palace secretly.

Though the duke was glad to get rid of his niece, Rosalind, he was concerned when it was discovered that his daughter Celia had really accompanied her.

Nor were these the only fugitives.

Orlando was also missing, and from the interest the young ladies had taken in him, it was believed he was now in their company.

And the whimsical jester, Touchstone, was likewise suddenly absent.

The duke was annoyed at these desertions, and ordered strict search to be made for the runaways.

The faithful old servant Adam discovered that Oliver de Bois had become so envious and inimical to his brother that he was plotting his destruction.

Full of anxiety Adam told this to Orlando, who resolved to escape at once.

But where?

That was the question.

He had no friends elsewhere, and no money, his unjust brother withholding from him even the one thousand crowns.

"Fear not, young master," said Adam; "I have saved some money—five hundred crowns—and you are welcome to it all. Let me still be your servant. Though I am old, yet I am as strong as many a younger one."

"Oh, generous old man, how can I thank thee?" exclaimed Orlando, much affected. "Come, then, with me, and if ever it is in my power, I will amply reward thee. We shall surely find somewhere a new means of living."

"Master, go on, and I will follow thee to the last gasp," answered Adam. "Farewell, old home, where I have dwelt from seventeen years old to nigh four score, and even if the worst comes, I but die in the service of the family."

PART II.

IN THE FOREST.

BEAUTEOUS was the summer time in the forest of Arden, whose leafy glades were now in full luxuriance.

Every tree wore its richest garb of green ; the turf beneath the feet was like a verdant velvet carpet, besprinkled with flowers ; sweetly murmured the rippling brooks, merrily sang the birds ; and oft in the distance glimpses of dappled deer and snow-white sheep could be discerned.

It was amid these bewitching and sylvan scenes that the banished duke and his faithful friends were now living.

They dressed as foresters of the olden time.

Their food was obtained in the woods and from the neighbouring farms.

They passed most of the days in the open air, and rested at night in a rustic mansion which the duke had made into a hunting-lodge.

"Is not this existence sweeter, my friends, than the painted pomp and empty glories of courts and cities?" the duke was wont to say, as he looked around him. "Here we have no anxieties, no formalities, no cares ; and but for being separated from my daughter and some of my old friends, methinks I have gained happiness by losing a crown."

The nobles and gentlemen with him and their attendants made but a small party—a great contrast to the large train the duke formerly had around him.

The principal of his exiled friends were named Amiens and Jaques—the latter celebrated for his musing and melancholy temperament ; and they all, like their patron, enjoyed this life of sylvan seclusion.

A splendid sunset was flooding the forest with a golden and crimson radiance, and the party were assembled around a primitive table, placed beneath a huge oak tree.

The repast consisted principally of venison and other game, all shot by the exiles during the morning's hunt, and there were fruits, vegetables and bread, wine and ale supplied by the shepherds and farmers of the district.

Yet the party were as merry and as well prepared to do justice to these viands as if the duke had been feasting in his gilded palace upon all the delicacies French cooks could produce.

"Now, my friends, all is ready," said the duke ; "we are waiting only for Monsieur Jaques. Can he have lost himself in the forest?"

"No, my lord, he was here not long ago," said one of the others. "I will go and seek him. But stay, he saves me the trouble, for I see him coming."

The melancholy gentleman, who was tall and thin, and clad in sombre-coloured attire, was just now unusually merry, as if he had just seen something that had mightily amused him.

"A fool, a fool !" he exclaimed. "I met a fool in the forest, a motley fool—a varlet clad in all the colours of the rainbow, who talked and talked such a mixture of folly and philosophy that I was infinitely diverted at him. He would be a treasure to you here, my lord."

"What fool was this?" asked the duke.

"A worthy fool," replied Jaques. "One who had been at court, and had travelled and knew the world, and jested so like earnest, and talked seriously so like jesting that I was e'en charmed with his humour. I think his profession would suit me exactly. I long to be a motley fool, too, and wear cap and bells like him."

The others laughed at the idea of the melancholy Jaques clad in the garb of a merry-andrew.

So Jaques, his head still full of the jests he had so recently heard from our friend Touchstone, now a fugitive in the forest, took his seat at the table, and the banquet was about to begin when something happened again to defer it.

Orlando, his sword drawn, and his aspect wild and disordered, rushed suddenly upon the party, exclaiming—

"Forbear, and eat no more !"

"Eat no more?" exclaimed Jaques. "Why, I have eaten none yet !"

"Who is this that so rudely disturbs our repast?" asked the duke.

"This is no time for formalities," exclaimed Orlando ; "I say, who ever begins eating until he has heard me shall die by this sword !"

"I think I shall eat some and take my chance," quoth Jaques.

"You would do better, sir," said the duke to the intruder, "to accost us civilly, and not with this violence."

Orlando replied—

"I almost die for food, so let me have it!"

"Sit down and feed, and welcome to our table," said the duke, more kindly.

"Pardon me this violence," said Orlando, dropping his sword, "but I am desperate. My lord, it is true that I am faint with hunger, yet I speak not on my own account. There is a poor old man, a faithful servant, who has followed me in my wanderings till he is half dead with exhaustion. It is for him I speak."

"Go, find him out," said the duke, "and bring him here."

"I thank and bless you!" answered Orlando, who then disappeared.

"You see, friends," said the duke, "we are not the only exiled wanderers in the wood. Here are those who are worse off than ourselves. Thus it must be in the theatre of life."

"Yes," said Jaques, "all the world's a stage, and all the men and women merely players. One man in his time plays many parts, and it is often tragedy as comedy."

Orlando came in, supporting the fainting weight of old Adam, who indeed looked in the last stage of exhaustion; these long wanderings and hardships had been too much for the man of eighty years.

"Welcome, friends," said the duke, as Orlando deposited his venerable companion on a seat, "heartily welcome to our banquet."

"I thank you most for him," replied Orlando.

"So you had need," said Adam faintly,

"'AH, MY OLD MASTER, SIR ROLAND, WOULD NEVER HAVE BEHAVED THUS TO ME,' SAID ADAM."

"for I have hardly strength to thank him myself."

"Fall to, then," said the duke, "and during the banquet let us have some music and a song."

The minstrels struck up, and Amiens, who was noted for his vocal powers, sang—

"Blow, blow, thou winter wind!"

the others joining in the chorus.

After the repast, the duke took Orlando aside, and told him that for his father—Sir Roland's—sake, he would gladly receive him and his aged retainer as members of their forest band.

Shortly before this arrival, in another part of the forest, three weary wanderers, almost as exhausted as Orlando and Adam, had reached an open space, and were looking around for shelter.

Touchstone the Jester wore his motley as before, but the other two could scarcely be recognised.

In appearance they were a rustic youth and a peasant girl.

The latter was a brunette, clad in a plain russet gown, only decorated with a few wild flowers. Upon her head was a wide-brimmed hat, similarly ornamented.

Her companion was also dark in complexion, and with eyebrows and short curls of jet black; a most dainty and prepossessing youth, attired somewhat like a forester.

In fact, it was the Lady Rosalind, who, with the aid of dye and other contrivances, added to her masculine attire, had thus transformed herself into Master Ganymede, while her cousin Celia had become Aliena the shepherdess.

"I can go no further. Oh, Jupiter, how weary are my spirits!" exclaimed

"' GO, SIR, AND FULFIL MY COMMANDS, OR YOU SHALL MEET MY HEAVIEST VENGEANCE,' SAID THE DUKE."

Celia, with a sigh, as she looked around at the scene.

"And how weary are my legs!" exclaimed the jester, seating himself on a grassy bank; "in truth, friends, it seems to me that none of us are fit for forest life. People must learn that, like all other trades, and I was never apprenticed to the art of walking twenty miles a day and sleeping out of doors at night."

"Ah!" said Rosalind, "and if I were not dressed like a man I should cry like a woman, I am so tired with this wandering. But cheer up, Aliena, and you too, Touchstone; remember you are no longer a court fool, but a forest yeoman."

"On the contrary, I feel I am a bigger fool than ever for coming to such a place as this. But look you, here comes some of the real forest folks; let us stand aside and observe them."

It was an old shepherd and a young one, the latter evidently in love, seeking

OLIVER DE BOIS.

advice from his senior as to his wooing.

But old Corin was scarcely competent to give counsel on this point.

So the youth soon left, sighing to himself—

"Oh, Phœbe, Phœbe!"

"Alas, poor shepherd!" exclaimed Rosalind; "he seems in an ecstasy of woe."

"Yes, lovers are strange creatures," observed Touchstone. "When I was in love I know I enjoyed being miserable above all things."

"I did not think a fool could fall in love," said Rosalind.

"Ay, but he can, and his doing so shows what a fool he must be," responded the jester.

Celia, who was in no mood for this lively converse, implored them to ask the old shepherd where they could get food and shelter.

Rosalind put the question to the rustic who answered respectfully—

" Young sir, I wish indeed I could aid you, but it is not in my power. I am but a poor shepherd, keeping sheep for a churlish master, who entertains no friends; besides, his house and property are now on sale, and as he is absent, there is nothing to eat in his dwelling."

" On sale !" said Rosalind; " ah, that is exactly what we want. We will buy this cottage and fields and flock of sheep, and live here as shepherds. Go, my good friend, and effect the purchase for us. We will make you our herdman."

" At increased wages," added Celia.

The old man was taken by surprise, but concluding Rosalind and Celia to be some young lord and lady, for some reason concealing themselves in the forest, he agreed to conduct them to the cottage.

The cottage suited Rosalind and Celia excellently, and by the aid of the old shepherd they were able to purchase it and its belongings on low terms.

They at once took up their abode there, passing as brother and sister.

Old Corin did all the rougher work.

Touchstone, who was not without a well-filled purse of his own, sometimes assisted, and the two ladies would watch the fleecy flock for hours, aided by Corin's old sheep dog, and enlivened by the songs of Celia, or the quips and cranks of Touchstone.

The pair enjoyed this primitive pastoral life very much, and felt that they could live thus in the forest all their lives.

As yet Rosalind had not met with her father, the exiled duke, for the forest was very large, and the two parties of wanderers knew naught of each other's whereabouts.

Orlando de Bois soon became one of the banished duke's intimates, but still he thought with bitterness of his unjust brother, who was in favour with the successful usurper, and who retained all the family estates.

Little, however, did Orlando think how soon retribution would come upon the unscrupulous Oliver.

Duke Frederick was highly displeased with Oliver's conduct.

" Sir," he said to him sternly, when De Bois was summoned to his presence, " I have heard of your injustice to your brother and of his disappearance. Go, find him out wherever he is, living or dead, within a twelvemonth from this time. If you do not you shall be exiled for ever, and all your estates confiscated."

" Your highness," stammered De Bois, taken aback by this; " I know my brother has offended you, but so far from taking his part, I always hated him."

" The more villain you !" exclaimed the despot. " Go, sir, and fulfil my commands, or you shall meet my heaviest vengeance."

So Oliver departed, much troubled, for he knew not where Orlando was, though he had an idea that he was a fugitive somewhere in the vast forest of Arden.

PART III.

ALL IN LOVE.

THE impression made upon Orlando by the Lady Rosalind had rather deepened with absence.

He longed to see her again, but feared he was parted from her for ever.

Wandering alone by moonlight, he reached an open space where he stood musing, and anon conned over a love-letter he had written in a poetical form.

" I will hang the verses on a tree here," he said, " and carve her beloved name upon the bark, that all passers-by may hear of her merits."

As luck would have it, Rosalind passed the spot the next day, and we may judge of her surprise at finding the freshly-carved name and the following effusion written upon a paper hanging on one of the boughs—

" From the east to western Ind,
No jewel is like Rosalind.
Her worth, when mounted on the wind,
Through the world bears Rosalind.
All the pictures, fairest lined,
Are but black to Rosalind.
Let no face be kept in mind,
But the face of Rosalind."

" A fine jogtrot rhyme, in sooth," said the jester. " I could keep on like that for years, meals and sleeping times excepted. Listen now—

" If a hart do lack a hind,
Let him seek out Rosalind.
If the cat is soft and kind,
So is gentle Rosalind.
Winter garments must be lined,
So must slender Rosalind.
They that reap, must sheaf and bind,
That's the work for Rosalind.
Sweetest nut hath sourest rind,
Such a nut is Rosalind.

" Peace, dull fool !" exclaimed the disguised lady. " I found this song on a tree."

" I never heard of verses growing on a tree before," remarked Touchstone. " It must be the tree of knowledge ; and here comes Madam Aliena, who has plucked some more fruit of the same kind."

Celia had indeed found another and still more impassioned poem nailed to a tree not far from the first.

From this it was pretty clear that Orlando de Bois was not far off ; at least so Celia thought, although, strange to say, her cousin did not at first suspect it.

" Do you know, coz, who has done this ?" she asked.

" I surmise it is a man," replied her lively cousin.

" Ay, but his name ?"

" Oh, wonderful ! As if you did not know without asking."

" Keep me not in suspense, but tell me," said Rosalind impatiently.

" Then I strongly suspect it is your Orlando—he who tripped up the wrestler and your own heart both at once."

" Orlando !" exclaimed Rosalind. " Ah, then you have seen him lately. When was it ? Where was it ? How did he look ? Did he inquire after me ? Where is he staying ?"

" I should need half-a-dozen tongues to answer so many questions," replied Celia.

" Alas !" cried Rosalind, " what shall I do with my doublet and hose ? Does he know that I am here in the forest disguised in man's attire ?"

" Perhaps," answered Celia. " And when I saw him last he was dressed as a forester, with bow and arrow. Cupid had also a bow and arrow ; you understand, cousin ? But soft, some one is coming."

" Heavens ! 'tis Orlando himself," ejaculated Rosalind. " Tis well, after all, that I am so disguised. He will not know me."

Orlando was not alone ; he was accompanied by the melancholy Jaques, with whom he had struck up a strange kind of friendship.

They bantered each other, and disagreed continually, but it was in a friendly way, for each recognised the merits of the other.

" I will now leave you, Monsieur Orlando," said Jaques, with mock ceremoniousness. " I thank you much for your company during the walk, although to tell the truth I would as lief have been by myself all the time."

" So would I," retorted Orlando, in the same tone, " and yet for fashion's sake, I thank you too for your society."

" Good-bye, then ; let us meet as little as we can."

" Certainly, sir. I hope we may be worse acquainted."

" I pray you," said Jaques, " not to damage any more of our trees by writing love songs on their barks."

" And I pray you, do not spoil any more of my verses by reading them so abominably."

" So Rosalind is your love's name," said the courtier. " In faith, I do not like the name."

" What a pity you were not consulted when she was christened !" exclaimed Orlando sarcastically.

" You are full of pretty answers," said Jaques.

" No more of this," said Orlando. " I am weary of you."

" By my troth," answered Jaques, " I was seeking for a fool when I found you."

" Oh, you want a fool ; go and look into the brook yonder—it is an excellent mirror."

" I will," answered Jaques ; " it will remind me of you. Farewell, Signor Love."

" Good-bye, Monsieur Melancholy," returned Orlando.

And with ceremonious bows they parted, each inwardly amused at the other's whimsical manner.

Orlando now saw approaching him a graceful youth in the dress of a forester.

Of course it was the disguised Rosalind.

Summoning up her courage she accosted Orlando as a stranger, and asked him the time.

" I can scarcely say ; there's no clock in the forest," he responded.

" Then," said Rosalind, " there can be no true lover in the forest, for lovers sigh regularly every minute and groan every hour, and they might tell the time by that."

" You are a smart youth," said Orlando, with a smile. " Where do you live ?"

" With this shepherdess, my sister, here on the skirts of the forest."

" Are you a native of this place ?"

" More or less," replied Rosalind.

" Your way of speaking is rather refined than rustic," observed Orlando, beginning to be interested in his young companion.

" Oh, yes," was the reply. " I was taught by my uncle, who was a learned man. But do you know there is some one haunting the forest spoiling our trees by carving ' Rosalind ' on the barks and hanging verses on the branches. I wish I could catch him."

" Supposing it was myself?" said Orlando.

" Impossible! You do not look sufficiently out of spirits for a lover."

" But I am one," protested Orlando. " I swear to you, fair youth, that I am the perpetrator of the poems."

" And are you as much in love as your rhymes make out?"

" More, more—beyond all rhyme and reason too !" exclaimed Orlando.

" Then I will undertake to cure you of that complaint," said Rosalind. " I'll tell you how. Suppose we pretend, for a few days, that you're in love with me, and that I, Master Ganymede, am the Lady Rosalind?"

" But you are not at all like her," answered Orlando. " She is fair—you are dark. She is taller than you appear, and moreover, she is many a mile away."

" No doubt ; but we are only pretending, you know. I will pretend to be Rosalind, and you can pretend to be in love with me, and I shall treat you in such a manner that you will soon be effectually cured of loving anybody."

" But I don't want to be cured," said Orlando. " However, I accept your proposal."

" Then you will come to see me every day ?" said the disguised lady.

" I will. Where is your house?"

" I will show you the way. Will you come now?"

" With all my heart, good youth."

" Nay, you must call me Rosalind. Come, sister, we will all go together."

The favour of the banished duke, and the friends he made among the nobles that surrounded him, much cheered Orlando de Bois in his exile.

But more than all, he was consoled by his growing acquaintance with his new friend, Master Ganymede.

Lady Rosalind, indeed, proved herself fascinating under every disguise; her lively waywardness and wit shone out in the character of the boy-wanderer.

At the same time she kept up the game of " pretending to be the Lady Rosalind," and plagued her adorer considerably by her wilful behaviour. Yet so well was she disguised, and so cleverly did she sustain this double character, that Orlando, who imagined the real Rosalind to be still with her uncle in the capital, did not suspect it was she to whom his mock addresses were being paid.

In short, they got on excellently together, and this augured well for the time when they might throw off all disguise, and confess their love.

But they were not the only couple who found life in the forest favourable for courtship.

The jester Touchstone, with his usual eccentricities and contempt for appearances, had found an honest and homely country wench, named Audrey, who tended a flock of goats in the forest, and whom he wooed in his quaint way.

She was beloved by a rustic named William, but he was no match in manners or knowledge for the court jester, who charmed the simple peasantess by his powers of speech, and she thought him the most wonderful man she had ever seen.

Stranger still, there was another rustic pair of lovers in the forest, Silvius and Phœbe, whose course of true love was disturbed by Rosalind.

Phœbe fell in love with Master Ganymede, an attachment which that young gentleman of course could not return.

This again shows the fascination the disguised Rosalind exercised on all who knew her.

Nor was her cousin, the lively Celia, long without an admirer, as we shall soon see.

But we have now to speak of the loves of those previously mentioned.

Audrey and Phœbe were both peasants— one a keeper of goats, and the other a shepherdess.

But there was a great difference between them.

Audrey was but an ignorant rustic, versed neither in books nor the fine manners of city life. She was homely in appearance, and awkward in demeanour.

Phœbe, on the other hand, had been more delicately nurtured ; she had been in service under a great lady of the court ; had learned to read, and had turned her reading to some account by perusing all the romantic stories and legends she could get hold of.

This had filled her mind with fanciful and ambitious ideas, and made her often dissatisfied with her humble position in life.

Moreover she was beautiful, with beauty of a more refined cast than could have been expected in a maiden of that rural community.

Her lover Silvius was also a youth of some education, and in all ways superior to William, the adorer of Audrey.

But when Master Ganymede came upon the scene, all the merits of Silvius seemed to Phœbe but poor in comparison.

Ganymede was altogether a being of a different order to any she had ever seen.

He realised all her ideals of the romantic and the poetic, and seemed less like a native of this every-day world than some fairy prince come from an enchanted and splendid region far away.

What other youth she had ever seen had such regular and clearly cut features, such purity of complexion, such a wealth of curled chestnut locks, such slenderness of form, and such grace and dignity of demeanour?

His voice, too, was melodious above all men's; his conversation so witty, sprightly, and yet at times tender and poetic, and his language one of great experience and cultivation of mind.

That he was something other than he appeared she was convinced.

Here, therefore, was a mystery—another powerful attraction; for Phœbe was fond of mysteries, and in all the legends and romances she had read were people who turned out to be somebody else greater than they were supposed to be.

Was it not probable that Master Ganymede was the youthful son of some rich lord, and would inherit wealth and a title?

If so, could Phœbe only secure his love, all her aspirations might ultimately be realised.

True, he was painfully cold towards her, but that, strange to say, only added fuel to the flame, and the difficulty of gaining his affection would only render it more precious when obtained at last.

Little did she deem that beneath this coy exterior beat a warm heart, overflowing with love—but, alas! it was for another, and not for the enamoured shepherdess.

Rosalind and Celia stood in front of their cottage; the former was silent and downcast, the latter had managed to preserve her usual high spirits.

"Never talk to me," sighed Rosalind. "I feel inclined to weep, and I will weep."

"Do so, by all means, good cousin; but please remember your new position, and that tears do not become a man."

"I care not; I am growing weary of this disguise, this constant and arduous sustaining of a part against my nature. I fear I shall one day betray myself in his presence, and then all will be over, for will he not hate me when he finds by what an unseemly device he was deceived?"

"I think not," responded Celia. "It strikes me, that, great as is his friendship for Master Ganymede, still greater would be his love for the Lady Rosalind should the metamorphosis take place."

"Do you think so?" asked Rosalind eagerly.

"Oh yes; I only think so," returned the provoking Celia, "for, my dear child, I want not to be too encouraging. After all, Monsieur Orlando may not bear love with you, but only, as you say, pretending."

"Ah! do not say that!" exclaimed Rosalind; "and yet his absence grieves and distresses me, and looks like an intentional slight. Why has he not come this morning as he promised?"

"Why, indeed," said Celia. "He swore he would come, but then lovers, it seems, will swear anything."

"Yesterday," said Rosalind, "I met the duke, my father, and had a long talk with him; of course, he had no suspicion whatever, so he asked me of what parentage I was. I answered 'Just as good as your own, my lord.' It was an impertinent speech from a poor forester to a nobleman, but he only laughed at my boldness, and let me go. But how can we talk of fathers when there is such a man as Orlando?"

"Oh yes, of course, Orlando is better than all the fathers in the world," acquiesced Celia; "but who comes here?"

It was the old shepherd, Corin.

"Good mistress and master," he said, "you have often inquired of the young shepherd Silvius, who is so deep in love with the proud, disdainful shepherdess Phœbe."

"Well, and what of him?" asked Celia.

"If you would like to see a little love scene well played," returned the old man, "come with me, and I will show you how the nymph and swain prosper with their wooing."

"Yes, let us go, by all means," said Rosalind. "I am rather interested in

love affairs just now, even other people's; besides, I may myself take part in their play."

Corin accordingly led the way to an opening in the forest, not far from the cottage.

Here they found Phœbe, the shepherdess, her crook in her hand, her fleecy flock grazing peacefully near, and at her feet knelt the gentle shepherd, Silvius, passionately urging his suit.

"Sweet Phœbe, do not scorn me," he pleaded; "if you really cannot find it in your heart to love me, tell me so, but not in bitterness. If you must strike death to all my hopes of happiness, be like the executioner, who shakes the hand and begs the pardon of his victim before raising the fatal axe."

Delightful as it was to the romantic mind of Phœbe to be addressed in this manner, she did not sufficiently consider the pain she was inflicting.

"I would not be your executioner," she said; "but since you say I have a killing glance, let it, at least, kill your misplaced affection; I can never be yours."

"Oh, why—why, dearest Phœbe, cruel that you are!" said the young shepherd, rising. "I see no pity in your eyes. May you, too, some day know what it is to feel the pangs of rejected love!"

Rosalind, Celia, and Corin, concealed behind a thick spreading bush, had watched this scene with much interest.

Rosalind now stepped forward and approached the lovers.

"I echo your wish," she said to Silvius. "May this proud and cruel maiden be punished for her pride and coldness, by being herself treated in the same manner."

Phœbe, who was much taken aback by the sudden appearance of the secretly-adored Ganymede, was too confused to speak.

"By what right do you scorn and insult an honest wooer?" said the supposed youth, turning to her angrily. "What, though you have beauty (although, let me tell you, not so much of it as you suppose), must you, therefore, be proud and pitiless? Why, what means this? Why do you thus gaze at me? Think not that I will fall in love with you, for all your black eyes and creamy cheeks. Foolish shepherd, why thus follow her? She is unworthy of you unless she at once fall on her knees, beg your pardon, and thank a bounteous Heaven for a good man's love."

"Oh!" exclaimed Phœbe, in raptures; "what beautiful language! Go on, sweet youth; I will listen for a year together. I would rather hear you chide than this man woo."

"I have naught for you but bitter words and frowning looks," said Rosalind. "Why do you look so upon me?"

"From no ill-will I bear you," answered the shepherdess in a softer voice. "It is, indeed, quite the reverse."

"I pray you do not fall in love with me," said Rosalind, "for I am false and wayward; besides, I like you not. Shepherdess, mark well my words. Shepherd, persuade her once more—until she be brought to reason. Farewell; my house stands yonder, if you need my advice. Come, sister, to our flocks."

This rebuff from Ganymede and the persuasions of Silvius was not without some effect upon Phœbe, although she would not all at once conquer her strange infatuation. But Silvius' hopes again revived.

Oliver de Bois, banished by Duke Frederick, was now feeling all the bitterness of disgrace.

He was bound to seek out his wronged brother, under pain of forfeiture of his estates, but it would be a hard task to find him, and humiliating to ask his forgiveness.

Oliver, however, bent his course towards the forest of Arden, but he was soon bewildered in its intricacies.

At length, weary with wandering, and faint with fasting, he came to a cave, where, after a scant repast of wild berries and a draught of water from a brook, he sat and rested till he fell asleep.

It so happened, shortly afterwards, that Orlando, who had been out hunting with the others, and had got separated from his party, came running past this spot.

With boar-spear in hand, he was pursuing a stag, which he had shot and wounded.

But a sight now met his eyes that turned him from this chase.

Near the mouth of the cave lay a man asleep, while round him hovered a gaunt wolf, preparing to spring upon his prostrate form.

Staggered by this sight, Orlando cautiously approached a few steps nearer, and his amazement reached a climax when he recognised his brother Oliver.

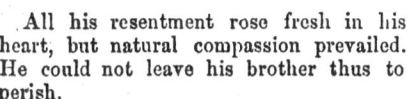

All his resentment rose fresh in his heart, but natural compassion prevailed. He could not leave his brother thus to perish.

Rushing at the wolf, he charged it with his boar-spear, dealing a severe wound.

The infuriated beast instantly turned upon him, and a fierce struggle began.

The wound which the wolf had already received had weakened him, and Orlando was fortunate enough to deal him another still more telling.

With a fierce howl, the creature fell to the earth, and Orlando despatched him with his hunting-knife.

Awakened by the noise of the conflict, Oliver started up, and was amazed to see a huge wolf lying dead near him, and Orlando, faint and bleeding from a wound in the arm, inflicted by the animal's claws.

A mutual explanation followed, and Oliver, having bound up the wound of his brother, assisted him to the dwelling of the exiled duke.

The next morning Celia and Rosalind were in the forest not far from their cottage, when they saw a strange gentleman approaching.

He was, like most of the ex-duke's party, clad as a forester.

"Good morrow, sir and madam," he said politely. "I have a message, and from your appearance, I believe you to be the right persons to receive it. Orlando de Bois commends himself to you both. and to that youth he in sport calls his Rosalind, he sends this bloodstained scarf."

"I am the—the youth you speak of," said Rosalind eagerly; "but where is he? and why has he not visited us as he promised?"

"An accident has prevented him," answered Oliver.

And he proceeded to recount his rescue, and Orlando's combat with the wolf.

Rosalind was so unnerved by hearing of her lover's danger that, at the sight of the stained scarf, she lost her presence of mind, and fainted.

"Oh, Ganymede, dear brother, what is the matter?" exclaimed Celia, throwing herself beside her.

In a few minutes Rosalind began to recover her senses.

"It was the sight of the blood," she said faintly. "Oh, I would I were at home!"

"We will lead you there," returned her cousin. "Kind, sir, will you be pleased to assist?"

"Be of good cheer, youth," said Oliver. "It was not like a man for you to faint."

"Oh, I was but pretending," she replied; "tell your brother so."

"Then it was very natural pretending," observed Oliver.

"Yes, I have played the part of Lady Rosalind till it was almost natural to me to act like a woman," explained the supposed Ganymede; "but pray, sir, tell your brother that the fainting was only pretence."

When next Orlando presented himself to Rosalind, he had his arm in a sling, and looked pale and weak. She was much concerned, but concealed her feelings under her usual lively demeanour.

The brothers had now made friends again, while between Oliver and Celia a love at first sight had sprung up.

The whole party were soon on the best of terms, and it now became Rosalind's turn to banter her cousin upon being in love.

"Do you know, Seigneur Orlando," said the pretended Ganymede one day, "that to-morrow is to be a grand wedding-day for all of us?—I mean most of us. In the first place, your brother is to marry Celia."

"I know it well," sighed Orlando, "for I am to go to the wedding. I rejoice at his happiness for his sake, but I grieve for my own, for I cannot be made happy in the same way."

"Oh, I am not so sure of that," replied his companion mysteriously. "Do you know I have learnt a little of the magician's art, and if you really love Rosalind —the real one I mean, and not your humble servant—I will undertake to find her to-morrow in time to make a double wedding of it."

"If you can do that——"

"I am sure I can, but here comes a lover of mine with a lover of hers."

It was, in fact, Phœbe and Silvius, the shepherd and shepherdess.

They were not yet quite reconciled, and Phœbe at once rushed eagerly to the side of Rosalind.

"Dear Ganymede," she exclaimed, "why have you treated me so unkindly?'

"Because it is my duty," replied Rosalind coldly. "I can never be yours, and it is your duty to love the faithful Silvius, who worships you as our friend Touchstone here worships his rustic lady-love."

"Yes, friends," said the jester, who led the peasantess Audrey, "we have fixed to-morrow for the grand ceremonial. Thus will the fool reach the climax of his folly."

"All are happy but myself," sighed Orlando; "my Rosalind is far away, and I can see her no more."

"Have I not promised to find her for you to-morrow?" said his companion.

"Mysterious youth!" he exclaimed; "and who, may I ask, is your lady-love?"

"No one. There breathes not a woman in the whole world whom I shall ever wed, unless it be Phœbe. But you shall see to-morrow."

The next day a large party were assembled outside the residence of the banished duke to witness the wedding of Oliver de Bois and Celia.

Rosalind attended, still disguised as Ganymede.

"So, my lord," she said to the duke, "you promise, if I bring your daughter Rosalind, to give her to Monsieur Orlando?"

"I promise," replied the duke.

And Orlando eagerly consented.

"And you promise you'll marry me if I be willing?" said Rosalind, turning to Phœbe.

"That I will, dear Ganymede, even if I die the hour after," exclaimed the enamoured shepherdess.

"'Tis well," said Rosalind. "We will go and do our best to satisfy everybody."

"A strange youth," said the duke, when Rosalind and Celia had departed; "and if he can do all he says, he is more powerful than I have ever been."

Touchstone and Audrey now appeared, arm-in-arm, the "motley Fool" and his rustic sweetheart causing much mirth to the courtiers by their whimsical appearance.

It was not long before Rosalind and Celia again appeared, having removed all disguise, and become as their former selves.

"Here I am; fetched hither by a magic messenger," said Rosalind, with a smile; "to you I give myself, for I am yours."

"My dearest daughter," said the duke, embracing her.

"My own Rosalind!" exclaimed Orlando, enraptured at this agreeable surprise.

All was soon explained, and matters were completed by the arrival of a young noble, who stated that the usurper Frederick, having been converted by a religious man to see the error of his ways, had determined to restore his brother his crown, and retire from the world.

It was, therefore, amid great rejoicing that the four weddings took place; for Phœbe, on discovering who Ganymede was, consented to bestow her hand on Silvius.

Never had so joyful a day enlivened the forest of Arden.

NOTICE.—"HENRY V.," being No. 10 of Stories from Shakespeare, will be ready on Monday, January 9. Orders should be given early to your Booksellers.

EDWIN J. BRETTS STORIES OF SHAKESPEARE
COMPLETE
KING HENRY V.

"'THE KING DESIRES YOU TO MAKE YOUR TERMS AS CONQUEROR,' SAID THE FRENCH HERALD."

"Boys of England Edition."

EDWIN J. BRETT'S

STORIES FROM

SHAKESPEARE'S PLAYS.

No. 10.—KING HENRY V.

CHAPTER I.

NOT only in London itself, but all through the little towns of England, the armourer's anvil was occupied, and every village gave forth the ringing clang, clang of the hammer as hauberk, and helm, and morion came hissing from the glowing fire.

England was at peace with all the world.

Then what could be the meaning of these warlike preparations?

Even the Scots were quiet, and the power of the fierce Northumbrian had been broken for ever.

Henry V., in the full blaze of his youthful manhood, was seated firmly upon the throne, and already statesmen, churchmen, and warriors were marvelling at the wondrous wisdom of one whose youth had been spent in riot and debauchery.

There had come a whisper from the court that the young king had laid claim to certain duchies in France, in right of his grandfather Edward.

Nothing definite was known about this.

It was a mere court rumour.

But there were those who came up from Portsmouth, and had seen there a noble vessel newly come from France with the French ambassador, though none what the purport of his embassy might guess.

The day after this news first became public, a man, clad in buckram, and with a huge sword dangling at his side, swaggered slowly down Eastcheap.

Alternate looks of aversion and merriment were directed towards him, and the apprentices especially seemed to pay little regard to his fierce swaggering bully air.

His nose was of enormous growth and as red as a beet; his face was covered with blotches and pimples.

In short, it was evident to the most casual observer that Lieutenant Bardolph, despite his warlike get up, had served Bacchus with far more energy than he had Mars.

"See you yonder swaggerer?" remarked a citizen to a neighbour; "he has just come from the court. I warrant you he could tell us some news an he listed."

"Wot ye not that is Lieutenant Bardolph, neighbour?" exclaimed the one addressed.

"Ay, marry!"

"One of the drunken followers of that drunken knight, Falstaff."

"Ay, marry. The one who used to be such great friends with the king when he was Prince of Wales."

"Ay, but he fell into sore distress, and was bidden not to show his face within ten miles of the court under penalty of death, so that we shall get no news from his henchman."

"You mistake there, neighbour," replied the first speaker, "you mistake. Our young king, though justly severe in his punishment of evil, is not so hard-hearted as to entirely desert his old companions."

"How now, neighbour; is the fat old knight in favour again? Then woe to England, for he is such a cunning mountain of flesh that it will not be long ere, with one specious argument or another, he contrives to inflame the king against all those who would counsel him truly."

"Nay—nay, neighbour; not so hasty," interrupted the first speaker. "I have it on the authority of neighbour Purswell that the fat knight is scarcely likely to trouble any of us again with his midnight brawls and indecent orgies, being, it is said, dying of a broken heart in consequence of the king's treatment of him——"

"Of a broken liver consequent of his excesses, more like."

"That may be—that may be. Nevertheless, the gossips have it that Dame Quickly, with whom he lodges, receives so much a day from the lord chamberlain for his support; and Bardolph has to go each day to court to get his money and hear the court news."

"Marry, if that be so, and the fat knight mend his ways, he is likely to have influence at court yet. I'll send him a venison pasty."

And full of ambitious hopes, the worthy cloth merchant made his way towards the hostelry where Sir John Falstaff lay seriously ill.

His companion made some audible remarks, expressive of contempt, and the true serving practices of some people, and went home to consult his wife about doing exactly the same thing.

Meanwhile Lieutenant Bardolph strolled leisurely down the street, until he neared the hostelry, when he perceived a fellow soldier in front of him.

Hastily stepping forward, he slapped him on the back, saying—

"Well met, Corporal Nym."

"Good morrow, Lieutenant Bardolph," replied the other, turning round, and exhibiting a face almost the exact counterpart of his companion; "have you news?"

"Ay, marry, that I have; and news too that will make your ears tingle with delight."

"Has the king made it up with the old knight?"

"That's as it may be. I fear he has made it up with a greater king than Harry."

"How now?"

"King Death and he are negotiating hotly."

"I am sorry to hear it."

"But come in and have a cup of sack. I have that which will rejoice you. By the bye, are Ancient Pistol and you friends yet?"

"For my part," returned Nym grimly, "I care not. I say little; but when time shall serve, there shall be smiles—but that shall be as it may be. You know I am a coward—I dare not fight—but I will wink and hold out mine iron. It is a simple one; but what though? It will toast cheese, and will endure cold as another man's will— and there's the humour of it."

"Nay, nay," said Bardolph hastily; "take the matter not so satirically. I will bestow a breakfast on you to make you friends, and we'll be all three sworn brothers, and to France. Let this be so, good Corporal Nym."

"Faith," replied Nym, still in an unrelenting mood, "I will live so long as I may, that's the certain of it; and when I cannot live I will do as I may. But what is this you tell me of France?"

"Glorious news. You must know I am just from the court, where the king has just given reception to the French ambassador. My faith, it was a sight to see! But this is dry work. Let us enter here. What ho! a cup of sack, and put not too much lime in it, or it may be that blows may arise. Knowing somewhat of the court, I contrived to get into the throne-room as the ambassadors were admitted.

"'Well,' said the king to them, 'you know we are a Christian king, therefore we pray you tell us how the French king received our message relative to certain dukedoms which we claimed in the right of our predecessor, Edward the Third? Tell us the Dauphin's mind?'

"'Sire,' replied one of the ambassadors, 'you have given us leave to speak plainly —thus much then in plain words. The prince, our master, says—

"'You savour too much of your youth, and bids you be advised there's naught in France that can with nimble galliard be won. You cannot revel into dukedoms there. He therefore sends you as fitter for your spirit this ton of treasure, and in lieu of this desires you to let the dukedoms that you claim hear no more of you.'

"'What treasure?' demanded the king.

"'Tennis balls, my liege,' replied the

Duke of Exeter. 'He has sent your majesty a ton of tennis balls.'

"Well, we all stood trembling, expecting that the king would have the ambassadors executed on the spot for this daring insult, the more especially as his brow grew as black as midnight.

"Then he rose from his throne. ·

"'We are glad the Dauphin is so pleasant with us,' he said. 'When we have matched our rackets to these balls, we will in France, by God's grace, play a set shall strike his father's crown into the hazard. Tell him he hath made a match with such a wrangler that all the courts of France will be disturbed with chases. So get you hence in safety, and tell the Dauphin his jest will savour but of shallow wit when thousands more than have laughed shall weep at it.'

"Then, descending from his throne, he gave orders that an expedition should be set on foot at once, so that ere a month elapses we may have reasonable thoughts of being in France and making fair pickings."

"This is good news indeed. Will the good knight go?"

"I fear, I fear; but nathless I would have you friends with Pistol."

"He did me foul wrong."

"Yes, but it is certain, corporal, that he is married to Dame Quickly, and it is also certain that she was engaged to you. But what then? 'Tis but the fortune of war, and maybe a French crossbolt may once more yield her to your arms."

"I cannot tell," replied Nym. "Things must be as they may. Men may sleep and have their throats about them at the time, and some say knives have edges."

Corporal Nym, as he said this, pulled his moustaches, and looked terrifically fierce.

"It must be as it may," he continued. "Though patience be a tired mare, yet she will plod. There must be conclusions."

At this moment who should enter upon the scene but Ancient Pistol and his newly-married wife, Dame Quickly.

For a moment the successful and non-successful rivals to her hand glared at one another, while Pistol's looks directed against Lieutenant Bardolph seemed to say—

"Could you desert me for a mean creature like that?"

"Good corporal," said Bardolph, in a whisper, "be patient now."

Then he added in a loud voice—

"How now, mine host Pistol?"

"Base tike! callest thou me host? Now, by this hand, I scorn the term. What, a warrior turn to a drawer of beer? Nor shall my Nell keep lodgers."

"No, by my troth," cried Dame Quickly. "Oh, well-a-day, if he be not drawn now! We shall see wilful murder committed. Good corporal, offer nothing here, I pray you. Lieutenant, put up your sword."

The blooming widow ran with great nimbleness between one another of the late bosom friends that were now so belligerently disposed to each other.

"Pish!" cried Nym.

"Pish for thee, Iceland dog!" roared Pistol, drawing also, "thou crop-eared cur of Iceland!"

"Good Corporal Nym," cried the dame, in great alarm, "show the valour of a man and put up thy sword."

"Will you jog off?" cried Nym to Pistol. "Some other time I will have you *solus*."

"*Solus*!" cried Pistol, who did not understand the Latin for alone. "*Solus*, egregious dog! Oh, viper vile, the *solus* in thy most marvellous face, the *solus* in thy teeth, and in thy—nay, I do retort, the *solus* in thy nasty mouth. For Pistol's back is up, and he will fight!"

"Pistol," said Nym, "you cannot frighten me with big words. If you grow foul with me I will scour you, Pistol, with my rapier as I may in fair terms. If you do not walk off I will prick you with my rapier, and that's the humour of it."

"Oh, braggard vile," yelled Pistol; "the grave doth gape, and doting death is near; therefore exhale!"

Both the men placed themselves in position, and in all probability this game of braggadocia would have ended in a real fight had not Bardolph interfered.

"Hear me what I say," he cried; "he that strikes the first stroke, I'll run him up to the hilt, as I am a soldier."

"An oath of might," cried Pistol, who was glad to get out of the scrape on such easy terms; "my fury shall abate. Give me thy fist, thy forefoot give; Nym, you are a fellow of tall spirit."

"Well, well," said Corporal Nym, "I will cut thy throat one time or another, in fair terms."

"*Coupe le gorge*, that's the word," yelled Pistol, "I thee defy again. Oh, hound of Crete, thinkest thou my spouse to get?"

When it seemed in all likelihood that the quarrel would be renewed, a good-looking page of some sixteen years of age entered and immediately burst out laughing.

He was servant to Sir John Falstaff, and knew these lying, brawling, swash-bucklers thoroughly.

"Pistol, mine host," said he, "you must come to my master, he is very ill; and you, mine hostess. Good Bardolph, put thy red nose between the sheets and do the office of a warming-pan, for he is very chilled."

"Away, you rogue!" cried Bardolph.

"Good husband," cried the dame, "come home quickly, I pray you; I fear he is about to die."

"Come," cried Bardolph, taking advantage of the incident. "Shall I make you two friends again? We must to France together. Why the deuce should we fly at one another's throats when there will be plenty of Frenchmen to plunder?"

"Let floods o'erswell and fiends for food howl on!" cried Pistol, afraid to be the first to give in a second time.

"Will you pay me the eight shillings I won of you at betting?" asked Nym.

"Base is the slave that pays," roared Pistol.

"That, now, I will have," cried Nym, "so there's the humour of it."

"As manhood shall compound," cried Pistol, drawing his sword and mindful of his friend's interference in the first instance. "Push home!"

"By this sword," cried Bardolph, "he that makes the first thrust, I'll kill him. By this sword!"

"Sword is an oath," cried Pistol, "and oaths must have their course. Corporal Nym, an thou wilt, be friends, be friends."

"Shall I have the eight shillings I won of you?" demanded the corporal firmly.

"A noble shalt thou have," replied Pistol, "and present payment. And liquor likewise will I give to thee, and friendship shall combine with brotherhood. I'll live by Nym and Nym shall live by me. Is not this just? Verily, we will to the English camp in France, and I shall sutler be, and profits will accrue. Give me thy hand."

"I shall have my noble?" reiterated Nym, who was not the least little bit taken in by all this grandiloquence.

"In cash most justly paid," cried Pistol.

As they were shaking hands Dame Quickly came running in with her apron over head, to tell them that Sir John was certainly dying, and that they must come to him at once.

But they got no further than the inn where he was staying, for all three were arrant cowards at heart, and now that their old commander lay dying, they were afraid to venture into his presence, being, like most bullies, woefully afraid of death.

So they sat in the bar-room down below, drinking sack at Pistol's expense, and discussing their plans—what they should do when the death of the knight should leave them free men.

The boy, whose name was Cherubino, and had been a present from Prince Henry to Sir John, alone had the courage to go up with the dame and see his dying master.

Presently the dame came in with a packet in her hand and announced that it was all over, that the good knight was dead, whereupon they all shed maudlin, drunken tears.

"This packet must you give to the king, Lieutenant Bardolph," said the dame; "if he have already gone to Southampton, you must follow him there, and you will be well rewarded."

"How died the poor knight?" asked Pistol, wiping away a few beery tears. "Boy, bustle up thy courage, for we must yearn therefor!"

"I would I were with him wheresoe'er he is," groaned Bardolph. "Left he aught for me?"

"Nay," cried Dame Quickly, unheeding the latter part of the question; "I am sure he is in heaven, for he made a fine end and went away just like any Christian child. After I saw him fumble with the sheets, and play with flowers, and smile upon his finger ends, I knew there was but one way, for his nose was as sharp as a pen, and he babbled of green fields. Then he bade me lay more clothes upon his feet. I put my hand into the bed and felt them. They were as cold as any stone."

"He died crying out against sack," said the boy, "so that may be a warning to you three. I would he had given me that despatch to carry to the king."

"Well, well," cried Bardolph hastily, "I must away. Maybe I shall make more by his death than he were alive, for the king was mighty fond of him, and now that he is dead, will pardon his faults."

"That is so, Bardolph," cried the others hastily; "we will go with thee and share thy good fortune."

"Illustrious Bardolph," cried Pistol; "were we not always thy bully boys? You will want nobles for the journey. Shall it not be Pistol who will furnish them?"

"Ah me," said the boy, "he saw a flea on Bardolph's nose, one day, and he said it looked like a black soul burning in hell fire."

"Well, the fuel is gone that maintained the fire," said Bardolph, "and that is all I ever got in his service."

"Wife," said Pistol, "we are going; give me thy lips my love. Look to my chattels and my moveables; let sense rule. The word is pitch and pay. Trust none, for oaths are straws, and men's faiths wafer cakes, and holdfast is the only dog, my duck. Yoke fellows in arms, let us to France like horse-leeches to suck. Touch her soft mouth, Bardolph, and march. Now, Nym."

"I cannot kiss!" cried Nym.

"And I would not," added Cherubino, much to the disgust of swaggering Pistol.

However, they were in great spirits as they marched off for Southampton, whither the king had gone to pitch his camp in order to collect men and ships for the invasion of France.

As they possessed no horses, and could steal none they were about a week on the road, to the terror of hen roosts and peaceable farmers whom they happened to pass on the way.

"More than once were they in danger of getting hanged, but the boy's wit saved them, and they easily induced some credulous people to believe that Sir John had regained his old influence with the king, now that war was about to break out.

But there were several people about King Henry's camp whom that despatch concerned deeply, and who, to get possession of it, would as soon hang up Sir John Falstaff's crew of disreputable swashbucklers, as they would a lot of carrion.

They made no secret of the fact that they were carrying a despatch from John Falstaff to the king to the various bands of free companies they met on the road to join the royal standard, but Bardolph was cunning enough to let no one see the contents.

So we will leave them for a while.

CHAPTER II.

THE harbour of Southampton swarmed with vessels of every description, from the open float to the stout caraval, all waiting the day of embarkation.

As each company arrived, it took up its place on the slope, and the knight bannerit unfurled his pennon.

The earls and dukes found lodgings in the king's palace, the knights were quartered in the town, while the captains and gentlemen at turns camped out in the open.

All day and night the air resounded with the clang and clamour of military preparations, and from the castle messengers were arriving and departing almost every minute of the day.

The utmost enthusiasm prevailed.

The flower of English chivalry had flocked to offer their services to the war-like young king, and the Church had come forward with sums of money unparalleled in the history of the Church.

In short, every one seemed to be happy and full of enthusiasm.

No one would suspect that under all this joyfulness, there lurked a woof of black treachery that was well-nigh successful in plunging England in gloom.

It was getting on towards evening when our four adventurers arrived at Southampton Castle, and set their wits to work to gain audience of the king.

How was it to be effected?

Occupied as he was with great military preparations, with a kingdom at stake, King Henry would care very little whether his old boon companion were dead or alive.

But Cherubino's wit brought them out of it.

Leaving Pistol and Nym to kick their heels outside the palace gates, he introduced Bardolph, and led him to the king's antechamber.

The king was just coming forth, and as

the chamberlains were pushing back the crowd, Bardolph resisted.

"What!" cried King Henry, catching sight of his red nose; "is that you, Bardolph? Did I not say that if Sir John came near our presence he should die? Take this bottle-nosed dog away and hang him, as a warning that we will have our laws respected!"

Poor Bardolph was so overcome that he could say nothing.

But the page, snatching the packet from him, fell on his knees before the king and handed it to him.

"Sire!" he cried, "my unhappy master has gone before a greater king than thou, and has sent this packet to you by his dying commands."

"Poor Falstaff," cried the king, as a sudden rush of tenderness came over him with the recollection of bygone days; "there will be many good and true men die for us in France whose death we shall less regret than this old wine-bibber."

Such is the force of association.

"How died he?"

"Peaceably, sire, but most anxious that you should get that packet and read it without delay."

The king paused a moment and then tore it open.

His frown became portentous as he read the following—

"From JOHN FALSTAFF, Knight, to HARRY, King of England.

"You used me, and you left me. If I was vicious, worse were you, for royalty may make vice seem virtue. As you have taken leave of your fast companions, put not too much trust in those of austere manners, and much prate of virtue. Ambition is more dangerous than the love of wine; so much the more dangerous to you are Lords Cambridge and Scroop, and the knight, Grey of Northumberland, the proof of whose treason whereof I enclose. For all your neglect may you prosper.

"JACK FALSTAFF."

Enclosed were indisputable proofs that the above-named noblemen had been guilty of taking money from the French king to assassinate King Henry.

How Falstaff obtained possession of it always remained a mystery.

The king retired hastily to the council chamber, where he was for some time closeted with his uncle Exeter.

When he once more came forth the hall was filled with royal guards.

They had neglected to take Bardolph away, not knowing exactly what to do with him.

"Summon hither the Lord Scroop, the Earl of Cambridge, and Sir Knight Grey of Northumberland.

"My lords," said King Henry, when they came into his presence, "we would ask your advice touching that wretched man yonder," and he pointed to Bardolph, "who yesterday railed against our person. We consider that it was excess of wine that set him on, and what think you if on his more advice we pardon him?"

"That's mercy, but too much security, my liege," said Lord Scroop, who enjoyed the privilege of sleeping with the king in order to protect him from assassination. "Let him be punished, my liege, lest example be bred by his escape."

"Oh, let us yet be merciful," said the king.

"Sire," said the Earl of Cambridge, "you show too great mercy if you give him life."

"Alas," replied the king, "your too much love and care for me are heavy orisons against this poor wretch. If little faults hanging on distemper shall not be winked at, how shall we stretch our eye when capital crimes, chewed, swallowed and digested, appear before us? We'll yet enlarge that man, though Cambridge, Scroop, and Grey, in their dear care and tender preservation of our person, would have him punished. And now to our French causes," he continued, as Bardolph was released, much wondering what it all meant. "Who are the late commissioners?"

"I am one, my lord," replied the Earl of Cambridge.

"And I, and I, my liege," said the other two. "Your highness bade me ask for mine to-day."

"Then, Richard, Earl of Cambridge," said the king, handing him a paper, "there is your commission; there yours, Lord Scroop, of Masham; and Sir Knight Grey, of Northumberland, this yours. Read them and know your worthiness. My lord of Westmoreland, we will aboard to-night. Why, how now, gentlemen, your complexions change? What see you in those papers that has chased all the blood from your cheeks?"

The three guilty ones turned deadly

white, and dropped to their knees confessing their crimes and praying for mercy.

"The mercy that was quick in us just now," cried the king sternly, "by your own counsel is suppressed and killed. You must not dare, for shame, to talk of mercy; for your own reasons against that poor man yonder, turn into your bosoms as dogs upon their masters. See you, princes and nobles, these English monsters have for a few light crowns agreed to kill us here in Southampton that France might not feel our vengeance. What shall I say to thee, Lord Scroop, thou cruel, savage,

Heaven acquit their souls. Bear them hence!"

There were tears in the king's eyes as he watched his late dearly loved friends being led away, and knew that ere the sun went down their heads would be grinning over gargantuas at the gates of the Tower.

"Now then, fellow," cried the king to Bardolph, "what favour wouldst thou have?"

"I would follow your majesty to France," cried Bardolph, shaking in his shoes.

THE DEATH OF THE DUKE OF YORK.

and inhuman creature, thou that didst bear the key of all my counsels, and knewest the very bottom of my soul? Did men seem dutiful? Why so didst thou? Seemed they grave and learned? So didst thou. Come they of noble family? So didst thou. Seemed they religious? So didst thou. Were they spare in diet, free from gross passion, or of mirth, or anger; constant in spirit? Such and all things didst thou seem; and thus thy fall hath left a blot to mark the full-fraught and best endued man with some suspicion. I will weep for thee, for this revolt of thine is, methinks, another fall of man."

Utterly confounded the baffled conspirators could make no word of answer.

"Arrest them and see that they suffer all three the doom of high treason, so may

"Humph," said the king; "you are not of the stuff a king may with safety reward, but since you ask, you and your companions may come, an you list. As you do valorously and well, so shall you be advanced. But if you, and Pistol, and Nym go back to your old practices, the king shall not save you from the provost marshal's cord. Fill this knave's cup with half-crowns. As for you, master page, you can re-enter our service or remain with Captain Pistol as you list. Now, lords," he continued, turning away, while Bardolph and Cherubino made haste to get away from so dangerous a presence. "Now, lords, let us deliver our puissance into the hand of Heaven, putting it straight into expedition. Cheerily to the sea, the signs of war advance. Embark all to-night.

THE ENTRY OF HENRY V. TO HARFLEUR.

By to-morrow we should be on the shores of France."

So saying, he led the way to the beach, where countless vessels were but awaiting the royal presence to make the welkin ring with salvoes of fierce-throated hurrahs.

The dying sun was reflected in a thousand glittering counterparts as the knights hung their glittering shields on the prow of green dragon and basilisk.

Then the anchors were weighed, and under the gentle evening breeze the whole expedition sailed for the coast of France.

CHAPTER III.

DAME FORTUNE seemed lavish of her favours to the young King of England.

A favourable wind from the north continued blowing all night long, so gently and evenly that the ships were enabled to keep all together, and by six o'clock in the morning were all run up on the broad, sandy, shallow beach, a little to the east of the fortified town of Harfleur, while the basilisks, sakers, demi-cannon and culverin thundered forth a deafening defiance at the dismayed Frenchmen.

These latter scrambled in behind their walls, and drew up drawbridge and closed their gates.

So rapidly had the young king's orders been obeyed, in the collection of men, that long before the King of France dreamt he was ready, he had landed in his territory.

However, the citizens resolved to defend the walls, and send to the Dauphin for help.

But by the second day the valiant young king, who had been the first to leap ashore, had made a breach in the walls, and with his own hand carried the scaling-ladder with which he was going to mount to death or glory.

The first attack they made, owing to a mine having been sprung, the English were driven back with terrible slaughter.

But brave King Harry, springing from beneath a pile of *debris*, led the way again.

" Once more to the breach, dear friends," he cried, " once more or close the wall up with our English dead! Stand you like greyhounds in the slips, straining upon the start. The game's afoot; follow your spirit, and upon this charge cry 'God for England and St. George!'"

Catching up the spirit of his war-cry, once more the English rushed forward in a mighty torrent, crying—"St. George! St. George!"

The brave French, on the other hand, shout "St. Denis! St. Denis!" and replied by showers of crossbolts, stones, and boiling oil and pitch, which they flung upon the heads of their assailants, so that many of them died in frightful agony.

Three times did the invincible king penetrate that deadly breach, and three times he was barely rescued.

But meanwhile, let us turn our attention to another part of the field, where our friends Bardolph, Nym, and Ancient Pistol, with the boy, are taking it easy.

Cherubino had been to the first assault, and was spent with exhaustion and covered with blood and dust.

"On, on to the breach," cried Bardolph without budging an inch, "ere they begin again!"

"Pray thee, good Bardolph, stay," cried Nym; "the knocks are too hot, and for my own part I have not a case of lives, that is the very plain song of it."

"The plain song of it is most just," said Pistol, glad of the excuse. "God's vassals drop and die."

"I would I were in an ale house in London," cried Cherubino, panting and wiping the blood from his face. "As for you two, you have not earned a drop of liquor."

Pistol was about to answer furiously when a little man, clad in complete armour, and with a face fiery red from excitement and choler rushed upon the scene.

It was the choleric Welsh captain, Fluellen, one of the best and bravest in the army, though a great oddity.

"Got's blood!" he cried, whipping out his sword; "up to the preaches you rascals, up to the preaches!" and without more ado began driving Nym, Pistol, and Bardolph before him as though they were a flock of sheep, thwacking them soundly with the flat of it.

"Be merciful, great duke," cried Pistol, "to men of mould! Abate thy rage—abate thy rage, thy manly rage! Use lenity, sweet chuck."

But all was of no avail.

He drove them up before him to the breach, leaving the boy whom he saw was

spent, and had been doing good work to regain his breath.

"Young as I am," soliloquised Cherubino, "I have observed these three swashers, but all they three could not be a man to me, for indeed three such articles do not amount to a man. For Bardolph he is white-livered and red-faced. For Pistol he hath a killing tongue but kills naught else. For Nym, he hath heard that men of few words are the best men, and therefore he scorns to say his prayers lest he should be thought a coward. He never broke any head but one, and that was his own against a post. They would have me as familiar with other men's pockets as mine own. I must leave them and win me a decent name in the prince's service. And now once more for death or glory."

"Captain Fluellen," cried Captain Gower, in another part of the field, "come to the mines, the Duke of Gloucester would speak to you."

"To the mines?" cried Fluellen; "tell the duke it is no good to come to the mines, for they are badly done."

"It is done under the direction of a valiant Irish gentleman, named Mac-Morris, Captain Fluellen."

"Then he is an ass!" cried Fluellen, getting even redder in the face.

"Here he comes to speak for himself," cried Captain Gower.

"Captain MacMorris," cried the fiery little Welshman, "look you, under your correction the mine is not well done. According to the description of the Romans, there is not many of your nation——"

"What is my nation?" demanded the Irish captain in a rage. "Is a villain, and a knave, and a rascal my nation?"

"Look you, Captain MacMorris," cried the Welshman; "if you take the matter otherwise than is meant, peradventure I shall think that you do not use me with that affability as in discretion you ought to use me, look you, being so good a man as yourself both in discipline of wars, and in the derivation of my birth and in other particulars."

"I do not know you to be so good a man as myself," cried the Irishman, "and I will cut off your head!"

They were rushing at one another's throats in good earnest when the trumpet on the walls sounded parley.

"Away!" cried Gower.

"Captain MacMorris," cried the little

Welshman to his gigantic antagonist; "when there is more better opportunity, look you, I will be so bold as to tell you I know the disciplines of war as well as yourself, and there's an end!"

He hastened away after Gower, and found that the king was speaking to the governor of the town.

"How yet resolves the governor of the town?" demanded the king; "this is the last parley I will admit. If I begin the battery once again, I will not leave the half achieved Harfleur till in her ashes she be buried. What say you?"

"Our expectations are at an end," returned the governor; "the Dauphin whom we entreated to send succour returns us that his powers are not yet ready to raise so great a siege. Therefore, enter, great king, and pray you have mercy!"

That night the victorious Henry entered Harfleur with his whole army, and on the following day despatched his Uncle Exeter to demand his claims from the King of France.

He was offered after months of tiresome negotiation the hand of the Princess Katharine, with a few petty dukedoms, which he could not in honour accept.

This was only done to gain time while the King of France got together a mighty army, outnumbering the English, as the sands upon the seashore.

On the other hand, King Henry, wearied of the negotiations, and being fearful of the sickness which had broken out amongst his soldiers, resolved to march them across the plains of Picardy, and with his base resting on the strongly fortified town of Calais, await supplies and recruits from England before making a further movement south towards Rouen.

But he had hardly started from his entrenched position before Harfleur ere an immense army, under the personal commands of the Dauphin, the Lord High Constable of France, and the French King, moved up to intercept him while he had scarcely nine thousand men, many of whom were sick from scurvy and dysentery.

————

CHAPTER IV.

THE English king halted upon the right bank of the river, or brooklet, and strongly fortified his position in front before the French came up.

He dug great pits in front of the position, which were covered over with poles and loose earth, and the bottoms filled with upright spears; behind these again he planted spears obliquely, so that when the bowmen were pressed by the cavalry they could retire behind these and were perfectly protected.

His right flank was protected by the river, which was here spanned by a small bridge.

On the hill behind him he posted his camp-followers, so that they looked like an army of reserve.

Harry of England had just completed his preparations when the horizon began to darken with the multitude of the French host, and as he was superintending a false posse in person, a man in herald's costume advanced at full gallop from the French lines and dismounted.

"Thy purpose?" demanded the king briefly.

"Thus says my king," replied the herald. 'Say thou to Harry of England, though we seemed dead we did but sleep. We could have rebuked him at Harfleur, but we thought it better to wait until we were sure of him Now we speak, and our voice is imperial. Bid him consider his ransom, which must be proportioned to the losses we have borne. His exchequer is too poor for the effusion of our subjects' blood; the muster of his kingdom, too faint a number, and for our disgrace his own person kneeling at our feet but a weak and worthless satisfaction. Tell him he hath betrayed his followers, whose condemnation is announced.' "

"Turn back and tell the king, thy master, that I do not seek him now," cried Henry, "because my people are weak, and feeble, and shy like so many Frenchmen. Yet here I am; my ransome is this frail, worthless trunk; my army but a weak and sickly guard. Yet, God before, tell him we will come on, though France himself and such another to back him stood in the way. We would not seek a battle; neither do we shun one, and if it must be so, we will dye your ground with French blood."

The herald, on receiving this answer and the customary largess, for heralds were the most honoured and courteously treated of all men in those days, rode slowly away, and the king once more addressed himself to the task of fortifying his position in which he was greatly annoyed by parties of French horsemen, who rode at the bridge and attempted to take it by a *coup de main*.

It was a short distance from here that Captain Fluellen met Captain Gower.

"How now, Captain Fluellen? Come you from the bridge?" he demanded.

"I assure you," replied the captain, "that there is very excellent service done at the bridge, in none so much as a valiant captain whom I saw do gallant service. My faith, his words were blood inspiring. He is as valiant as Mark Antony, and yet he is a man of no estimation."

"What do you call him?"

"Pistol—Ancient Pistol is he called."

"I know him not."

"See," cried Fluellen, "here he comes."

"Captain," cried Pistol, coming towards them, "I beseech thee do me favours. The Duke of Exeter doth love thee well."

"Ay," replied Fluellen, "I praise God I merit some love at his hands."

"Bardolph, a soldier firm and stout of heart," continued Pistol, "hath stolen a *pix*; fortune frowns on him, and he must be hanged unless we can save him. Let not my friend's gallant neck be cut with edge of penny cord."

"Ancient Pistol," said Fluellen, "I do understand thee."

"Why then rejoice?" asked Pistol.

"Certainly, Ancient, it is not a thing to rejoice at, for if he were my own brother he should hang, seeing that discipline must be kept up."

"Die, or be hanged!" cried the enraged Pistol; "a *figo* for thy friendship."

"Very good."

"The fig of Spain, measly Welshman," cried Ancient Pistol, going off, seeing that his mission was sure of failure. "I do retort the fig in thy teeth."

"Why, Fluellen, this is an arrant counterfeit rascal. I remember him now; a scoundrel—a cutpurse," said Captain Gower.

"I assure you he uttered brave words at the bridge," said Fluellen, looking somewhat crestfallen at having been taken in; "but 'tis no matter. I warrant you I shall see him again. Here now comes the king."

"How now, Fluellen?" asked the king. "How goes the bridge?"

"It is well maintained, my liege," replied Fluellen.

"What men have you lost?" asked the king anxiously.

"Marry," replied Fluellen, "for my part I think the duke has lost never a man but one that is like to be executed for robbing a church—one Bardolph, if your majesty knows the man—his face all bubukles, and whelks, and knobs, and flames of fire; and his lips plough at his nose, and it is like a coal of fire; but his nose is executed and his fire's out."

"We would have all such offenders so cut off," replied the king; "and we give express charge that in our marches through the country there be nothing compelled from the villages, for when lenity and cruelty play for a kingdom the gentle gamester is the soonest winner."

The king then gave orders that all who were not on the watch should spend the night not devoted to needful rest in prayer for victory, and he in person visited the outposts to see that nothing was overlooked.

In the French camp, which was not fifteen hundred yards from the English, the utmost riot and debauchery held sway.

The knights and men-at-arms gambled for the English which were to be taken prisoners next day, and even the Lord High Constable was heard to brag that he would take a hundred prisoners with his own hand.

While the king was taking a solitary ramble amongst the outposts he ran across Pistol.

"Who goes there?" demanded Pistol.

"A friend," replied the king.

"What's thy name?"

"Harry le Roy."

"Harry le Roy," exclaimed Pistol; "a Cornish name. Art thou of the Cornish crew?"

"No," replied the king, "I am a Welshman."

"Knowest thou Fluellen?"

"Yes."

"Tell him I'll knock his leek about his pate upon Saint Davy's day."

"Do not wear a dagger in your cap that day lest he should knock that about yours."

"Art thou his friend?"

"And his kinsman too."

"A *figo* for thee, then."

"I thank you. God be with you."

"My name is Pistol called."

"It suits well with your fierceness."

Pistol blustered a little longer, but

finally went off as a couple of soldiers of the guard came up and demanded of the king who he was.

Desirous of ascertaining the feeling of his army, the king entered into a long conversation with the honest soldiers, and from them discovered that they cared not a jot whether his cause were a right or wrong one; they were bound to obey him by virtue of their oath of allegiance, and that all the blood that was shed would be called to account for at the last day.

The king attempted to defend himself, but did so so lamely that the soldier jeered at him, and reproved him sternly, all the time thinking him but a common soldier.

At last the king said—

"I should be angry with you if the time were convenient."

"Let it be a quarrel between us, if you live," cried the soldier eagerly. "Here is my glove; give me another of thine. This will I wear in my cap. If ever thou dost come to me and say after to-morrow this is my glove, I will take thee a box on the ear."

"Well, I will do it," replied the king, "though I take thee in the king's company."

"Thou darest as well be hanged," cried the soldier.

And so they parted.

Early in the morning the king was busy getting his army in position when the Duke of Westmoreland rode up to him.

"Oh, that we now had here but one ten thousand of those men in England who do no work to-day!" he cried.

"I would not have one more," replied the king, in a loud voice so that all the army heard him. "If we are marked to die, we are enough to do our country loss, and if to live the fewer men the greater share of honour. Rather proclaim it through the host, good cousin Westmoreland, that he who hath no stomach for the fight, let him depart. We would not die in that man's company."

Wild and enthusiastic cheers greeted this gallant speech, and ere they died away about two thousand French knights, anxious to win the day before the men-at-arms, thundered down upon the English position.

They were followed by a reserve of two thousand more who came galloping madly at their heels, and in their eagerness forgetting all the rules of war.

The men-at-arms rushed after them, fearful lest the knights should get all the spoil, and so infantry and cavalry got mixed up.

The king at once bade his knights dismount and fight on foot, and at a signal retreated behind the *chevaux de frise.*

On came the exultant crowd, and yet not an arrow fled from the English ranks.

The knights and captains were busy restraining their men, and keeping them in strict discipline.

Suddenly down went the front line of French knights, and tumbling over them came the second.

Then came the hot words of command, and as the air darkened with the clothyard shaft, the bill and bowmen rushed forward and captured the horses.

At the same moment the English knights got to horse and charged through and through the French infantry, who, imagining that their own knights had turned on them, gave way to panic and fled.

In the meanwhile English arrow and English pike had done terrible work amongst the overthrown French knights, who, once unhorsed, were helpless.

In fact, except for a charge, when their weight told on infantry, French knights were not much good against English bowmen, who sometimes sent their cloth-yard shafts right through and through them.

A reserve of five thousand knights, seeing the disaster, advanced to the rescue, and charged through their own infantry to get at the English cavalry.

But the old Duke of Bedford, who was in command of the squadron, was too wary a man to give them battle.

He immediately wheeled and retreated behind his infantry, who in turn retreated behind their *chevaux de frise*, and poured forth a deadly cloud of arrows.

Once more the knights fell headlong into their foes, and were slaughtered without mercy as they struggled to get out.

Once more the French infantry was charged by the exultant cavalry, and this time the slaughter was fearful.

The rout became general, and a fearful carnage ensued.

Three times the English king had his crown shorn off his helmet, and once he

was beaten to the earth, where a Welsh knight stood over him and kept the assailants at bay until assistance came.

Three hundred French knights had bound themselves by an oath to capture the English king.

Not one of them left the field alive, but twenty of the bravest knights of England paid with their lives for their desperate defence.

At one time it was said towards the close of the battle that the French had killed the boys and captured the luggage of the English army.

Fearful that this was the result of renewed confidence on the part of the French, and as they were still more than three to one, every Englishman killed his prisoners.

Thus, in a few moments, ten thousand French were put to death.

"Here comes the French herald," said Harry of England; "his mien looks humbler than it was wont. What is it?"

"The king bows his head to the judgment of God, and desires you to name your terms as conqueror."

"Tell him," replied the king, "that we will dictate our terms from Troyes. What castle is that yonder?"

"Agincourt, your majesty."

"Then this field shall be called the battle-field of Agincourt, and this victory shall we celebrate each year at the feast of St. Crispin."

"What ho! Captain Fluellen," he called out to the Welsh captain, who was passing; "wear thou this favour for me," and he handed him his glove. "If any man challenge this he is a traitor; if thou encounter any such, apprehend him as thou lovest."

The little Welshman was delighted, and walked off on his mission, but the king sent a company of soldiers after him to see that he got into no mischief.

He had not got far, however, before Williams the soldier saw his glove, and without more ado marched up to him and bestowed on him a box on the ear.

They were about to come to mortal blows when both were arrested and taken before the king.

"Give me thy glove, soldier," cried the king; "look, here is the fellow of it. 'Twas I indeed thou promised to strike, and thou hast given me most bitter terms. How canst thou make me satisfaction?"

"All offences come from the heart, my liege," cried the soldier stoutly; "and never came any from mine that could offend your majesty."

"Here, Uncle Exeter," cried the king, "fill this glove with crowns and give it to this honest fellow. There is another whom I met in my rounds last night, Pistol is he called. Fluellen, he hath promised to break a leek about your pate St. Davy's Day; see you, look to it. Come, lords, we will send our terms to France."

CHAPTER V.

OUR friend Pistol was not idle.

He carefully kept in the rear of the fight until it was all over, and then captured a French knight who was running away.

"Yield, cur!" he cried in a mighty voice.

"*O Seigneur Dieu!*" called out the Frenchman.

"Oh, Signieur Dieu should be a gentleman," replied Pistol, who did not understand a word of French. "O Signieur Dieu, thou diest on the point of fox, unless thou givest me most egregious ransom."

"*O, ayez pitie de moy!* (have pity on me.)"

"Moy shall not serve," replied Pistol; "I will have forty moys, or I will fetch the rim out at thy throat in crimson drops."

"Oh, monsieur," replied the Frenchman, "*est il impossible d'eschapper la force de ton bras?* (Is it not possible to mitigate the force of your arm?)"

"Bras, cur!" cried Pistol; "thou damned mountain goat, offerest me brass?"

"*O pardonnez moy!*"

"Is that a ton of moys?"

Fortunately for the unhappy Frenchman, Cherubino came in at this moment and explained to Pistol that the Frenchman was willing to give him five hundred crowns for his life, whereupon Pistol graciously consented to spare him, and bade him be off to his tent under guidance of the boy.

But Ancient Pistol's triumph was short-lived, for as he was congratulating himself upon the possession of five

hundred crowns, the Welsh captain, Fluellen, came towards him, surrounded by several others, and wearing a leek in his hat.

"Got bless you, Ancient Pistol, you scurvy knave," cried the little Welshman; "here is my leek. I pray you eat it."

"Ha, art thou Bedlam?" cried Pistol; "dost thou thirst, base Trojan? Hence! I am qualmish at the smell of leek."

"I beseech you to eat this, knave," cried Fluellen, "because, look you, you do not love leek, and your digestions do not agree with it."

"Not for Cadwallader and all his goats."

"There is one goat for you," replied Fluellen, and gave him such a thump on the jaw that it ached again. "Will you be so goot as to eat it now?"

"Base Trojan," roared Pistol, "thou shalt die!"

"You say very true, scald knave, when God's will is; I will desire to live in the meantime. Eat your victuals—there is sauce for it," and he gave him another thumping box on the ear; "if you can mock a leek you can eat a leek."

"Must I bite?" demanded Pistol, now thoroughly cowed.

"Yes, certainly."

"By this leek I swear most horrible revenge. I eat and eke I swear——"

"There is not enough leek to swear by, so eat it all up," striking him again.

"All hell shall stir for this," cried Pistol, devouring the leek to the utmost part, and then walking hastily off the field.

"Never mind," he added, after a moment's reflection. "I'll be off to England with my spoil. I will cover my face with patches and scars. There will I ruffle and swagger it with the reputation I got in the Gallic wars."

CHAPTER VI.

OUR story now draws near a conclusion. Henry V. moved slowly on towards Troyas with his army, intending to overrun the whole of France.

But by the exertions of the Duke of Burgundy, who showed him a portrait of the beautiful Katharine, daughter of the French king, he was induced to modify some of his demands, and negotiations were straightway put, in order that he should marry her, and that he should be declared the heir to the French throne instead of the Dauphin, whom he pursued with bitter hatred in consequence of his practical joke.

The King of France having any occasion to write for matter of grants, had to add the following—"By permission of our dear son Henry, King of England, and heritor of the French throne," with this addition in Latin—"*Præclarissimus filius noster Henricus, rex Angliæ et hæres Franciæ.*"

"Well, sweet Katharine," cried King Henry, entering the apartment of the lovely French princess, where she was surrounded by her lords and ladies, "everything is settled save your consent, and now you must give me grace, and listen to a soldier's wooing. Fair Katharine, and most fair, will you vouchsafe to teach a soldier terms, such as will enter a lady's ear?"

"Your majesty shall mock me," replied the queen; "I cannot speak your English."

"Oh fair Katharine," replied the royal lover, "if you will love me with your French heart I will be glad to hear you confess it brokenly with your English tongue. Faith, Kate, my wooing is the better fit for thy understanding. I am glad thou canst not speak no better English, for if thou couldst thou wouldst find me such a plain king that thou wouldst think I sold my farm to buy a diadem. I know no way to mince in love, but directly say I love you. And so, if you say yea, clap hands, and a bargain. How say you, lady?"

"Me understand very well," said the queen. "Is it possible that I should love de enemy of *la belle France?*"

"No," replied the king; "it is not possible you should love the enemy of France, Kate, but in loving me you should love the friend of France, for I love France so well that I will not part with a village of it. I will have it all mine; and when France is mine, Kate, and I am yours, then yours is France, and you are mine."

"I cannot tell vat dat is."

"It is as easy for me to conquer a kingdom, Kate, as to speak so much more French; but, Kate, thou canst understand this much in plain English. Canst thou love me?"

"I cannot tell," replied the queen. "Dat is as it shall please de king, my father."

"Nay, it will please him, Kate."

"Den it shall content me."

"Upon this I will kiss your hand and call you my queen."

"Oh, my lord," cried the queen rapidly, in French, "you do me too much honour. I would not that you should so throw off your grandeur and abase yourself as to kiss my hand."

"Then I will kiss your lips, Kate," said the king, and to the surprise of the whole court he took her in his arms and imprinted a hearty kiss upon her lips, telling her at the same time that there was more eloquence in a sugar touch of them than in all the tongues of the French council, and that they should sooner persuade Harry of England than a general petition of monarchs.

The French king was overjoyed that the English king had fallen in love with his daughter, and that he had by this means got out of a dilemma which threatened to deprive him of his kingdom.

The Dauphin's claims as Heir Apparent to the throne of France were set aside in favour of English Harry and his heir by marriage with Queen Katharine.

Shortly afterwards the wedding of the English king and the French princess was solemnised with great pomp and ceremony, and when the king returned with her to England, after having received the oaths of the nobles of France, the fountains of London ran with wine.

Until the day of his death King Henry V. held a firm grip of France, and was considered the wisest and most warlike of all the English kings.

Cherubino, the page, rose to be a captain in the army, under command of Lord Talbot, and never ceased to rejoice at the day he parted company from Bardolph, Nym, and Ancient Pistol.

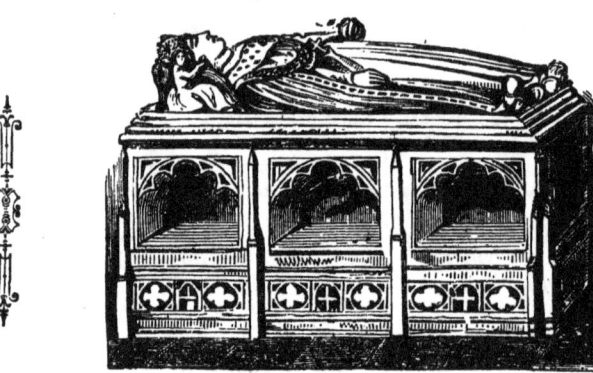

TOMB OF HENRY V.

NOTICE.—"HENRY VI.," being No. 11 of Stories from Shakespeare, will be ready on Monday, January 16. Orders should be given early to your Booksellers.

EDWIN J. BRETT'S STORIES of SHAKESPEARE

COMPLETE

KING HENRY VI.

THE DEATH OF YOUNG JOHN TALBOT.

"Boys of England Edition."

EDWIN J. BRETT'S

STORIES FROM

SHAKESPEARE'S PLAYS.

No. 11.—KING HENRY VI.

CHAPTER I.

DURING the reign of Henry V. that warrior king kept a firm grasp on France, and it was not until his death, after a short but glorious reign, that the French once more made an effort to throw off the English yoke.

Henry V. had taken the precaution of having his infant son crowned at Paris, and most of the French nobility swore allegiance to him.

By his will he left his brother protector to the young king until he should have attained his majority, while another brother, the Duke of Bedford, was created Regent of France, having under his command, as Grand Marshal of France, Lord Talbot, a general only second to himself in military renown.

To his uncle Henry Beaufort, the Bishop of Winchester, he left no power whatsoever, having reason to dread his ambition.

To the ceaseless efforts of this prelate to gain power, in which efforts he was aided by several powerful nobles with whom the reader will become acquainted as our story progresses, was due the fact that the English gradually lost their hold over France.

Taking advantage of the dissensions amongst the English nobles, the Dauphin, Charles, son of the French king whom Henry V. had defeated at the battle of Agincourt, determined to throw off the English yoke, and accordingly he raised the standard of revolt.

The whole of France, except that part under the dominion of the Duke of Burgundy, flocked to his standard.

But for months the military genius of the great Talbot kept them at bay, and the Dauphin was unable to make headway against him.

Unfortunately, though he sent messenger after messenger to England imploring men and money, the great English nobles were too much occupied in wrangling amongst themselves at home to afford him timely aid.

Town after town threw off the yoke, and the valiant Talbot found himself in the position of a victorious leader marching through an enemy's country, and only able to maintain himself by forcing the Dauphin into pitched battles when he could find him.

Notwithstanding the odds against him he became the terror of the French, and the Dauphin retreated before him as he laid siege to and captured one town after another.

He was laying siege to Orleans when our story, illustrative of the reign of Henry VI., opens.

On a summer morning during the year 1428, it was *fete* day in the little village of Arc, in the department of the Indre-et-Loire, on the borders of the Forest of Orleans, some miles from the town of that name. This was the capital of the Duke of Burgundy, then a staunch ally to the

English, and a personal friend of the great Talbot, whom, despite the defection of his followers, he staunchly supported.

"Joan! Joan! you lazy hussy, will you be lying in bed all day?"

The speaker was one of the peasant class, outside a miserable hut not far from the forest.

As he spoke he gathered his sheep together in no very amiable frame of mind.

"I am coming, father," replied a peevish voice.

"Ay, coming, art thou, thou lazy hussy? 'Twas ever thus. By the mass, the grass will be dry under the scorching sun ere thou takest the hood of sleep from thy drowsy eyes."

"Why this clamour, good father?" said a handsome young woman, at that instant appearing from the hut. "'Tis scarce ten minutes past sunrise, and I have seen that which would have kept thee staring all day."

"Go to, go to, thou lazy slut; 'tis another of thy foolish visions, I warrant--- visions that have made thee the laughing stock of the village."

"I care not for their laughter or sneers, good father," she replied. "Who would care for the opinion of those who can laugh and make merry when our unhappy country is delivered over to the mercy of these accursed English?"

"Go to, go to, wench," replied the old man. "What is that to thee? Attend thy sheep, and leave to thy betters the task of understanding these things."

The rich blood crimsoned a face at once handsome, haughty, and sullen.

In person, despite her mean attire, Joan was exceedingly handsome; almost masculine in stature, her beautifully developed limbs were well calculated to bear the weight of armour which she was subsequently destined to wear, while her raven locks and midnight eyes might well cause one to believe her the beautiful sorceress the English subsequently called her.

"I understand them well enough," she replied bitterly; "our beautiful young king retreating before that butcher Talbot, who they say drinks the blood of babes to give him terrible strength. Our beautiful country laid waste and desolate by these ravening wolves, and all the while the lazy hinds in the village will stir nor hand nor foot to help our gracious king."

"Marry, what treason is this, thou trull?" cried the old man in a rage. "Wouldst thou have me lose my life for thy vapourings? Go, tend thy sheep, and mend thy ways. Knowest thou not that our good lord of Burgundy is friends with Lord Talbot, and does not recognise the pretensions of the Dauphin?"

"I know the Dauphin will drive our enemies from France," said the girl, with an intense look upon her face. "Yea, those that were as brothers shall become bitter enemies."

"What ails thee, Joan? what ails thee?" cried the old man, impatiently; "I believe that thou hast become bewitched lately."

"And if I have," replied she, "it is the saints and our Holy Mother that have bewitched me.

"Hear me, sweet mother!" she cried, lifting her hands to heaven in a sort of religious ecstasy, "hear me, Mother of God! vouchsafe to give thy handmaiden one more sign, and I will obey thy sacred call though it should lead me to the stake.

"See, see," she added, pointing to the hill before her, whose summit was crowned by a dense patch of woodland; "dost not thou behold her and all the company of the saints in yon fierce blaze of glory? Ave Mary, I come, I come!"

"I see nought but the sun rising over the hills, thou foolish wench," cried the old man in a sudden fit of spleen; "an thou dost not move on quickly with thy sheep this stick shall become acquainted with thy lazy back."

Joan heeded him not.

Apparently she was wrapped in a trance. Her gaze was fixed, her hands clasped together in an attitude of devotion.

"Here is that will recall to thee that it is necessary to obey my commands," said the old man, giving her a sharp blow across the shoulders with his stick.

But to his surprise it broke in half, while she appeared unconscious of the blow.

"I heed thee, sweet Mother," continued the girl, "no weapon framed by man shall have power against me until I have delivered our rightful king and driven these dogs of English from the soil."

"She is bewitched; she is bewitched," groaned the shepherd. "Oh, that I should live to see my only child a prey to the evil one!"

"Foolish old man," cried Joan. "Do you not know that I am destined to deliver France? A virgin shall dull the edge of their swords and put their haughty pride to shame. A woman unaided and alone shall put to flight the foes of France."

So saying, she walked forward with her gaze steadfastly fixed in the direction of the little village of Arc.

"The priest must see to this," said the shepherd, as he followed her footsteps. "A curse on all foul fiends, it will cost me eight groats ere I get the good father to exorcise her."

Unheeding her father's lamentations the girl walked steadily forward until she reached the village green, where a number of peasants were keeping up the *fete* of "Our Lady of Orleans," by dancing.

Joan stopped here and addressed them in a voice of mingled anger and scorn.

The men she lashed because they could give way to mirth and merriment while France was being overrun with the English; while the women came in for their share of opprobrium because they permitted their lovers to stay at home when the Dauphin wanted every arm to aid him.

The dance stopped.

All was confusion.

Overcome by her eloquence they remained silent and ashamed.

It was the voice of her father which broke the silence.

"I do assure you, good people," he cried, "this treason is none of my begetting. The wench, as ye know, was ever a dreaming, lazy baggage, and I doubt not some evil spirit hath persuaded her to our undoing."

"Peace, peace, old man!" cried Joan. "I tell you I am a prophetess, selected by our Holy Mother to deliver our unhappy king from his enemies."

At this there was a universal burst of laughter.

"Why," cried one, "who is this that addresses us in this lofty strain? Is it not the old shepherd's daughter, Joan—lazy Joan—who cannot mind her sheep without going to sleep in the noon-day?"

"Ye lie, knave—it is the visions that overcome me. It is our Holy Mother that doth appear to me when ye deem me asleep. She hath told me to arise and drive the English from the land, that the Virgin may be honoured.

"Sacrilegious wretch!" cried out one; "Wouldst thou dare tell us that the Holy Mother would appear to such as thou?"

Another shouted "to the river with the witch—to the river!"

The cry was taken up by a hundred voices as the speaker advanced to put his threat into execution.

But scarcely had he laid his hand on her ere he dropped down dead.

The crowd fell back horrified and terrified.

"Told I you not that I am under the protection of the Virgin?" cried the girl in a voice thrilling with religious enthusiasm. "This place is called Arc, and ere this year has passed I, Joan of Arc, shall have my name in all men's mouths."

As she ceased speaking, a priest approached to know the cause of the uproar.

He had a merry, cunning eye. One it would appear that could tell character at a glance.

While they were telling him of the events which had just happened, he surveyed Joan of Arc critically.

Her features, lit up with enthusiasm, beamed like those of an angel, while her immense height and commanding appearance enabled her to overawe the crowd which surrounded her.

In short, if there was religious enthusiasm to be created and a crusade to be made, here was the instrument.

"And so you would fain see the king, maiden?" said the priest, approaching.

"Holy father," cried Joan, "I would deliver him from the power of his enemies."

"Thou wilt please his eye, at all events," muttered the priest to himself, "and therein I spy advancement for me, if we should gain the day."

"It is to thee that I was about to go, holy father," continued the maid, "for the Virgin hath commanded me to pray and fast with thee all night, before the high altar of St. Croix, ere I take the enchanted armour there awaiting me."

"Good people," said the priest, turning to the mob, "this night will I spend in prayer with this maiden. Assemble all of ye to-morrow, and we will then learn if this is a miracle of our Holy Mother, or whether it be the device of the Evil One. The Bastard of Orleans passes this way to-morrow," continued the wily priest to himself; "it will go hard with me but what I persuade him to a miracle shall obtain me a bishop's mitre."

All night was spent in prayer.

In the morning, Joan, robed in white,

made her way to the high altar, and to the surprise of everybody (except, perhaps, to the wily priest) took from behind it a suit of armour inlaid with gold, which fitted her exactly.

By the side of the armour was a silken banner, covered with *fleur-de-lys*, having in the centre a crimson cross.

Advancing to the steps of the altar, Joan raised her voice.

"By this sacred banner, which, with the armour I now wear, has been sent to me from the Virgin, I swear to deliver France from her enemies!"

While the organ pealed forth its sonorous notes to this, a cry arose—

"The English, the English!"

Instantly a panic arose.

But Joan was equal to the occasion.

"The Lord hath delivered them into our hands," she cried; "follow me, and see the wonders that will be wrought."

Rushing out of the church, with her bright sword flashing in her hands, and her silken white banner waving in the sun, she found waiting for her a horse gaily caparisoned,

Shouting, "*La Pucelle! La Pucelle!*" she dashed down the road, where a convoy of English were passing.

Followed by the maddened peasantry, she threw herself into the midst of them.

The English, not expecting an attack, and seeing the banner of the *Fleur-de-lys* (the royal banner), supposed that they must be surrounded by the army of the Dauphin.

However, after the first surprise they resisted stoutly, but were cut to pieces just as trumpets in the distance announced the arrival of the Bastard of Orleans, the Dauphin's brother, with a company from the south.

"By my faith, fair maid," said he, when Joan's doings and wonderful narrative had been narrated to him, "an I carry not to my brother the reinforcements he expected, at least he will have somewhat to console him in thee."

"Bastard of Orleans," said Joan impressively, "thou wilt have thy reinforcements ere we reach Orleans, and within this month this banner shall be hanging on its outer walls. Arms! arms! ye peasants," she continued, raising her voice; "St. Denis aid us, and this day month shall see the bloody Talbot driven from French ground."

Lord Talbot was laying vigorous siege to Orleans, and the Dauphin, with an army numerically stronger, was endeavouring to raise the siege.

But the bull-dog and desperate courage of the English had disheartened them.

They had no stomach for the fight.

Meanwhile Talbot had sent again and again to England for succour that never came.

Leaving Orleans and the adventures of the Maid of Orleans for the present, let us see how it fared at the court of Henry VI.

CHAPTER II.

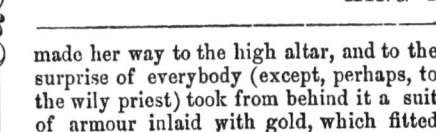

THE young king was surrounded by a host of unscrupulous and ambitious nobles, not the least of which was the Bishop of Winchester, who, with the Duke of Suffolk, was plotting a disgraceful peace with France, which might give him a cardinal's hat.

But all their intrigue availed not, so long as the Lord Protector remained in power.

They, therefore, directed their attention towards undermining him.

But he was so popular with the masses that this was almost a hopeless task.

The king trusted him utterly, but as he grew up so did his pernicious counsellors endeavour to persuade him that the Protector was aiming at the throne.

Finding this of no avail, they determined that the king should marry some one who would be a tool in their hands, and who would gradually wean the king's affection from his uncle, Gloucester, and lead to his overthrow.

But while these persons were plotting his overthrow, one person, who was destined to upset them all, was also occupied with his plans.

This was Richard Plantagenet, who became first of all Duke of York, and afterwards the head of the Yorkist or White Rose faction, while his rival, Somerset, became the head of the Red Rose faction.

The quarrel between these two took place in the Temple Gardens, over a quibble of law, which was in reality a mere paltry excuse to cover their deep-dyed enmity to one another.

Those who have read Henry V. will remember that he, prior to his departure from France, caused the Earl of Cambridge, Richard's father, to be beheaded for plotting to place Mortimer, Earl of March, his brother, on the throne.

The Duke of Somerset taunted Richard Plantagenet with this fact, and he, not knowing why his father was executed, paid a visit to his uncle Mortimer in the Tower to find out.

To his astonishment he learned from the dying earl that by right he was more entitled to the throne than the king.

And this was how the dying earl explained it—

"Declare the cause why my father, the late Earl of Cambridge, lost his head," said Richard.

"That cause, fair nephew, which hath detained me all my flowering youth within this prison here to pine, was cursed instrument of his decease."

"Discover more at large what cause that was, for I am ignorant and cannot guess."

In a long dying speech, he explained to Richard Plantagenet how it was that he was the rightful heir, and perfectly convinced him that the throne should be his by right.

He concluded by saying—

"Thou seest that I no issue have, and that my fainting words do warrant death. Thou art my heir; the rest I wish thee gather. But yet be wary in thy studious care."

Richard promised faithfully to work for the dethronement of the king and the elevation of himself to the throne.

He had hardly vowed this ere the old earl expired.

He resolved, as soon as his plans were developed, to take into his confidence all his partizans who had accepted the White Rose, plucked in the Temple Garden, as their badge.

Meanwhile he worked hard to provoke the growing enmity between the Bishop of Winchester and the Lord Protector, knowing that both of them must fall ere he could hope to be strong enough to establish his claim to the throne.

The young king was weak and foolish, the prey to religious and superstitious fears, and distracted by the contentions of his fierce nobles, who had not, like Richard Plantagenet, the wit to keep their plans to themselves.

He so fomented the quarrel between the noblemen that the prelate's followers and those of the Lord Protector were constantly in a state of brawls, and blood was shed like water between the retainers of each in the streets of London.

While matters were in this state, the Governor of Paris came over to take the oath of fealty to the young king.

But he had scarcely begun the ceremony ere a courier arrived from Paris with a letter to the king, which filled the court with anger and dismay.

This was from Henry's staunch supporter in France, the Duke of Burgundy, and ran as follows—

"To the King,—I have upon special cause, moved with compassion of my country's wreck, together with the pitiful complaints of those on whom your oppression feeds, forsaken your pernicious faction and joined with Charles the rightful King of France."

Hardly was the herald's back turned upon the court, where he had filled them with consternation and dismay at the threatened loss of France altogether, than the nobles again began quarrelling.

The king, in order to pacify them, hastily organised an expedition to France.

And now that we have carried our story so far, and seen the intrigues of the English court laid bare, let us once more cross the Channel and see how it fared with the Maid of Orleans.

CHAPTER III.

HARLES OF FRANCE was gnawing his fingers with rage and impatience before the city of Orleans.

In vain they attempted to drive back the English.

At last the Dauphin spoke up.

"Let us leave this town," he said, "for they are hare-brained slaves, and hunger will enforce them to be more eager. Of old I know these English. Rather with their teeth will they the walls tear down, than forsake the siege."

At this moment the Bastard of Orleans entered, and was heartily welcomed by the Dauphin.

"Be not dismayed," said the Bastard,

"for succour is at hand. A holy maid, hither with me I bring, which, by a vision sent to her from heaven, ordained is to raise this tedious siege, and drive the English forth the bounds of France. The spirit of deep prophecy she hath, exceeding the nine sibyls of old Rome. What's past, and what's to come she can descry. Speak, shall I call her in? Believe my words, for they are certain and infallible."

"Go, call her in," said Charles. "But first, to try her skill, Reignier, stand thou as Dauphin in my place. Question her proudly, let thy looks be stern. By this means shall we sound what skill she hath."

Reignier assumed the Dauphin's place, and as the Maid of Orleans entered, he asked her in a haughty voice if she could do all the things she pretended.

"Reignier," cried the Maid, "stand thou back, and let me see the Dauphin. Thou art not he."

While all stood amazed, the abashed prince came forward, and she continued—

"Be not amazed, there's nothing hid from me. In private will I talk with thee apart. Stand back, you lords, and give us leave a while. Dauphin, I am by birth a shepherd's daughter, my wit untrained in any kind of art. Heaven, and our Lady gracious, hath it pleased to shine on my contemptible estate. Lo, whilst I waited on my tender lambs, and to sun's parching heat displayed my cheeks, God's mother deigned to appear to me, and, in a vision full of majesty, willed me to leave my base vocation and free my country from calamity. Her aid she promised, and assured success. In complete glory she revealed herself. And, whereas I was black and swart before, with those clear rays which she infused on me, that beauty I am blessed with, which you see. Ask me what question thou canst possible and I will answer unpremeditated. My courage try by combat, if thou darest, and thou shalt find that I exceed my sex. Resolve on this—Thou shalt be fortunate, if thou receive me for thy warlike mate"

"Thou hast astonished me with thy high terms," replied the king. "Only this proof I'll of thy valour make—In single combat thou shalt buckle with me, and, if thou vanquishest, thy words are true, otherwise, I renounce all confidence."

"I am prepared," said Joan, "here is my keen-edged sword, decked with five *fleur-de-lys* on each side. The which at Touraine in Saint Katharine's churchyard, out of a deal of old iron I chose forth."

Accordingly they retired outside, and in a few rounds the Maid of Orleans beat the Dauphin to his knees.

In vain he tried every feint and guard, and so hurt was he at thus having his pride taken down by a country wench that he would have killed her if he could.

But it was all to no purpose.

And at last, chagrined at his want of success, he flung down his sword, and swore that she should be his mistress.

The maid gravely assured him that she could not think of love until she had driven his foes from France.

"Heaven protects me," she said, "else assuredly I had not prevailed against your majesty, and now I prophesy that I will crown you king at Rouen. Come, let us begin and drive away these English dogs!"

This raised them to the greatest pitch of enthusiasm.

No less was it so with the volatile Frenchmen.

The fame of her prophecies had spread abroad, and, when she went to review the troops, the common soldiers regarded her as one sent from Heaven.

"When shall we begin to raise the siege?" inquired the Dauphin.

"Now!" cried La Pucelle. "Now is the time; soldiers of France, to-day is victory amongst you."

In a spirited harangue she wrought the French soldiers up to a terrific pitch of enthusiasm.

A holy fire animated them.

Rushing into the fore front of the battle, she drove the awe inspired and superstitious English soldiers before her like chaff before the wind.

In the meanwhile, a chance shot had wounded to the death the Duke of Salisbury, and John Talbot was mourning over his old friend, when news came that the English troops were everywhere retiring before the French.

He rushed into the battle-field full of fury, and saw his troops in full flight pursued by Joan.

"Ha! here she comes," he cried; "I'll have a bout with the devil, or devil's dam. Blood will I draw thou art a witch. Straightway will I give thy coat to him thou servest."

In a moment they closed, and then began a dire conflict.

"Ha, ha!" laughed the scornful laugh of the virgin in his ears. "It is I that must disgrace thee, proud Talbot."

"Heavens!" cried Talbot, as he leaned back after a furious bout in which he in vain endeavoured to beat her to the earth. "Can you suffer hell to prevail? My breast I'll burst but what I will chastise this high-minded impostor."

But Joan of Arc, for all her vaunt, had had quite enough of old Talbot, and could not assure herself that she would come scathless out of the fray should she engage again.

fight, or tear the lions out of English coats. Renounce your soil, give sheep in lion's stead. Sheep run not half so timorous from the wolf as you fly from your oft-subdued slaves."

In vain the English soldiers tried to rally to their great commander's passionate appeal.

Again and again they were driven back.

And at last Talbot saw that the day was lost.

"It will not be," he cried sullenly. "You all consented to Salisbury's death

MARRIAGE OF HENRY VI. AND MARGARET.

Besides her purpose had been gained. "Talbot, farewell," she said, "thine hour has not yet come. I must go and victual Orleans forthwith. Overtake me if thou canst. I scorn thy strength. Go cheer up thy hungry starved men, or help Salisbury to make his will. This day is ours!"

Then with a ringing laugh of triumph and defiance she mixed amongst a group of soldiers and entered the town, leaving the great English commander raving with rage.

"Heavens!" he cried. "I know not where I am nor what I do. A witch I fear, not force, drives back our troops. They called us for our fierceness English dogs, now we like curs are running away. Hark, countrymen! Either renew the

since none of you will avenge him. Return to your trenches. Pucelle has entered Orleans in spite of us or aught that we could do. Oh, would I were to die with Salisbury! The shame of this will make me hide my head!"

———

CHAPTER IV.

MEANWHILE inside the town all was in the greatest state of jubilation.

Where before all had been starvation, now all was plenty.

And the citizens knelt down and kissed the ground the holy maid had pressed as she passed along.

Joan went to the cathedral, where she returned thanks for the victory, and then went out on the city walls surrounded by a wild crowd of enthusiasts who now believed in her thoroughly.

"Advance our waving colours on the wall," she cried, while all listened to her as one inspired. "Rescued is Orleans from the English wolves, thus Joan hath performed the first part of her vow."

"Divinest creature," cried the effeminate and sensual French king, who had fallen desperately in love

PORTRAIT OF HENRY VI.

with her. "How shall I honour thee for this success? France, triumph in thy glorious prophetess. Recovered is the town of Orleans. More blessed hap did ne'er befall our state."

"Why ring not out the bells throughout the town?" cried Joan.

"Dauphin, command the citizens make bonfires, and feast and banquet in the open streets to celebrate the joy that Heaven has given us."

"All France will be replete with mirth and joy when they shall hear how we have play'd the men," said the Bastard.

"'Tis Joan," said Charles, "not we, by whom the day is won, for which I will divide my crown with her and all the priests and friars in my realm shall in procession sing her endless praise. A statelier pyramis to her I'll rear than Rhodope's, of Memphis, ever was. In memory of her, when she is dead, her ashes in an urn more

QUEEN MARGARET.

precious than the rich-jewel'd coffer of Darius, transported shall be at high festivals before the kings and queens of France. No longer on Saint Denis will we cry, but Joan la Pucelle shall be France's saint. Come in, and let us banquet royally after this golden day of victory."

We shall see presently how the base king performed these promises.

They entered into the king's palace and spent the night in riotous debauchery, so that the English heard their exultant cries.

But Joan little knew the fierce and vigilant commander to whom she was opposed if she imagined that one victory or one bit of ill-success would make him lose heart.

In the middle of the night he summoned his forces in silence, together with his ally, the Duke of Burgundy, who had not yet turned recusant.

The joyful French had neglected their outposts and sentinels, and in a few moments a swarm of desperate English, headed by their fierce leader, Talbot, were in the town.

Then rang out the fierce cry "St. George! St. George! A Talbot! a Talbot!"

Cutting, hewing, slaughtering the surprised and panic-stricken French, the English swarmed all over the town.

Some leaped the wall in their night-shirts, others hid themselves in cellars.

The slaughter was terrific, and the victorious English everywhere searched for the Maid of Orleans, who had given them such a scare in the earlier part of the day.

She succeeded in making her escape with the Dauphin, who, like most cowards, immediately turned round on his preserver. "Is this thy cunning, thou deceitful dame?" he said to her as they were running along in full flight. "Didst thou at first to flatter us withal make us partakers of a little gain, that our loss might be ten times as much?"

"At all times will you have my power alike?" retorted Joan. "Sleeping or waking must I still prevail? Improvident soldiers, had your watch been good this sudden mischief never could have fallen."

The principal nobles then began wrangling as to who was to blame for the want of care, and were on the point of falling out amongst themselves, when Joan managed to pacify them, and persuaded them to retreat with their scattered forces towards Bordeaux, and there having augmented the army, they would once more offer battle to the bold English commander.

She contrived to persuade them that it was only when she was asleep that she was not invincible.

Brave Talbot was obliged to retreat from the town he had so hardly won.

Animated by the wild enthusiasm of La Pucelle, the country everywhere rose against the English.

Burgundy's soldiers began to desert in masses, food could hardly be procured, and it was only after repeated messages that the weak-minded Henry VI. at last decided to send the two rivals, Richard Plantagenet of the White Rose, and Somerset of the Red to his assistance.

But, animated by mutual jealousy, they tried to hinder each other in every possible way, and in the meanwhile unfortunate Talbot had to contend against overwhelming odds.

Each one of the commanders was so occupied in sending accounts of the shortcomings of the other commander to the king, that they had no time to heed the imploring letters and messengers which came daily from Talbot, who, like a bulldog that is dying, never relinquished his grip on the victorious French, but with a mere handful of followers held them in check.

But in the other parts of the country victorious Joan drove the English before her, and the Dauphin, who had now become her paramour, was solemnly crowned King of France at Rouen.

At last the two divisions of the English army, one in command of Somerset, the other under the leadership of Richard Plantagenet, Duke of York, moved slowly up the plains of Gascony to Talbot's support.

Talbot was in front of Bordeaux, and a mighty army under the command of the Dauphin was between him and the relieving forces.

He despatched a gallant knight—Sir William Lucy—for aid, and he succeeded in breaking through the French forces, and made his way to the Duke of York.

He thus addressed him—

"Thou princely leader of our English strength, never so needful on the earth of France, spur to the rescue of the noble Talbot, who now is girdled with a waist of iron, and hemmed about with grim destruction. To Bordeaux, warlike duke; to Bordeaux, York, else farewell Talbot, France, and England's honour."

"Oh Heaven!" replied the Duke of York, "that Somerset, who in proud heart doth stop my cornets, were in Talbot's place, so should we save a valiant gentleman by forfeiting a traitor and a coward."

"Oh, send some succour to a valiant and distressed gentleman," reiterated Sir William Lucy.

"He dies," replied York; "we lose; I break my warlike word. We mourn; France smiles, all along of that traitor Somerset."

"Then," replied Sir William Lucy earnestly, "Heaven take mercy on brave Talbot's soul, and on his son, young John; whom, two hours since, I met in travel towards his warlike father! This seven years did not Talbot see his son; and now they meet where both their lives are done."

"Alas," replied the Duke of York, "what joys shall noble Talbot have to bid his young son welcome to his grave? Away! vexation almost stops my breath, that sundered friends greet in the hour of death. Lucy, farewell; no more my fortune can, but curse the cause I cannot aid the man. Maine, Blois, Poictiers, and Tours, are won away, along all of Somerset and his delay."

"Thus," soliloquised Sir William bitterly, "while the vulture of sedition feeds in the bosom of such great commanders, sleeping neglection doth betray to loss the conquest of our scarce-cold conqueror, that ever living man of memory,

Henry V. Whiles they each other cross, lives, honours, lands, and all, hurry to loss."

So saying, he made his way to where the Duke of Somerset was advancing on another route, to whom he addressed the same piteous appeal for help.

Somerset replied—

"It is too late; I cannot send them now. This expedition was by York and Talbot too rashly plotted. All our general force might with a sally of the very town be buckled with. The over-daring Talbot hath sullied all his gloss of former honour by this unheedful, desperate, wild adventure. York set him on to fight and die in shame, that, Talbot dead, great York might bear the name. York should have sent him aid."

"And York," replied Sir William, "as fast upon your grace exclaims, swearing that you withhold his levied host collected for this expedition."

"York lies," replied the Duke of Somerset. "He might have sent and had the horse. I owe him little duty and less love, and take foul scorn to fawn on him by sending."

"The fraud of England, not the force of France, hath betrayed my noble commander," said Sir William bitterly. "Never to England shall he bear his life, but dies betrayed to fortune by your strife."

Finding that he could not get assistance, the valiant knight resolved to return and perish with his commander.

He found him on the eve of battle, imploring his young son to fly while there was yet time.

But young John steadfastly refused.

"Oh, my son," said his father passionately, "I did send for thee to tutor thee in stratagems of war, that Talbot's name might in thee be revived when sapless age, and weak unable limbs, should bring thy father to his drooping chair. But—O malignant and ill boding stars!—now thou art come unto a feast of death, a terrible and unavoided danger; therefore, dear boy, mount on my swiftest horse, and I'll direct thee how thou shalt escape by sudden flight. Come, dally not; begone!"

"Is my name Talbot?" asked young John, "and am I your son?—and shall I fly? Oh, if you love my mother, dishonour not her honourable name. The world will say—'He is not Talbot's blood, that basely fled when noble Talbot stood.'"

"Fly, to revenge my death if I be slain."

"He that flies so will ne'er return again."

"If we both stay we both are sure to die."

"Then let me stay; and, father, do you fly. Your loss is great, so your regard should be; my worth unknown, no loss is known in me. Upon my death the French can little boast; in yours they will, in you all hopes are lost. Flight cannot stain the honour you have won."

But of course his father resisted this, and both father and son resolved to fight and die together.

They had barely bade each other adieu, resolved to show the French how brave Englishmen could die, when the battle became general.

Animated by the courage of their leaders, the English fought like furies, and in vain the Holy Maid of Orleans endeavoured to press them backward to flight.

Though, they were as sands upon the seashore compared to the English, they could not make the latter fly; rather did they prefer to fall where they stood.

In the midst of the fight the victorious Joan rushed up to young John Talbot and challenged him to fight her, as he was doing prodigies of valour, and equalled his father in daring and high courage.

Joan was afraid of encountering the father; she thought she would have an easier victory over the son.

So she taunted him as follows—

"Thou maiden youth, be vanquished by a maid!"

But, as he turned away from her to another part of the field, where he saw the coronet of the Dauphin, he answered, in a voice full of majestic scorn—

"Young Talbot was not born to be the pillage of a giglot wench."

And so left her proudly, not deeming her worthy to fight.

But, as we said before, he espied the Dauphin, and cutting his way through the thick of the fight, with one blow he sheared helm and coronet, bringing him to his knees.

But a dozen devoted noblemen threw themselves between the young lion and his prey.

While the Dauphin was helped to his feet, they pressed on young John, who would have been either killed or taken prisoner then, but that his father came raging to his rescue, with frantic shouts of "St. George and victory! Fight, soldiers—fight!"

Again he implored his son to leave the field; but the young man would not, although he saw that now, thanks to the overwhelming odds, there was no hope for the English.

At last Talbot received his death-wound, and was supported a little way in the rear by one of his retainers.

"Where is my son?" he cried. "Where is valiant John? Triumphant death, his valour makes me smile at thee. He left me suddenly to rush into a cluster of French."

"Alas, my lord!" cried one of the servants, "yonder is borne your son, desperately wounded."

"Bring him here!" cried old John; "let him die in these arms. Ha! the English fly at last; the Talbots are not there to reanimate their courage.

"Come, come, and lay him in his father's arms; my spirit can no longer bear these harms. Soldiers, adieu! I have what I would have, now my old arms are young John Talbot's grave."

As he finished speaking, he fell back dead, just as the triumphant Maid of Orleans came rushing over the plains.

They found the terrible warrior and his son clasped in one another's arms.

"Ha!" cried the French king, "the day is ours; but had York or Somerset brought rescue in we should have found a bloody day of this!"

At this moment the heralds announced the arrival of Sir William Lucy.

"On what submissive message art thou sent?" inquired the Dauphin.

"Submission!" retorted Sir William haughtily. "'Tis a mere French word; we English warriors know not what it means. I come to know what prisoners thou hast taken."

"There is the chief of those thou seekest," replied the King of France.

"Is Talbot slain?" cried Sir William, in a burst of passionate grief. "Talbot, the scourge of France! Give me their bodies, that I may bear them hence, and give them burial as beseems their worth!"

"Go, take them hence," replied the king. "So we be rid of them, do with them what thou wilt; and now to Paris, in the conquering vein, all will be ours now bloody Talbot's slain!"

The King of France accordingly retired to the gay dissipations of the capital, giving no thought to the advancing forces of Somerset and York.

But the remorse caused by Talbot's death to both of them, caused them to forget their bickerings for awhile and to advance to revenge him.

In vain Joan of Arc, the warlike Maid of Orleans, implored the king to hasten forward and intercept the junction of the two armies.

He paid no heed to her.

In fact, Charles was heartily sick of his paramour, the warlike Amazon.

She had served his turn, and another favourite reigned in her stead, and was the mistress of the sensual king.

But he dared not quarrel with Joan openly, for the soldiers still believed her to be inspired.

Besides, he wanted to conclude a peace with England, and the wily Bishop of Winchester, for his own purposes, wished to conclude a peace too, no less than the ignoble boy, Henry VI., who was gradually losing what his father had so valiantly won.

Each side in fact was anxious to bring the war to a close, and diplomacy was constantly undermining the effect of valour in the field.

The pope was requested to use his influence to bring about peace; and the price to be paid was a cardinal's hat for the Bishop of Winchester, who would thus be a greater man in England than his hated rival, the protector Gloucester.

CHAPTER V.

BUT all these diplomatic relations were put to flight by the fact that the Dukes of Somerset and York joined their forces, and forced upon Charles the alternative of flight or a pitched battle before Angiers.

Again the warlike virgin resumed her sway, much to the disgust of the king, who would now fain have concluded peace and got rid of his Amazon at any price.

Prophetesses became stale as well as every other kind of novelty in this world, and Joan found to her sorrow that she no longer inspired the same amount of enthusiasm since it was alleged that she had allowed the king to become her paramour.

The French and English forces met with a terrible shock before Angiers, the former no longer under the maddening influence of the maid, while the English were burning to avenge the death of their beloved Talbot.

The issue was not long in doubt, and it was then alleged by the English that La Pucelle, finding her saints forsake her, invoked the aid of the fiends.

Shakespeare makes her invoke their aid on the field of battle; and they refuse, telling her that her hour is come.

Almost immediately afterwards she is captured by the Duke of York, who says to her—

"Damsel of France, I think I have you fast; unchain your spirits now with spelling charms and try if they can gain your liberty. A goodly prize, fit for the devil's grace. See how the ugly witch doth bend her brows, as if, with Circe, she would change my shape."

"Changed to a worser shape thou canst not be," replied La Pucelle.

"Oh, Charles the Dauphin is a proper man; no shape but his can please your dainty eye," responded York.

"A plaguing mischief light on Charles and thee," replied the maid, "and may ye both be surprised by bloody hands in sleeping on your beds."

"Fell banning hag," cried York, "enchantress, hold they tongue."

"I pray thee," retorted the maid, "give me leave to curse awhile."

"Curse, witch?" cried the enraged York. "Thou wilt curse when thou comest to the stake, whither thou shalt presently be led."

And so the unhappy enthusiast was led away to prison.

In the meanwhile, the Earl of Suffolk had captured Margaret, the daughter of Reignier, titular King of Naples.

He fell violently in love with her and she consented to being his mistress, provided he married her to the foolish King of England and concluded a peace with France.

Suffolk knew no surer way to power than by having the wife of the king his mistress.

He hoped by this means, aided by his friend the Cardinal Bishop of Winchester, to overthrow the Lord Protector Gloucester and become the first man in England.

A most disgraceful peace was therefore concluded, by which nearly every English possession was given back to France.

But in return the dastardly French King Charles abandoned the "Witch of Orleans," as she was now called, to the fury of the English soldiers.

After a mock trial, she was sentenced to be burnt for a witch in the market-place of Rouen, now known as the Place de la Pucelle, and thus consummate one of the most despicable pieces of revenge of which English soldiers have ever been guilty.

But as this execution needs a deal of description, we will begin another chapter.

CHAPTER VI.

IN vain—in vain, had the unfortunate Joan implored the wretched French king to save her form the cruel fate which awaited her.

Occupied with his new mistresses, and plunged into a sea of pleasure which the new treaty with England gave him leisure for, he paid no heed to her passionate supplications.

In fact he was animated by two ideas—a desire to please England, and a wish to be rid of one whose only fault was that she loved him too well and mistook for a holy mission and inspiration what was in reality merely a passionate love for her country and her king.

Vast crowds filled the market-place of Rouen as the maid was led out, surrounded by priests, to the centre, where a vast pile of faggots awaited her.

A peasant came forward to acknowledge her as his daughter, but she averred that this was but a trick of her enemies to bring her into contempt, and she would not acknowledge her father.

Then the shepherd burst out in a rage.

"Burn her, burn her!" he cried, "hanging is too good."

"Ay," cried York, who was eager to avenge the death of his friend Talbot, and who hated Joan because she had robbed him of what he deemed would be his possession as soon as he had matured his plans and seized the English throne. "Take her away," cried York. "Take her away, for she hath lived too long to fill the world with vicious qualities."

"First," cried the maid, "let me tell you whom you have condemned. Not one begotten of a shepherd swain, but issued from the progeny of kings, virtuous and holy; chosen from above by inspiration of celestial grace, to work exceeding miracles on earth. I never had to do with wicked spirits, but you, because you want the grace that others have, you judge it straight a thing impossible to compass wonders,

but by help of devils. My blood will cry for vengeance at the gates of heaven."

"Ay, ay!" bellowed York, "away with her to execution."

"And hark ye, sirs," cried Warwick, "because she is a maid, spare for no faggots, let there be enough. Place barrels of pitch upon the fatal stake, that so her torture may be shortened."

"Now Heaven forefend! the holy maid with child!" sneered the Duke of York.

In despair, then, the unfortunate maid told them that she was about to become a mother, and was consequently entitled by law to a reprieve.

"The greatest miracle that e'er ye wrought," cried the brutal Earl of Warwick, who was afterwards known as the King Maker; "have all your miracles come to this?"

"She and the Dauphin have been together," said York. "I did imagine this would be her refuge. Well go to; we will have no illegitimate kings."

"You are mistaken," cried the maid; "it is Alencon who is father of my child."

"Alencon!" exclaimed York; "it dies if it had a thousand lives."

"Oh, give me leave," cried the unhappy Joan, at her wits' end what to say to preserve her life. "It was Reignier, King of Naples."

"Why worse and worse—thy words condemn thee," replied York; "use no entreaty for it is in vain."

"Then hear me," cried the unhappy martyr. "With thee I leave my curse. May never glorious sun reflect his beams upon the country where you make abode! But darkness and the gloomy shade of death environ you, till mischief and despair drive you to hang yourselves."

"Light the faggots," cried York. "Break thou in pieces, and consume to ashes, thou foul accursed minister of hell."

As the brutal flames shot upwards, cries and groans, and lamentations arose from the common people.

They would have broken through and rescued her, but that they were driven back by the fierce spears of the English soldiers, who feasted their eyes on her agony.

But, after her last passionate appeal for life, Joan closed her eyes and folding her hands as if in prayer, remained silent while the flames crept upwards.

Suddenly a piercing, thrilling scream escaped her lips.

She opened her eyes, and lifted them in one imploring appeal to Heaven.

Then her head fell forward on the iron collar.

She was dead!

Almost at the same instant a white dove circled in the air over her head, and then rose heavenward.

None knew whence it came, and it was taken as the soul of Joan, pure and unsullied, mounting to heaven.

So perished the gallant and enthusiastic Maid of Orleans, in the zenith of her fame, a prey to revenge and cowardice.

She left a blot on the escutcheons of France and England which will never be removed.

After her death, and the conclusion of the truce between France and England, both armies broke up, and the great nobles went back to assist at the marriage between the wretched boy, King Henry VI., and Margaret of Anjou.

The nobles once again began their plotting for power, each one in turn supposing that they could pluck the reins of government from his weak hands.

With the marriage ceremony of the king to Margaret, the mistress of Suffolk, the first part of the reign of Henry VI. is properly speaking brought to a close; want of space will prevent our giving elaborately the details of his second reign. We will conclude the chapter by giving the speech of the Duke of Suffolk, when he went to fetch the queen. "Thus," exclaimed he; "Suffolk hath prevailed—and thus he goes, as did the youthful Paris once to Greece, with hope to find the like event in love, but prosper better than the Trojan did. Margaret shall now be queen, and rule the king; but I will rule both her, the king, and realm."

CHAPTER VII.

AFTER the king's marriage each nobleman was so occupied with his own affairs that he paid but little attention to the intrigues of his neighbours.

But all were united in endeavouring to bring about the ruin of the upright Lord Protector, the Duke of Gloster. This they finally accomplished by swearing that his wife was plotting the death of the king by witchcraft.

She was made to walk through the streets dressed in white, and then banished to the Isle of Man.

The king took the staff of office from the

Protector by the advice of his queen and her paramour, Suffolk, aided by the machinations of the cardinal.

Then he was committed to the Tower to be brought to trial for high treason.

However he was so popular with the House of Commons that they did not dare bring him to trial on the frivolous charges they had trumped up against him.

Accordingly Suffolk and the cardinal conspired to compass his death, which they did by having him violently murdered.

Great was the horror and indignation expressed at this, and the powerful Earl of Warwick boldly accused the Duke of Suffolk of being his murderer.

In this accusation he was supported by the Commons and the Duke of York, who had secretly made alliance with him, with a view of his own ultimate elevation to the throne.

Suffolk was banished the kingdom, and on his passage to France was murdered by pirates.

The cardinal bishop, died in the most frightful agony, betraying that he was an accomplice in the murder.

There was now only the Duke of Somerset, representative of the House of Lancaster, between the Duke of York and the throne.

In order to get power, the Duke of York solicited a command in Ireland, where after a short time he found himself at the head of a large army.

Meanwhile he had arranged with the Earl of Warwick, and his father, the Duke of Salisbury, to assist him with their influence, promising Warwick that next himself he should be the greatest man in the kingdom.

To give a colour to his movements, he incited a reckless rough, named Cade, to get up a monster rebellion by declaring that he was the son of Mortimer, and heir to the crown.

Supported by all the rabble of the country, Cade marched on London, promising his followers that the gutters should run with wine, and that after he was made king there should be no more ladies and gentlemen.

He invented a distich for their edification, which they shouted as they went forth to plunder—

> "When Adam delved and Eve span,
> Who was then the gentleman?"

The rebels were victorious for awhile, and the king fled to Oxford.

Speedy messengers informed the Duke of York of the revolt, and making it a pretext, he returned at the head of a powerful army, in the meantime sending out spies to inform Salisbury and Warwick to come to his aid.

That his advance after Cade's rebellion had been put down and the leader slain was only a pretext, may be gathered from the following speech he made—

"From Ireland thus comes York, to claim his right and pluck the crown from feeble Henry's head. Ring, bells, aloud; burn, bonfires, clear and bright, to entertain great England's lawful king. Ah, *sancta majestas!* who would not buy thee dear? Let them obey that know not how to rule; this hand was made to handle nought but gold. I cannot give due action to my words, except a sword or sceptre balance it. A sceptre shall it have."

The king sent in haste to him to know what he meant by coming at the head of such an army, upon which he replied that he accused the Duke of Somerset of high treason, and if he were committed to the Tower he would disperse his forces.

The weak king consented, or pretended to consent to this.

But when he got him, as he imagined, in his power, revealed the fact that his rival was still at liberty.

At this York burst into a violent rage. "How now!" he cried. "Is Somerset at liberty? Then, York, unloose thy long-imprisoned thoughts, and let thy tongue be equal with thy heart. Shall I endure the sight of Somerset? False king! why hast thou broken faith with me, knowing how hardly I can brook abuse? King did I call thee? no, thou art not king; not fit to govern and rule multitudes, which darest not, no, nor canst not, rule a traitor. That head of thine doth not become a crown; thy hand is made to grasp a palmer's staff, and not to grace an awful princely sceptre. That gold must round engirt these brows of mine; whose smile and frown, like to Achilles' spear, is able with the change to kill and cure. Here is a hand to hold a sceptre up, and with the same to act controlling laws. Give place; by Heaven, thou shalt rule no more o'er him whom Heaven created for thy ruler."

"Oh, monstrous traitor! I arrest thee, York," cried the Duke of Somerset.

"Here come my two sons then to be my bail," cried the Duke of York.

" Call hither Clifford," cried the queen ; " bid him come amain to say if these boys of York shall be surety for their father."

But when Clifford came with the forces, to the surprise of everybody his forces were matched by those of the sons of the Duke of York, so that it was beyond his power to arrest him.

" Why, what a brood of traitors have we here !" cried Clifford.

" Look in a glass and call thine image so," cried York. " I am thy king, and thou a false-hearted traitor. Bid Salisbury and Warwick come to me."

" Hence, heap of wrath," cried Clifford, " foul undigested lump, as crooked in thy manners as thy shape."

The king bitterly rebuked the Duke of Salisbury and his son, the Earl of Warwick, but all to no purpose.

They were resolved, they said, to support the Duke of York as king.

Hot and furious words ensued, each one calling the other traitor.

At last Buckingham arrived to help the king, and both parties being evenly balanced, a bloody battle ensued, at the end of which King Henry VI. fled to London.

Here, practically speaking, the reign of the weak King Henry VI. ended, and the House of York was triumphant, although the whole country was plunged into the wars of the White and Red Roses.

A tremendous battle ensued between the king and the Duke of York's party, in which the king's party got the worst of it, and were obliged to flee to London.

Here, in the House of Parliament, the Duke of York seated himself on the throne, but finally he consented that the king should reign during his lifetime, but that after his death the crown should revert to him and his sons.

He then retired to his castle in Yorkshire.

But Queen Margaret was in a state of perfect fury when she heard that the foolish King Henry VI. had disinherited by this act his own son.

She hastily organised an

JOAN OF ARC.

army, and surprising the Duke of York in his castle, defeated him and slew him.

The sons escaped, and being joined by the powerful Earl of Warwick, they defeated Queen Margaret, and fearfully revenged their father's death.

King Henry VI. was deposed, and Edward, Richard Plantagenet's eldest son, reigned in his stead.

Queen Margaret fled with her son to France, to solicit assistance from the French king.

But thither also came the powerful Earl of Warwick, on an embassy from King Edward, to solicit the hand of the French king's sister.

He had won the French king over to his cause, when messengers arrived stating that King Edward had altered his mind, and married the beautiful Elizabeth Woodville.

This slight so incensed Warwick and the French king, that they both joined Queen Margaret, and invaded England.

The king's brothers deserted him, with the exception of Richard.

He was defeated by Warwick and obliged to fly.

Soon after he returned with a powerful army and defeated the king-maker.

In the battle of Tewkesbury he defeated Queen Margaret, and captured both her and her son, whom he and his brothers murdered.

Meanwhile, his brother, Richard the Crafty—Richard Crookback—was plotting to gain the throne.

He contrived to get his two brothers assassinated, and, on the king's death, had himself proclaimed Lord Protector.

When he had thus secured the reins of power, he had the two young princes, heirs to the throne, barbarously murdered in the Tower.

No sooner was this accomplished, than he had himself proclaimed king under the title of Richard III., which forms another of Shakespeare's plays.

NOTICE.—" TAMING THE SHREW," being No. 12 of Stories from Shakespeare, will be ready on Monday, January 23. Orders should be given early to your Booksellers.

No. 12.]   [Price One Penny.

EDWIN J.BRETTS STORIES of SHAKESPEARE

COMPLETE

TAMING THE SHREW.

"'I THANK YOU, SIR,' SAID KATHARINA, VERY HUMBLY."

"Boys of England Edition."

EDWIN J. BRETT'S

STORIES FROM

SHAKESPEARE'S PLAYS.

No. 12.—TAMING THE SHREW.

CHAPTER I.

IN the days when Italy and all the states on the Gulf of Genoa were split up into petty dukedoms, each ruler anxious to elevate himself into undue importance at the expense of his neighbour, the life and liberty of peaceable traders and merchants were subject to the caprice of every petty despot.

As their calling led them from one dukedom to another, they, more than any other class of people, were subject to the petty jealousies and fits of spleen to which these petty despots were alternately a prey.

At such a time, on a lovely morning in June, two strangers might have been observed crossing the Prato-della-valle, in Padua.

Unheeding the many solicitations of the market people, who were holding their fair, they held their way until they got opposite the church of San Antonio, and halted under the monument to Petrarch, where were a number of students gathered together from all parts of the world, for the purpose of disputation.

One of them, by his rich apparel, was evidently a gentleman, while his companion's mien and apparel proclaimed him to occupy the position of confidential companion or upper servant.

"Well, here we are at last, Tranio," cried the more richly-apparelled of the two. "Faith, I marvel at the richness of this wondrous place after Pisa. It is like jumping from the shallows into the deep."

"True, Master Lucentio," responded Tranio, "I have seen worse places than Padua. I've no doubt we shall manage to enjoy ourselves here very much."

"Enjoy ourselves, Tranio?" cried the other; "am I not come here to improve my mind by travel? To study virtue and philosophy?"

"That's all very well, master mine," replied the companion, who made a very vinegar face when Lucentio talked of philosophy; "but if you will be guided by me, you shall study all these and still enjoy yourself."

"Explain, Tranio," retorted Lucentio. "I know you will not be wanting in an excuse to turn study into play."

"Why, then, here it is, master mine," replied Tranio, with a grin. "You come to study rhetoric, study it in your common talk, and that will be as beneficial as if you had all the learned philosophers chopping logic with you."

"Well, next?"

"Music and poetry you must learn, find some sweet maid to teach you——"

"And mathematics and metaphysics, sirrah?"

"Fall to them as your stomach serves you," cried Tranio, making another wry face, "which," he added in an aside, "I promise myself will not be often if once he tastes the sweets of this gay capital."

"Well dost thou advise," cried

Lucentio, laughing; "I wish that Biondello, my valet, were come ashore with the things, so that we could go and hunt up some lodgings, where we may entertain such friends as we happen to make in Padua."

"Come, that's better than talking of dry learning and practising all the morals," said Tranio, with a pleased smack of his lips. "Halloa, here comes a curious-looking old curmudgeon; what is he so excited about, with those two young gallants? Let's stand aside, master, and watch them. I promise you there is some fun here."

"Heavens! Saw you ever so beautiful a face as that young girl's?" cried Lucentio, pointing to the younger of the two girls, who had now come close to where they stood.

"Hush!" said Tranio, "listen to what the old party is saying."

"Gentlemen," cried the old citizen, in a loud voice, "importune me no farther. You know me. I am Baptista, and my word is my bond. I tell you that I am resolved that no one shall marry my younger daughter, Bianca, until her elder sister, Katharina, is married. You can come courting if you like, but until Katharina is married, Bianca shall not have a husband!"

"But, sir——" cried the young gallant, who was called Hortensio.

"No buts for me," cried the old merchant, Baptista; "if either of you love Katharina, you can have her, and the other can marry her sister."

"Katharina is too rough, she may go hang for me," cried Hortensio.

"And for me, too," cried his companion, who was known as Gremio; "I like not women with such a temper as she has, I promise you."

Both the young men turned away in disgust.

Katharina, who was evidently the elder of the two sisters, a tall, queen-like looking woman, with a hard, imperious face, stamped her foot furiously, and a flash of anger mounted her cheek.

"How dare you make me so cheap amongst these men, father?" she cried.

"Faith, maid, you are too dear for me," cried Gremio.

"Ay," added Hortensio, "unless you were of milder, gentler mood, like your sweet sister Bianca."

"I would I were married to you but only for a day, you saucy jack," cried Katharina, "I warrant I'd comb your noddle with a three-legged stool, and paint your face with my finger-nails."

"From all such devils, good Lord deliver us," cried Gremio, while Katharina fairly hissed with rage.

"Stay, master," cried Tranio, as Lucentio advanced; "this maid is mad, or else the worst vixen of a woman I have ever seen."

But Lucentio had paid no heed to his servant.

He had fallen violently in love at first sight with Bianca, and could not take his gaze off her face.

Whenever Tranio spoke a word to him, he answered in an absent manner, by wild ejaculations of praise to her beauty.

"Now, Bianca, my child, that they may know that I am in earnest, get you into the house, and remember that though in this matter I am resolved, I will love you none the less."

Bianca immediately burst out crying.

"Put your finger in your eye, cry baby cry," cried Katharina scornfully.

"Sister," cried Bianca humbly, "mock me not; since it is my father's pleasure I am content."

"Sir," cried Gremio excitedly, "will you mew her up to gratify this she fiend, whom no one will marry?"

"I am resolved," cried the old merchant; "but if you know any teachers expert in music and poetry, I pray you send them to me, gentlemen, for I am resolved that she shall not want for pleasure during her maidenhood. Come in, Bianca, I have something to say to you. Katharina, you can stay behind with the gentlemen."

"Why," cried Katharina, "do you dare appoint hours and places for me to go and come, as though I knew not what to take and what to leave?"

"You may go," cried Hortensio, "we are glad to be rid of your company. Now look here, Gremio," he continued, as her back was turned, "we are both rivals for Bianca's love."

"Well, what of it?"

"Let's put our heads together and contrive to get Katharina married to some one. Once she is out of the way we can become rivals once more, and may the best man win."

"Agreed," cried Hortensio, and the two young men strolled away together, arm-in-arm, consulting how they should

entrap some one into marrying Katharina. Meanwhile, Lucentio had not moved from the place, and continued to talk in the most rapturous manner.

"Look here, sir," cried the ready-witted servant man, "since you have fallen so terribly in love with that maid, I pray you bend your wit to achieve her, and stay not there all day sighing like a furnace."

"Tranio," cried Lucentio, "I saw her coral lips to move——"

"Master," said Tranio, "if you go on like that, nothing can be done; but if you listen to me, I have a plan by which you may get access to her"

"Explain, good Tranio."

"Heard you not the old man say he wanted a music teacher for her?"

"Certainly. Marked you her——"

"Pish! very well then, you will be her music teacher, or her Latin master. So you will listen to my plan."

"Not possible," cried Lucentio; "for who will take my place, entertain my friends, keep house, and do the honours worthy of my father, Vincentio, the rich merchant of Pisa?"

"Content thee, master, and change cloaks with me. I will be Lucentio for the time being. They have not seen our faces yet at the lodgings, and know not the master from the man."

"But, my servant, your companion Biondello?"

"You shall instruct him to pay the same reverence to me as he does to you—in fact, to call me Lucentio."

Biondello came up just as they had arranged that Tranio was to personate Lucentio, and go amongst the other suitors to Baptista's house, while Lucentio was to be introduced to Baptista as a very learned Latin scholar.

Having settled these matters to their satisfaction, they went off in search of their lodgings, resolved to wait until next day before they began the campaign.

―――

CHAPTER II.

ALMOST at the same time Petruchio arrived at Hortensio's house.

He was the wildest, most reckless gallant in Verona, and like Lucentio, had come to visit Padua, partially to have some sport, partially to mend his fortunes by a good match.

Like master like man.

His servant, Grumio, was as great an oddity, and was just as eccentric as his master, as the following incident will show—

"Knock me here roundly," said Petruchio, when they had arrived at the gate.

"Knock you, sir?" cried Grumio. "Who am I that I should knock my master?"

"Villain, I say, knock me at this gate," cried Petruchio; "and rap me well, or I'll knock your knave's pate!"

"My master has grown quarrelsome," cried Grumio pathetically. "I know if I knock him he will knock back."

"Then I'll wring," cried Petruchio, making a sudden leap forward and catching his servant man by the ear, which he wrung lustily.

The din and clamour brought Hortensio down, who parted them, and expressed himself delighted to see them.

"My master is mad, Signior Hortensio," cried Grumio, lying on the ground and rubbing his ear vigorously.

"Good Hortensio," cried Petruchio, "'tis a senseless villain. I bade him knock upon your gate, and could not get him to do it."

"Knock at the gate!" cried Grumio. "Oh Heaven! Spake you not these words—'Sirrah, knock me here. Rap me here. Knock me well, and knock me soundly?'"

"Sirrah," cried Petruchio, "begone, or talk not, I advise you."

Grumio's glib tongue would have procured him another thrashing had not Hortensio interfered.

They entered the house together, and then Petruchio made his friend acquainted with the fact that his father was dead, and that he had come to Padua to get a wife, provided she had money with her.

"Petruchio," cried Hortensio eagerly, "I know the very wife you want. She is very rich. The only drawback is that she is such a fearful shrew, and has such an abominable temper that I fear she would doom you to a life of misery."

He then briefly told him how the case stood with regard to Katharina.

"Hortensio, my friend," said Petruchio, "few words suffice; as wealth is the burden of my wooing dance, one rich enough to be Petruchio's wife, be she as foul and ill-favoured as was Florentin's love, as old as Sibyl, and as curst and shrewish as was Xantippe, or worse, she moves me not, or moves me but affection's edge in me, therefore let us go and see."

"Why, look you," said Grumio, who, despite the fact that his ear was still aching, must needs put his oar in again. "Give him gold enough, and marry him to an old trot with ne'er a tooth in her head."

"Her name?" cried Petruchio, slapping his thigh in great good humour.

"Katharina Minola, daughter of a wealthy merchant, Baptista Minola."

"I know her father, though I know not her. I will not sleep, Hortensio, until I see her," said Petruchio.

"We cannot go before to-morrow, Petruchio," said Hortensio, "and then I want you to do me a favour."

"Name it," cried Petruchio, who was in great good humour.

"You know I am in love with Bianca, the youngest, and cannot get access to her, wherefore, I pray you, present me as a schoolmaster, well learned in music. I will disguise myself so that old Baptista shall not recognise me."

In the evening while they were at supper, Hortensio's friend, Gremio, looked in and informed the former that he had secured the services of a scholar, who, while he read to Bianca, would tell her of his (Gremio's) love for her and plead his cause.

Petruchio and Hortensio kicked each other under the table at this, for was not Hortensio going in person?

However, in order that our readers may not needlessly be mystified, we will tell them that the learned man whom Gremio had engaged to plead his cause was no other than Lucentio, who, thanks to Tranio, had obtained the post.

Petruchio, in great good humour, amused himself by listing to Grumio's sarcasm, until he got too saucy, when it became equally amusing to cuff him.

Tiring of this, he went to bed to dream of conquest on the morrow.

CHAPTER III.

ON their way to Baptista's house on the morrow, Hortensio met Gremio, accompanied by Lucentio, who was disguised as a poor scholar.

"You are still resolved to woo this wild cat, Signior Petruchio?" said Gremio, who seemed to be on very good terms with himself. "I hope you will win her."

"I wish I was as sure of a dinner," grumbled Grumio.

Just as they arrived opposite Baptista's house they encountered Tranio, who was got up in gorgeous apparel, and attended by Biondello.

He demanded of them the way to Signior Baptista's house, declaring that he was an old friend of his father, and that he had come to woo his daughter.

"My name," said Tranio, "is Lucentio, old Vincentio's son."

A terrible quarrel arose amongst the two lovers—Hortensio and Gremio—at this, each one contending that Bianca belonged to him.

But Petruchio, finding that he was after Katharina, made peace between them all, and gave him directions how to arrive at the house, arguing that, as none of them could get Bianca until he chose to wed Katharina, he had the most to say in the matter.

So they all arrived at the house.

Meanwhile, Katharina had indulged in one of her fits of rage.

Because Bianca would not tell her which of her suitors she loved best, she tied her hands together, and slapped her until she cried.

Her cries brought her father to the rescue, whereupon Katharina bitterly accused him of favouring Bianca more than her, and then made her escape to an inner room, there to cry off her rage, just as all our gallant lovers arrived in a body; Gremio, with Lucentio disguised; Petruchio, with Hortensio as a musician; and Tranio, with Biondello, bearing a lute and books.

When the salutations had been exchanged, Petruchio, who did not know what modesty was, began the conversation abruptly.

"My good sir," he said, "have you not a daughter called Katharina, fair and virtuous?"

"I have a daughter called Katharina!" sighed the old man, looking at Petruchio, as much as to say—

"You are a forward sort of customer."

"You are too blunt!" said Gremio, in alarm.

"You wrong me, Signior Gremio!" cried the unabashed Petruchio. "I am a gentleman of Verona, sir; that, hearing of her beauty and her wit—her affability and bashful modesty — her wondrous qualities and wild behaviour—am bold to show myself a forward guest within your house; and, for that I may be welcome, I here present you with a man of mine, cunning in music and the mathematics. Accept of him, or else you do me wrong."

"You're welcome, sir," said the old Baptista. "But for my daughter Katharina, she is not for your turn, the more my grief."

"I see you do not mean to part with her," answered Petruchio; "or else you like not of my company."

"Mistake me not!" cried the old man, "I speak but as I find. What is your name, sir, and whence come you?"

"I am Petruchio, Antonio's son."

"I know him well; you are welcome for his sake."

In spite of the efforts of Gremio to get a word in edgeways, Petruchio monopolised the old merchant's attention, until he was ready to beat him.

But at last he gave him an opportunity of presenting Lucentio (disguised.)

Then Tranio came forward, and presented a packet of books and a lute, stating that his name was Lucentio, and that he begged he might be allowed to be one of the suitors for Bianca's hand also.

Old Baptista readily gave his consent, saying that he knew Lucentio's father, Vincentio, very well.

He sent the tutors in to see his daughters, and invited Gremio, Tranio, and Petruchio to walk with him in the garden.

"Sir," said Petruchio, with the most wonderful coolness, "I cannot come every day to woo. You know my father well: I am his sole heir. Tell me, if I get your daughter's love, what dowry shall I have with her?"

"After my death, one half my lands," cried the old merchant, fairly carried away by the bluntness of Petruchio's speech, "and in possession twenty thousand crowns."

"And for that dowry," said Petruchio, "I'll assure her widowhood. Now let specialities be drawn——"

"Ay, when the special thing's obtained —her love—for that is all in all!" cried the other, marvelling more and more at Petruchio's assurance.

"Why, that is nothing, father," cried Petruchio, "for I tell you that I am as peremptory as she, and so she yields to me; for I am rough, and woo not like a babe."

"Well, Heaven speed your wooing!" cried the old man.

And just as he had finished his speech, Hortensio entered, with his head broken, and told a piteous tale how she had broken his lute across his head, and called him twangly Jack, and a dozen other vile names.

"Now, by the world!" cried Petruchio, slapping his thigh, "'tis a lusty wench; I love her more than ever. I pray you let me have some conversation with her."

"Well, well," said the old man, "I'll send her out to you. Signior, do you come with me to my younger daughter; she's apt to learn, and thankful for good turns."

Away went Hortensio, thankful for good luck; and presently Katharina entered, evidently not in the best of humours.

"Good morrow, Kate," cried Petruchio, strolling towards her carelessly; "for that's your name, I hear."

Although she was a tall, finely-developed woman, he was as the oak to the willow beside her.

"They call me Katharina that do talk of me," she cried, looking scornfully at Petruchio.

"You lie in faith; for you are called plain Kate," cried Petruchio, bending over his plumed hat until the feathers swept her face and irritated her beyond endurance, "and sometimes Kate the curst! But Kate, my super-dainty Kate, for dainties are all cates, take this of me for thy consolation; hearing thy mildness praised in every town, thy virtues spoken of, and thy beauty sounded, myself am moved to woo thee for my wife."

"Let him that moved you hither remove you hence!" cried Katharina, trying in vain to get that aggravating feather out of her face. "I knew you at the first; you were a moveable."

"Why, what's a moveable, Kate?"

"A joint stool."

"You were right. Come, sit on me, Kate."

"I've borne enough from you," began Kate, and broke forth into a torrent of abuse.

"Come, come, you wasp!" cried Petruchio. "Faith, you are too angry."

"If I am a wasp, best beware my sting."

"Why, where should your sting be, Kate? In your tongue?"

"There!" cried Katharina, utterly unable to sustain this war of words any longer. "Now you feel my sting!"

And she fetched him a clip on the ear that made it ring again.

"I swear," cried Petruchio, catching her hand suddenly in a vice-like grip that made her shrink with sudden terror, "I'll cuff you if you do that again!"

"So may you loose your arms," she whimpered. "If you strike me you are no gentleman."

"And if no gentleman, why then no arms, Kate," returned Petruchio, with imperturbable good humour. "What is your crest? A coxcomb?"

"No, Kate."

"You crow too like a craven."

And she attempted to escape.

"Nay, nay, my sweet Kate!" cried Petruchio, still retaining her without any apparent exertion in that wonderful grip which she was powerless to resist, "in sooth you go not so. Now listen to me."

"I chafe you if I tarry. Let me go," pleaded Kate.

"No, not a wit!" retorted Petruchio. "I find you passing gentle. 'Twas told me you were rough, and coy, and sullen, and I find report to be a liar. For thou art pleasant, gamesome, and passing courteous. But slow in speech, yet sweet as spring-time flowers. Thou canst not frown, thou canst not look askance as angry wenches will. Nor hast thou pleasure to be cross in talk. Oh, slanderous world! Let me see thee walk."

"Go, fool!" cried Katharina, as he released her, "and whom thou ownest, command."

"I shall command you, Kate."

"Yes; keep you warm."

"Marry, so I mean, sweet Katharina. Wherefore setting all this chat aside, this much in plain terms. Your father has consented that you shall be my wife, and, will you nil you, I will marry you. Now, Kate, I am a husband for your turn; for, by this light whereby I see thy beauty—that beauty which doth make me love thee well—thou must be married to no man but me, for I am he was born to tame you, Kate. Here comes your father, never make denial. I must and will have you for my wife."

As he concluded old Baptista entered, accompanied by Gremio and Tranio to ascertain how this wild wooing speeded.

Katharina flew at him at once, while Petruchio continued carelessly seated with legs crossed as if he had not a trouble in the world, and fairly beamed on Katharina as she broke out to her father in a perfect torrent.

"How speed you with my daughter?" asked old Baptista.

"How but well, sir, how but well?" replied Petruchio. "It were impossible that I should speed amiss."

"Call you me daughter?" burst forth Katharina, in a rage. "I promise you you have shown a fatherly regard to wish to wed me to one half-lunatic, a madcap ruffian and a swearing jack, that thinks with oaths to face the matter out."

"Father," cried Petruchio, with a calm smile on his face, "'tis thus yourself and all the world that talked of her have talked amiss of her. If she be curst it is for policy, for she is not froward, but modest as the dove; and to conclude, we have agreed so well together that upon Sunday is the wedding day."

"I'll see thee hanged on Sunday first!" said Katharina.

"Hark, Petruchio," cried Gremio, "she says she'll see thee hanged first."

"Be patient, gentlemen," cried Petruchio, rising, and going over to where Kate was, who shrank back from him in terror. "I choose her for myself. If she and I be pleased, what's to do with you? 'Tis a bargain betwixt us twain that she shall still appear curst in company, but when alone I tell you 'tis incredible to believe how much she loves me. Oh, the kindest Kate! She hung about my neck, and kiss on kiss she gave so fast that in a trice she won my love. Give me thy hand, Kate (for Kate was about to speak), I will unto Venice to buy apparel 'gainst the wedding day. Provide the feast, father, and bid the guests. I will be sure my Katharina shall be fine. Father, and wife, and gentlemen, adieu. Kiss me, Kate, we will be married on Sunday!"

Bewildered by his rapid talk, the pressure of his hand, his wild, roving eye, and reckless deportment, utterly panic-stricken, and driven out of her usual self, Katharina suffered Petruchio to kiss her heartily and then fled from the room, upon which Petruchio also took his departure, promising to return on Sunday, and leaving the spectators of his strange wooing in a state of unutterable astonishment.

As for Katharina, she was so ashamed and mortified, that she retired to her room unable to summon up enough courage to deny what he had said.

And the more she thought of the swaggering, handsome, blustering, good-

CHAPTER IV.

DURING the week preceding Petruchio's marriage, Lucentio and Hortensio had things pretty nearly their own way with Bianca.

Katharina was too much occupied with preparations for her approaching marriage to pay any heed to the music teacher and

"'I WILL NOT SLEEP, HORTENSIO, UNTIL I SEE HER,' SAID PETRUCHIO."

humoured, fierce Petruchio, the more she became convinced that it would not be such a bad match after all, so she resolved to let matters take their course.

Gremio and Tranio then fell a-wrangling for Bianca's hand, the latter, of course, for his master, Lucentio, whom he was personating.

Baptista sold her to the highest bidder, and Tranio bid three times as much in land and ships as Gremio, subject to his father's approval.

Latin master, or she would soon have found out that these gentlemen thought more of teaching a lesson in love than in Latin or music.

While Tranio, the false Lucentio, was entertaining all Padua, and was at his wits' end to find some one to personate old Vincentio, his master's father, his master was making love to Bianca, without the least suspicion, except perhaps from his watchful rival, Hortensio, who, in the *role* of music master, was also endeavouring to gain her affections. The jealousy of these two rivals at last brought them to downright quarrelling.

Bianca, who of course saw through their shallow artifice, was excessively amused by their wrangling, and kept on encouraging first one and then the other.

At last came the day before the wedding, and each felt that they must speak out.

But each one was in the other's way.

"Fiddler!" cried Lucentio, "forbear! You grow too forward."

"Wrangling pedant," cried Hortensio, "when we have spent an hour in music, your lecture shall have leisure for as much."

"Prepo sterous ass!" cried Lucentio.

"Sirrah!" cried Hortensio. "I will not bear these braves of thine."

"Why, gentlemen," cried Bianca, "you do me double wrong. I'll not be tied to hours nor 'pointed times, but learn my lessons as I please myself. Here sit we down; take your instrument, play you the while. His lecture will be done ere you have tuned."

LUCENTIO AND BIANCA.

"Where left we last?" cried Bianca, sitting by Lucentio.

"Here, madam," cried Lucentio, casting an exultant glance at Hortensio.

"Construe these lines," said Bianca.

Now was Lucentio's long waited for opportunity, and he began—

"*Hic ibat*, as I told you before. *Simois*, I am Lucentio. *Hic est*, son unto Vincentio of Pisa. *Sigeia tellus*, disguised thus to get your love. *Hic steterat*, and that Lucentio who comes a-wooing. *Priami*, is my man Tranio. *Regia*, bearing my port. *Celsa senis*, that we might beguile your father."

"Dash it," cried the jealous Hortensio, who could not hear a word of what passed but judged from Bianca's looks that something more interesting than Latin was going on. "He is making love to her, the wretched scholar. I dare swear I must put a stop to this. Madam, my instrument is in tune."

"Let's hear," cried Bianca, who however had not been disturbed. "Oh, fie, man!" cried she, as Hortensio advanced, playing, "the treble jars."

"Try again, man," cried Lucentio.

"Now," continued Bianca, as Hortensio retired very much mortified, "let me see if I can construe that Latin. *Hic ibat Simois*, I know you not. *Hic est Sigeia tellus*, I trust you not. *Hic steterat Priami*, take heed he hear us not. *Regia*, presume not. *Celsa senis*, despair not."

"Madam," cried Hortensio again, "the instrument is in tune."

"All but the bass," cried Lucentio, anxious to gain a little more time.

"The bass is right," cried Hortensio in a rage, "'tis the base knave that jars. Now, for my life, that knave doth court my love."

"In time I may believe, yet I mistrust you just a little now. You may go walk in the court, sir; my lesson in music is not in three parts."

"I believe that musical knave is making love to her," grumbled Lucentio, as he walked off, leaving the delighted Hortensio to supply his place.

"Madam," cried Hortensio, "will please read the gamut of Hortensio."

She read the following—

"I am the ground of all accord,
To plead Hortensio's passion.
Bianca, take him for thy lord,
That loves with all affection.
One clef two notes have I;
Therefore show pity ere I die.

"Call you this a gamut? Tut, I like it not. Old fashions please me best. But here comes my Latin master again."

And her eye rested on Lucentio.

"Therefore I must send you both away, for to-morrow is my sister's wedding day."

"I have cause to pry into this pedant," cried Hortensio, in a rage that she should prefer the humble schoolmaster to him. "Yet if thy thoughts be so humble, Bianca, as to be satisfied with him, I'll be no competitor."

Bianca had by this time fully made up her mind which of her two lovers to accept.

But as nothing could be done until after her sister was married, she dismissed the matter from her mind in as summary a manner as she had dismissed her lovers.

CHAPTER V.

AND now the eventful day arrived, and all were in the greatest state of expectation about the wedding.

Old Baptista had made extraordinary preparations to send Katharina off on a grand scale, he was so heartily glad to get rid of her, and to such a good husband too, for the old merchant knew that though Petruchio was young and eccentric he had plenty of good sound common sense and often used his apparent madness to conceal some settled purpose.

Katharina too had been in better temper all the week.

For all his bluster he was a gentleman, and a wealthy and proper looking man.

She had come to the conclusion that she was fortunate to get such a match, and promised herself that once she was married to him she would soon get him under her thumb.

But when the eventful day came, and ten, eleven, and half-past eleven, yet no Petruchio, all the guests were filled with dismay.

Even old Baptista for once sympathised with his daughter.

And she, as they waited for him in the garden, so as to save time should he come at the last moment, felt that she should sink into the earth with shame if he came not ere the clock struck twelve.

"Signior Lucentio," said the old Baptista, "what will be said? What mockery will it be when the priest attends and there is no bridegroom! What say you to this shame of ours?"

"No shame but mine!" cried Katharina bitterly. "I must be forced to give my hand unto a mad-brained gallant full of spleen, who wooed in haste, and means to wed at leisure. I told you he was a frantic fool, hiding his bitter jests in blunt behaviour. To be noted for a merry man he'll woo a thousand whom he never means to wed. Now must the world point at poor Katharina and say ' Lo, there is mad Petruchio's wife an it would but please him to come and take her.' "

"Patience, good Katharina!" cried Tranio. "I'll be bound he means well."

"Would I had never seen him," cried Katharina, bursting out weeping and going into the house, followed by her sister Bianca, who tried in vain to give her some comfort.

Just when things were about their worst, Biondello came rushing up the street open mouthed.

"Lord, lord!" he exclaimed, "Petruchio is coming; listen. In a new hat and an old jerkin, a pair of old breeches, a pair of boots that have been candle-cases, an old rusty sword taken out of the town armoury, with a broken hilt and without a sheath. His horse is hipped with an old mothy saddle and odd stirrups. The horse has the glanders, full of wind-galls, sped with spavins, and ready to drop with the staggers. You may see his ribs sticking out like the eaves of a three-hundred year old house. He drives him with a headstall of sheep's leather, which ever and anon being pulled suddenly to keep him from stumbling, hath burst in a thousand pieces and is thereby knotted. A woman's crupper behind, sewn with packthread and patched all over."

"Who comes with him?"

"Oh, sir, his man, Grumio, for all the world caparisoned like the horse, with a linen stock on one leg, and a kersey boot-hose on the other—a monster, a very monster in apparel."

"'Tis some old humour pricks him," cried Tranio.

"I'm glad he's come, anyhow," cried the old merchant, with a heavy sigh.

As he uttered this exclamation Petruchio entered, calling out in a loud voice, as he stumbled off his sorry old nag who was liked to have fallen down with the shock—

"Come, where be these gallants? Who is at home?"

"You are welcome," cried old Baptista in a faint voice; "and yet you are not so well apparelled as I could wish you were."

"Were it not better I should rush in thus than come late?" said Petruchio. "But where is Kate—where is my lovely

bride? Gentles," he added, "methinks you frown? Do you see some prodigy?"

And he clapped his hand on his sword.

"Why, sir," cried old Baptista, "you know this is your wedding-day. First we were sad, fearing you would not come, now sadder that you come so unprovided. Fie, doff this habit, shame to your estate, an eyesore to our festival."

"And tell us what misfortune hath so long detained you from your wife and sent you here at last so unlike yourself?" added Tranio.

"It is too tedious to repeat," cried Petruchio; "suffice it I am here. But where is Kate? I stay too long from her. 'Tis time we were at church. The morning wears."

"See not your bride in these unreverent robes," cried Tranio, who began to believe the joke was going too far; "I will lend you some clothes of mine."

"Not I, believe me," cried Petruchio. "Thus I'll visit her."

"But thus, I trust, you will not marry her," cried the old merchant, bursting out with sudden anger.

"Even thus," cried Petruchio; "therefore have done with words. To me she's married, not unto my clothes. But I am a fool to chat with you, when I should see my bride and seal my welcome with a loving kiss."

"Let him alone," cried Tranio to the old merchant aside; "he hath some meaning in this mad attire."

Just as Petruchio was rushing into the house, Katharina, having heard of his arrival, appeared at the door and almost fainted at the sight of him.

Ere she had time to fly even, Petruchio caught her in his arms and gave her a thumping kiss, and clapped her on the crupper of his saddle.

Holding her there firmly he called out, like a Bedlamite—

"Who ever is for church, follow me; we have no time to lose. Those of you who like to come and witness the uniting of two loving hearts can come. Those who don't may stay behind."

In vain Katharina screamed and tried to get off.

Petruchio held her on with a grasp of iron, and Grumio whipped up the crazy old nag.

In vain the unhappy girl cried and screamed and buried her mortified face in her hands.

Petruchio chose her to believe that her tears were caused by the fact of her leaving her home for the last time, and kept on consoling her and calling her his sweet pretty turtle dove.

But as these consolations were intermingled with fierce oaths at Grumio and the horse, distributed freely amongst them, and sundry raids into a crowd of small boys that followed the procession beating the pans and yelling like fiends, it is not to be wondered at if they did her little good.

In short the bride reached the church more dead than alive, escorted by her mad groom, and a hooting yelling mob.

Some of the wedding guests followed on for very shame's sake, while others, who could not summon up enough courage to face such a sorry expedition stayed at home.

The result was that the church was filled quite as much with the rabble as with the wedding guests.

The poor priest was frightened out of his wits at what he saw.

"Come, priest," cried Petruchio, bearing Katharina up to the altar, "marry us off hand; and for that thou mayest know everything is all right, here is my best man."

And he lugged Grumio forward by the ear.

"Will this maiden be your wife?" asked the priest, in trembling tones.

"Ay, by *gog's-wouns*!" cried the fierce bridegroom, and swore so loud that, all amazed, the priest let fall the book; and as he stooped to pick it up the mad-brained bridegroom fetched him such a cuff that down fell priest and book, and book and priest, whereupon Petruchio swore at both bride and his best man for not helping to pick the reverend father up.

As for poor Katharina she stood there as white as a sheet and trembling in every limb.

Then when the ceremony was over he called for a glass of wine and drank the bride's health, throwing the slops in the sexton's face for no other reason but that he said his beard looked hungry and seemed to ask for the slops as he was drinking.

This done he took the bride about the neck and kissed her lips with such a clamorous smack that all the church did echo.

Some of the guests left for very shame.

But it made no difference to Petruchio.

He got his dainty bride to horse again, and trotted off home to her house, followed by half the yelling of Padua.

Katharina dared not say anything while in church, or in the public streets, for fear of making matters worse, but she vowed that once the iron gates shut out the mob, she would revenge herself on her bridegroom.

In this belief her courage gradually came back to her.

But she was speedily undeceived in this as in other matters, for no sooner had they arrived in old Baptista's courtyard than Petruchio, addressing the assembled guests, said—

"Gentlemen and ladies, I thank you for your pains. I know you think to dine with me to-day. But so it is, my haste doth call me hence, and, therefore, here I mean to take my leave."

"Is it possible you must away to-night?" cried the old merchant, in amazement and anger.

"I must away to-day before the night comes," said Petruchio. "Make it no wonder; if you knew my business you would entreat me go rather than stay."

"Nay, then," cried Katharina, "do what thou canst, I will not go to-day. No, nor to-morrow; nor until I please myself. The door is open, sir; there lies your way. You be jogging. 'Tis like you'll prove but a surly husband that take it upon yourself at first so roundly."

"Oh, Kate," cried Petruchio; "pray thee be not angry."

"I will be angry. Gentlemen, go forward to the bridal dinner; I see a woman may be made a fool of if she had not spirit to resist."

"They shall go forward, Kate, at thy command," cried Petruchio. "Away to the feast; carouse, drink her health, be mad and merry, or go hang yourselves. As for my sweet Kate, she must with me. Nay, look not big, nor stamp, nor fret. I will be master of what is mine own. She is my goods, my chattels; she is my house, and here she stands. Touch her who ever dare. I'll bring my action on the proudest he that stops my way in Padua. Grumio, draw forth thy weapon; we are beset with thieves. Rescue thy mistress if thou be a man. Fear not, sweet wench; they shall not touch thee. I'll buckler thee against a million."

And with his drawn sword in his right hand the mad bridegroom snatched up his wife under his left arm, and carried her screaming to his horse.

"Now let him go, in Heaven's name," cried one of the guests. "We are well rid of them."

So the guests returned to the house, and during the feast Lucentio took such opportunity about pressing his suit that Bianca resolved to elope with him if she could get her father out of the way.

Tranio, who was still impersonating Lucentio, resolved to get some old man to personate Lucentio's father so that while he and the old merchant should be wrangling about settlements, the two young people should have a chance to get married on the sly.

He was lucky in this. Having found an old man newly come to the city from Mantua, by persuading him that the duke was resolved to kill any one that came from Mantua, he induced him to represent himself as Vincentio, father of Lucentio, and to arrange with old Baptista about the settlements.

Leaving affairs in this condition we will follow the journey of our mad bride and bridegroom.

CHAPTER VI.

PETRUCHIO carried on in such a frightful manner, swearing he would kill any one that looked at her sourly, that until they left the town Katharina was fain to hold her tongue.

But when they got into the country she found her tongue, and began to rail again.

But the more she railed the more he vowed she was all sweetness and good temper, and that it was a wonder she did not lose her temper with so many things to cross her.

Then he would yell and storm and swear at the top of his voice, and beat the unfortunate horse, or beat Grumio, who, in turn, would howl like mad.

The horse reared and kicked and plunged until she had to stop railing at him and hold on for her life.

On their way home, about half the way, they fell in with a band of robbers, who commanded them to halt and deliver up their purses.

"Told I you not that ill would come of our setting out?" cried Katharina bitterly. "Good people, take our purses and let us go, but if you would do me a good turn I pray you release me of this lunatic and escort me back to my father's house. He will pay you well."

"What! you rascals," cried Petruchio; "stand you there without taking off your hats to my bonny bride? My faith! this is foul shame. They shall bend the knee to thee, my sweet; they shall own thee the fairest maid in Padua and twelve miles round."

Hardly were the words out of his mouth ere he and Grumio fell upon the astonished robbers with such suddenness that they presently knocked over two of them, and the rest took themselves off in sudden fright, while Katharina stood by looking at the conflict.

"Said I not that they should kneel to thee?" said Petruchio. "Bring up those knaves that dare to look crossly at my beauteous wife. Now kneel, my sirrahs, and swear she is the most beautiful lady in all Italy."

Terrified no less by his terrible ravings and antics than by their defeat, the bandits hastened to do homage to Katharina, under the impression that Petruchio was an escaped lunatic.

"Shall I cut off their heads, sweet Katharina?" he demanded.

"I wish they had cut off yours," she replied bitterly.

"Nay, then, as thou hast so commanded, off with their heads, Grumio," cried Petruchio, waving his sword above his head.

"Oh, sweet mistress," cried one of the prisoners, "I pray you entreat for us; we were poor starved men."

"Spare them," cried Katharina.

"Do you entreat?" cried Petruchio.

"I entreat you—I that have never asked favour of man before."

"I am content, good wife," cried Petruchio. "Get ye gone, ye knaves. Here are purses for you from the fairest lady in all Italy. Sweet Kate, angels would listen while you plead."

It might be imagined that after this incident they would get along peaceably.

Katharina could not hold her tongue, and something that she said sent Petruchio into a towering passion (with Grumio of course).

He swore at him and the horse, swearing they were enough to vex a saint, much less the sweetest-tempered lady in Italy.

Thereupon, just as they came to a mire, he fell to beating the old wreck of a horse

until it staggered and rolled over in the mire, with its mistress underneath.

Instead of helping her up he swore this was Grumio's fault, and beat him until Katharina managed to free herself from the fallen steed, and crawling through the mire, pull her husband off his man-servant, begging with tears and sighs for the love of Heaven not to be the cause of the poor man's death.

"Go forward, sir, and announce our arrival," cried Petruchio sternly. "Sweet Katharina, they are all in league against thee, but I will be thy mainstay. Even the very horse is dead. Never mind; we will walk, my sweet one; 'twill give us an appetite for our dinner."

And so he led her a twenty mile dance, through bog and mire, until she was liked to have dropped from fatigue and mud and dirt.

At last she prayed him, for the love he bore her, either to let her lie down and die, or take her to some house.

Upon this he snatched her up in his arms, and swearing that his sweet Katharina should never know pain, carried her to the house.

Here all the servants were collected to meet them, having been carefully trained by Grumio beforehand.

"You peasant swains," he yelled when he was come to the house, "you malt-horse drudges, told I not you to meet me in the park, to welcome your mistress? Go, rascals, go and fetch my supper in. Sit down, Kate; welcome home. I will make these villains love you."

Poor Katharina had sunk exhausted on the sofa.

"Come, good Kate," he continued as the servants entered with the supper, "be merry. Off with my boots, you rogues, you villains. Out upon you, you villain, you pluck my foot awry; take that, and mend your plucking. Be merry, Kate. Where are my slippers? Shall I have some water? Come, Kate," he continued, as a basin was presented, "wash, and welcome heartily."

The servant let the basin fall, and Petruchio fell upon him like a fury.

"Patience, patience, my good lord!" cried Katharina, in a terror; "'twas a fault unwilling"

"'Twas done to flout you, Kate," he said, desisting. "You know how I love you, I will not see you imposed upon. But come, I know you have a stomach."

She was half dead from hunger.

"What's this?" he burst out presently. "Mutton?"

"Ay, sir."

"Who brought it?"

"I, sir."

"'Tis burnt, and so is all the meat. What dogs are these? Where is that rascal cook? How durst you villains bring it to me that love it not?"

So saying, he snatched the dishes and pelted his servants with them, pretending to be in a perfect fury, and all for love of Katharina.

"I pray you, husband," cried the shrew, "be not so disquiet, the meat was well if you were so contented."

"I tell thee, Kate," cried Petruchio, "'twas burnt, and I am expressly forbid to touch it, for it engenders choler, planteth anger; and better 'twere that both of us did fast, since we are both of us given to anger, than feed it with such over-roasted flesh. Be patient; to-morrow it shall be mended, and for this night we'll fast for company."

But it was just the same when she went to bed starving.

He railed and swore at everybody, swearing the sheets were damp and not fit for the likes of her, so that, in short, she was fain to sit up all night, and at last fell asleep from sheer exhaustion in a chair.

The next morning it was just the same, and at last she managed to get rid of him for a moment, and came into the dining-room where Grumio was, and begged him to get her some food.

"Faith, I dare not for my life," said Grumio.

"The more my wrong, the more his spite appears," cried poor Katharina. "What! did he marry me to famish me? I, who never knew how to entreat, am starved for meat, giddy for lack of sleep; and that which maddens me more than anything else is that he does it under the name of perfect love! I pray thee get me some repast. I care not what it be so it be good wholesome food."

"What say you to a neat's foot?"

"'Tis passing good. I pray thee let me have it."

"I fear it is too choleric a meat," said Grumio mournfully. "How say you to a fat tripe broiled?"

"I like it well; good Grumio, fetch it me."

"I cannot tell, I fear it is choleric. What say you to a piece of beef and mustard?"

"A dish that I do love to feed upon."

"Ay, but the mustard is hot."

"Why, then the beef, and let the mustard stand."

"Nay, then I will not; you shall have the mustard, or else you get no beef of Grumio."

"Then both, or one, or anything thou wilt," cried Katharina, losing patience.

"Why, then," cried Grumio, "the mustard without the beef."

"Go, get thee gone, thou false deluding knave," cried Katharina, and beat him with such return of temper as she had not shown since she left her father's house.

Grumio made his escape just as Petruchio entered, bearing a dish he had made himself.

He was accompanied by his friend Hortensio, who, having been jilted by Bianca, resolved to come down and see his friend Petruchio.

"That's right," cried Petruchio. "See, love, how diligent I am to dress thy meat myself, and bring it thee. I'm sure, sweet Kate, this kindness merits thanks. What, not a word? Nay, then, thou lovest it not, and all my pains have gone for nothing."

"I pray you set it down," cried Katharina, as he was taking it away.

"The poorest kindness is repaid with thanks," cried Petruchio, "and so shall mine be ere you touch the meat."

"I thank you, sir," said Katharina humbly, for in sorry truth she was starving.

"And now, my honey love," cried Petruchio," when she had finished her repast, "we will return to thy father's house, where I hear thy sister is about to be married; but first of all, thou must have some clothes to wear, and here, by good luck, comes the tailor."

Katharina felt a good deal better now that she had a full meal, and more inclined to stand up for her rights.

"Here is the cap your worship did bespeak," said the tailor.

"A cap!" cried Petruchio. "Call you this a cap? Why, 'twas moulded on a porringer! Come, let us have a bigger."

"I'll have no bigger," cried Katharina. "This doth fit the time, and gentlewomen wear such caps as these."

"When you are gentle," said Petruchio, "you shall have one; not till then."

"Why, sir," cried Katharina, who felt all her old spirit cropping up now that she was going back to her father's house; "I trust I may have leave to speak, and speak I will. I am no child. Your betters have endured me say my mind, and if you cannot, you had best stop your ears."

"Why, thou sayest true," cried Petruchio; "it is a paltry cap, a custard coffin, a bauble, a silken pie. I love thee well, in that thou likest it not."

"Love me or not," cried the shrew, "I like the cap, and it I will have, or none."

"Thy gown?" cried Petruchio. "Why, ay; come, tailor, let us see it. Oh, mercy, Heaven! What masking stuff is here?"

"I never saw a better fashioned gown," cried Katharina. "Belike, you mean to make a puppet of me!"

"Why, true, Kate; he means to make a puppet of thee. Take it away, thou knave, thou thimble, thou yard, three-quarters! What, braved in my own house by a skein of thread?"

And so saying, he banged the unfortunate tailor about the head with his own yardstick, and tore both gown and cap to ribbons, while Katharina wept with rage.

"Well, come, my Kate," said he, at length, "we will unto your father's house even in thine honest mean habiliments. Our purses shall be proud, our garments poor. Let us see, 'tis now some seven o'clock, and well we may come there by dinner time."

"I dare assure you, sir, 'tis almost two," cried Katharina; "and 'twill be supper time ere we come there."

"It shall be seven ere I go to horse," cried Petruchio, in a rage. "Look, what I speak, or think, or do, you are still crossing it. Sirs, let it alone; I will not go to-day, and ere I do, it shall be what o'clock I say it is."

CHAPTER VII.

ETRUCHIO stuck to his word, but the following day at the same hour, he announced that it was seven o'clock, and he would start.

Katharina was wise enough not to contradict him this time.

She was beginning to see that the more she gave into him, and the less she showed of her temper, the better it was for her.

"Come along," cried Petruchio, waking up from a reverie, after they had been for some time on the road. "Lord, how brightly the moon shines to-night."

"The moon!" cried Katharina; "the sun! It is not moonlight now."

"I say it is the moon that shines so bright," cried Petruchio.

"I know it is the sun that shines so bright," cried Katharina.

"Now, by my mother's son, and that's myself," cried Petruchio, in a sudden burst of anger, "it shall be moon, or star, or what I choose, or ere I journey to your father's house. Fetch our horses back again. Evermore crossed and crossed, nothing but crossed."

"Say as he says," whispered Grumio, "or we shall never go."

"Forward, I pray you, since we have come so far," cried Katharina; "and be it sun or moon, or what you please—and if you please to call it a farthing candle—it shall be so for me."

"I say it is the moon," said Petruchio.

"I know it is," said Katharina.

"Nay; then you lie. It is the blessed sun."

"Then God be blessed," said Katharina, "it is the blessed sun. But sun it is not when you say it is not; and the moon changes even as your mind. What you will have it named, that it is, and so it shall be so for Katharina."

"Petruchio," cried Hortensio, in a loud tone, "thou hast won the day!"

"Soft," cried Petruchio, spying an old man whom they had overtaken on the road. "Tell me, sweet Kate, and tell me truly, hast ever beheld a fairer gentle-woman? Fair lovely maid, once more good day to thee. Sweet Kate, embrace her for her beauty's sake."

"Young budding virgin," cried Katharina, "fair and fresh, whither away? Happy the parents of so fair a child."

"Why, how now, Kate?" cried Petruchio, while the old traveller looked in blank astonishment from one to the other. "I hope thou art not mad. This is a man, old, wrinkled, faded, and not a maiden as thou sayest he is."

"Pardon, old father," cried Katharina, "my mistaken eyes that have been so bedazzled with the sun that everything I look on seemeth green."

From the old man they ascertained that he was Vincentio, the father of Lucentio, who had come to Padua in search of his son.

Petruchio told him that his son was by that time married to his wife's sister.

And so chatting pleasantly they

entered the town together, and Petruchio conducted Vincentio to his son's lodgings.

It so happened that at the very time Tranio was with the mock Vincentio upstairs with old Baptista, humbugging him over the preparation of a lot of marriage settlements, and keeping him engaged while Lucentio and Bianca were getting privately married.

Vincentio then invited Petruchio and Katharina to come in, and began knocking, at which the bogus Vincentio put his head out of the window, and demanded who was there.

"I pray you, sir, tell Signior Lucentio that his father is come from Pisa," cried old Vincentio, "and is here at the door."

"Thou liest!" cried the bogus Vincentio. "His father is here."

"What?" cried the old man; "call thou thyself his father?"

"Ay, sir," replied the impostor Vincentio, "if I may believe his mother."

In short the conspirators resolved to brave it out, and shouted for the guard to come and arrest old Vincentio, while Katharina and Petruchio laughed heartily.

Just as matters were getting to a desperate pass, Lucentio, returning from church with Bianca, saw his father about to be arrested, and at once put matters right while Tranio, Biondello, and the impostor ran off, trusting to Lucentio to win their pardon for them.

The old merchant was at first very indignant at having been so tricked, but as the real Vincentio offered to make good all the sham Vincentio had promised, and as the deception was only a *ruse* to gain the girl's affection, he finally forgave them, and they all went in to dinner.

In the evening Hortensio came to join them, and then it became known that when he found he had no chance with Bianca against Lucentio, whom he had taken for a common school teacher, he had gone off and married a widow.

During the evening they began to rally Petruchio on having married a shrew, and when the ladies had retired and the wine flowed, had many a laugh at his expense.

"Now in good sadness, son Petruchio," said the old merchant, "I think thou hast the veriest shrew of all."

"Well, I say no," said Petruchio quietly; "and therefore for assurance let each one send for his wife, and he whose wife is most obedient to come at first when he doth send for her shall win the wager."

"Content," cried the other two husbands. "What shall it be?—twenty crowns?"

"Twenty crowns!" cried Petruchio. "I'd venture as much upon my hawk, but twenty times as much upon my wife. Make it a hundred."

"Biondello," said Lucentio, "bid your mistress come to me."

Presently Biondello returned, saying that his mistress said she was busy and could not come.

"Sirrah, Biondello," cried Hortensio, "go and entreat my wife to come."

"Ho, ho, entreat!" cried Petruchio.

Presently Biondello returned.

"She said you have some goodly jest in hand. She will not come but bids you come to her."

"Grumio," said Petruchio, "go to your mistress; say I command her to come to me."

They all laughed at this, but the laugh went the other way when Katharina the Shrew entered and said in a mild voice—

"What is your will, sir, that you did send for me?"

"Go fetch your sister and Hortensio's wife," cried Petruchio.

And away went Katharina.

"Lord," cried the company, "wonders will never cease. Petruchio hath wrought a miracle."

"And now, Katharina," cried Petruchio, "tell these women the duty they owe their husband."

In an instant Katharina began, and in an eloquent speech upbraided them for having set their husbands at defiance.

The old merchant was so delighted with the change in his daughter that he bestowed upon Petruchio half his fortune.

As for Katharina and Petruchio, they lived together in love and perfect happiness, for the once arrogant headstrong vixen had found the only thing she wanted to make her a good woman, and that was a temper as fiery as her own, and a will inflexible.

NOTICE.—This Number completes the Volume of "Stories from Shakespeare's Plays." Now Ready, price One Shilling, in a Handsome Wrapper. Orders should be given early to your Booksellers.